Mahler,
Consciousness and Temporality

Mahler,
Consciousness and Temporality

David B. Greene
Wabash College
Crawfordsville, Indiana

GORDON AND BREACH SCIENCE PUBLISHERS
New York   London   Paris   Montreux   Tokyo

Copyright © 1984 by Gordon and Breach, Science Publishers, Inc.

Gordon and Breach Science Publishers

1 Park Avenue
New York, NY 10016
United States of America

42 William IV Street
London WC2N 4DE
England

Post Office Box 161
CH-1820 Montreux
Switzerland

58 rue Lhomond
75005 Paris
France

48-2 Minamidama
Oami Shirasato-machi
Sambu-gun
Chiba-ken 299-32
Japan

Library of Congress Cataloging in Publication Data

Greene, David B.
    Mahler, consciousness and temporality.

    Analysis of Symphonies no. 5, 8, 9, and 3.
    1. Mahler, Gustav, 1860—1911. Symphonies.
2. Symphonies — Analysis, appreciation.   I. Title.
ML410.M   785.1'1'0924   83-11632
ISBN 0-677-06160-9

Contents

Preface

In company with only a few other composers, Mahler speaks to us
directly about joy and finitude, courage and ordinariness, love and
emptiness. He confronts us with matters that are too momentous to
grasp at once and too important to be allowed to slip away. If we are
to tighten our grip on them, we would do well to begin by describing
the vehicles by which they come to us: Mahler's musical processes.
We need to be attentive not just to the moods evoked by his suggestive
melodies and his brilliant orchestration, but also to the way he
divides one section from the next and how he joins what he has
separated. To this end, I have analyzed in detail four of Mahler's
symphonies. Because they are as innovative musically as they are
compelling emotionally, I have found that analogies with traditional
forms (such as sonata-allegro, scherzo and rondo) are often more
misleading than helpful. Consequently, I have described the shape of
some movements without using these terms; I have sometimes given
traditional analytic concepts a different force, and have occasionally
invented new terms.

Music analysis does not have a vocabulary for ultimate matters.
For help in pointing toward the vision that the music carries, I have
turned to the phenomenologists of our century — particularly
Husserl, Heidegger and Sartre — who have concerned themselves
with many of the same matters as Mahler. They have systematically
thought about the nature of human existence, and, in that context,
about the experiences of finitude and joy. The particular meaning
they give to consciousness and temporality encapsulates their thinking.
I am not using their terms, however, in order to "interpret" Mahler;
what I am doing is not like translating a message from one language
into another. Instead, I am setting Mahler's vision and theirs next to

one another; I want to let his musically projected images become sharper by comparing and contrasting them to the conceptually projected images. What I am doing is comparable to literary critics comparing two poems on the same theme by different writers.

The terms of both musical and phenomenological analysis are directed toward Mahler's music with the same intention: to deepen and refine our response to his music. But using two sets of concepts, both of them formidable, makes this a difficult book to read. I have tried to make it possible for someone who is familiar with Mahler's music but is unfamiliar with the vocabulary of music analysis to skim over the technical sections and still follow my descriptions of Mahler's temporal processes and the images of ordinary and transfigured consciousness that these processes project. Fewer concessions are made to the reader who may be impatient with phenomenology and its demands, for the intention to describe Mahler by metaphors drawn from Heidegger and Sartre affects the musical analysis at every step.

For the reader's convenience, an unusually large number of charts, sketches and musical illustrations have been included. All the music in the figures has been transposed to concert pitch. These examples were drawn by Terry Nichols of Los Angeles and are reproduced with the permission of Mahler's publisher, Universal Edition of Vienna.

DAVID B. GREENE

Introduction

In each of Mahler's symphonies, some passages seem to be building on what has already taken place in the piece; other passages seem blatantly to refuse to build, and others seem to ignore their past as they build. His music sometimes arrives at the event toward which it has been building, sometimes lets the moment for such an event pass by unobserved and sometimes arrives at a climax or closure that is unwarranted by and unresponsive to its past.

Listening habits and analytic tools developed in connection with eighteenth- and nineteenth-century music presuppose that the memory of prior passages and the anticipation of coming ones qualify the experience of every moment in the piece. A composer is supposed to guide our memory and anticipations and thereby to fashion patterns out of tones, so that as sounds, like life itself, keep slipping through our fingers, the patterns survive. These patterns are like the plot in a narrative; they are supposed to transcend and at the same time give meaning to the episodes, the continuously passing fragments.

A musical continuity that presupposes remembering and expecting has its roots in the temporal process that, we usually suppose, structures our lives. According to this supposition, the temporal process — that is, the way the past, the present and the future are related — is coherent, and the nature of its coherence is reflected in our concept that past events cause present events and present events cause coming ones and in our concept that the past and the present provide a context in which present, future-shaping decisions are made. Husserl (in his *Cartesian Meditations,* 1929) and other phenomenologists have argued that some such understanding of the temporal process is implicit in the nature of human consciousness. Only if consciousness were different would it be possible for the temporal process to be different. If a piece of music refuses to comport with this process, either it is poorly made music, or the nature of consciousness must be reconsidered. And because our consciousness is so close to us, it is not easy to imagine that its nature could be disputed.

Most of Mahler's detractors and his champions share these suppositions. His detractors are bothered by the difficulty in discerning an overarching pattern because of the moments when coming musical events can not be anticipated or when past events seem not to be relevant. They find that he is not sufficiently a master of musical materials to make them cohere with each other. Or else they suspect that he is confused about continuity: perhaps in his self-pity or in his megalomania he is insufficiently aware that remembering and expecting do in fact impinge significantly upon present experience and that no present event is ever isolated. Mahler's champions hear a profound continuity in the flow of his music, but maintain that it is achieved in extraordinary ways: it is a continuity that is more all-embracing than previous music, because it incorporates more aspects of life, or it is a continuity using larger units of its past as building blocks for its future or using more subtle motivic connections than his listeners are usually prepared for, or it uses orchestral color to generate the thrust and articulate the form where prior composers were more dependent on melody and harmony. In any or all of these ways, Mahler is said to expand our concept of continuity and at the same time to confirm our ideal of coherence. His music is significantly novel and demanding, and precisely therein lies its importance.

The burden of this book is to champion Mahler, but to do so by candidly acknowledging the experiences that bother his detractors: his music does in fact violate the standards of coherence and continuity that traditional music presupposes and that seem to be implicit in human consciousness and its temporality. His defenders' claim that the discontinuities are apparent, not real, and that they function to project a more profound confirmation of this ideal coherence is not convincing. For the more closely one pays attention to Mahler's music and the details of its twists and turns, the more one realizes that its processes cannot be said to exemplify the temporal process in which we usually think we live. And if Mahler is to be championed by agreeing with his detractors, then we are put into the uncomfortable position of having to dispute the supposedly indisputable nature of consciousness and temporality.

Mahler's music itself disputes our usual concepts of consciousness and temporality in the sense that it embarks on processes that are analogous to those of cause and effect or of decision-making and then rejects these familiar processes for the sake of more disturbing ones. These other processes are not, however, altogether unfamiliar, for they have analogies in aspects of our experience that, like Mahler's music, contradict our usual concept of consciousness and temporality. These contradictions intimate that there is a gap between our consciousness as it is and our consciousness as we think it is. Indeed, it may be that when consciousness reflects on itself it is bound to understand itself as Husserl and common sense do, but that there are acts of consciousness that this understanding cannot accommodate — that, in short, there is a confusion buzzing through consciousness itself. If so, Mahler can be seen as reflecting and responding to this confusion.

In any case, a brief look at experiences that challenge our usual concepts of consciousness and temporality will be used to introduce Mahler's music. Before turning to those experiences, it may be helpful to lay out what is here being called the "ordinary" or "common-sense" concept of consciousness, and to show how consciousness seems almost bound to think of itself this way. It is also important to show how this concept seems to dictate that the temporal process must be one in which the past, present and future are related to one another as they are in processes of mechanical cause and effect or of decision-making, or in some model similar to these. For as one sees this tight link between consciousness and temporality, one also sees why one must either consign Mahler's music, to the extent that it fails to comport with this temporality, to the wastebin of nonsense or one must open oneself to the possibility that the temporal process and consciousness may not be what they seem to be.

1. Consciousness, Temporality and Coherence

Consciousness is invisible. We experience through it, but we never experience it. We can hardly talk about it except by describing its structure. This structure, Husserl says and common sense agrees, is temporal. Consciousness is always the consciousness of an object, and this object — my dog, or my dog chewing my slipper — is always temporal, for it consists not merely of what I am now perceiving, but of a synthesis of the present perception with what I remember and what I expect. The object of awareness includes the dog's fourth paw, which I remember but which is now hidden from view, as well as the inside of the slipper's toe, which I have never seen but would expect to see if I shone a flashlight into the slipper. The object of which I am aware is already temporal; it does not become temporal by persisting, but is a synthesis of recollection, present perception and anticipation just in being an object of awareness.

Husserl's insight comports with many of our intuitive notions about the nature of human consciousness. That it seems to describe consciousness as it actually is can be confirmed by noting the apparent absurdities into which we fall if we try to imagine its contrary. Let us, for example, try to imagine that consciousness is radically pastless in the sense that it has no possibility of remembering the past or even being aware of the category of the past and therefore cannot even be said to have forgotten anything. When we try to imagine such a consciousness, we seem to have negated not just pastness but consciousness itself. Trying to think of a pastless consciousness seems to be like thinking of a round square: one is not thinking of anything at all. For a pastless consciousness would be one in which each moment would be the first instant of consciousness. Having no past, one could not expect that what one is now seeing might change, and if it were somehow possible to expect change, one would have no idea of how it would change. The three-legged slipper-chewing dog I am now perceiving could as easily turn into a ten-legged, cigar-smoking cat as into a four-legged bone-eating dog. And pastlessness implies that regardless how the object of perception changes, I would not be aware of the change. I would have no memory of perceiving the three-legged dog when I see the four-legged dog or the ten-legged cat.

Radical pastlessness would also entail that the subject of consciousness would not synthesize itself with the subject of prior awareness, and since self-awareness entails such a synthesis, it could have no concept of itself, and hence no sense of a distinction between itself and that of which it was conscious. The object of present awareness would totally fill the consciousness.

Radical pastlessness would imply futurelessness. If there were no past, there would be no basis for expecting anything in particular or even for any change at all; there would be no self-aware subject of consciousness, synthesized with the subject of past awareness, to do the expecting; and if some sort of future were somehow to survive these problems, pastlessness would imply an undifferentiated future, that is, a future in which there would be no distinction between a near and a distant future, for the former would be the past to the latter, and so would contradict the hypothesis of pastlessness.

Let us try to imagine a radically futureless consciousness, a consciousness that does not have even the possibility of expecting. Now we find that the notion of having a past also is either radically changed or annihilated. Radical futurelessness would imply a past in which the differentiation between the near and the distant past would have to disappear inasmuch as the former would have been the future of the latter. If we synthesize memories of past perceptions with a present perception but have no expectation of future perceptions, each instant would be experienced as the last moment of time. Surviving to a subsequent moment could not be experienced as contradicting the finality of the prior moment, for such a contradiction would deny the hypothesis of radical futurelessness. If the subject of consciousness did not synthesize itself with some awareness of possibilities, it would not be able to see itself at all, hence it would be no different from unself-consciousness entities. It would not envision itself as doing anything or acting upon the objects it is encountering in any way. The subject of consciousness would be as passive as the most inert object. It could be a self-guided agent no more than a stone can be. A radically futureless consciousness, like one that is radically pastless, is so different from ordinary consciousness that we are likely to be repelled or at least amused by the odd notion. That its absurdity seems so obvious shows how deeply the temporal articulation of consciousness is imbedded in our assumptions. To imagine a consciousness that is not characterized by temporal articulation is to invent a fundamentally different concept of consciousness.

The process of synthesizing expected with remembered and present perceptions entails that there are limits to what may be expected and that these limits are crucial to the process of consciousness. If I take the object of consciousness to be a slipper-chewing dog, I may not expect it to become a cigar-smoking cat in the next five minutes, and if it does, the object of consciousness changes from what I thought it was. Either I was wrong in supposing that I saw a dog or I am now wrong in thinking that I see a cat or I am wrong in thinking that the two awarenesses are of the same object. If I shine a flashlight into my slipper, I may not expect to see an entrance into a secret garden through which I may pass, spend the afternoon and reemerge five minutes before I first turned on the flashlight. I may be wrong about the particular limits that define a given object, but I may not assume there are no limits. If there are no limits to what I may expect, I may expect anything, and in synthesizing that sort of expectation with the presently perceived and remembered objects of perception, I find that the object of consciousness has become so amorphous as not to be an object at all. Consciousness that is not aware of some more or less definite object is not consciousness at all.

The way that consciousness entails expecting and expecting entails limits is encapsulated in our sense of a universe. This idea is the assumption that all that is somehow constitutes a single totality. According to Husserl, the nature of consciousness necessarily requires that there be some sort of preconceptions concerning the nature and limitations of reality. We must assume that there is some sort of coherence between what is and what will be, and that to the extent that we grasp the coherence we know what we may expect. When it turns out that we have expected wrongly, we assume that we have misunderstood the nature of coherence; we do not assume that there is no coherence. Nor do we assume that there are multiple sets of conflicting and equally valid rules. Even if we live in a variety of kinds of reality and pass back and forth from one to another, we assume there are rules (which we happen not to know) governing the relations among them. Without a sense of the universe, however sketchy our idea may be or however wrong we may be about particulars, we could not expect anything. The toe of the slipper may well turn into the entrance to a garden, and we could not suppose that the change was odd. We could not synthesize expectations with remembered and present perceptions, there would be no limits to make the objects of awareness definite, and consciousness would be radically futureless.

Because consciousness reflecting on itself must assume that we live in a universe, we find it appropriate to try to explain events. Such efforts amount to an attempt to discover the nature of the universe's coherence or to apply the rules as we know them to particular events. Without a sense, however indeterminate, that we live in a single totality, it would never occur to us to look for explanations. But given the sense that we do live in a universe, we do attribute grounds to events, even if we do not know what these grounds are, and usually we feel compelled to try to identify them.

Generally speaking, there are two different kinds of explanations: those based on mechanical causation and those based on the decisions of a free, self-reflective individual. Fundamentally different ways of explaining events, both kinds of grounds express one's sense of a universe, of the limits to possible perceptions, and of the temporally articulated structure of consciousness. Some people are tempted to see only one kind of ground, mechanistic causation, and reduce human decision-making to it by explaining putatively free choices in terms of their biological context. Such a reduction more easily sustains a sense of a universe.

But even if one maintains that decisions are a basically different kind of ground, they function as an explanation and comport with the sense of a universe in which ungrounded events are unintelligible and unintelligible events are impossible. We believe that it is appropriate to justify our decisions; we believe that decisions are rational to the extent that they may be universalized. Both beliefs express the assumption that consciousness may and must synthesize remembered and expected perceptions. That is, on the basis of this assumption, it makes sense to ask whether a particular decision comports with what any rational person would have chosen to do and to try to describe the characteristics that any rational person instantiates. Difficulties in synthesizing what takes place with what has been expected may be interpreted as a discrepancy between what persons have chosen and what they ought to have chosen. Even when free choice is not seen as implying a need for justification or universalization — even when events grounded in a free choice may be seen as radically unpredictable — the same nest of assumptions may be expressed, for enacting decisions may be regarded as actualizing a non-empirical self that becomes concrete only through this process. Even the most unpredictable and apparently capricious decision expresses the non-empirical self which functions as the ground of the resulting event and explains it; the apparently capricious event is to be synthesized with the non-empirical self. On the basis of this assumption, it makes sense to ask to what extent what actually comes to pass coincides with what the decision-maker intended. Difficulties in synthesizing what is with what was expected come about, one may believe, because the self knows itself or external reality inadequately or because external reality resists being shaped in such a way that the self may be fully actualized.

2.   *Consciousness and Temporality in Confusion*

Reflection on consciousness seems to make it impossible to suppose that events may simply happen and that we might not feel compelled to explain them by finding their ground. It is hard to suppose that people just happen to make decisions and that one might not feel compelled to ground them in a prior reality, whether the empirical world or the non-empirical self. Yet there is evidence that consciousness, before it reflects on itself, is after all capable of such suppositions. And if it is, then the temporal process and hence consciousness too must be different from what our reflection on them suppose that they must be.

In the eighteenth century, for example, Newtonian scientists were able to accept the law of universal gravitation without wondering why bodies attracted one another and why they were not, instead, simply indifferent to one another. The law served as the ground of coherent motion, but it itself had no ground other than the belief that God made things that way. By ascribing the origin and the pattern of motion to God, they expressed their need for coherence. But as Hume later pointed out, they knew nothing about the nature of God beyond the assumption that he is the unmoved mover. Consequently, this ascription amounted to simply putting a name on the mystery that material bodies attract one another. Eighteenth-century scientists could not explain the connection between the putative ground of gravitation and the actual fact of it. This inexplicableness did not bother them, for putting a label on it had the effect of masking the fact that gravitation was mysterious. The label made it possible to ignore the fact that they did not understand the ground of gravitation; so far as their understanding went, the law of gravity simply happened to be the case. Goethe made himself unusual by managing to become explicitly aware of the fact that the ground for gravitation itself (as opposed to the ground for attributing gravitation to all masses) was utterly mysterious. His Faust expresses an awareness that the ground of gravity itself has thus far been unapprehended when he longs to "learn what holds the world together/There at its inmost core:/See the seeds of things, and power."[1]

Instead of probing Faust's question and substaining by deepening the sense that the future may be synthesized with the present, contemporary physics has been forced by various phenomena to give up the traditional notion of mechanical causation. For example, elementary particle theory today requires, as Norwood Hanson writes, "that the nucleus of every unstable isotope be identical with every other nucleus of that type." The theory also requires that these nuclei decay in an unpredictable way — it is in principle impossible to predict which nuclei will decay. Given these premises, one cannot explain why the particular ones that decay do decay, for they are, until the moment of decay, identical to those that do not.[2] The behaviour of the aggregate is explicable as a caused event, but not the decay of the particular nuclei. It is possible to predict how many nuclei will decay in a given time, but not which ones. Cause as a statistical phenomenon is very different from cause as a principle of the continuity that seems required by our reflection on consciousness, and the synthesis of expected with present perceptions and consequently temporality and consciousness itself must accordingly be different as well.

Just as contemporary particle physics seems forced to give up the notion of mechanical cause as grounds for events, so Sartre's phenomenology seems obliged to give up a non-empirical self as the ground for consciousness itself. Husserl supposes that the act of consciousness is the act of a subject — the transcendental Ego. The Ego is transcendental in that it logically precedes consciousness and transcends both the act of consciousness and that of which consciousness is aware. In *The Transcendence of the Ego* (1937), Sartre argues that the concept of a transcendental Ego is unwarranted, unnecessary and pernicious. Consciousness generates itself in a radically spontaneous way, he says, and the sense of an "I" is the product, not the ground, of this utterly ungrounded event. Sartre's analysis has a parallel in the work of psychologists who identify the mind with brain activity. For them, consciousness is nothing other than electro-chemical events, whose pattern can be described, this pattern defining the structure of the brain. There is no self or mind that controls the brain's activity. The sense of a self results from and does not ground the work of the brain.

Husserl's idea of a transcendental Ego comes from Kant, who supposes that a non-empirical self is what makes decisions and thus grounds the kind of activity on which moral judgments are appropriate. Kant himself, however, is able to countenance the possibility of an ungrounded event. In his *Critique of Judgment* (1790), Kant interprets beautiful objects in a way that makes them exemplify an ungrounded event. A beautiful object, he says, is one in which we find disinterested pleasure. Pleasure in beautiful things, whether natural or manmade, cannot be explained in terms of cognitive concepts nor in terms of sensuous gratification nor in terms of utility. Insofar as they are beautiful, they are useless. Although they are purposive, both in the sense that they sustain disinterested pleasure and in the sense that their internal parts may be said to serve purposes in relation to one another, they are not grounded in a concept that may be said to be their purpose and the explanation of their origin. While it is inconceivable that a wagon, for example, could be built without a concept of its use, there is no determinate concept of the beautiful object that could control its construction. Artists may have a concept of symmetry, and they may create objects that exemplify this concept, but if these objects are beautiful as well as symmetrical, they are not beautiful *because* they are symmetrical. They may also be designed to serve a moral end or satisfy an appetite, but if they are beautiful as well, the beauty is not grounded in the purpose.

Had Husserl considered the beautiful and understood it in Kant's way, he would have had to recognize that, in judging the beautiful, one is synthesizing remembered and expected perceptions of only that object. One may be, of course, simultaneously comparing and contrasting it to other objects — the cognitive faculties do not necessarily become dormant — but wider syntheses have nothing to do, Kant would say, with the strictly aesthetic pleasure. A beautiful artwork may, of course, reflect the nature of the universe, but, in Kant's view, it is not beautiful *because of* this reflection. Even though a beautiful artwork may turn out to have limits self-imposed by the artist and dictated by the medium, and even though these limits may reflect the limits of reality, one may experience an object as beautiful without presupposing that there is a universe or that it has limits. While I may have certain expectations as I listen to a piece of music, for example, all of the limits implicit in these expectations (except the expectation that I will not become bored) may be transgressed without the music failing to be beautiful.

Art critics generally recoil from the notion of disinterested pleasure because the term seems ill chosen for an experience that is so absorbing and because it seems too rigidly to abstract aesthetic experience from other experiences. Nevertheless, the influence of Kant's Third Critique has been extensive. Building on its principles, Schelling in 1800 makes the aesthetic intuition the cornerstone of his transcendental idealism and identifies aesthetic intuition as the point of non-difference between the intuition of natural causality and the causality of a free decision. He believes the aesthetic intuition reveals the deepest self, a sort of consciousness that is distinct from that in which cause and effect are observed or in which free choices are made. The distinctiveness of the aesthetic consciousness vis-à-vis what may be called the Husserlian consciousness is critical to understanding the latter and seeing it as even possible, for mechanical causality and human freedom invalidate each other: if one accepts the first, then one must admit that supposedly free choices have natural causes, and freedom is an illusion; if one accepts the second, then one must say that the human mind unconsciously posits the world in order to have an arena in which to exercise its freedom, and natural necessity has no objective status. Either alone may be valid, but in order for both to be possible, there must be, Schelling says, a point of indifference — the aesthetic intuition — from which the other two processes differentiate themselves.

Johan Huizinga in *Homo Ludens* (1938) widens Kant's notion of the beautiful into the concept of play. He calls attention to the activities in which human beings indulge without having any purpose at all. Play is misunderstood, he says, if it is taken to be functional. Although it does serve functions — one may learn through playing, and diversion may rejuvenate one to resume work with renewed vigor — serving these purposes is not central to the nature of play. Indeed, these purposes are usually met less well to the extent that the playful activity is designed or entered into with them in mind.

To the extent that consciousness indulges in beauty and play, understood as Kant and Huizinga think they are understood, it accepts the possibility that some things simply happen and take place without any grounds. If one thinks that only mechanical causality and free decision-making can ground events and that ungrounded events are inconceivable and impossible, then one cannot entertain Kant's concept of the beautiful or Huizinga's of play. Freudian art criticism, for example, reduces the supposedly beautiful to mechanistic processes, such as the sublimation of repressed drives, and Marxist art criticism reduces it to artists' decisions which either reflect or criticize society and for which society must hold them morally responsible.

Art critics who reject reductionist interpretations of artistic beauty sometimes say that it is grounded in the artists' genius, not their craftmanship. It is not groundless after all, but as the word "genius" suggests, this kind of grounding is very different from that of mechanical cause or free choice. We would probably do better, however, to say that beauty is ungrounded, for natural causality and free choice so control over notion of grounding that the word "genius" almost inevitably slips into becoming a special case of one or the other. We might do better to admit that while we understand craftmanship, the beautiful object simply comes into being and we use the word "genius" not to name the ground but to say that we do not understand how it can happen.

Certain kinds of religious events are inexplicable in much the same way. In the Dionysian rituals of the pre-Socratic Greeks, the god appeared to the celebrants. The rite was effective only if the god's presence was genuine. Even though each re-presentation of the god might be temporally distinguishable, each was identical to the god himself, hence identical to each other. For medieval Catholics, the celebration of the mass was miraculously identical to Christ's crucifixion and resurrection; their religious experience implied that the same historical event could occur at various times and places. Krishna was believed to make love simultaneously to innumerable cowmaidens. All these are impossible events in the sense that they can not be understood on the basis of the kind of continuity presupposed by concepts like cause and effect or decisions made by a free agent. The temporal process in which people practicing these religions were living is radically different from the one in which we live when we feel the need to make explanations and try to specify grounds. We can say that the divine reality itself grounds these events, but only if we construe the relation of the ground to the event as radically different from the relation of cause to effect or decision to result. As with the word "genius," we might do better to say that the name of the god is used not to name the ground of the religious event but to say that we do not understand how it can happen.[3] We can, of course, dismiss these religious experiences either by saying that the temporal process in which we live is so different from what they presuppose that we can form no viable concept of the religious consciousness or by saying that these experiences reflect the underdeveloped consciousness of the primitive mind. But if we do not feel inclined to dismiss them, they suggest that our own consciousness may not be what our reflection on it says it must be.

Events that are impossible in the sense that we do not understand how they can happen are not always so positive as beauty, play and religion. We get a sense of the range of impossible events when we confront a dreadful accident — an event whose outcome is so disproportionate to its causes that we find we cannot understand it in terms of its causes. If a driver turns briefly to reprimand a child, skids on a patch of ice into a motorcycle, whose rider is killed, we can say that the child, the reprimand and the ice caused the cyclist's death, but recognizing these causes does not express our horror at the event. As an empirically observable event, it can be related to its grounds; and a horrible event, it is groundless. Our notions of mechanical causality and of free choice may compel us to cry out, "Why didn't you watch out for the ice?" but our sense of an accident makes us realize there can be no adequate answer. If the driver answers, "I made a mistake," and someone asks, "Why did you make a mistake?" we feel that the force of "mistake" has not been felt. If a mistake can be explained, can it still be called a "mistake"? The momentary inattention simply happened. The sense of moral responsibility that free choice ordinarily implies is suspended. While culpable, the driver is far less so than if he shot the cyclist in order to steal his money.

An accident understood in this way is a slur on the concept of a universe. Until it is felt, the horror of the cyclist's death is as inconceivable as the beauty of the artwork that tomorrow will bring. To the extent that the future is unimaginable, it is in principle unpredictable. To the extent that it is in principle unpredictable (and not merely that particular predictions turn out to have been incorrect), the nature of the universe fails to be what our reflection on consciousness and its temporal structure supposes that it must be. Perhaps for this reason, some people refuse to understand dreadful accidents as events that simply happen. The supposition of coherence requires that monstrous events must have monstrous causes, and so they attribute things like the momentary inattention to latent moral perversity or to subconscious drives, the one explanation seeing the accident as a particular mode of decision-making and the other as an instance of a causality analogous to that in nature.

play and accident as well as those of mechanical cause and free decisions. The perplexingly intermingled operation of the apparently contradictory kinds of temporal processes suggests that consciousness itself may be confused. To some extent, consciousness and temporality seem to be what our reflection on them assumes they must be; to some extent, consciousness deals with events that have no grounds, and with a future that is accordingly indeterminate and cannot be synthesized with the present.

3. Consciousness, Temporality and Mahler

Mahler's music pulls us into this confusion, and responds to it by creating a kind of coherence that our usual assumptions find startling, mystifying and perhaps even unacceptable.

Many aspects of Mahler's style are responsible for arousing the sense of confusion. Sometimes he begins a passage which promises to comport with our usual notions of continuity and whose process closely resembles that of an event causing a subsequent event or of a decision, made by a free agent, shaping a future; but then the passage subverts this continuity and leaves us feeling at the end that what has transpired has simply happened, its process resembling that of events like nuclear decay, beauty and accidents for which no ground may be determined. Sometimes he blurs the distinction between an event that, like an event in nature, seems to unfold out of the event preceding it, as though the new were implicit in the old, and an event that, like an event shaped by a free decision, seems to mark a new beginning, as though it were responsive to the preceding music but not determined by it. He begins ideas that fizzle out; new ideas enter from nowhere; the banal is harshly juxtaposed to the sublime; interruptions and interpolations upset the continuity. Although some principle of continuity is always operative, different principles — some of them incompatible with one another — prevail from one section to the next, and sometimes two contradictory principles operate at the same time. Things happen that respond to no actual past; events that are evoked are sometimes not even partly actualized. The more ungrounded events take place and grounded ones fail to materialize, the more listeners feel not so much that expectations are frustrated as that expecting anything at all is sometimes inappropriate to this music. In short, Mahler's way of coming off a past and arriving at a future frequently fails to comport with our common-sense presuppositions about temporality. It fails to reflect the aspiration for the kind of coherence that the nature of consciousness seems to require. In this respect, his music resembles some of the processes embodied in works by his Viennese contemporaries, such as Schnitzler, Klimt and Kraus, as well as other twentieth-century works, like Proust's *Remembrance of Things Past,* Heidegger's *Being and Time* and Sartre's *Being and Nothingness.*

In some passages of Mahler's music — some passages from the Third and Fifth Symphonies, for example — the future becomes so indeterminate and the past seems so irrelevant that both the future and the past begin to disappear even as possibilities, and the temporal process approaches radical futurelessness and radical pastlessness.

Yet Mahler's symphonies are not simply confused. While they pull us into the confusion consciousness has about itself, they also project temporal processes that cohere with one another and thereby respond to this confusion. The responses may be classified into two types. First, some of his movements appeal both to our common-sense presuppositions about temporality and also to our sense that some kinds of events are groundless. They do justice to both of these by creating a kind of continuity that is fundamentally different from what our usual reflection on consciousness seems of necessity to ascribe to the temporal process. These movements imply an understanding of consciousness that accordingly is basically different. Perhaps they understand consciousness as it actually is, not as we would like to think that it is.

Second, some of his movements suggest a totally unfamiliar temporal process that differs from the temporality of groundless events as much as the latter differs from a world in which events are assumed always to have a ground. These movement lead us into transformed temporalities that are different from those of causation, decision-making and ungrounded events, all three. Perhaps they understand consciousness as it might be, not as it actually is.

Neither of these two responses is peculiar to Mahler: the first has affinities with Schubert, Bruckner and perhaps Liszt; the second has affinities with Wagner (at the end of *Tristan* and *Götterdämmerung*), Strauss (*Tod und Verklärung*) and Schoenberg (*Verklärte Nacht*). Both responses have affinities with some pieces by Stravinsky, Messiaen, Stockhausen and Cage, namely, those that minimize continuity and closure and deliberately deny an analogy with processes in which events have grounds.[4]

In Mahler's Fifth Symphony and in much of the Third we see him responding in the first way. In the Finale of the Third, all of the Eighth and the outside movements of the Ninth, we see the second kind of response. In this book, these four symphonies (one from each of his style periods) will be analyzed, the temporal processes they exemplify will be delineated and the kind of consciousness which these processes imply will be indicated. In other words, the analyses will try to identify the assumptions about temporality which the music embodies and which the listener must share, at least provisionally, if it is to make sense.

Mahler's music so obviously deals with weighty matters like death, resignation, resurrection, courage, creation, love and peace that his commentators are tempted to dwell on these themes to the neglect of the more tedious work of source criticism and careful formal analysis. By using concepts like temporality and consciousness, which usually belong to the philosophers' domain, this book apparently joins the ranks of these interpretative studies. These concepts will not be used, however, to sidestep technical analysis, which will in fact be detailed if not wearisome (but less detailed in each successive chapter). Rather the concept of temporal process will be used to gather up a number of assumptions about continuity, coherence, fulfillment and closure that are implicit in the music (and in any music critic's analysis, no matter how narrowly technical it may profess to be). Because a concept of consciousness is so tightly linked to a concept of temporality, becoming clear about the temporal processes Mahler is exemplifying may help us to know how to assimilate his allusions to matters of the soul.

The meaning of "exemplify" that is being used here is the one developed by Nelson Goodman. In *Languages of Art,* he argues that music, or any art, exemplifies a property (such as a temporal process) that it both possesses and shows forth. To be precise, Goodman would have us say that Mahler's music, like music generally, metaphorically (not literally) exemplifies temporal processes. Music provides literal examples of things like oboe sounds, silences, repetitions, contrasting amplitudes of sound and changes of pitch. Working together, these things may suggest or express or metaphorically exemplify things like progression, striving, fulfilling tendencies, arriving at a climax, not arriving at a climax, and closure. These things in turn work together to exemplify metaphorically a temporal process.

To say that a passage metaphorically rather than literally exemplifies fulfillment (for instance) is not, however, to say that it does not actually possess the property that is labeled by the term "fulfillment." Rather, it is to acknowledge that there may not be a label that refers to the property literally and that the most apt way to refer to it is to apply a label from another realm of discourse. The reassignment is influenced by our old habits of using the term: what we know about the process of a person attaining fulfillment may lead us to see some sort of resemblance, for example, between it and the process projected by a musical passage. The musical property and the term seem to attract each other. At the same time, Goodman argues, the new application may be said to be "metaphorical" only if this attraction has a resistance to overcome — only, that is, if the new application is also "to some extent contra-indicated"[5] : fulfillment presupposes something like desire or striving; the music, being insentient, is not literally desirous. One might argue that "fulfillment" labels the feeling literally felt by the listener, and the term is applied (non-metaphorically) to music that evokes the feeling. But it is the case that listeners may and often do recognize that a passage of music is expressing desire even when they themselves do not really care whether the expressed desire is satisfied; that is, they recognize the aptness of this label for a property that the music actually possesses in spite of the fact that neither they nor the music literally has the property of desiring.

Critics may well be asked how they know, or what evidence they have, that a property such as a climactic resolution is in fact exemplified by the music. But for two reasons the question must be deflected. First, musical climax cannot be reduced to a set of empirical features that are present whenever it is exemplified. Because it is always a somewhat different (though sometimes only slightly different) set of literally exemplified features that metaphorically exemplifies this concept, its instances are analogous, not identical, to one another. Second, seeing an exemplification is a matter of recognizing the aptness of the metaphor (that is, a label, such as "climax") for the property. It means simply recognizing that a configuration of sounds possesses the property and therefore resembles other things that have a similar property. Seeing the resemblance is not a matter of applying a concept to an observation. When it is appropriate to speak of exemplification, one sees this resemblance between the configuration of sounds and that of which it is an instance in the very act of hearing the sounds. Hearing the configuration and seeing the resemblance is one act, not two. There are, of course, other resemblances which are not seen immediately, other properties that the music possesses but that are inferred, and they may not be said to be exemplified. For example, a Mahler movement has a certain length, which may be identical to the length of, say, a trip to the grocery store, but it does not show forth or exhibit this resemblance. The music itself provides the context that determines which of its properties it merely possesses and which it also exemplifies. While critics cannot say conclusively how they know that a property is exemplified, they can and should describe their understanding of the context that differentiates between exemplified and unexemplified properties.[6]

The project of describing the temporal processes that Mahler's symphonies metaphorically exemplify may be initiated by studying several of Mahler's paired phrases. For in these phrases, one hears events that seem to be ungrounded or that seem to be both grounded and ungrounded (a study of the phrases' contexts would presumably determine which). Within a short span, these phrases sometimes encapsulate and sometimes foreshadow the kinds of relations that characterize large sections of Mahler's works. Accordingly, analyzing these phrases may aptly serve to introduce the subsequent chapters' analyses of entire symphonies.

In the exposition of the First Symphony's opening movement, there are two instances of the following syndrome: a four-bar group generates an answering subphrase, which seems to be responsive to the first one; in fact, however, some sort of interference disturbs the continuity so that the "answering" subphrase is not genuinely responsive, but the unresponsiveness is disguised by the flowing contrapuntal lines. The first instance, quoted in Figure 1, begins at S:6 (rehearsal number 6 in the score). The first four bars following S:6 are unmistakably analogous to the antecedent subphrases of Classic period music. The second violin strikes up the consequent subphrase at five bars after S:6. Like the Classic consequent, this one begins with the same motif that begins the antecedent, although it is decorated by the falling sevenths (D—E) in the second violins. In the next measure, the ear follows the second violins and their stepwise line descending from D. But this line turns out not to be the line that will lead the phrase to closure. By the beginning of the consequent's

FIGURE 1
Mahler, First Symphony, first movement

third measure, the second-violin line has petered out, and the subphrase is brought to its end by the first violins, whose line is hidden, at the beginning of the consequent, beneath the second violins' line. The second measure of the consequent in the first violins is exactly the same as, but an octave higher than, the second bar of the antecedent subphrase. What the ear hears in the consequent is a line that begins but that does not end (the second violins) and a line that ends but that has no beginning (the first violins). The closure at nine bars after S:6 simply happens in the sense that the line in which it takes place is cut off from the beginning of the gesture that is responding to and is generated by the antecedent's mobility. The nine bars are a developmental elaboration of the main theme masquerading as an antecedent-consequent group.

Critical to this effect is the fact that the second-violin line opens with a decorated version of the antecedent's opening motif, signaling the beginning of the consequent, and continues in the fore of the listener's attention until the third or fourth beat of the next measure. Studying the score may lead an analyst to suppose that the first violins in bar 6 after S:6 simply continue, an octave higher, the consequent begun in the previous measure by the second violins, but this interpretation ignores the extent to which the second-violin descent from D holds our attention. (And, of course, a conductor may interpret the passage in such a way that the second-violin descent in fact does not hold our attention; here, as always, one must refer to a particular performance of the music.) The listener who does not pick up the cue that the consequent begins with the second violins may hear a conventional four-bar antecedent beginning at

S:6, extended in a fairly routine way into a five-bar group, and followed by a conventional four-bar consequent (although this way of hearing the passage must face the awkward fact that the first bar of the putative consequent is identical to the *second* bar of the antecedent). Expanded phrases in Classic and Romantic music usually have the effect of postponing closure, thereby making it more satisfying. But if we hear Mahler's nine-bar phrase as the result of a break in continuity (a consequent that begins but does not end), we realize that his extension undercuts and does not merely postpone closure.

The other instances begins at eight bars before S:8 (see Figure 2;

FIGURE 2
Mahler, First Symphony, first movement

here as elsewhere, passages are identified by the bar number of their first downbeat, not of its upbeat, if there is one). The trumpet and then the cellos, one bar apart, state the main theme canonically. After two bars, the trumpet's line is carried forward by the oboe and clarinet. In spite of the change of timbre, the first four bars of the trumpet and oboe-clarinet line sound enough like a four-bar antecedent subphrase to lead the listener to expect the oboe-clarinet continuation to function as a consequent. Yet this line stops on E without coming to closure. The cello line also groups itself into a four-bar antecedent and a continuation that likewise stops without reaching closure. A violin figure that comes from nowhere closes the phrase (at S:8). Although the violins begin on the pitch where the oboe-clarinet leaves off (E), the change of timbre and, even more, the inappropriateness of the violin line as a continuation of the oboe-clarinet line (it descends too quickly and the turn from A to D at its end is too precipitous) make it a separate gesture, not a continuation of the oboe-clarinet line. Nevertheless, the violins' closure obscures the fact that neither of the putative consequent subphrases attains satisfactory closure. What the antecedent subphrases evoke never really comes to pass. If either the oboe-clarinet or the cello consequent reached closure, the descending violin line would be heard as a bridge to the next eight-bar unit (beginning at S:8). As it is, the violin line must be heard as the closure to the eight-bar group ending at S:8, but, as in the phrase beginning at S:6, this closure is not part of a gesture that is generated by and that is responding to the mobility of an antecedent.

The pairing of an antecedent to a consequent phrase is essential to the Classic style. Almost every nineteenth-century composer alludes to and manipulates this technique. The Vienna of Mahler is also the Vienna of Johann Strauss, who uses it so incessantly that his waltzes would be totally unintelligible if one were to ignore the phrase pairings — as if one could! With Mahler, it is often used much less obviously; sometimes it is only implicitly present,[7] and still his audiences were sure to hear the allusion.

The critical difference between Classic paired subphrases and the phrases quoted in Figures 1 and 2 is that Mahler's closures are only tenuously related to the evoking gesture. In the Classic-period paired subphrases, the cadence ending the first subphrase and articulating the division between the two subphrases is unstable enough that the first subphrase as a whole thrusts forward and evokes the second even while it seems somewhat closed and separate from the second. The separation between the subphrases makes the second sound like a fresh gesture and not the mechanical continuation of the first; at the same time, the second ends more stably than the first, and because it does, the second seems genuinely a response to and a fulfillment of the first. The consequent member of the pair seems to be grounded in its past, but, as a fresh gesture, it also seems to be grounded in something other than its past. Thus the pair as a whole resembles the process of a free, non-empirical self enacting a decision, and thereby making itself concretely actual, for the second subphrase seems to have been genuinely summoned by its past and yet as a fresh gesture it is more like the result of a free decision than the outcome of a mechanically operating cause in nature. Because of the cadential separation, the second subphrase does not sound as if it were implicit in the first, an unfolding of what the first has made inevitable, yet because the second ends more stably than the first, it fulfills what the first asks and makes actual what the first evokes.[8]

The two phrases from Mahler's First explicitly allude to the same process: in both cases, the first subphrase evokes a future, and the satisfying closure at the end of the second makes this evocation seem to be fulfilled, but the breaks in continuity that occur during the second subphrase suggest that a certain degree of serendipity has inserted itself into the process. The closure that happens only seems to be part of the responding gesture that begins with the beginning of the paired subphrase; in fact this beginning peters out without coming to a close, and the gesture that brings the phrase to closure has no beginning. It is not rooted in the previous process; it just happens. Other music, of course, has its fortuitous moments. For example, the middle section of the slow movement in Mozart's *Eine kleine Nachtmusik* — an agitated, anxious passage — seems serendipitous when it happens. But with Mozart, as with Beethoven, Brahms and others, the effect is temporary. Subsequent events build on the contrast created by the serendipitous moment, giving it a justification that erases the sense of mere fortuitousness in favour of an all-embracing coherence or of a struggle (sometimes deliberately unsuccessful in Beethoven and Brahms) to project a comprehensive unity. Mahler, by contrast, sometimes simply lets the fortuitousness stand and become an aspect of the overall temporal process that his movement is projecting.

The interweaving contrapuntal lines are indispensable to Mahler's effect. They represent a kind of continuity, different from that at the beginning and the ending of a passage, that makes it possible for the apparent fulfillment to happen without being rooted in the process it is closing. Thus these lines hide the way that the closure in fact violates the principle of continuity evoked at the beginning; they help hold the groundlessness together with the sense that the ending is grounded in something resembling a free decision. The process exemplified by these phrases is one in which outcomes seem to have grounds but in fact simply happen, as though the self enacting itself accepted more responsibility for the outcome than it had and fancied itself to be more concretely actualized than it really was. (Incidentally, this description is not asserting that the phrase seems to have been grounded in, say, Mahler's character but in fact simply happened to turn out as it did, or that he claimed more responsibility for its final form than he had, as though it were a whim and not a decision that gave the phrase its shape, or as though the beginning and the ending were written on different days, and Mahler had literally forgotten the one when he wrote the other. These assertions may, of course, be true, and if they are, the compositional process would literally exemplify the same process that the music itself exemplifies metaphorically. But that question is not the concern of this book.)

The Second Symphony offers a more complex example of the same process. In its opening movement, the first sustained melodic line begins in the oboe seven bars before S:1 (Figure 3). The melody seems to be a continuously unfolding process, as though each new segment were implicit in the previous segment. In this respect, the oboe line that runs from seven bars before S:1 to ten after S:1 exemplifies a process that resembles the way Newtonian nature unfolds, each event caused by and in that sense implicit in the previous event.[9] The sense that what has happened is what must happen is supported by the ostinato bass line. From five before to ten bars after S:1, the bass repeats exactly the same line it had in the previous fifteen measures. The literal repetition conveys the feeling that an ironclad destiny is unfolding and that it pays no heed to new dynamics. Nothing, one feels, that is not inherent in the process from the beginning can affect it. At the same time, it does not do violence to the oboe melody to hear it as a series of four four-bar subphrases (the first with a one-bar extension) which group themselves into a pair of pairs (see Figure 3b). It is possible, in short, to hear the oboe melody as a simple march with a straightforward symmetry. In this respect, the oboe line alludes to Classic paired phrases and suggests the kind of temporal process in which outcomes are grounded both in the past and in a decision-making and self-actualizing agent.

One can, of course, insist that one process will dominate the other and that the symmetrical organization is merely incipient and ornamental, its four-bar units suggesting plateaus along the inexorably unfolding pathway. But this interpretation is difficult to maintain in face of the strong contrast between the opening seventeen measures and the passage quoted in Figure 3a. The first seventeen bars sound very much like an introduction; having no trace of four-bar organization, they seem to be groping toward a themelike structure. When the oboe melody begins, it sounds very much like that which has been introduced; one is anticipating a four-bar organization, and the oboe melody does not frustrate this expectation.

Although the oboe tune suggests two kinds of temporal processes, it does not reconcile or synthesize them, for each has the effect of undercutting the other. To the extent that the future seems to be evoked by analogy to causation in nature, the validity of something like a free agent is attenuated, and to the extent that something like

FIGURE 3
Mahler, Second Symphony, first movement

a free agent seems to ground the process, the validity or something like natural causation is attenuated. In other words, each kind of grounding weakens the force of the other with the result that the outcome seems ungrounded at least as much as it is grounded. One is reminded of the old maxim that if two arguments are needed to support an idea, both may be suspected to be weak. The sum of two principles of continuity may be less than one.

When the first violins enter at S:1, they seem to be involved in a motivic play. They seem simply to be imitating the oboe's motif and filling in the gap between its subphrases. This way of hearing the violins' gesture at S:1 is confirmed when the oboe line recommences at three bars after S:1. When the violins reenter in the next measure, *molto espressivo,* they again seem to be imitating and embellishing the main melody. But the violin line refuses to stay in the background. It supplants the oboe as the bearer of the main melody. Two bars later, it is the oboe that is imitating the violins instead of the other way around (note the motifs marked with an asterisk in Figure 3a). It is the oboe's statement of the motif that overlaps the beginning of the fourth subphrase (just as it is the violins that overlap the beginning of the third subphrase). By the end of the oboe's fourth subphrase, the violin line has completely dominated the foreground, and the oboe line has been submerged without coming to closure. The violin line does not reach closure at ten bars after S:1 either, but presses ahead across the end of the oboe's fourth subphrase and the end of the bass's repetition. Closure finally comes at seventeen bars after S:1.

The exchange of background and foreground gestures — like the way figure and ground change places in some of Escher's and Pollock's paintings — is impossible in a Newtonian universe, or, some would say, in any self-consistent universe. The nature of space is contradicted when a point is said to be both further and nearer than another point. Because the violin line at first puts itself in the background behind the oboe line and then puts itself in the foreground in front of the oboe line — because, in short, both the violin and the oboe are both foreground and background to each other — the passage in Figure 3a is more disjointed, less analogous to ideally coherent processes than it may seem.

If there were no quasi-pairing of the phrases, the ear probably would not hear a tentative differentiation between foreground and background, and the two lines would simply be woven with the bass line into a single fabric, as their analogues in Baroque music are. Conventional phrase-pairing implies a differentiation between melody and background, and Mahler's paired-phrases grouping is just strong enough to force us to hear a foreground against a background. But then the repeated inversion of background into foreground prevents the lines from defining a single, self-consistent space. Imitating one another, the violin and oboe threads appear to be woven; not moving in the same space, the threads only appear to be woven. The imitation makes the process seem continuous as now the oboe and now the violin moves the process forward, but because of the inversion of foreground and background there is in fact no single kind of continuity from the beginning to the end of the passage. There is always some kind of continuity and there is closure, but the closure is not the outcome of the sum of the threads any more than it is the outcome of either one of them. Closure happens more groundlessly than it may appear.

A similar equivocation between mechanical cause as the ground of an event and the responsible self as the ground characterizes the first phrase of the slow movement in the Sixth Symphony (bars 1–10, Figure 4a), and here too the equivocation creates a sense that the

FIGURE 4
Mahler, Sixth Symphony, third movement

event has no ground at all or that it is both grounded and ungrounded. The first two measures set an antecedent subphrase into motion. The caesura between B-flat and D in the second measure resembles the articulation that typically divides a Classic subphrase into two balancing parts. The second part, however, extends itself beyond the expected length of two measures as a result of the G-flat in bar 4. The G-flat interferes with the conventional unfolding of the phrase, and resolving the G-flat lengthens the antecedent by six beats. The B-flat on the third beat in bar 5 begins a restatement, a third higher, of the opening motif. As a restatement, it seems to launch an answering phrase, but the sense of a consequent is attenuated by a metric dissonance: the restatement tries to make the third beat correspond to the downbeat of the antecedent.

The metric dissonance is resolved in bar 7. The last two beats of bar 6 extend the consequent's counterpart to beats three and four of bar 1. Beats one and two of bar 6 correspond to the third and fourth beats of bar 1, and the last two beats of bar 6 are an extension that enables the D of bar 7 to fall where its counterpart (the E-flat of bar 2) falls, namely on the downbeat. The putative consequent divides itself into two parts at the caesura between the D and D-flat of bar 7, but the caesura comes two beats too late to divide the consequent symmetrically (that is, the conventional caesura would have come after beat 3 of bar 6 and before the second beat of bar 7). By resolving the metric dissonance of bar 5, the articulation in bar 7 is dissonant with the meter of the consequent (that is, having heard beat 3 in bar 5 as a downbeat — though a displaced one — the listener expects beat 1 in bar 7 to be a weak beat). This second metric dissonance could have been avoided by deferring the resolution of the first one until the end of the consequent. Just how disturbing the metric dissonances are can be determined by comparing Mahler's phrase to the version given in Figure 4b, in which small changes turn the passage into a conventional pair of subphrases.

One finds, of course, both metric dissonances and extended subphrases in the music of Schumann, Brahms and other Romantic composers. They usually have the effect of suggesting the struggle (and often failure) of a self-actualizing agent to manifest itself concretely. When, however, the metric dissonance is combined with a clear restatement of the phrase's opening, as in bar 5 of Figure 4a, the effect is different. In this case, the reappearance of the opening motif signals the beginning of a consequent, but the metric dissonance, weakening the force of bars 5—10 as a consequent subphrase, has the effect of making the ten bars as much like a continuous unfolding or spinning forth of a single motif as like a pair of subphrases. Yet the hint of paired phrasing is too strong to allow bars 1—10 unambiguously to exemplify the process of mechanical causes producing predictable effects. One has a lingering sense of the difference between ending an antecedent and beginning a consequent even though the metric dissonance prevents one from locating the sense in a specific moment of the music. Something like a free decision is exemplified by the putative consequent subphrase. Listeners are led to and abandoned in a never-never land where neither kind of ground — neither the mechanical cause nor the self-actualizing agent — is wholly effective and where things happen without either kind of possible explanation. A sense of groundlessness which results from the inversion of foreground and background in the example from the Second Symphony is created here without the use of contrapuntally woven lines.

Mahler sometimes conflates an antecedent and a consequent gesture into a single phrase. In these phrases, the image of the self-actualizing agent appears and then evaporates. Typical is the four-bar subphrase quoted in Figure 5 from the Fourth Symphony. Identified

FIGURE 5a
Mahler, Fourth Symphony, first movement

as subphrase *a* in Figure 5b, it occurs three times in the exposition. It also occurs at the onset of the recapitulation (bars 234-240) where its first three bars are tucked away in the end of the development section, and the beginning of the coda (341) alludes to it. Each of its four complete appearances is followed by a four-bar subphrase — each time a different four-bar unit (the *x* subphrases in Figure 5) — which invariably summons an answering subphrase (the *b* subphrases in Figure 5), whose first two bars are always the same. The *x* and *b* subphrases pair themselves to one another as clearly and tightly as any conventional antecedent-consequent pair.

FIGURE 5b
Sketch of Mahler, Fourth Symphony, first movement, exposition

mm.	1—3	4—7	8—11	12—17	18—21	22—25	26—31
	Intro- duction	a	⌐x	b⌐	a	⌐x	b⌐

32—37	38—57	58—71	72—76	77—80	81—84	85—91
Bridge	2nd th.	Expo- sition closing	Intr.	a	⌐x	b⌐

But the *a* subphrase is strange, and its relation to the *x* subphrase is also strange. On the one hand, *a* seems to grow out of the introduction, which seems to launch an unfolding that continues through the *a* subphrase into the *x* and *b* subphrases. On the other hand, each *a* subphrase also begins as though it were an antecedent phrase, and it ends with the finality of a consequent phrase. Its closure is so strong and the forward thrust at its end is so minimal that it cannot be heard as generating or evoking the *x* subphrase, which is ushered in only by the repeated note pattern which the winds or brass take from the introduction. Because the *a* subphrase has the traditional length and because its beginning so clearly instantiates the listener's concept of an antecedent, the *x* subphrase seems to be a consequent. But it cannot be; the *a* leaves no residual tendencies for *x* to carry to completion, no mobility for it to absorb. It simple happens. The sense that the *x* subphrases only seem to be grounded in the *a* subphrases is underscored by the fact that all of them are different. Although they seem to be grounded in the unfolding process that begins in bar 1 and although they follow a subphrase whose beginning is generating a consequent, they also seem to exemplify a fortuitous, groundless occurrence both because they are not in fact generated by their immediately prior subphrases and because they do not base themselves on the other subphrases which occur in the analogous position between the *a* and the *b* subphrases. The *x* subphrases would not seem so strange were not the beginning of the *a* subphrases so analogous to the conventional antecedent and the relation of the *x* to the *b* subphrases so analogous to the conventional antecedent-consequent relation.[10]

Events on higher architectonic levels in Mahler's music also exemplify ungrounded occurrences. The Fifth Symphony, which Chapter I will analyze, is a good example. Each of its five movements may be described using the terms of a conventional form — a march, a sonata-allegro, a scherzo, a song form and a rondo. Like the paired subphrases described above, each movement begins by alluding to the temporal processes that we ordinarily assume to characterize consciousness, and in various ways it sustains these allusions during at least part of the movement. But during the course of the second, third and fifth movements, that kind of temporality is held together with one in which events simply happen — groundlessly and without arousing a need for an explanation. These movements reflect our confused consciousness that both demands coherence and unquestioningly accepts incoherence, that attributes events to mechanical causes or to decisions but also deals with events like beauty and accidents which, by the criteria of continuity which the concepts of causes and decisions reflect, are inconceivable and impossible. The Finale clarifies the nature of a consciousness in which the future and the past have meanings that are fundamentally different from what our ordinary reflection on consciousness says they must be.

In the Third Symphony, which Chapter II will analyze, Mahler seems to be continuously shifting the rules of continuity. Music is not easy to understand when the basic rules of what can appropriately follow what — of what second phrase can succeed a first phrase, of what can count as climax and what can count as closure, for example — are constantly changing. The absence of a single underlying mode of continuity suggests that some important musical events take place without justifying warrants or grounds. For the most part, Mahler's musical material is easily accessible, sometimes nostalgic, sometimes effortlessly beautiful,[11] but when in the Third Symphony and elsewhere he keeps changing the rules of continuity, he has alternatively baffled and infuriated listeners. Such changes might suggest that his symphonies are simply a mess, that he has dared more than he has succeeded, and that the great lengths of his symphonies bespeak a failure of organization more than cosmic comprehensiveness.[12] If the changing rules of continuity betoken an inability to compose, the beautiful material becomes sentimentality.

There is, however, another possibility. The shifting rules of continuity may suggest changes from one temporal process to another. Fundamental changes in temporal processes may be interpreted as changes in the nature of consciousness. The Third leads us through temporal processes that associate themselves variously with with unconsciousness, semi-consciousness and full consciousness. The conflicting kinds of continuity and temporality are presented as a procession. In the Finale, Mahler goes not only beyond the usual concept that consciousness has of itself, but also beyond a consciousness in which grounded events coexist with events that simply happen. Mahler seems to be suggesting a radically new temporality that may characterize a post-human consciousness or a transfigured consciousness. It is a kind of consciousness of which human beings have at most only occasional, shadowy intimations. This introductory chapter and most of the following two chapters concern themselves primarily with Mahler's assault on the temporal process that consciousness reflecting on itself seems to require and with his presentation of temporal processes that may more nearly comport with the confused consciousness that we may actually live. The last two chapters will focus on the transformed temporalities presented in the Eighth and Ninth Symphonies and the transfigured consciousness that each of them implies. The two parts of the Eighth exemplify in different but complementary ways a temporal process that feels strange and disorienting. Both parts have texts that deal with redemption, inviting us to suppose it is Mahler's vision of redeemed consciousness whose temporality the musical processes exemplify. Neither part pays much attention to a world in which things take place by mechanistic causation or by human choices or in which they simply happen to take place. It is not the transformation of temporality but transformed temporality that is presented. Longer and richer than the Third Symphony Finale, each movement gives us a fuller presentation of a new temporality and a new consciousness.

Both the first and the last movements of the Ninth Symphony lead us through a process which resembles that transversed by the Third as a whole. Each of these movement begins with one kind of temporality and ends in another. And, as the temporal process is transformed, the implied nature of consciousness is also transformed. The two endings differ in subtle ways that are important enough to force us to compare them.

We are not transfigured simply by listening to these movements. We may learn what a new temporality and a transfigured consciousness may be like (and what Mahler envisions them to be like), but to understand this music does not imply that one's consciousness is changed or even that it can be changed. After all, these movements metaphorically exemplify processes of which we have no concrete experience. Mahler is providing figurative examples of processes for which we may have no literal samples. We may have no prior experience that his music may be illuminating, clarifying and modifying. Even intensely religious people for the most part claim no more than anticipations or foreshadowings of the redeemed state. We may be perplexed by the Fifth Symphony and the first five movements of the Third because they simultaneously promise and withhold conventional continuity and contradict the way we may prefer to think about consciousness. But at least these movements purport to present the temporalities in which we actually live. The Finale of the Third, all of the Eighth and the outside movements of the Ninth may well be more perplexing, because they lead us into temporal modes which, outside this music, structure our experiences only fragmentarily, or not at all.

Notes

1. *Faust*, part one, scene 1, lines 29—31, trans. Randall Jarrell (1976).

2. *Patterns of Discovery* (1958), p. 92.

3. Arthur Danto, in *The Transfiguration of the Commonplace* (1981), pp. 18—20, 76—77, mentions these three religious experiences as a way of distinguishing "re-presentation," which they instantiate, from "representation," which is what happens when anything stands as proxy for something else. Experiences understood as re-presentations have to be reinterpreted as representations when the relation of the divine reality to the event is construed as analogous to that of cause to effect or decision to result.

4. See Leonard B. Meyer, "The End of the Renaissance?" in *Music, the Arts and Ideas* (1967), pp. 68—84, and Jonathan Kramer, "Moment Form in Twentieth-Century Music," *Musical Quarterly*, vol. 64/2 (1978), pp. 177—194. Kramer calls attention to the relation of musical discontinuity to contemporary experience: "To remove continuity is to question the very meaning of time in our culture" (p. 178). He also notes Stockhausen's quest for eternity through discontinuity: "A given moment is not merely regarded as the consequence of the previous one and the prelude to the next . . . This concentration on the present moment — on every present moment — can make a vertical cut, as it were, across horizontal time perception, extending out to a timelessness I call eternity" (*Texte I*, p. 199, trans. Seppo Heikinheimo, *The Electronic Music of Karlheinz Stockhausen* [1972], pp. 120—121; quoted in Kramer, p. 179). Neither Stockhausen's goals nor his means are so different from Mahler's (especially in the Eighth Symphony) as the difference between their sonorities might lead one to believe.

5. *Languages of Art* (1968), p. 69. For a rigorous analysis of the concept of "metaphorical exemplification" and for a careful argument that this concept is the only consistent way to understand what the term "expression"in music criticism can mean, see pp. 52—71 and 85—95. Since this book appeared, much of the philosophical discussion of artistic expression has been based on the exemplification theory. Its importance becomes particularly clear when Danto uses it (*op. cit.*, pp. 189—194) to clarify the logic of metaphor and the relation of art to the rest of reality.

6. This important amplification of Goodman's exemplification theory is spelled out by Monroe Beardsley in "Understanding Music," in *On Criticizing*

32   *Mahler, Consciousness and Temporality*

Music: Five Philosophical Perspectives, edited by Kingsley Price (1981).

7. Wilfred Mellers, "Mahler as Key-Figure" in *Studies in Contemporary Music* (1947), pp. 115–117, rightly points out that the cumulative effect of Mahler's manipulation of the antecedent-consequent structure — stretching and loosening the phrase — is both to revert to the principles implicit in the polyphony that prevailed in Italian music before the advent of paired phrasing and also to anticipate the kind of melody characteristic of expressionist music. "To reconcile these principles [of the Italian polyphonists] with the dramatic symphonic ideal was the real struggle . . . behind his working life." Without disagreeing with Meller's generalization, this book tries to indicate the effect of Mahler's manipulation in particular passages.

8. For a detailed argument of the claim that the paired phrases and sections of sonata-allegro movements in the Classic period exemplify a process closely akin to that of a free self making decisions, see David B. Greene, *Temporal Processes in Beethoven's Music* (1982), pp. 17–24.

9. For an elaboration of the idea that a continuously unfolding line, in which each new segment seems to have been implicit in the previous one, resembles a Newtonian temporal process, see Greene, *op. cit.,* pp. 7–10.

10. Other interpretations of the peculiarities of Mahler's phrase structures may, of course, be offered. An important example may be found in the first comprehensive study of Mahler's music, Paul Bekker's *Gustav Mahlers Sinfonien* (1921), which has greatly influenced conductors, musicologists and record-jacket commentators over the years. Like the paragraphs analyzing Figures 1 through 5, Bekker calls attention to the "continuous growing, interweaving, budding and blooming" that characterizes Mahler's themes. However, he sees an "unending thematic becoming" which makes it "useless and indeed untenable to try to hear periodic grouping" (p. 41). Bekker seems to be suggesting that the Mahlerian theme is analogous to the natural processes of growth that characterize all living organisms, but he also speaks of the "absolute freedom of pure fantasy" which they exhibit, as though they were analogous to neither nature nor rational human consciousness as ordinarily conceived.

Bekker does not seem to notice that Mahler explicitly alludes to periodic grouping at the same time that he makes periodic grouping, in the end, untenable. Consequently, Bekker misses the possibility that Mahler's phrase structure may evoke the common-sense concept of consciousness in order to reject it and replace it with a different understanding of consciousness.

Schoenberg, in *Style and Idea* (1975), pp. 460–462, overlooks the metric dissonance in the theme to the Andante in the Sixth Symphony and interprets the theme as a four-bar antecedent, extended by half a measure, followed by a four-and-a-half-bar consequent, extended by a full measure. Nevertheless, he does not contradict an analysis involving the idea of a metric dissonance when he says of the theme, "This is not the *tour de force* of a 'technician' — a master would not bring it off, if he made up his mind to it in advance. These are inspirations which escape the control of consciousness, inspirations which come only to the genius, who receives them unconsciously and formulates solutions without noticing that a problem has confronted him."

Theodor Adorno's *Mahler: eine musikalische Physiognomik* (1960) elucidates Mahler's dialectic of simultaneously affirming and denying. According to Adorno, Mahler sets the hurly-burly of everyday routine — what Hegel calls the "course of the world" — into his music, and then contradicts it by the appearance of that which is new and other to that process and which consequently ruptures the musical flow. For example, the climactic entrance of the brass fanfare at the onset of the reprise in the opening movement of the First Symphony is heard as "a tear in the musical fabric. Something that comes from beyond the music's own intrinsic motion is interfering with the musical process" (*Gesammelte Schriften*, vol. 13, p. 153). Such moments are a rupture in the musical process because they lack musical warrants. They are like events which, from the perspective of the endless succession of public events — the world's course — are unheard of and impossible. Indeed, from the perspective of public events, only the outer shell of the new can be seen, and, unable to appreciate its inner core, this perspective must reject the new as stupid and meaningless, just as some of Mahler's critics have seen the ruptures in his musical flow as evidence of compositional incompetence and the lack of craftmanship. From a perspective that does not see the emptiness of routine activity, the rupturing events simply happen, for they are the diametric opposite to events that have the customary grounds and explanations.

One might suppose that the rupturing event would exemplify the process of free individuals setting themselves against routine, and that the new seems simply to happen groundlessly only from a false perspective on human activity, but that in fact it has the decision of a free agent as its ground. In other words, it is not groundless, but has a different kind of ground. Adorno, following Kant and Hegel (and Beethoven), assumed the possibility of such a different kind of ground, but then he goes on to admit that the new — the other that would concretize the free individual whether in accord with or contrary to the course of the world — is not in fact actualized. The rupture protests against the world's course, but it only appears to actualize its opposite. The reason is that "the manifestation of the rupture is disfigured by what is required for the rupture to take place" (pp. 159—160). While the rupture exemplifies an experience that is inimical to the logic of art, it needs art to manifest itself. Indeed, it must enhance art; Mahler must, and does, invent new artistic techniques for the sake of manifesting his vision of the new taking place, and precisely for this reason the rupture fails to become an actuality. It is an artistic image of the rupture as much as it is the rupture itself. Mahler's music remains in the grip of a dialectic: "To realize the rupture musically means to testify at the same time that it has failed to become an actuality" (p. 154). For Adorno, this dialectic reflects the fact that society is immanent within musical form, and the opposite to society cannot become immanent within the form that is derived from society. In that it realizes the new, the rupture is intelligible as grounded in the free self, but unintelligible to the course of the world. In that the new is not realized, the musical events that appear to manifest the rupture are in the end somewhat clumsy from both perspectives. The free self may see this clumsiness as grounded in the way its opposite — the course of the world — is in spite of the self persistently immanent in the music, but it can see no ground for this persistence. The clumsiness bespeaks an arbitrariness — a brute facticity — at the very core of human reality.

Adorno's dialectic may be applied not only to putative climaxes which both do and do not embody the new that tears the musical fabric apart but also to their lower-level analogues within the paired phrases quoted in Figures 1 through 5. All of these both allude to the reject Classic periodic groupings and the way such groupings exemplify the process of a free agent making a decision and actualizing itself while fulfilling its past. In the examples from the First and Second Symphonies, the closure represents a fulfillment that is in fact a rupture because the process that appears to have generated it in fact does not. The persistent immanence of society asserts itself in the appearance of generating the closure, that is, in the way that Mahler hides the arbitrariness of the ending behind his contrapuntal facility. The fifth measure of the example from the Sixth Symphony, where an answering phrase that would exemplify the force of something like a free decision both does and does not begin, represents both the appearance and the non-appearance of the new. As Adorno interprets this moment (p. 253), it is both the beginning and the ending of a phrase; as a beginning it shows the new asserting itself, while as an ending it shows the opposite of the new asserting itself. In other words, as mediating between the balanced, periodic groups of Classic music, and the spinning forth that is reminiscent of Baroque music, the phrase as a whole embodies the rupture as both taking place and not taking place. In the example from the Fourth Symphony, Adorno's rupture is exemplified both by the end of the *a* subphrases and by the onset of the *x* subphrases. For the analogy to Classic paired groups leads listeners to expect the one to end with forward thrust and the other to respond to that thrust, but instead the first ends with an unexpected closure (so there is no thrust to which the second may respond), and the self-generating quality consequently felt at the beginning of the second shows the presence of something like Adorno's rupture.

Adorno's interpretation explicitly assumes that it is the relation between the individual and society that makes the appearance of the new a dialectical process. It implicitly assumes, along with western post-medieval thinking generally, that human consciousness must suppose that events have grounds and that every present involves the expectation of a future on the basis of knowing those grounds. Adorno makes the same assumptions in his study of the late Beethoven, and what he says about Mahler closely resembles what he says about the late Beethoven. The difference between them is apparently that Beethoven gives us early symptoms of the futurelessness that comes with the loss of individual autonomy while Mahler is much closer to that futurelessness itself, which finally takes place in the serial music of Arnold Schoenberg.

The difference between the late Beethoven and Mahler is, then, a difference in degree of explicitness. The implied lack of genuine difference runs contrary to Adorno's attachment to the Hegelian-Marxist notion of historical development, but this contradiction fits Adorno's interpretation of nineteenth-century music: the very lack of genuine difference signals the individual's loss of freedom; historical stagnation inevitably accompanies the loss of autonomy. This implication is carefully elaborated in Rose Rosengard Subotnik, "The Historical Structure: Adorno's 'French' Model for the Criticism of Nineteenth-Century Music" in *Nineteenth-Century Music*, vol. 2 (1978), pp. 36—60. For an analysis of Adorno's remarks on the late Beethoven, see Prof. Subotnik, "Adorno's Diagnosis of Beethoven's Late Style: Early Symptoms of a Fatal Condition" in *Journal of the American Musicological Society*, vol. 29 (1976), pp. 242—275.

One may wonder whether Adorno does justice to the difference between late Beethoven and Mahler. To be sure, both of them simultaneously allude to and reject Classic paired groupings. But Beethoven gives us consequents that lack closure because they are not fully responsive to their antecedents and residual energy attenuates the sense of embodying fulfillment, while the examples from Mahler give us a closure that is unearned, not the result of a process, hence arbitrary. It would seem that while Beethoven really is exemplifying Adorno's dialectic, Mahler is exemplifying a radically different kind of temporality — one in which groundlessness is not impossible — from that which Adorno assumes.

Adorno might have been more consistent to his own assumptions as well as more faithful to Mahler's music had he said that an individual who undergoes the dialectic exemplified in Beethoven will come to experience events as ultimately groundless, as exemplified in Mahler. In other words, the temporality of Adorno's dialectic has, in Mahler, transformed itself into a new kind of temporality. One might interpret the history of the nineteenth-century symphony as the history of this transformation, looking for it primarily in the symphonies of Schubert and Bruckner, rather than in those of Schuman, Mendelssohn and Brahms (see Bekker, *op. cit.*, pp. 11—19). For while the latter may justify Adorno's implication of historical stagnation, Schubert and Bruckner developed modes of continuation that differed significantly from Beethoven's. (Although this book will not enter into the debate about the extent of the resemblance and debt of Mahler's music to Bruckner's, it may be noted in passing that some of Mahler's modes of continuation — namely those in which a passage whose motifs, though clearly chiseled, succeed one another in such a way that its shape seems amorphous is gradually transformed into a passage with themelike shapeliness — significantly resemble Bruckner's, even though Bruckner's motifs and themes are much more abstract in that they do not suggest, as Mahler's do, qualities like restlessness, torment, anger and peace.)

11. Donald Francis Tovey speaks for many when he writes, "There is no class of composer, diabolist [e.g. Liszt] or purist, for whom a first impression of Mahler will not cause pangs of jealousy . . . In every technical direction — form, counterpoint, and instrumentation — his musical facility is . . . enormous . . . What we composers find so disconcerting about Mahler is that every aspect of his work shows all the advantages of an unchecked facility and none of the disadvantages." *Essays in Musical Analysis*, vol. 6 (1939), pp. 74—76.

12. Donald Jay Grout in *A History of Western Music* (1960) typifies the reaction of many musicologists to Mahler. He sees Mahler as attempting to join dualistically opposed elements whose combination would constitute a total cosmos and notes that the attempt is "not always with success" (pp. 574—575).

CHAPTER I

The Fifth Symphony

Mahler's Fifth Symphony leads us through moods of sadness, anger, jubilation, lilting cheerfulness, intimate serenity to triumphant affirmation. It is easy enough to put labels like these on the various movements or even on successive passages within each movement, but what label shall we use if we want to know how each mood qualifies the others? What is the precise nature of each of these moods in the context of the others? And how does Mahler get us from one mood to the next: does he portray the changes of mood as simply happening, or as being willed by their subject, or as being caused by an external force? What must be the nature of consciousness and temporality in order that this procession of moods be convincing and coherent? These questions are important, because the affirmation at the end is triumphant only if the process of getting there is plausible. If we resonate to Mahler's ending, we must also find that his way of coming upon that ending has parallels in the way our lives unfold. If it does not, either we must admit that the ending is not convincing after all, or we must change the way we think about the temporality of our own experience.

These questions are sometimes answered by quoting Mahler's comment, "the symphony is the world; it must embrace everything." But the question has been rephrased, not answered: how does the Fifth hold everything together?

Some listeners have responded in the negative: the ending is not psychologically convincing; Mahler does not hold his world together. These listeners have variously interpreted his music as the autobiography of a composer or the autobiography of a culture. As personal autobiography, the symphony exposes the childhood scars made by his siblings' deaths, or his loneliness in an alien world, or his conflict between loving life and resigning himself fatalistically to its loss; the exuberant Finale is a brave face that only hides the man's agony and pretends to overcome his inner strife. As the autobiography of a culture, the symphony's incongruities, non-sequiturs, dislocations and disruptions and the lack of a fit between its climaxes and their preparations, all of which are combined with grandeur and heroism, express the decay of Western society. Written in 1901–1902, ten years before *commedia* figures incongruously appear on Naxos in Strauss's *Ariadne*, the Fifth Symphony incongruously juxtaposes a jaunty march to a tragic cry and a poignant murmur in its second movement; its Scherzo incongruously sets nostalgia down in the midst of frenzy; and its Adagietto–Rondo puts an elevated, soulful meditation next to a thumping peasant dance. Every atmosphere is overcharged, and the excess exacerbates the incongruities. Or, if it makes each mood so overbearing that the others do not impinge on it, the excess insulates each section against the incongruity. Like Klimt, Schnitzler and Freud, Mahler is in some sense aware of impulse and instinct and how they generate what to the rational mind are non-sequiturs. Like his contemporaries, Mahler is aware that the old values are irretrievably lost, but he is too keenly imbedded in his culture to construct new ones. Mahler's defects are symptoms of a society that has lost its center and helplessly mourns the loss.

Mahler's more single-minded enthusiasts, of course, simply deny that his music is marred by dislocations. If Mahler imports an incongruous idea, they say, he puts his own stamp on it, and makes it appropriate. The putative disruptions are simply postponements that are longer than usual, the inevitable and justifiable result of painting on a vast canvas. Mahler's "mastery of form" fits the preparations to the climaxes and the climaxes of contrasting sections to one another.[1] This assertion is typically justified by pointing to his complex network of interconnected motifs. But motivic cross-references by themselves do not unify a work or hold a world together.

One suspects that the disruptions would be more candidly acknowledged were it not that Mahler's melodies so fill the mind and his orchestration so compels respect for each event that the listener is lured away from structural problems. A climax carried by such a melody and such a sound is so convincing that one may unconsciously assume that it must fit its preparation. Some conductors have supported this inattentiveness by building their performances around the lyrical and the climactic passages and glossing over the details that might have disturbed the continuity; this style of performance may have also supported the judgment that Mahler is *Kitsch*.

For Mahler's more balanced enthusiasts, the incongruities are real, but instead of marring his music, they suggest that it is working from an ironic perspective: the jaunty march in the second movement mocks the heroic fanfares of the first; as the Scherzo becomes more and more demonic, it caricatures the whirl of life off of which it spins; the Rondo mocks the sentiments of the soulful Adagietto by turning its theme into an open-air romp. But the situation is more complex than these critics have imagined. For Mahler is not only ironic: the music confirms the values of heroism, poignancy, lilt or good cheer at the same time that it mocks itself for being heroic, poignant, lilting or jocular, and it mocks those who unreflectively applaud heroism, poignancy, lilt or good cheer at the same time that it mocks those who unreflectively mock all these dispositions. Like the perspective in the cubist style that Picasso is going to initiate in 1906, the point of view in the Fifth is multiple. In order to get to the bottom of the matter, one must deal with the question, what is the nature of consciousness such that multiple attitudes are possible? And its corollaries, what kind of temporal process articulates a consciousness with multiple perspectives; what is the nature of the temporal process such that one can move from tragedy and anger to joyful affirmation by way of non-sequiturs?

The burden of this chapter will be to develop some new terms and concepts that can be used to describe this complex temporal process in which the triumph comes and to define the affirmation itself more precisely. Tracing this process will be a matter of patiently following Mahler from one section, even one phrase to the next throughout the symphony, asking at each point how what we have heard relates itself to what we expect to come. Along the way, help will be sought in analogies between Mahler's music and works by Schnitzler, Klimt, Kraus, Heidegger and Sartre. These analogies may suggest that Mahler was influenced by his contemporaries, or that the phenomenologists were moved by the Viennese artists, or that all of them were children of their age and of its excesses, agonies and wrenches, or that Mahler was indeed the amanuensis by which the declining Austrian empire was writing its autobiography. But this suggestion will not be developed. The analogies are intended to illumine Mahler's music and not to argue that his music is the product of a man in torment or a society in upheaval.

1. Part One

Part One of the Fifth Symphony comprises two movements. The first movement is a dirge whose fanfares and marches paint a picture of death and its scars on public and private life. The second movement opens with a storm of bitter anger, a response to death and its inescapability. Driven by a motif suggesting uncontrollable rage (see Eigure 10, bar 1), the storm reappears four times (see Figure 6). Between the five "anger" sections there appear four contrasting sections that use a family of motifs derived from the first movement.[2] In all but the third of these sections, these motifs come from the trio sections of the first movement (see Figure 7). These motifs

FIGURE 6
Sketch of Mahler, Fifth Symphony, second movement

sections using anger motif	sections using first-movement motifs	chorale
1–73	74–140*	
141–187	188–253*	
254–265	266–315†	(316–322)
323–355	356–463*	464–519
520–576		

*compare bars 78–115, 214–221 and 356–392 with first movement, bars 323–369, and bars 116–124, 222–229 and 400–427 with first movement, bars 203–220

†compare bars 266–277 with first movement, bars 121–132. The passage from 278 to 315 grows out of the quotation of the first-movement march, though it also uses some of the anger motifs.

FIGURE 7
Sketch of Mahler, Fifth Symphony,
first movement

fanfare	march	trio
1–34	35–60	
61–88	89–152	
153–154		155–232
233–262	263–316	
317–322		323–376
377–415		

contain the upward stepwise motion that permeate Mahler's works and that, according to Philip Barford,[3] Mahler associates variously

FIGURE 8
Mahler, Fifth Symphony

with aspiration, upsurging inspiration and longing loneliness. In the case of the first-movement prototypes, where the next to last note in the rising line is repeated, becoming dissonant to the bass (at * in Figure 8a), and resolving upward (sometimes into a dissonant interval against the bass), the rising gesture suggests a struggle — a laborious aspiration. Barford has shown that elsewhere Mahler frequently, almost obsessively, follows the rising line with an upward leap that, he says, symbolizes liberation — that is, release from the tension generated by the rising figure, fulfilling its goal (although sometimes, as in the Tenth Symphony, it is distorted into agonizing frustration) — and then with a falling whole-step motif which Barford links variously with serenity, exhaustion, death — either self-transcendence through love (as in the last movements of the Third and the Eighth) or self-negation through resignation to death (as in "Der Abschied" from *Das Lied von der Erde*). In the second movement of the Fifth, the rising line is indeed followed by a leap and then a falling whole step (at ‡ in Figure 8b). In the context of this symphony, these elements seem to connote a quest for liberating peace; they extend the attempt, begun in the trio sections of the first movement, to understand or transcend or resign oneself to the fact of death that is so grimly presented in the first-movement march sections.

Toward the end of the second movement, Mahler gives us a brass chorale that is as glorious as any ever written. Exploiting techniques of effective brass writing that one also finds in Wagner, Bruckner and Strauss as well as Mahler's earlier symphonies, it suggests an exuberant, public jubilation whose outward expression matches an inward intensity.[4]

As a sequel to the anger aroused by death and the struggle to deal with one's feelings in face of it, the public jubilation in the chorale near the end of the movement may seem monstrously inappropriate. Does alternating between stormy anger and a quest for peace and then making a thrilling affirmation exemplify a process like facing and then willfully turning one's back on the negative aspects of existence? Or is the chorale appropriate because it exemplifies courageously affirming what can be affirmed in spite of the negativities? These possibilities presuppose that the mode of continuation embodied in the movement resembles the way a free decision shapes a future which genuinely responds to its past and that the way the contrast between what has been, what is and what is to come is experienced in this movement resembles the way this contrast is experienced by a decision-making self. Ought one to presuppose instead that the movement somehow exemplifies a process like that of a past determining a future? That is, if we look more closely at the sections suggesting anger and the quest for peace, shall we see that in them the brass chorale is already implicit? Or does the brass chorale function not as that which has been determined by its past, but as one of the determinants of the future, namely a future in which the anger theme dominates (as it does in the section, bars 520–576, that follows the chorale) and in which death is all the more horrible because the jubilation has made clear precisely what it is that we lose because of death?

In short, just what is this rejoicing that can take place on the heels of sorrow and rage? The following analysis will approach this question by asking a subsidiary (and more manageable) question: Precisely how does Mahler's music relate the stormy sections and the peace-questing sections to one another? And both of these to the shout of joy? A preliminary answer is that the contrasting sections do not so much alternate with each other as converge upon one another, and as they do so, they also converge upon the shout of joy. For although the first anger and the first peace-questing sections seem to be utterly different, as though opposites were meaninglessly juxtaposed, there are latent and profound relationships that come to the surface in subsequent statements. This confluence happens in such a way, however, that it unambiguously exemplifies neither a process like that of an earlier state of affairs determining a later one nor a process like that of making and actualizing a free, future-creating decision, but rather a process that is similar to both of these in some respects and different from them both in others. Consequently, the temporal process of this confluence — the sense in which the anger and the quest for peace have the convergence as their future and are the past of the convergence — must be delineated with particular care.

(1) Anger and the Quest for Peace

Mahler relates the five sections stating the anger motif to the peace-questing sections in four ways: they have some motifs in common; in successive appearances, motifs from each one contaminate the other so that the contrast between them becomes blurred; there are significant analogies between the structures of their phrases; and a variety of techniques are used to connect the end of one section to the beginning of a contrasting section.

(i) Motifs Shared by the Anger and the Peace-Questing Sections

The anger sections are conspicuously different from the peace-questing sections in tonality, mood, tempo and melodic configuration. Nevertheless, their background textures have two important features in common. Both of them use repeated eighth notes in the brass or winds (compare, for example, bars 3—4 and 29—30 to 74—86 and 115; see Figure 9), and both of them use an upward leaping minor ninth or variants thereon (in, for example, bars 6—8 and 74—76; see Figure 10). Moreover, the stepwise triplets that do much to give the peace-questing sections their particular character are anticipated, somewhat fleetingly to be sure, in the first anger section (compare bare 48 to 117).

The presence of these features links the two kinds of sections not only to each other but also to the first movement. For the first four notes of the symphony (the fanfare: ♫♩|♩) as well as the accompaniment in the second trio of the first movement (bars 323—351) use the repeated-note idea that is so important in the second movement, first in helping to establish the mood of anger and then in creating a throbbing background during the quest for peace. And the leap of a minor ninth is foreshadowed by the abrupt leap to the dissonant G-flat that drives the "passionately wild" first trio of the first movement (bar 155), and is explicitly anticipated by the upward leaping minor ninths in the accompaniment to the second trio (violas, bars 323—336). The persistent recurrence of these motifs as well as the reappearance, as noted above, of foreground motifs from the first movement in the foreground of the peace-questing sections, consistently reminds the listener of that movement. The reminder thickens the second movement's atmosphere by maintaining the force of the first movement's tensions, even producing a sense that the dirge has not ended.

Or, better, it confirms the impression created by the first move-

FIGURE 9
Mahler, Fifth Symphony, second movement

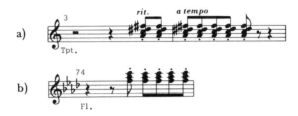

FIGURE 10
Mahler, Fifth Symphony, second movement

ment itself that it does not come to an ending. The dirge consists of a succession of sections which either peter out or are interrupted before reaching closure. The funeral procession — when, as it were, we see the cortege moving past us — takes place in bars 35–60, 89–152 and 263–316 (See Figure 7).[5] These march sections are preceded and interrupted by heroic fanfares and by two trio sections. The first fanfare prepares, though it does not lead into the march proper, in two ways. First, it opens up the tonal space in which the march will take place. And second, it modulates the contrast between the highly regular phrase structure of the march (in which eight-bar phrases are paired to one another, and each eight-bar phrase consists of two four-bar subphrases that are also paired to each other) and a more undifferentiated structure in which each successive geature seems more to extend than to respond to the previous one and gestures do not come to clear, cadential endings. The fanfare brings about this modulation by beginning with a passage (bars 1–14) which does not divide itself into subphrases that evoke and respond to one another and then giving us gestures (bars 15–20, 21–24, 25–28 and 29–34), each of which sounds more and more like a phrase that will summon a responding pair into existence. While each successive gesture sounds more and more like a phrase paired to the previous gesture, such pairing does not take place until the hearse begins to move in bar 35, its black crepe absorbing all the light flashing from the fanfares.

In bar 61 the fanfare returns. In fact, the return has begun to happen before the end of the march; the last eight bars of the march allude to the last eight bars of the first fanfare. Partly because the return inserts itself in this way, it does not seem to be a response evoked by the march. Rather it is as though the focus of attention were simply shifted away from the public event and turned inward, contemplating once again the heroism and nobility of the dead person. Although heroism is implicit in the march sections, the fanfare makes it explicit, just as sadness is more implicit in the fanfare and more explicit in the march. The fanfare is grander this second time. By delaying the climax in bars 72–74 (in comparison to bars 12–13), Mahler makes it more thrilling. This change and other small variations make this statement of the fanfare more an entity in its own right than a preparation for the march. The meditation on human courage and greatness simply dies away at the end of the second fanfare, and the march resumes as if it had not been interrupted; it is as unchanged as if a fanfare had not intervened.

The march is interrupted again, this time by the first trio. In this passage, the sadness that pervades the fanfares and marches bursts out in a terrible scream for release from grief. The march does not generate this outburst. Once again, it is as though our attention drifted from the public event, this time to make explicit the horrible pain associated with the death of the person whose corpse is passing by. In gestures of uncontrollable agony we cry out for release from the pain. Fragments of the fanfare come to the surface during this trio, suggesting that it is human greatness that makes death so unintelligible and unbearably painful. The trio does not reach closure. Although it does not attain a resolution, our attention drifts away from its concerns in bar 233, where the fanfare is restated. For the fanfare marks the beginning of a new section; it is not a continuation or a further unfolding of the trio. Still less is the fanfare a resolution to the trio or an answer to its cry for release from pain. It is as though the pain and tensions of the trio were temporarily suppressed while attention is refocused on heroism.

The rest of the movement repeats the pattern made by bars 1–232, alternating between the inner and outer worlds and, in the inner world, between celebrating heroism (the fanfares) and seeking release (the trio) from the grief generated by the combination of heroism and death. The cortege seems to reach the end of its journey; ending in the major in bar 316, the march closes somewhat more conclusively this time.[6] But its finality does nothing to bring the other two kinds of music to a satisfactory close. In the second trio, the quest for liberation from pain begins calmly but ends in a shriek that is even more dreadful than the outburst in the first trio. The music does, of course, come to a stop. But at the end of the movement there is no resolution to the search for release from pain, no resolution to the tension generated by juxtaposing heroism to death. The situation and feelings that the movement lays bare are still raw and exposed at its end. The force of these unresolved tensions is maintained throughout the second movement by the persistence of first-movement motifs. Consequently, what happens at the end of the second movement happens to the first movement's tensions as well. Mahler is not being arbitrary when he groups the two movements together as Part One of the symphony.

(ii) The Exchange of Motifs between the Anger and the Peace-Questing Sections

The contrast between the angry and the peace-questing sections of the second movement is stark in spite of the important motifs that they share with one another and with the first movement. But although their atmospheres seem entirely alien in their first appearances, the two sections come to resemble one another in subsequent statements. Anger-section motifs that initially helped produce the contrast between the two sections enter peace-questing sections and seem at home there. Figure 11 lists these exchanges.

FIGURE 11
Exchange of Motifs

motifs from the "anger" sections	that appear in a "peace-questing" section
22—25 (violins)	238—241 (cellos)
37—41 (violins)	362—370 (violins)
44—46 (trumpets)	230—233 (cellos), 242—244 (horns)

The exchanges of motifs show that the peace-questing sections are more compatible with the elements of the anger sections than the initially strong contrast would seem to have allowed. The underlying attitudes suggested by the two kinds of music may have a complementarity that their contrast initially conceals. After all, the anger is, in an importance sense, world-affirming: if life in the world were not valuable and worthy, one would feel no anger over its loss. And the quest for peace is a yearning for that which can be affirmed.

(iii) Phrase Structures and Their Similarities

One aspect of the music that facilitates the motivic exchanges and makes them seem musically appropriate when they take place is a close similarity between the phrase structures of the two sections. There are two kinds of structures that pervade both sections on various architectonic levels. First, both sections repeatedly articulate a pattern that consists of a statement, an intensifying repetition and an arrival. (Using the techniques of rhythmic analysis developed by Cooper and Meyer,[7] this pattern may be described as a double-anacrusis — thesis, ∪ ∪ —; the term "anacrusis" is used to refer not only to a forward-directed weak beat but also to a group of several bars that generates the next passage, which in turn functions as the focus or thesis of the anacrustic measures. As Cooper and Meyer have shown, a group may function as an anacrusis even if it is a forceful statement in its own right.)

And, second, both sections consist of a series of three groups in which the pairing between subphrases is stronger in each successive group: the initial, somewhat amorphously structured groups seem preparatory, the second group seems to be an arrival, but its quality of arrival is surpassed by that in the third group. The procession from an introduction to a statement that turns out to be introductory to an emphatic statement is a higher-level analogue to the double-anacrusis — thesis patterns that are articulated on lower architectonic levels. The higher- and lower-level structures support one another.

The following two subsections will study these phrase structures closely and develop the concept of "having decided" as a way of describing their distinctive quality. This concept is important not only because it seems to characterize these structures but also because, as the analysis later will suggest, it aptly refers to important aspects of both the convergence upon the shout of joy and the jubilant brass chorale itself. For the similarities between the structures in the first anger and peace-questing sections not only facilitate the subsequent exchange of motifs but also, it turns out, have significant ramifications for the convergence of the two on the brass chorale.

(a) Phrase structures in the first anger section. The movement opens with two instances of the double-anacrusis — thesis pattern

(bars 1—6 and 7—9; See Figure 10), and the two together function as a double anacrusis to a coming thesis. Both instances consist of a figure that is stated and then twice repeated. The third statement alters the repeated figure so that it both absorbs the pressure generated by the first two statements and also makes the set as a whole press on urgently to something else. Figure 12 sketches this opening (in the sketch, the symbol ⊔̄ indicates a passage that initially sounds thetic in relation to what has preceded it, but turns out to be anacrustic to what follows it).

FIGURE 12
Sketch of Mahler, Fifth Symphony, second movement

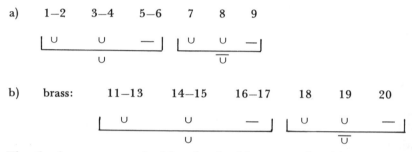

The thetic passage evoked by the double anacrusis of bars 1—6 and 7—9 begins with the upbeat to bar 9. Bars 9—18 group themselves into a phrase that seems to be paired to bars 20—30. Although bars 9—30 may create the impression of an unstructured torrent, two features account for the analogy to conventional phrase organization: first, bars 9—18 are so fragmentary and urgent (and increasingly fragmentary and urgent, for as successive elements are briefer and briefer, the pace quickens) that they generate an expectation for a longer gesture; and, second, the two phrases, typical of paired phrases, begin with the same melodic idea and both of them are introduced in the same way (compare 7—9 to 18—20). Moreover, each phrase somewhat vaguely suggests the shape of a pair of subphrases. The first phrase has a caesura after its fourth downbeat (violins in bar 12), precisely where a conventional subphrase would end. What follows (that is, bars 13—18) responds to the first subphrase in that its rising line (bars 13—15) mirrors the falling line of bars 9—12; and its last two bars are a compressed version of the first subphrase. The phrase ends on the unstable second degree of the scale (the violins' B in bar 18), so that bars 9—18 as a group summon a paired phrase. The answering phrase also consists of paired subphrases (bars 20—23 and 24—30).

But in both phrases, Mahler overlays elements that attenuate the paired subphrases structure. The ending of the introduction (bar 9) overlaps the onset of the first phrase, so that one does not have a clear sense when it begins; it is clear only that it has begun. Moreover, the trombones spell out a rising line (bars 11—13) that overlaps and obscures the separation between the two subphrases of the first phrase. Then, bars 14—15 give a compressed version of the same rising line, so that the two statements together press toward the horn call in bars 16—17. As Figure 12b shows, the structure of the brass parts in bars 11—17 is an exact analogue to bars 1—6. Bars 11—17 press toward bars 18—20, a repetition of bars 7—9, just as urgently and forcefully as bars 1—6 have pressed toward bars 7—9. In other words, Mahler has laid over the first phrase a redoing, hence an intensification of the introduction. We hear another double anacrusis in 11—20 at the same time that we hear the response to the double anacrusis of 1—9.

In the second phrase, the articulation between the subphrases in bar 23 is also obscured, though to a lesser degree, by the way the violins in bars 22—23, 24—25 and 26 make a rising sequence which is laid over the subphrase structure. The partial submergence of the paired subphrases in both phrases makes them sound as much like a statement (9—18) and its varied repetition (bars 19—30) as like a set of paired phrases. As a statement and repetition, they make still another double anacrusis to some coming event, analogues to the way bars 1—2 and 3—4 lead to 5—6, to the way bars 7 and 8 lead to 9, and to the way 1—6 and 7—9 lead to 9—18.

Hearing bars 9—18 and 19—30 as two anacrustic passages, the second pressing forward more urgently than the first, makes sense when a new theme strikes up at the upbeat to bar 33. Gushing like a torrential river, yet more themelike and more clearly organized than anything prior to it in the movement, it sounds like the beginning of that for which everything else has been the introduction, the arrival of that toward which everything has been pressing. At the same time, bars 9—30 function not only as a second anacrusis pressing to this arrival, but also as an arrival in its own right. Although the pairing of its groups is to some extent swept away by the overlaid sequences that press toward bars 31ff., it is more themelike than bars 1—9. It modulates the contrast between material that is clearly not paired (bars 1—8) and material that is strongly paired (bars 31ff.). Mahler does not take us directly from preparation to arrival, but takes us through a middle stage that shares some characteristics of both striving and fulfillment.

The final stage is motivically connected to the first two stages. The final stage uses a melody that is a decorated stepwise descent of a sixth, from F to A; the descent is preceded by an anacrustic E (see bars 35–37, 41–47 and 51–54). The same falling sixth has already been articulated in bars 9–10 (whose anacrustic E is in bars 7 and 8) and in bars 29–30. See Figure 13. Moreover, the compulsive, repetitive drumming on the interval from C to A at the ends of phrases in the third stage (bars 37 and 54–56) has appeared at the very opening of the movement, and in the middle stage bars 21–24 drum on the interval from C-sharp to E.

FIGURE 13
Mahler, Fifth Symphony, second movement

The paired-phrases structure of bars 31ff. is not so straightforward as the paragraphs above may suggest. Following two bars of introductory strummings, the first phrase begins on the upbeat to bar 33 and ends on the downbeat of bar 42. It divides itself into two paired subphrases, the articulation coming after the A in bar 38. In passing, one should note that the first subphrase is yet one more instance of a statement-repetition-arrival pattern (33 34 35–38). The beginning of the second phrase (upbeat to bar 42) overlaps the end of the first phase. The strings' melody of bar 42 reappears in bar 51; the recurrence helps to divide the second phrase into two subphrases (bars 42–50 and 51–59). In the first subphrase, the strings' melody is submerged by a trumpet call (bars 43–46) that the horns answer (bars 47–50). This brass interpolation both extends the subphrase beyond the length of the subphrases in the first phrase and provides a double anacrusis (again, statement and repetition) to the second subphrase. Consequently, bars 42–50 relate themselves to 51ff. in two ways: both as a subphrase summoning a pair and as a double anacrusis. The double relationship, of course, recalls the double relationship of 9–18 to 19–30, where two brass calls in bars 11–20 (statement-repetition) lay a double anacrusis over an antecedent. The melody of the final subphrase ends in bar 54, its fourth downbeat and the place where a conventional subphrase ends, but it is extended by the false cadence (F instead of A in the bass). The final subphrase does not come to a clear-cut and decisive ending; instead, the structure gradually becomes more and more amorphous. By bar 67 the music's energies are waning, and do not seem to be summoning a paired phrase. The future, compared to the future impinging on bars 33—42, has become unclear.

(b) Phrase structures in the first peace-questing section. Bars 74—78 are shaped exactly like bars 1—6. Like 1—6, 74—78 articulate the double-anacrusis — thesis pattern. And bar 76 echoes bars 74—75 (as bars 3—4 echo bars 1—2), while bars 77—78 give two overlapping statements of the same motif (as bars 5—6 give two compressed statements of the motif from 1—2 and 3—4). See Figure 14.

FIGURE 14
Sketch of Mahler, Fifth Symphony, second movement

mm.	1—2	3—4	5—6	7	8	9
mm.	74—75	76	77—78	79—82	83—86	87

Bars 79—87 parallel bars 7—9. As bar 8 repeats bar 7, so bars 83—86 repeat bars 79—82, and as bar 9 both states a second repetition of bar 7 and also begins a new gesture, so bar 87 gives a second repetition of bar 79 and at the same time launches the next wave of music.

Listeners may not notice the parallelism of structure because the difference in kinetic energy is so striking. Bars 7—8 explicitly and urgently press upward, while bars 79—87 do not seem to be pressing toward anything; indeed they hover so long on A-flat (in an F-minor context) that the A-flat begins to seem stable, contradicting the usual tendency of the third of a chord to press downward to the tonic (see Figure 15). A contrast in length is relevant to the contrast in energy. While each statement in bars 7—9 takes only half as much time as each statement in bars 1—6, each statement in bars 79—87 takes twice as long as each one in 74—78. Bars 7—9 suggest the activity of a person who is too furious to think or wait; in bars 79—87, the immobile A-flat suggests the inactivity of a person who inwardly feels no compulsion to change or to react in spite of the outward appearances of heavy pressure to respond to some event.

Like bars 9–18 and 19–30, bars 87–94 (clarinet) and 95–102 (viola, then first violin) seem in many respects to be a set of paired phrases, each phrase consisting of a set of paired subphrases. But as in 9–30, this regular, conventional shape is obscured to some extent. During bars 79–85, the clarinet has been part of the background texture behind the cello in the foreground. The cello continues to

FIGURE 15
Mahler, Fifth Symphony, second movement

hold the foreground when the first subphrase begins in the upbeat to bar 87. When the clarinet begins to play on the second beat of 87, it is submerged in the sound of the cello. Although Mahler instructs the clarinet to come to the foreground, the ear will continue to follow the cello until about the fourth beat of bar 87. To listen to bars 87–88 is to hear a foreground and a background reversing themselves: what begins as decoration (the clarinet) becomes the central figure; what is initially at the center of attention (the cello) trails off into a vaguely shaped background figure, only to reassert itself in the upbeat to bar 90, so that the reversal may be repeated in bars 91–92 (Figure 15). The same process occurs two more times. Beginning with the upbeat to bar 95, the foreground clarinet and the background viola exchange places, and beginning with the second beat of bar 95 the foreground viola and the background cello gradually change places (or almost change places; the viola does not yield the foreground entirely during bar 97).

All four instances exemplify a continuation (the clarinet, the clarinet, the violas, the cellos) of something that has not begun (the beginning of these lines, being inaudible, is not a concrete, actual event), and the first three exemplify a beginning (the cellos, the cellos, the clarinet) that has no continuation. In other words, at bars 87, 91 and 95 one hears the beginning of a subphrase — a melody, set against a background, that is pushing toward a cadential close — but in each case, the line that actually falls to a cadential close is a different line. Were it not for the cadences that fall at regular intervals, the pairing of subphrases and the differentiation between foreground and background, we might well hear bars 87–102 as a tapestry woven of the continuous unfolding of several different voices, now one, now another of which is dominant. In a different way, the brass episodes in bars 11–19 and the violin sequence in bars 22–27 are also continuations that have no beginnings, for what has begun comes partially to rest in bars 12 and 23, respectively, and the overlays, by obscuring these articulations in the phrase, obscure to some degree the continuation of what has begun and they themselves continue something that has not begun. This process is not uncommon in Mahler's music; the introductory chapter has described some of its appearances in the First, Second and Fourth Symphonies. It is critically important in the second movement of the Fifth, for it appears not only in bars 11–19, 22–27 and 87–95, but also later in the movement.

A similar process almost entirely structures many of the short stories written by Arthur Schnitzler, a Viennese playwright and novelist who practiced medicine briefly before turning to literature. His 1892 story, "Dying," is a good example.[8] It tells of a young man, Felix, dying of tuberculosis. Marie, his mistress, insists when she first learns of his condition that she will kill herself on his death-bed. Although she does not really believe he will die, she believes she is deciding to die with him. Later, as she comes to see that in fact he is dying, she also realizes that she has decided not to commit suicide, even though there is never a moment when she makes this decision. At the beginning of the story, Felix decides that Marie must not die with him; in fact, he decides not even to tell her about his disease. But later, without ever deciding anything to the contrary, he cannot face dying alone, and he gradually (and at most only dimly) realizes that he has decided that Marie must not only be with him as he dies, but she must also die with him. He has come to feel that death is not the overwhelming reality it appears to be if Marie can freely choose to die with him, as though the power to choose death were a kind of power over death, a power of which Felix's tuberculosis had robbed him.

At every point, the story is propelled not by decisions, but by what has been decided. Decisions — contrary to our idea and ideal of ourselves as rational creatures who actualize consciously considered decisions and thereby actualize ourselves — are always in the present perfect tense: it is what I have decided to do, not what I decide to do, that constitutes my life. My putative decisions are beginnings that turn out not to have continuations (I do not in fact enact the decisions); and what is followed through has no beginning (there is no moment when I decide to pursue this course). "Having decided" means that I accept responsibility for this course, even though it is not a continuation of a process that has begun with an identifiable decision. "Having decided" means that if it makes sense to think of a non-empirical self that actualizes itself by enacting decisions, it must be a self that is more elusive than our ideal of the rational self would like, for "having decided" means linking a present course of action with a past decision that never was a present decision. Yet neither Schnitzler nor Mahler suggests in any way that this process — "having decided" — is unusual. In fact, they make it seem so familiar that by contrast to it both the picture in which human behavior is determined by forces like mechanistic causes and not by free decisions and the picture in which a self creates its own future by actualizing rational decisions seem to distort the way human experience in fact proceeds.

The last of the four subphrases in bars 87—102 ends less stably than the first three. While the first three end with a falling second (decorated by a cambiata in the third subphrase), the fourth ends with an upward leap of a fifth that denies the set of phrases any conclusiveness. One leap follows another, the line goes higher and higher, and the size of the leap becomes a sixth (bar 105), an octave (bars 105, 107, 109) and a minor ninth (bars 111—112). Thus the motif opening the peace-questing section has been reestablished; the nearly stable set of nearly paired phrases has opened into a powerful forward surge, and when a clearly themelike, clearly structured gesture arrives in bar 117, we realize, as we have realized in bar 33, that all the previous music has been an introductory preparation for this arrival. As in the anger section, here too we are led from non-paired gestures to nearly paired gestures to fully paired phrases (bars 117—124 form a pair with bars 125—133; the first phrase consists of a set of paired subphrases, bars 117—120 and 121—124).

And just as there are motivic connections among the three stages of the anger section, so here also motivic connections help tie the three stages together and make them parts of a single process. The melody that begins in bar 117 has three elements: a line rising upward by steps, a leap and a stepwise downward resolution. (And, as Barford suggests, these elements metaphorically exemplify, respectively, an aspiration for release from the pain caused by confronting death, the actual liberation, and the serenity for which one has aspired and which the release brings.) The preceding section, mediating between preparation and fulfillment, has anticipated this melody; it too has these three elements, although their presence is less forceful because of the decorating turns (bars 88, 92, 100) and because of the way the subphrases "have begun" without ever beginning.

At its cadences, the melody of bars 87–116 combines two elements from bars 74–86. First, the downward resolving appoggiature that occur six times in bars 74–86 occur as significant elements of the melody in bars 89, 93 and 94 (see Figure 15). And, second, all the subphrases of bars 87–116 end with the melody on the third of the chord (though the chord itself differs from one cadence to the next) and in this way join the stability of the cadence to the instability of the downward tending melody. Poised above a bass, yet resisting the pressure to move downward as though it did not feel the force of gravity, the suspended third at these cadences exemplifies more explicitly and more forcefully the same serene immobility in the face of external pressure to move and to be moved as does the lingering A-flat in bars 79–86.

In bars 74–86, the downward resolving appoggiature sound like fragments within the background texture. When the cello strikes up in the upbeat to bar 79, it sounds like the beginning of a foreground melody against that background; the cello with its hovering third seems to launch a process that will have consequences. But when the paired subphrases begin in bar 87, we realize that bar 79 has not begun the process, but rather has disclosed another of the elements with which the process will work. And in the first two subphrases, the downward resolving appoggiatura comes into the foreground.

Because of the motivic connections between bars 74–86 and 87–116, the latter are not only a middle stage between introduction and the beginning of an arrival but also a reworking of the first preparation. The attempt in the first phrase (87–94) of the middle stage to generate a future depends on what precedes it; its particular way of working toward a future uses elements disclosed in bars 74–86. Bars 87–94 sound like a reaffirmed, more forceful, better focused effort to generate the same future that bars 74–86 have tried to evoke.

The phrase in 95–102, which is paired to 87–94, serves as the arrival of that future until it is surpassed by the beginning of the third stage (bar 117). Once again, we hear a first phrase working toward a future, once again using and reworking previously heard elements. Much of the distinctive quality of the stage beginning in bar 117 is the way it supercedes a prior effort to create and actualize an appropriate future.

The structure of the first peace-questing section resembles that of the first anger section in several important respects. Both sections have three stages. The beginning of each stage initially seems to be the beginning of a regularly organized theme, but the first two stages turn out to be introductory. The second and third stages relate themselves in two ways to the previous stage: they are at once the arrival of that which the prior music has generated and a more incisive restatement of the somewhat more vaguely paired phrases of the prior section.[9] (It is not uncommon, of course, for paired phrases to be preceded by an introduction and for the introduction to foreshadow the materials of the paired phrases. What distinguishes Mahler's processes is the double relation of the three stages to one another.) Both sections thus exemplify a process that is also exhibited by a person who makes a decision but then instead of enacting it rejects it as having been too vague, makes a fresh decision to create a certain future, which, surprisingly, turns out to be a more forceful version of the same decision, but again, instead of enacting it, rejects it as too vague and once again makes a new decision that turns out to be the old decision, only clearer, more profoundly engaged with its context. Like the examples of continuing without beginning in bars 87–102, but in a different way, the third stage in both sections metaphorically exemplifies "having decided."

(iv) The Joints between the Anger and the Peace-Questing Sections

The last of the clearly paired subphrases in the first anger section ends in bar 54. The false cadence extends the shelter of the clear structure for several bars, but by bar 61, it is clear that entropy is setting in: just as the section has moved in three stages toward clearer shape, so now it is falling away from shape. In bars 67–72, the winds plunge into an abyss that swallows their energies. For a full measure we hear nothing but a very soft tympano roll. There is a rupture between the sections. Consequently, when the peace-questing section begins in bar 74, it is almost as though a new piece were beginning, as though bars 1–73 had not happened at all. Only the thin thread of the strings in bars 69—71 leads across the rupture as the next section begins by repeating their motif, using the C to which the strings in 69—71 have led as the point of departure. See Figure 16.

FIGURE 16
Mahler, Fifth Symphony, second movement

The ending of the first peace-questing section is altogether different. While the third stage of the anger section begins on its tonic (A minor), and loses harmonic clarity at the same time that it is losing structural certainty, the third stage of the peace-questing section begins on its submediant (that is, D-flat), which is the beginning of a strong, clear progression to its tonic (F minor). This progression as a whole together with the clarity of the phrase structure constitutes the arrival of the future generated by the first two stages. The paired phrases of the third stage end in bar 133. But instead of falling away from shape, as do the last bars of the anger section, the music makes a fresh effort to encompass even more within a structured gesture. This gesture is supported by the six-four chord in bars 133—136, leaning toward the dominant, which comes in 137—140 and in turn summons the F-minor tonic. This rally is abruptly cut off in bar 141 by the sudden, unsuspected and unmotivated reassertion of anger. The harmonic progression that would have signified the completeness of the third-stage arrival in the peace-questing section is aborted.

The second anger section (bars 141—187) lapses into entropy at its end, but since it achieves less internal structure than does the first anger section, its falling away from shape is less remarkable.

The second peace-questing section (188—253) precedes its more definitely shaped stage with a longer preparation than does its proto-type and follows this stage with an even stronger effort to reach a fuller, more embracing climax. Consequently, the rude eruption of the anger motif in bar 254 has an even more devastating effect here than in bar 141.

The third anger section has even less semblance of a paired-phrases structure or even the push toward one than the second anger section.

It presses mightily, however, toward some sort of climax, especially in bars 262–265, which recall the way bars 7–9 push ahead.

The sudden appearance of thoroughly conventional paired phrases in bar 266 is just as astonishing and devastating as the rude interruption of the push forward in bar 254. The unexpectedness is increased by the way this gesture reprises the march theme of the first movement but omits its first two beats! The omission makes us feel that the march must have been in progress, its force implicitly felt, for some time, and that we have just now turned our attention explicitly to it. Some unclarified impulse directs our attention away from our feelings of anger to the external event that has given rise to them.

The violin counterpoint to the march theme uses repeated upward leaps, holding the upward minor-ninth leap in force during the march reprise. These leaps occupy the foreground beginning in bar 280 and grow in size from minor sevenths to a diminished octave (bars 283–284) and finally to a minor ninth in bars 287–288.

As soon as the minor ninth is achieved — that is, as soon as the music closes the gap between the march reprise and the second movement's anger and searching — the mood changes drastically. The minor ninth resolves downward by a whole step instead of the anguished semitone, the tonal context suddenly becomes A-flat major and the tempo picks up to become a cheerful, perhaps even jaunty march (bars 288ff.).[10] The music continues to press forward in this optimistic, slightly cocky mood. The push in bars 308–315 toward a climax recalls and reviews the thrust felt at the end of the second peace-questing section (bars 234–253). The interval of a descending second, which launches the jaunty march (F–E-flat in bar 288), dominates the renewed thrust toward a peak. The climax which is denied at the end of the second peace-questing section comes when the descending second reaches a joyous F-sharp–E, the trumpets doubling the violins (bars 316–317). The somewhat trivial connotations of the preceding march are burned off instantly in the bright splendor of this thrilling moment.

As if the glory were not yet earned, however, the moment sustains itself for only six measures. But before it is abruptly cut off, the shout of joy intensifies itself and manages to reach up one more step and becomes G-sharp–F-sharp in bars 320–321.

The sudden suppression of joy happens at the hands of the anger motif, more furiously urgent than ever, mollified in no way by the achievements of the preceding section. The renewed statement of anger even takes the major ninths and major seconds of the preceding section and puts them to its own service (bars 326–327). The structure is articulated somewhat less crisply than in the first anger section, but more clearly than in the two preceding, much briefer anger sections. We hear introductory gestures in bars 323–332, analogous to those in 1–9, and nearly paired phrases in 333–351, analogous to those in 9–30. But where the analogy to the opening section calls for the clearly paired phrases of patently themelike material of bars 31–54, we get instead the material associated with the first stage of the peace-questing section: instead of restating bars 31–54, as the analogy of 323–351 to 1–30 leads us to expect, bars 356–362 restate bars 79–86 and 214–219.[11] This restatement leads into a gesture that integrates motifs from the anger section (compare bars 362–371 with 37–41) with motifs from the peace-questing section (compare bars 372–391 to 125–140 and 230–253), and then proceeds to regain the ground abruptly lost to the anger motif in bar 323. That is, the music presses forward once more to a shout of joy. Using motifs that recall the two previous attempts to arrive at and sustain a climax (bars 234–253 and 288–315), the passage from about 420–463 retraces their steps. While the first attempt is cut off by the anger motif before it arrives at the shout of joy and while the second attempt is cut off after only six measures, this time the climax comes in the full dress of a brass chorale and sustains itself for a full statement (464–519).

(2) The Shout of Joy

The brass chorale is the culmination of both the anger sections and the peace-questing sections. Looking at the ends of sections of both kinds, one sees that they lead to the brass chorale, indeed that each subsequent one leads more urgently to it. We have just observed how they do not lead to each other, the one entering after the other's structure has disintegrated, its energy spent, or the one brusquely interrupting the other and pushing it aside. But not leading to each other, they do move toward the same thing, converging upon it, as it were, from different sides. Neither one would be able to support the climax without the other; it is only as they converge upon the climax that it can take shape.

(i) The Convergence of the Anger and Peace-Questing Sections

But as they converge upon the same thing, they also converge upon one another. First, in each subsequent statement of peace-questing music, motifs from the anger music make themselves more and more forcefully felt. That the motifs seem suitable in their new context, in spite of the stark contrast between the moods of the anger and peace-questing sections, is partly the result of the similarities of phrase structures which, from the very beginning of the movement, have underlain the contrast. Second, all three of the drives to the great shout of joy — the drive that fails (bars 234—253) and the one that leads to a short-lived shout (bars 288—315) as well as the successful one — mix and integrate the two kinds of motifs. For example, the jauntiness of the march in the second of these largely depends on blending the rhythm of the one with the melody of the other (Figure 17).

FIGURE 17
Mahler, Fifth Symphony, second movement

The two converge on one another in another sense. In the fourth anger section, the listener discovers that the anger music can flow into — it can prepare, its third stage theme can be replaced by — a version of the peace-questing section. This event is remarkable, for previously in the movement there has been no forward thrust from an anger into a peace-questing section, and the reentering anger sections have rejected the forward thrust that the peace-questing sections have not been allowed to spend. Musical processes have been left suspended at the end of sections, and now these suspensions are answered by the explicit, straightforward coupling of the two kinds of music.

In fact, it would probably be more accurate to say that only *because* the two kinds of music begin to converge upon each other do they converge upon and thereby support the shout of joy. That is, only as their motifs begin to exchange places does a push toward some goal begin. A motivic exchange that is associated with generating forward thrust takes place in the second anger section and in the second peace-questing section. The second anger section (bars 141–187) is less clearly organized internally than the first (its gestures less clearly separate themselves from and lead toward one another). Nevertheless, it begins to establish some sort of event beyond itself as its goal by incorporating an important feature of the peace-questing music: the motif shown in Figure 18a (in bars 171–173, derived from bars 95–97 and 125–127; see Figure 18b). In the second peace-questing section (at bar 230), a gesture referring explicitly to the anger section appears as a counterpoint to the Figure 18b motif and so contaminates it that it can no longer unambiguously connote serenity. Indeed, it is precisely this combination of motifs that sets into motion the forward pressing section that begins with bar 234 and is frustrated with such devastating effect in bar 254.

FIGURE 18
Mahler, Fifth Symphony, second movement

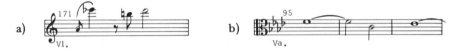

Moreover, the motifs that the two kinds of music share (the upward leap of a ninth, the repeated note and the triplet) begin to take on the character of pushing ahead as the other motifs begin to exchange places. For example, various permutations of the leap of a ninth followed by downward stepwise resolution are more prominent at the end of the second anger section (bars 174–184) than before and exert more forward pressure, but clearly not toward what we are given in bar 189. Further permutations of this motif appear in bars 262–265 (which Mahler marks "always still pressing"), though what follows immediately thereafter, again, interrupts and temporarily sets aside the process which this motif is urging.

The repeated note motif is more prominent in the fourth anger section than in the first or the second (it is not used in the third). In the fourth, it is modified so that, like the version of it used in the peace-questing section, it begins on the upbeat, or it is intensified into a triplet (bars 342–348). The figure contributes significantly to the push (bars 352ff.) into the reprise of the peace-questing gesture that comes at the place where the third stage of the anger section might have been, and it continues during that reprise so that it helps not only to link the two sections but also to sustain the push forward, a push that this time culminates in the shout of joy. And it is the persistence of these repeated notes as well as the upward leaps, the triplets and the exertion of anger-section motifs (see Figure 19) that makes this section, in which the peace-questing motifs are also persistently present, push so vigorously and convincingly into the brass chorale.

FIGURE 19

passages in the last peace-questing section that use anger-section motifs:	derived from:
372–375 (cello)	11–15, 60–64 (trombones)
379, 381 (upward arpeggio)	43–47 (horns), 157 (trumpet), 168 (violin)
444–446 (bassoon, cello, bass), 448ff. (second violin), 456–463 (cello, bass)	1–6 (bass parts), 21–26 (violin) and 54–56 (horn)
450–455 (horn)	43–46 (trumpet)
457–463 (horn)	48–49 (horn)

As the anger and the peace-questing music are integrated by exchanging and blending motifs and by pressing to a common goal, they create a new mood — a new attitude, a new way of looking at things and experiencing reality — that is like and unlike both of them.

(ii) The Brass Chorale

The new mood, expressed in the brass chorale, is like the anger sections in that it is world-affirming: what happens and takes concrete shape in the public realm matters. But the brass chorale obviously differs from the anger sections in that it places a positive value on what happens in the world. The chorale also seems to express the same sense of fulfillment, the sense of being beyond a struggle, that the upward leap and falling second in the peace-questing sections connote. But the outer-world associations of the chorale obviously distinguish it from these elements of the peace-questing music and their connotations of inner release. In fusing the attitudes of the anger and the peace-questing sections, the chorale seems to express the attitude of a person who is fully willing to participate in all the world's struggles, sharing its joys, risking its pains, so that what happens really counts, and yet who maintains a positive basic outlook, no matter what happens. No pain, however deep, no loss however devastating can or will undermine the underlying affirmation of life.

This way of describing the brass chorale either makes the attitude that it exemplifies seem self-contradictory or it makes life's losses seem cheap. It seems unrealistic — it seems one is not genuinely facing what actually happens — to determine to maintain a sense of fulfillment in the face of all eventualities.

But Mahler has after all led us to face death, the death of one who is heroic and noble, and it is not the case that the anger and bitterness involved in confronting that death have simply exhausted themselves or that the brass chorale emerges because a positive attitude has defeated a negative one in a war of attrition. Although the anger sections exchange motifs with the peace-questing sections, anger sustains its force. The pressure in the later anger sections toward what turns out to be a brass chorale thus suggests the search for release *within* a world in which death can happen, not release *from* the world. That the peace-questing sections and the exchange of motifs do not overcome the force of anger is indicated by the way the brass chorale alludes continuously and explicitly to the anger motifs. That is, the attitude of the anger sections continues to make its presence felt throughout the shout of joy because there are both strong motivic similarities and clear structural analogies between the anger sections and the brass chorale.

One way to take into account the presence of anger within the culminating shout of joy would be to say that the chorale presents and celebrates courage to accept whatever happens, to be resigned to living in pain. Yet in the peace-questing sections Mahler has embodied a desire for genuine serenity and fulfillment, not simply the courage to face turmoil and non-fulfillment. And these sections sustain this connotation in spite of the exchange of motifs with the anger sections. Like the latter, they press toward the shout of joy, and their force is maintained during the culminating shout in that the chorale has motivic similarities and structural analogies to the peace-questing sections.

In other words, the chorale represents the convergence of the two kinds of music not only in the sense that both lead into it as they exchange motifs with one another, but also in the sense that it holds them together by integrating the motifs and structures characterizing each of them. By describing its similarities and analogies to the prior sections, then, one may become able to describe the way it sustains the force of each while overcoming the contrast between them.

The anger section makes its presence felt during the chorale primarily through two motifs. First, there are the circling thirds in bars 488–491 and 498–499 that press toward higher and higher climaxes. They are new versions of the circling thirds that open the movement and that later reappear within peace-questing sections, contributing to their forward thrust. In the brass chorale, these circling thirds in fact combine features of the two kinds of sections, for here they whirl in triplets, a rhythmic figure as clearly associated with the peace-questing as with the anger music. See Figure 20.[12] Second, a rhythmic figure from the anger music, ♩ ⁊ ♪ ♩ , which also insinuates itself within the peace-questing sections and contributes even more significantly to their forward thrust, occurs in the brass chorale three times (bars 468–469, 473–476, 491–496). Sounding each time like the crack of a whip, this figure helps generate the climaxes in bars 476–477 and 496–497. Moreover, the diminished-seventh chord, which helps set the bitter mood in the opening of the movement (bars 2–6, 66–73, and again in 322–325) is used to create local dissonances in the passage of the chorale that leads to its high point (bars 492, 494 and 496). And the melodic fragment spit out by the trombones in bars 11–15 and elsewhere, rising from the fifth to the eighth degree of the scale, occurs in the brass chorale in bars 479–480 and 510–512. Both occurrences are gestures that sustain the level of the fervor without striving to increase it.

The peace-questing sections make their presence felt through the falling-fourth motif in bars 482–483, 484–485 and 504–505 (see bars 96, 126 and elsewhere). This motif is critically important in determining the character of the peace-questing sections, and it is equally significant in the brass chorale.

Even more important is the way the chorale suspends the third of its scale (F-sharp in the D major scale), explicitly recalling the suspended thirds (A-flat in the F minor scale) in the peace-questing sections. It is no exaggeration to say that the entire brass chorale is a prolongation of F-sharp. F-sharp is crucially important to the climactic beginning of the chorale (climactic because this chord is consonant, sustained for a whole note by trumpets and trombones in their upper register, following a long, quickly moving, dissonant passage), and so to prolong F-sharp is to sustain the sense of culmination. The F-sharp occurs in the chorale melody at bars 485 and 500, and each time it sounds like an arrival that is stable and does not press toward a goal in spite of the fact that the tonic of the chord is not in the melody.[13]

The F-sharp at the beginning of the chorale has an uncanny quality whose impact the listener needs to recognize fully. F-sharp (= G-flat) has already been stated in bars 460 and 462, where it resolves upward leaps of a major ninth. These G-flats, although they resolve the appoggiature on the downbeats, are dissonant against the

FIGURE 20
Mahler, Fifth Symphony, second movement, brass chorale

bass (a six-four chord in 460 and a diminished-seventh chord in 462). The reason why a climactic quality is effused in bars 464 is that this same note is now surrounded by notes to which it is not dissonant. What seems uncanny about the F-sharp in bar 464 is that it is climactic not because it resolves the dissonance in bars 460–463, but because the dissonance simply disappears. The dissonance vanishes, but not as the result of a melodic or a harmonic process of which the F-sharp is a part. The climactic quality of the F-sharp in bar 464 cannot be said to result from a struggle exemplified by a melodic progression (such as the resolution of an appoggiatura) or a harmonic progression (such as the resolution of a dominant; for there is no sense of a strong root movement from bars 460–463 to 464). The musical process is like a metamorphosis or transformation in which something becomes something else while sustaining an identity with itself (a dissonant pitch becomes a consonant pitch without changing). Not moving and yet arriving, the F-sharp — like the second-stage theme of the peace-questing music — belongs to a temporal process in which the usual distinction between continuing and beginning must be reformulated. Arriving without having moved is like "having arrived," which means seeing a present sense of attainment as the continuation of a past actualization that never was a present actualization. "Having arrived" must belong to a temporal process in which "having decided" also makes sense.

The other two F-sharps are less strange. Although there is nothing about the process from 460–463 to 464 that resembles natural causation or the decision of a free self, the latter process may be associated with the other two F-sharps in the chorale. Both of these F-sharps come after a three-part gesture that consists of a twofold exertion (bars 471–473, 474–475 and 492–493, 494–495) and release (bars 477 and 497). The F-sharps arrived at in bars 485 and 500 maintain and intensify the sense of fulfillment projected in 477 and 497. Although the F-sharps do not consummate a struggle, they seem to exemplify moments of realizing the full implications of release or of enjoying its effect to the fullest.

The sense of struggle and release in 471–477 and 492–497 can be accounted for by the way both passages bring together three features that have characterized previous sections of the movement. First, they instantiate the pattern of statement — intensifying-repetition — goal, a pattern that structures bars 7–9 and much of the movement on various architectonic levels. Second, both 471–477 and 492–497 repeatedly use the downward whole step which here as in the peace-questing sections connotes the serenity that follows release. Even bars 473 and 475 have this connotation, in spite of the fact that at the same time they are part of an exertion forward. Third, the upward leaps preceding these downward whole steps are permutations of the upward-leaping minor ninth that permeates both the anger and the peace-questing sections. The interval covered by these leaps grows from a fifth in bars 473–474 (F trumpet), to a sixth in bars 475–476 and again in 491–492 and 493–494 and finally to a seventh — most explicitly reminiscent of the minor ninth — in bars 495–496.

Because of features like the increasingly wide leaps, the chorale seems continuously to be growing toward something, working to concrete, visible, outer-world actualizations. Yet what it grows toward in fact — what is actually realized — is the same outer-world reality that is established at the beginning of the chorale, or, more accurately, *before* the beginning of the chorale. The F-sharp is established as a climax as the chorale begins, and the chorale as a whole sustains it as a hovering fulfillment that grows in richness and splendor but is never surpassed by any concrete actualization.

In other words, although all three F-sharps have a climactic quality, none of them actualizes a surpassing peak. The F-sharps in bars 460–463 are the peak generated by the swelling energies of bars 442–462, but the persisting dissonances in 460–463 deny these F-sharps a climactic quality. When the dissonances mysteriously disappear in bar 464, a glorious sense of climax shines forth. The F-sharp in 464 discloses and confirms that the peak has been attained; what it actualizes turns out to have been already attained.

The other two F-sharps function similarly. Although they are climactic, they do not actualize a peak that surpasses the peaks attained in 477 and 497. The relationships of all three F-sharps to what immediately precedes them is analogous to the way the third-stage themes in the anger and peace-questing sections relate themselves to what precedes them. Just as the third-stage themes seem to be making and enacting something fresh, like a new decision, and to be that for which the two prior stages have been the preparation, but in fact enact more resolutely, as it were, a decision that has already been made, so the F-sharps function as final arrivals, but ones that do not surpass arrivals that have already been attained. In a temporal process in which decisions are in the present perfect tense, climaxes are too.

The hovering quality of the F-sharps — the way they are downwardly mobile, yet are stable — is critical to the temporal process of these climaxes. Not only does the hovering third maintain the force of the peace-questing music, but also it sustains the instability and mobility that has been present throughout the movement first in the form of the stark contrast between the violently juxtaposed sections and then, when the two kinds of music begin to converge, in the form of a push forward. Because the hovering F-sharp is as stable as it is mobile, it can function as the resolution to the tensions between prior sections and as the outcome of the forward-thrusting passages. As stable, the F-sharps have a thrillingly climactic quality, but as hoveringly mobile they do not move beyond the climax attained in the gestures that precede them. The F-sharps have a double musical meaning.

And when we remember that the chorale as a whole is a prolongation of F-sharp, we realize that the chorale as a whole is related to the rest of the movement in the same way that the F-sharp is related to the chorale: the chorale also has a double musical meaning. It is the consummation of the movement, but at the same time it does not achieve anything that is not already present in the combination of the juxtaposed and then converging sections of anger and peace-questing music.

As implicit in the rest of the movement, the chorale is like the unfolding of necessity, like an event that is so completely determined by its past that it is implicitly contained in the past and is thus inevitable. But as a genuine climax, analogous to climaxes in Beethoven and Brahms, it is like a fresh event, something new that responds to, more than it is caused by, the movement's tensions and thrusts. In that the chorale is genuinely climactic, moving into the climax is like making and concretely enacting a decision. In that the chorale actualizes what has already been attained, moving from the previous sections into the chorale is like having decided. The relation of the chorale to the rest of the movement is like and unlike both the process of a past state of affairs determining a future, which thus discloses what that state of affairs implicitly contains, and of a free decision injecting something into the temporal process that is at once new and responsive to the past. In other words, the chorale can almost be explained on the basis of one kind of ground (one resembling causation in nature) and at the same time almost on the basis of another kind of ground (one resembling free choice); it is as though the movement were almost satisfactorily coherent in each of two ways. But it is not as though the two kinds of grounds were complementary, each explaining what the other left unexplained. In the end, one must admit that by appealing partly to each of two kinds of coherence but referring without reservation to neither, the movement is coherent in its own way. Its kind of coherence differs from both causation and decision-making as much as it resembles them. In differing from them both, it resembles events like miracles, beauty, play and accidents which, by comparison to the other kinds of processes, seem to have no grounds at all.

Another way to reach this understanding of the brass chorale is to examine its phrase structure. Mahler fashions his phrases so that they relate themselves to one another simultaneously in two ways that are not only different but also, common sense would say, mutually exclusive.

Ends of subphrases fall in bars 470, 478, 486, 497, 510 and 520. The six subphrases thus articulated are not merely strung out next to one another, but they form groups. The clearest grouping is that of bars 500—510 with 511—520: these subphrases form a pair with each other. The first of these is a condensed and more stable version of the B-flat trumpet in bars 464—478. (The comparative instability in 464—478 results from the powerful forward thrust generated when

G—E [in bar 465–466] is held for an extra measure [that is, the F-sharp–D expected in 466 is delayed until 468]. This irregularity in the rhythm makes the D—B at the end of the phrase [469–470] mobile, and before its mobility is discharged the repetitions in 471–478 whip up further pressure. The subphrase in bars 500–510 has no such rhythmic irregularity, and the only mobility at its end is that generated by stopping on the fifth degree of the scale instead of the tonic.) Bars 479–486 are very similar to 511–520, the differences having the effect of making the latter stabler, more final than the former. Thus bars 464–486 as a whole are both analogous to and less stable than 500–520, and so the phrase in 464–486 and the phrase in 500–520 together comprise an antecedent-consequent pair.

There are two equally valid ways of hearing the intervening material (bars 487–497). Bars 492–497 make a clear analogue to 471–478, and bar 511 would form an excellent continuation to bar 497, so good, in fact, that bars 498–510 seem to be an interpolation. On the strength of the analogy between 471–478 and 492–497, one hears 471–478 and 479–485 as forming a pair with 492–497 and 511–520. The interpolation between 497 and 511 closely resembles bars 464–470 and has the effect of reinstating the force of 464–470. If bars 498–510 preceded bars 492–497 (that is, if 498–510 and 492–497 came in the same order as their analogues, bars 464–470 and 471–478), then the six subphrases of the chorale would be orderly in an easily intelligible and predictable way (because more closely analogous to other, more familiar music). Then we would have two phrases, each consisting of three parts, and the two phrases would be paired to one another. See Figure 21.

FIGURE 21

phrase 1			phrase 2
464–470	corresponds to		500–510 (introduced by 498–499)
471–478	”	”	492–497 (introduced by 487–491)
479–486	”	”	511–520

Both 492–497 and 500–510 are preceded by introductory passages. These gestures consist of whirling thirds that keep the surface motion active while enlarging the separation between the end of one phrase and the beginning of the next. The articulation thus created by bars 487–491 is by far the strongest in the chorale. These measures create the sense that what precedes them is a single unit (divided by the weaker articulations in 470 and 478 into three

parts) and that what follows them is also a single unit (divided by the weaker articulations in 498—499 and 510 into three parts). In short, bars 487—491 clearly signify the beginning of a second phrase and confirm the feeling that bars 464—486 are a phrase paired to the phrase in 492—520.

The other, and equally valid, way of hearing bars 487—497 hinges on the fact that the introductory whirls in 498—499 seem to suggest that what follows them is also the beginning of a phrase. Bars 487—491 having taken on the function of separating phrases, the allusion (although abbreviated) to that material in bars 498—499 seems to have the same function. This intimation is strengthened considerably by the obvious similarity of bars 500—510 to 464—470. Together, these two features divide the chorale into three parts (464—486, 487—497 and 498—520) just as clearly as the correspondences listed in Figure 21 divide it into two parts (464—486 and 487—520). The subphrase in bars 492—497 (introduced by 487—491) is not the (misplaced) middle part of the second phrase, but the beginning of the second of the chorale's three phrases. Figure 22 sketches the two different ways of hearing groupings within the chorale.

The tripartite grouping is supported by two other aspects of the chorale. First, bars 471—478 have served as the middle of the first phrase, and so the allusion to that material in 492—497 more easily sounds like the onset of the middle of three phrases than like material that would appropriately follow the chorale's only major articulation. Second, the climax that arrives in bar 500 sounds like the climax of the whole chorale and as clearly the beginning of a phrase as is bar 464, not a merely local climax tucked away within its second part.

In the tripartite grouping, the climax at bar 500 is a final fulfillment, the concrete actualization of that toward which the chorale and the whole movement have been struggling; Mahler has written *Höhepunkt* over the bar, indicating that his verbal as well as his musical thinking recognized its climactic character. But it is an achievement that has already taken place: the bipartite grouping and the sense it creates that the climax begins in bar 492 are not superceded. The F-sharp that projects the climax in bar 500 has already been achieved. If bars 500—510 had been placed before 492—497 (as in Figure 21), the F-sharp climax in bar 500 would have been far less equivocal. But in the music that Mahler actually wrote, the F-sharp in bar 500 is both a *Höhepunkt*, analogous to a more or less conventional climax, and a continuation of a previously attained peak. Once again, the F-sharp has a double meaning.

Thus the chorale as a whole articulates a temporal process in

FIGURE 22

Sketch of Mahler, Fifth Symphony, second movement, brass chorale

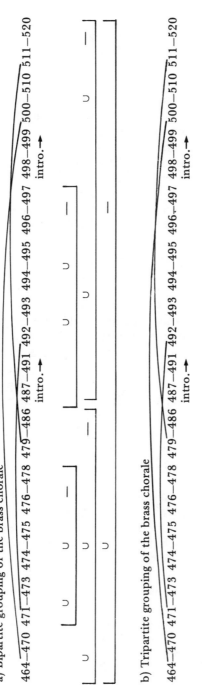

a) Bipartite grouping of the brass chorale

464–470 471–473 474–475 476–478 479–486 487–491 492–493 494–495 496–497 498–499 500–510 511–520

intro. →   intro. →

b) Tripartite grouping of the brass chorale

464–470 471–473 474–475 476–478 479–486 487–491 492–493 494–495 496–497 498–499 500–510 511–520

intro. →   intro. →

Arched lines above bar numbers link similar gestures.

which one is simultaneously reaching toward fulfillment (hence
engaging the listener in a process that is like that of shaping a future
through making decisions, taking risks and understanding oneself as
being what one expresses oneself to be through one's way of creating
a future) and at the same time finding that what counts as fulfillment
has already arrived (hence finding oneself beyond risk-taking in that
climax means the moment of realizing what has been decided, what
has been achieved, and seeing that fulfillment was already there even
when risks were still being taken). The chorale projects this temporal
process in a number of different ways on a number of different levels:
the poised F-sharp is both mobile toward a goal (a metaphorical
instance of moving in a concrete way to a concrete goal) and stable
(a metaphorical instance of feeling fulfilled no matter what the
course of present events may be); again and again in the chorale,
F-sharp is established as a goal, but a goal that, when it arrives, does
not surpass an already actualized goal (a metaphorical instance of
genuinely moving toward actualization and at the same time already
being fulfilled); because of the overlay of a tripartite on a bipartite
structure, the third subphrase in the first phrase begins as if it were
the first subphrase in the second phrase, but ends as the completion
of the first phrase, though a completion that does not surpass the
degree of completion already projected by the second subphrase; and
the simultaneous projection of a bipartite and a tripartite shape for
the chorale as a whole keeps fulfillment in the future until bar 500,
while already projecting fulfillment before then. In all these ways,
Mahler is exemplifying a process in which making decisions, taking
risks, and arriving at goals are in the present perfect tense: it is what
one has decided, what one has risked, what one has achieved that
counts, not what one is deciding, risking and achieving. There is no
moment in which these things actually happen, for although at every
moment one is looking ahead and working toward a future, when the
expected future comes, one finds one has already been there.[14]

We have already noted that this process is exemplified in both the
anger and the peace-questing sections. But there it is presented more
vaguely, less forcefully. Its presentation in the brass chorale is like
the third-stage themes and peace-questing sections in that the chorale
sounds like the beginning of that which the rest of the movement has
been introducing by converging on it and pushing toward it, but
turns out to be a more definite and compelling statement of a process
that has already been underway. The chorale thus brilliantly affirms
life and liberation from life's doomed struggles as well as a temporal
process in which these are, surprisingly, both possible. In affirming

decisions and fulfillments, the chorale affirms the validity of the anger sections' attitude; in making decisions and fulfillments a matter of having decided and having attained, (which no present reality, however grizzly, can take away or, however glorious, can enhance), it affirms the validity of the quests for peace.

"Having decided" may have negative connotations. Insofar as it applies to Schnitzler's "Dying," it may suggest that decisions are in the present perfect tense because one is unable to face them and hence makes them unconsciously. "Having decided" may suggest that the gloomy present forces one to reevaluate the past as more of an achievement than it felt when it was the present. Drawing these implications, however, presupposes that there is only one kind of temporal process and that its nature is such that "having decided" and "having attained," as they have been construed in this chapter, are nonsense. On the basis of this presupposition, these processes are apparent, not real — the result of the mind playing tricks on itself and on reality. But the brilliance of Mahler's brass chorale — the exuberance of the shout of joy — makes it impossible to construe the double relationships of the F-sharp within the chorale and of the chorale within the movement as connoting anything negative. The double relationships project a process that is like one in which we both struggle to effect changes and also discover, when the changes have been achieved, that they have been embodied in the past, and then find that we are false to our experience if we reduce either of these to the other. The affirmative connotations of the brass chorale invite us to think that a temporal process characterized by having decided and having attained may at least be possible.

Hearing the chorale's relation to the rest of the movement in this way is supported by the chorale's use of materials that are at first contrasting and then converging. The contrasting materials are initially juxtaposed with very little or no transition to modulate the contrast. When these materials, in spite of their contrast, converge upon one another, the confluence is like the F-sharps within the chorale and the chorale within the movement as a whole: the convergence has a double meaning. On the one hand, it is the outcome of a struggle; as the violent contrast is overcome, a genuine change takes place that is encapsulated in the shout of joy; the motivic exchange is like an event that does not have to happen, but does. On the other hand, the parallelism of the phrase structure in the anger sections to that in the peace-questing sections suggests that the two kinds of music have an underlying similarity and that the convergence is implicit in their initial statements; the contrast is more apparent than real, and when the motivic exchange surmounts the contrast, no genuinely basic change takes place. One can hold the two meanings together by saying that, because of the structural parallels, the convergence exemplifies a process like that of having decided, for genuine change takes place, but when it does it turns out to have already happened.

Overlapping the last tones of the brass chorale, the motif of anger recommences, and the final section of the movement is given over to a reprise of the motifs of the opening section: the circling minor thirds, the upward leaping ninth, the diminished-seventh chord, the repeated eighth notes, and the melodic figure that moves down a sixth (F to A, bars 559–560; compare to bars 9–10 and 35–37). For only about twenty-five measures is this last outburst of anger loud enough to be a scream (522–547). It is significant that this outcry is entirely in the relaxed key of the subdominant D, the key of the brass chorale. When the movement's tonic returns, the music is soft, and the movement ends quietly. The contrast in tonality and dynamic level between the opening and closing sections, in spite of the use of identical motifs in the two sections, makes it impossible to hear the ending as a return to the mood of the opening. This contrast dramatizes the effect of the movement's process and its glorious encapsulation in the shout of joy: although anger persists to the end of the movement — the affirmation of life necessarily risks feeling the pain of death — it is no longer a frantic anger that overwhelms everything else. At the close of the movement we hear anger, pain and bitterness in the context of persistently affirming life, involving oneself in its struggles and decisions, thrilling to its joys and risking its grief while remaining tranquil and free in all eventualities, for deciding, risking, attaining turn out to be having decided, having risked and having attained.

2. Part Two

The Scherzo turns its back on death, heroism and the quest for peace. A horn call that summons itself from nowhere moves us into the glittering world of the Ländler and the Viennese waltz, an infectiously cheerful whirl in which the future and the self are sometimes forgotten, sometimes suppressed and sometimes affirmed.[15] If we hold to our usual assumptions about consciousness and temporality, the movement must seem to wobble between aimlessness and chillingly conventional directedness, like an exalted madness that is alternatively as unpredictable as the wind and as predictable as a golem. And indeed, the music evokes these assumptions, but it brings them to mind in order to reject them and in rejecting them to lose a standard against which its behavior could be seen as mad.

Repetitions of the opening horn call (bar 1, Figure 25) in bars 174 and 490 somewhat imperiously and ungraciously (how different it would be if it had an upbeat!) divide the huge Scherzo into three sections (Figure 23). Section one has seven waves; at the beginning of each wave, the music is aimless in the sense that it seems quite self-contained and, in spite of sharing motifs and a common tonic with its past (the previous wave) and its future (the next wave), it seems neither to grow out of the one nor to evoke the other; yet the end of each wave arrives in a conventional way at conventional goals. The waves in section two are goal-directed at their beginning but drift into aimless wandering and then disappear without closing on their goals. While these ways of relating the present to the future seem to be mutually exclusive, both are presented with the complacent authority of people who suppose that the temporal process they live

FIGURE 23
Sketch of Mahler, Fifth Symphony, third movement

section one		first wave	second wave	third wave
1— 39	first subsection	1— 15	16— 26	27— 39
40— 83	second subsection	40— 72	73— 83	—
84—135	third subsection	84—120	121—135	—
136—173	Trio			
section two				
174—201	first subsection	174—188	189—201	—
202—489	second subsection (extn. of Scherzo/ reprise of Trio)	241—307	308—428	429—489
section three				
490—526	first subsection	490—504	505—516	517—526
527—579	second subsection	527—562	563—579	—
580—763	third subsection (Trio)	580—632	633—661	662—763
coda		764—790	791—819	—

is the only one that is plausible. Section three obliterates the distinction between the processes of sections one and two, as if their contrast were more apparent than real. But then the coda, as if to sweep aside the possibility that moving from contrast to non-differentiation were a resolution that reasserts the validity of our usual views of temporality, undoes the obliteration and redoes it in a new way.

(1) Section One

The first section has three subsections plus a trio. Each of the three subsections uses the thematic material laid out in the first twenty bars, and each comes to closure on a decisive, strong cadence. The three subsections are separated from one another not only by these cadences but also by several bars of an introductory scherzando motif (Figure 24, bars 40–47 and 83–93).

FIGURE 24
Mahler, Fifth Symphony, third movement

The first subsection of section one consists of three waves, each of which seems complete and self-sufficient both because it consists of stably paired phrases and because it ends on a strong tonic cadence. At none of these cadences is there any residual energy from within the phrase that would thrust forward into the next phrase. The second and then the third waves seem to create themselves *de novo*, to push themselves along, to respond to their own impulse, not to the previous wave. And each wave ends with such final closure that it seems to generate no pressure toward and to demand nothing of the next wave. Each wave lives for itself; it does not live from its past nor toward its future. Thematically similar, they have no more to do with each other than do three strangers who happen to be wearing the same dress and happen to be in a train station at the same time. Both the second and third subsections consist of two waves, the second as unrelated to the first as are the three waves to one another in the first subsection. Thus, section one of the Scherzo consists of seven waves which, like the various sections in a round of dances, are all self-sufficient and independent of one another in spite of motivic similarities and a persistent dance rhythm.[16] At the same time, the past seems somewhat relevant to the end of the three subsections in that the three final waves are more exuberant and more straightforwardly organized than the three first waves.

Much the same could be said of the three subsections of section one in relation to one another. Each starts with a fresh impulse and ends with little residual energy. At the same time, there is one respect in which the past impinges on the second and third subsections in spite of the fact that they do not seem to be evoked by the previous subsection. The first wave of both the second and the third subsection chromatically distorts the main thematic material by bending it into the key of the relative minor (see bars 48ff. in Figure 31 and 94ff.), warping whole steps into half-steps and major thirds into diminished thirds; to hear these passages as distortions implies a connection with both the past and the future — that is, a recollection of what is now being heard in a distorted form and an expectation that the distortion will somehow be rectified. And the moments, near the end of these waves, when this expectation is met and the tonic, D major, returns (bars 67 and 115) are glorious indeed.

(i) First Subsection

The first wave not only refuses to generate the second wave, but also it so combines conventionalities with irregularities that the listener both has specific expectations about the immediately future notes within this wave and at the same time has no expectation of a future at all.

The paired phrases sound thoroughly conventional, but in two respects the end of the first and the beginning of the second are not so clear as their apparent conventionality suggests they ought to be. First, the last bar of the first phrase (horns, bars 1–8; see Figure 25) and the first bar of the second phrase (flutes and oboes, 8–15) overlap. The second phrase consists of two four-bar units, 8–11 and 12–15. The first of these is hidden in the shadow of the horns. Nevertheless, the second is sufficiently conventional that it seems to have been generated by and paired in the traditional way to the first. Second, the phrasing is blurred by the clarinets and bassoons in the background. They spit out a triple meter each of whose beats consists of two beats as written and each of whose measures consists of two bars as written (see Figure 26).

The metrical independence of the foreground and background from each other comports with the connotations of their motifs. There is a kind of innocent swagger about the opening horn call: it insists on filling our consciousness as though it were totally unaware that anything else might have a claim on it. The clarinet—bassoon

FIGURE 25
Mahler, Fifth Symphony, third movement

FIGURE 26
Sketch of Mahler, Fifth Symphony, third movement, clarinets—bassoons

rising scale in bar 5, imitating the horns' scale, is also exuberantly oblivious to everything else, and, in bar 6, strikes up a three-quarter time dance rhythm (shown in line b) of Figure 26) that spins us into the self-forgetting whirl of life. Both this rhythm and the waltz rhythm of the triple meter as written are like a force which is external to the self and in which the self can lose itself.

The cross rhythms resulting from the metrical autonomy of the background affect the foreground structure in two opposite ways. On the one hand, the coincidence of strong clarinet—bassoon downbeats with the first beats of bars 8 and 12 powerfully underscores the beginning of flute—oboe subphrases at those points. On the other hand, when the strong beats in the background meter fall on the second beats of the foreground meter (bars 7, 9, 11, 13, 15), the cross accents attenuate the regularity of the horn or flute—oboe meter, thereby weakening the sense that a conventional four-bar subphrase is in progress. This attenuation is particularly unsettling in bar 15 where the flute—oboe comes to a decisive downbeat, which is followed, on beat two, by a silent downbeat in the clarinet—bassoon meter. The dissonance between the two meters compounds the confusion that Mahler has built into the opening horn call, even before the clarinet—bassoon strikes up, for although he writes the first note of the movement as a downbeat (Figure 25), the listener may as easily hear the downbeat falling with the third note (as in Figure 27a). And the flute—oboe tune, until its last measure, could be heard with its downbeats as shown in Figure 27b.

The multiple downbeats within a single measure reinforce the hubbub and confusion created by the overlapping phrases. Indeed, the overlapping phrases are a higher-level version of multiple downbeats, for we hear the four-bar groups in the horns and flute—oboe as four-beat measures (each measure consisting of a dotted half-note), and on this architectonic level both bar 8 (in terms of the four-bar groupings to be created in the flute—oboe) and bar 9 (in terms of the four-bar groupings projected by the horns in 1—8) must be heard as downbeats. Moreover, the opening horn phrase consists of two-bar as well as four-bar groups; the two-bar groups have their strong beats in bars 1, 3, 5, 6 and 8. The multiple downbeats in the third of these two-bar groups (5—6) partly set up the multiple downbeats that occur in bars 8—9 on the four-bar level.

FIGURE 27a

FIGURE 27b

The confusion created by the multiple downbeats is compounded by the fact that in some measures in some voices the sense of a downbeat is almost entirely lost. In measures like the clarinet—bassoon in bar 5, the first beat is nearly undifferentiated from the second and third beats, and each of the three beats is anacrustic to the downbeat in bar 6. The number of anacrustic beats is continuously

changing, and this variation also adds to the disarray. In the clarinet—
bassoon accompaniment, bars 8 and 10 are preceded by a half-beat
anacrusis, bar 12 by four anacrustic beats and bar 15 by one and a
half. The horns in the first measure begin abruptly and flatfootedly
on a downbeat (as Mahler bars the first measure and as the ear
subsequently realizes), and then proceed more graciously as two-beat
anacruses lead into the downbeats in bars 3, 5, 6 and 8. The flute—
oboe tune has two-beat anacruses that lead into bars 10, 12, 14
and 15 and a half-beat anacrusis to bar 11.

FIGURE 28

The cumulative effect of the overlapping phrases, multiple downbeats and irregular anacruses is to pull listeners into the middle of the
process such that they cannot tell its contours very precisely. One is
reminded of several paintings by Gustav Klimt, such as "Pear Tree"
(1903), "Farmhouse in Upper Austria" (1911/1912) and "Avenue in
Schloss Kammer Park" (1912), in which orchards and trees reach out
toward their viewers, reach over their heads and continue indefinitely
behind. Klimit treats these trees the way many painters treat the sky,
which at the horizon recedes indefinitely from the viewer and,
toward the top of the canvas, reverses its direction, comes toward its
viewers and continues infinitely over their heads into the distance
behind them. Although no one supposes that Klimt's trees are
limitless, they so surround the viewers that they cannot tell where
the limits are. The usual connotation of "viewer" — one who views,
detached from what is being viewed — cannot apply. Listeners to
Mahler's Scherzo are surrounded, washed along in the wave. As
though they are participating in the process, they cannot see what
they are creating. They hear paired phrases, but cannot tell very

precisely where the first ends and the second begins.

Figure 28 offers a Scherzo beginning which uses Mahler's ideas in a way that is regular, pleasant and not totally uninteresting, although no one would mistake it for a piece of Mahler's writing. Comparing it to Figure 25, one sees at once how irregular Mahler can be without failing to sound in some respects quite conventional. The point of the contrast is not to suggest that to hear Mahler properly involves hearing the discrepancy between some ideal regularity and the actual irregularities he has composed and then expecting the discrepancy to be resolved in some way. Nor is it to suggest that Mahler has improved upon the trivial and the banal by introducing complexities to challenge the listener. Mahler is neither departing from the norm in order to reestablish it more profoundly nor enriching the ordinary in order to make the music correspond to a loftier image of human experience. Instead, he is immersing us in a whirl in which there are many voices making many demands on our attention; each has a past (and some of these pasts coincide with one another), and each presses to its own future (and some of these expectations are actualized). The process exemplified by the music is like one in which a person is too self-forgetting to want regularity or even to feel its absence.

It is not maximally disorderly, however: the tonality is stable, and there are recurring motifs as well as several clear-cut four-bar units. Many of the orderly fragments appear in the next wave. The kaleidoscope has turned, however, and they fall into a new arrangement. The horn's first four-bar subphrase (bars 16—19; see Figure 29) is identical to its bars 4—7, but what at the onset of the movement are the last and the first downbeats (that is, bars 4, 5) in different four-bar groups here are the first and second downbeats (bars 16 and 17) of a single subphrase.

For an answering subphrase, the horn must wait until the upbeat to bar 22 (one may hear 23—26 as a tidy four-bar subphrase, so retrospectively one may well hear 21—22 as a four-and-a-half-beat anacrusis to 23—26). Meanwhile, the violins are singing a four-bar subphrase (bars 18—21) and beginning another one. The first downbeat (18) that falls in one of the violins' four-bar groups coincides with the third downbeat in the horn's tune. The violins in bars 15—17 have played an obbligato ornamenting the horn's tune, but it turns out that this embellishing figure also functions as a seven-and-a-half-beat anacrusis that, like winding up a music box, impels the violins' own ditty in 18—21. The violins in 15—17 might also have sounded like the beginning of a four-bar subphrase, except that our attention is attracted more to the familiar horn tune than to it, and the violins do not move into the foreground until bar 18, where the horn's motion stops temporarily. The violins give the downbeat to the answering subphrase (bar 22) before the horn gets to its, but the horn quickly takes over, and by bar 24 the violins have receded into a non-tuneful background, and one loses track of the end of their answering subphrase.

FIGURE 29
Mahler, Fifth Symphony, third movement

One of the most significant aspects of this wave is its use of first beats that serve very little as the focus of a three-beat group but rather push toward a coming downbeat. This technique, which resists the focal force usually associated with a first beat, has already occurred in the first wave (clarinet—bassoon, bar 5), but it is more extensively used in the second wave. The first beats in bar 16—17 (violins) and in bar 22 (horn) do not unambiguously function as the focus to the two beats that follow them. Instead, they are more analogous to the anacrustic gestures in 15 and 21, and continue the push toward a focal gesture. In other words, the push in 16—17 and 22 toward a focus is far less clearly differentiated into weak and strong beats than are bars 18—21 (violin) and 23—26 (horn). The fact that the first beats of 16—17 and 22 do not behave like downbeats but rather like extensions of the anacrusis begun in the previous measure means that the listener cannot be sure that downbeats will be coming at regular intervals. Making first beats not sound like downbeats reduces the comfort and certainty — or oppressive predictability — that regularly recurring downbeats produce.

Interpolating the violin subphrases between the horn subphrases has the same effect: for three first-beats, the horn does not move; the downbeat that the previous four downbeats might lead us to expect in bar 19 simply does not materialize.

Changing the meaning of the horn's tune in bars 4–6 when it recurs in bars 16–18 has the same effect on a higher architectonic level. Figure 30 places bars from the second wave directly beneath the bars to which they are identical in the first wave and indicates how the new placement of the music within the phrase changes the rhythmic meaning of bar 16: it is focal (analogous to a downbeat) while the bar it copies is analogous to an afterbeat (since its first beat, being tied to the previous measure, is not articulated).

FIGURE 30
Sketch of Mahler, Fifth Symphony, third movement,
obbligato horn, bars 1–19

1	2	3	4	5	6	7	8
—	∪	—	∪	—	—	∪	—

16	17	18	19
—	∪	—	∪

What is particularly remarkable about the process into which Mahler spins us is that we come not to expect regular downbeats. Given our listening habits, we probably continue to feel an implicit waltz rhythm but to a significant degree we do not hear the non-thetic first beats as the non-occurrence of something that "ought" to happen. To that extent, the music is taking us into a temporal process which does not presuppose that there are principles of regularity and to which even the concept of regularity is absent. Consciousness in such a temporal process would be futureless in that no expectation (of what, say, an object might be if we viewed it from a different angle nor of what an event might be if we made a certain decision) would bear on the present object of consciousness. There would be no way to find an object or event different from what we expected. Having no basis for expecting anything in particular, we would have no basis for expecting at all. Expectation would be no different from what we usually call "fantasy." We would continue to synthesize present perceptions with past perceptions (just as in Mahler's music, one associates the horn in bars 16–18 with the horn of bars 4–6 and one associates consequent four-bar groups, such as bars 23–26 in the horn and 22–26 in the violins, with prior antecedents), but it would never occur to us that this association might provide the basis for an expectation (just as in Mahler's music one does not hear the non-downbeats as the erosion of downbeats; the absence of down-beats is not experienced in contrast to an "ought").

In the third wave (bars 27–39) Mahler pulls us back somewhat from this self-forgetful, nearly futureless world. We hear two sub-phrases that are clearly paired to one another (29–32 and 35–39), the first clearly exemplifying a future-generating and the second a past-generated gesture. Moreover, both subphrases are set into motion by long anacruses (seven and a half beats and eight beats respectively). Thus, we hear a clear distinction between a gesture that energizes a subphrase and the subphrase itself; the process distinguishes between the activation of an impulse (the past) and the result of that potential (the future of that past). In that the wave uses the same tonality and musical material as the previous wave, it is continuous with its past. At the same time, however, the third wave as a whole is pastless in the sense that its long subphrases ride on the energies of their own anacruses and not on any residual energy from the previous wave. This pastlessness confirms that the previous wave is as futureless as it seemed to be when it was going on.

(ii) Second Subsection

The second subsection of the first section opens with what Bekker aptly calls a "stamping motif"[17] (bars 40ff.; see Figure 24), which energizes the paired subphrases of bars 50–53 and 56–59. Because all the first beats in bars 40–42 sound as anacrustic as do the second and third beats and because the wind entrances in 43–47 are imitative, it is unlikely that one will hear anything in 40–47 as the beginning of a paired group. That the anacruses in the violins in bars 16–17 and 26–28 function more like these introductory measures than like the downbeats within a subphrase confirms the validity of hearing 16–17 and 26–28 as multi-measure anacruses.

Mahler's dazzling skill in writing two lilting, magically tuneful melodies in counterpoint to one another, a skill already exhibited in bars 22–23, becomes more conspicuous in bars 48–51. He gives us two tunes simultaneously, each of them so like a foreground melody with the other as part of its background that hearing the two together is like centering one's awareness completely on each of them, as though one were living at once in two different presents.[18] The bass instruments strike up the tune the horn had in bars 22–23 while the violins give a chromatically warped version of their bars 16—17 (Figure 31). But it is not only the tune that is warped: the basses are trying to make an antecedent subphrase out of what had been a consequent subphrase (compare basses in bars 48—51 to the horn in 23—26). The would-be consequent (54—56) to this would-be antecedent falls silent after its third measure, and the violins, playing what had been a background figure, turn out to be carrying the foreground melody.

The violins' two subphrases (50—53 and 56—59), each of them preceded by a long anacrusis (48—49, 54—55) make a phrase that summons a pair. But just as if that process were not going on, the winds interrupt for a cute pair of subphrases (60—67) — like the violins interrupting the horns' paired subphrases in 18—21, only more blatantly. The horn call in bar 67 summons us back to the other reality, and the phrase evoked by 50—59 comes to actuality (69—72, preceded by a five-beat anacrusis).

FIGURE 31

Mahler, Fifth Symphony, third movement

By whirling us through two worlds — at first simultaneously, then in abrupt, meaninglessly transitionless juxtaposition — Mahler leaves us feeling we are in no world. We are no place where there are firm rules of continuation. Even more than in the first subsection, we are moved toward a futureless consciousness.

The second wave in the second subsection comes from nowhere. Its energy surpasses that of the first wave. One does not expect the subsection to have a third wave, but neither does one expect it not to. The second wave ends with the same upward scale that ends the first and second waves of the first subsection. The third wave of the first subsection ends with a descending scale. If one takes an ascending scale as a sign that a third wave is coming and if the third wave of the first subsection establishes three waves as a norm, then one expects a third wave to the second section. But there is no third wave, and the section does not seem truncated. It is not as though the return of the stamping motif in bar 83 sounds too soon or too eager.

(iii) Third Subsection

The first wave of the third subsection sounds more like a development section than a round of four-bar dances. The opening stamping motif covers more ground than before. It activates the winding figure (bars 94–95, violins) that we have come to associate with an anacrusis to a four-bar group. But no such group materializes, and about the time we realize that none is going to, the horns strike up a four-bar group. Not responding to the violins, it too is activated by the impulse conveyed in the stamping measures. Before the horns' subphrase can evoke a pair, the cellos–basses begin another four-bar group, over-lapping the horn's fourth downbeat and using the motif of the opening horn call (bars 102–105). This subphrase also fails to evoke a paired subphrase.

As in the first wave of the second subsection, we are spun off into the winds' world for eight bars, and then get a four-bar consequent phrase (bars 117–120, plus a five-beat anacrusis) that responds to no very clearly stated antecedent.

The second wave of the third subsection has two four-bar groups (woodwinds, bars 121–124, and trumpet, bars 127–130). The two groups seem oddly unhinged from one another. The tune played by the trumpet is a fragment of what has functioned in bars 8–11 as the antecedent subphrase of a consequent phrase. The trumpet in 127–131 also sounds like the beginning of an eight-bar group, leaving the winds' antecedent subphrase in 121–124 without a consequent. The trumpet's answering subphrase also fails to materialize. Never-theless, the winds' subphrase and, even more, its extension in bars 125ff., as well as the strings' scales swirling in the background throughout the wave, are sufficiently analogous to closing gestures in other pieces of music that the ending in bar 131, in spite of the false cadence, seems final enough to conclude not only the wave, and not only the third subsection, but section one as a whole.

Thus the section as a whole, just like each subsection as a whole and like each wave within each subsection, ends as unproblematically and conventionally as its internal processes are irregular. Although the tunes in section one are so ingratiating that we keep thinking their organization must be as glitteringly clear as they are lilting and elegant, the organization is, by the canons of rational lucidity, in fact always under a cloud. The use of waves and subsections that live off their own impulses instead of spinning off an instability felt at the end of the previous wave or subsection moves us toward a world in which one does not experience a contrast between what-is and what-has-been because what-is is not experienced as the coming-to-be of expectations that constitute part of what-has-been. And the use of antecedent phrases that have no consequent, of consequent phrases that have no antecedent, of pairs of subphrases that separate a consequent from its antecedent, and of subphrases that so overlap that none of them clearly evokes a coming subphrase — all these techniques in the second and third subsections, like the unpredictable downbeats in the first section, have the effect of moving us toward a temporality in which consciousness does not experience a contrast between what-is and what-is-to-come because it gives up having expectations. We are nearing a consciousness in which the self would be lost along with its past and future, for the self would lose its contrast with its no-longer-itself and its not-yet-itself as well as with objects.

Each wave, each subsection, and the section as a whole, however, end as crisply and conventionally as its internal organization is fuzzy. These endings are arresting, but not so much because they are novel or intrinsically brilliant as because their sharp profile sits strangely with the somewhat vague internal structure and they supply precisely what the brilliant melodies may have led us to expect. Coming to these endings is not only like reaching a goal; it is also like reaching a goal that has been defined by custom and reaching it, moreover, in the customary way. In this respect, we are experiencing the kind of temporal process experienced by a self that makes no distinction between itself and humanity in general. Its goals are not unique to itself, but are the goals that an impersonal "one" has, and it reaches them not in its own way, but in the way that "one" reaches them. As Heidegger might say, human existence has become lost in the they-self.[19] To summarize the movement as a whole thus far, we can say that Mahler presents us with a process resembling one in which the self, attaching itself to a vitality external to itself (that is, the dance rhythm), begins to lose touch with its past and future and itself. And then suddenly the self and its goals seem to be remembered — but it is a self that is controlled by convention and habit, not a radically particular self, that pops up.

What comes next could transform the meaning of the section one material. It could, for example, redo the material in such a way that the downbeats and phrase groupings were clearer. Then we would re-interpret section one as setting up a very particular kind of dissonance to be resolved by the rest of the movement. Then we would take section one to be directed toward a specific future, and the process exemplified would be that of a very original self struggling toward its own altogether unique and particular future.

(iv) Trio

What comes next is, of course, a new dance in a new tempo and a new mood, like the traditional Trio that follows the traditional Scherzo, and for a time we are moving through a comfortably recognizable process. To be sure, the opening eight-bar phrase refuses to divide itself into two four-bar groups, and the bassoon counter-point, in 142—143, putting a bit of the violins' ingratiating tune across the end of the first eight-bar phrase, obscures to some extent the articulation that separates this phrase from its pair (Figure 32). Moreover, the tune passes from the violins to the cellos for the last six beats of the second phrase, and this transferral diverts the listener from the fact that the phrase has only seven instead of the conven-tional eight measures. Nevertheless, a pair of phrases has clearly been articulated by the time of the cadence in bar 150, and we expect another pair, an answering pair, to follow.

The second eight-measure phrase in this answering pair is clear enough: it consists of the four-bar subphrase in the horn and violas of bars 166—169 and the four-bar subphrase in the first violins of bars 170—173. But the preceding group (151—165), to which 166—173 is paired, gives only the illusion of conventional clarity. In bars 151—165 we hear several four-bar groups, each of which proclaims itself as the beginning of an eight-bar phrase. (These four-bar groups either sing out simultaneously [in 151—154 both the oboe and the violins give a four-bar tune, and in 160—163 the flutes give a four-bar subphrase while the cellos begin one, which they do not complete] or they overlap one another [the first violins start a group in bar 162 before the flutes or the cellos have completed theirs].) Each of these four-bar groups seems to begin the group that is evoked by the fifteen-bar group in 136—150; each of them behaves as though it were the first thing to happen since bar 150.

Thus, we are twirled into a process in which what is happening both has and does not have a past. In that each four-bar group responds to 136—150, the past is relevant, and what is beginning now

FIGURE 32
Mahler, Fifth Symphony, third movement

is understood as the completing, or at least the carrying forward of
what had been begun before. But in that each successive four-bar
group during 151—165 responds so much more to 136—150 than to
previous segments of 151—165, the immediate past seems irrelevant
or, better, almost non-existent. In this respect, these groups represent
an analogue, on a lower architectonic level, to the way each of the
three waves in the first subsection and each of the three subsections
of the first section of the movement succeed one another without

responding to one another, energized almost entirely by impulses intrinsic to themselves, as though they were ignorant of any past.

The eight-bar group in 166—173 responds to bars 151—165 as if they did not exemplify this anomaly (and, indeed, they are not experienced as anomalous). The four-bar groups in 166—173 are as clearly paired to one another as those in 150—165 are not, and the close of this phrase sounds completely analogous to the close of a pair of eight-bar phrases (as though 151—165 were the first member of this pair). Yet, ending on the dominant, it is an unstable closing, more mobile than the end of the Trio's first pair of phrases (bar 150), and summons a future that will respond to this instability.

(2) Section Two

What we get has nothing to do with that instability. Instead, our faces are slapped by an audacious, impulsive trumpet call, which, like its model (the horn call in bar 1), is not even graced by an upbeat. The call launches the reprise of the Scherzo. Although the Trio seems incomplete — not only does it end unstably, but its thirty-eight bars seem too few to balance the 135 of the Scherzo — nevertheless, the trumpet call seems so full of itself that we are not sure whether we are permitted to expect the Trio to complete itself later.

The first subsection of this section of the Scherzo comes in two waves, bars 174—188 and 189—201. Bars 174—188 are essentially a reprise of bars 1—15. Bars 189—201, which are as unrelated to 174—188 as bars 16—26 are to 1—15, consist of a new mixture of the motifs used in the movement's first section, drawing at its end from the closing-like gesture of 121—131 (compare especially the violin in 195—196 to the winds in 121—122).

As before, the stamping motif (at bar 201) introduces the second subsection. More frenzied, more contrapuntally elaborated than in either of its appearances in the first section, it is also much more extended,[20] and when it gives way (bar 241) to periodically organized material, it is not to the Scherzo's main theme (as it was before) but to a motif that both serves as a counterpoint to the stamping motif (see bars 224, 237 and 239) and recalls the Trio's main motif (though the latter decorates its recurring pitch with lower neighbor tones and the motif in bars 241ff. decorates with an upper auxiliary) as well as its subsidiary oboe motif (see bar 151).

The material that follows bars 241 up to the horn call that announces section three of the Scherzo comes in three waves. The

Scherzo maintains its presence in all three waves by allusions to the opening horn call (bar 252), by various extensions of the stamping motif (bars 352–359, for example) and by quotations of the opening Scherzo (in bars 464–469, 472–474 and 479–481). At the same time, each wave alludes to the Trio more explicitly than its predecessor. The mood evoked by the horns in bars 241ff. comports more with the nostalgic Trio than with the exuberant Scherzo. The second wave introduces the pizzicato accompaniment, which is very important to the Trio's character, and quotes the Trio's theme in places (for example, 329–334), and the third begins straightaway with the Trio's main motif. For this reason, the three waves gradually take on the function of carrying forward the Trio, which was so rudely shoved underground by the trumpet call in bar 174. In fact, it is as true to the music to say that bars 241–489 are the continuation or the reprise of the Trio and that 174–240 are a contrasting section within the Trio as to say that bars 174–489 are the reprise of the Scherzo. Bars 174–240 and 241–489 thus have dual meanings: in relation to the Scherzo (1–135), bars 174–240 function as a return to the beginning of the cycle; in relation to the Trio, they function as a step forward, leading to the return of the Trio; bars 241–489 function in relation to the Trio (136–173) as a return to the beginning of the cycle, and in relation to the Scherzo (1–135 and 174–240) as an extension-development.[21]

In general, a Scherzo and its reprise are like paying attention to the ongoing, cyclical processes in whose context specific events occur, and a Trio is like a specific event taking place in that context. When Mahler gives us a Scherzo reprise that is also the Trio's trio, he gives us a gesture that is at once part of the context of an event (the Scherzo, including its reprise, is the cyclical background against which the Trio takes place) and an event itself against another background (the Scherzo reprise is also the Trio's trio, an event against the cyclical context created by the Trio in 136–173 and its reprise in 241ff.). Similarly, bars 241ff. are both part of an event (the Trio) taking place in a context (the Scherzo) and part of the context (the Trio) in which an event (the Trio's trio) takes place.

Kolomon Moser's poster for the Secession's Fifth Exhibition in 1899 is a good visual analogue to Mahler's procedure. The background and foreground interchange with one another throughout the poster in a way that, Alessandra Comini suggests, echoes the androgyny of its central figure, a flat-chested long-haired angel.[22] The olive in the background becomes foreground when it is outlined in yellow; some of the lettering is olive against yellow, while some of it is yellow against olive. (The technique goes back at least to some of the Middle Kingdom Egyptian bas-reliefs in which an incision into the stone serves sometimes to indicate what is further from, sometimes what is nearer to the viewer.) Just as Moser presents us with a visual space in which something is both nearer to us and farther away than something else, and in which this contradiction of Newtonian space is not experienced as a contradiction, so Mahler gives us a temporal process in which a return to the beginning of the cycle is also, non-contradictorily, a step forward.

To the extent that the first three waves of the movement erase expectation as an aspect of the temporal process (by erasing the focal power of certain downbeats on various architectonic levels), the first subsection offers a temporal process in which one does not experience the present as the arrival of the past's future — that is, the coming to actuality of what a past gesture prepared. The dual meaning of bars 241—489 is a higher-level instance of this same temporality, for if a gesture is both a return and a step forward, it is not clear that anything is actually taking place or that it makes sense to think of the present as something prepared by the past or of the past as the context of the present. Both ambiguities experienced in bars 174—489 — that the reprise of the Scherzo (174—241) is also the Trio's trio and that the reprise of the Trio (241—489) after its trio is also the extension of the Scherzo — indicate a process in which one gives up or backs off from expecting a particular future and what comes is not experienced as the actualization of the past's struggles. Not expecting a particular future is also the result of the way 174ff. and 202ff. do not seem to be generated by their past and are not the coming-to-actuality of something prepared by a past.

The Scherzo's reprise in bars 174—201 might reasonably lead us to expect that 202ff. will redo the material from bars 1—135 in such a way that the cloudiness of their organization might be removed. But far from resolving section one, the three waves beginning at 241 present processes that are, in fact, the obverse of the processes in bars 1—135. While there we are presented with waves and subsections that are self-sufficient and neither respond to the preceding one nor evoke the next one, here we are presented waves that, like the first statement of the Trio (bars 136—173), press ahead to a coming event. Or rather, the three waves in 241—489 initially press forward to the next section, but they disintegrate before the future they try to evoke becomes actual. The details of this disintegration and its effect are somewhat different in the three waves.

After the stamping-motif introduction, the first wave begins with an antecedent phrase (bars 241—250 in the horns, then trumpet) that presses toward a consequent. But the answering phrase is cut off by an impetuous reappearance of the stamping motif (251—253) and the horn call (252—253). Although the winds' *pianissimo* background in bars 241—250 has maintained the rhythm of the stamping motif, it seems like bad manners for the stamping figure to assert itself *fortissimo* in 251—252 and suppress the answering phrase. The assertiveness of the stamping is evidently more than the shape-begetting process can bear: the same motif continues to prevail, but regularity becomes more and more elusive. Fragmentation becomes increasingly characteristic until, for the fairly long passage from 270 to 307, we are further from shapeliness and nearer to entropy than ever before in the movement. The downbeat is eroded by the dissonance between the ongoing triple meter of the waltz and the duple meter of the violins in 262—264, of all the instruments in 266—269 and especially of the horns' entrances in 271—274. The downbeat is all but lost in the subsequent *ritards* and *fermati*. The melodic motif is consistent, but meanders without defining a goal for itself.

The wave as a whole suggests the transformation of a gesture controlled by a self-aware agent, struggling to actualize itself, into a gesture which does not seem to be controlled by a goal and to which the very idea of struggling and self-determining becomes questionable.

A fresh impulse toward a rational process is felt in bar 308. Although this wave (308—428), like the preceding one, ends in aimless meandering, the exertion toward shape sustains itself much longer. Four times between 308 and 343 we hear the first phrase of a pair, but before the evoked pair is actualized, either the process is cut off (bars 314, 326) or it fades away (bars 334ff. and 342ff.). We are being reminded of the Trio's temporal process in bars 151—165 as well as its motifs. From bar 344 to bar 378, one four-bar group washes in after another, each one overlapping the one before. Each of them is designed to evoke a responding group, but because of the overlapping, no responding phrase ever takes place. It is a little like being in a room that is contiguous to three or four other rooms in each of which someone is singing, each one being oblivious to the other voices; now we hear this one, now that one; now we hear this scrap of meaningful shape, now that one, but the scraps do not cohere to make an overarching shape. And it is like the characters in Schnitzler's stories who decide very firmly now to do this, and now to do that and never become aware that they follow through on none of their decisions. The fragmentation is more palpable in 379ff., where even the first four-bar group fails to materialize.

Beginning in bar 389, the effort is more promising: we are given an eight-bar group that consists of two tidy four-bar groups, but the responding group trails off into shapelessness after four bars. Bars 403–410 and 411–418 are eight-bar groups each of which is anacrustic to some coming focus, but no focus comes. Instead, aimlessness sets in deeper during bars 419–428, though we are not so far from human struggle and the hope of actualization here as we are at the end of the first wave.

The third wave is even friendlier to human aspiration: bars 432–439, 440–447 and 448–455 are all eight-bar groups, each consisting of two tidy four-bar groups. Each of them is anacrustic to some coming group, and while none is the answer to its predecessor's evocation, they do not ignore but rather intensify one another. But this process breaks down abruptly — not gradually as in the first two waves — at bar 460, where a new eight-bar group begins at the point where a second four-bar group might, given the preceding music, have been expected.[23] What we get at 460ff., however, is not an eight-bar group, for this gesture is interrupted after only four bars by the bass voices in bar 464 (plus upbeat) insisting impetuously on *their* eight-bar group and alluding to the Scherzo explicitly (see bars 9–12). At its sixth measure, the horns butt in with their four-bar group, which the trumpets cut off after only three bars. In counterpoint to the violins' quotation of bars 48–49, the trumpets begin a new eight-bar group (472–479) exactly where the bass voices indicated that one ought to begin. Bars 472–479 heighten the push forward begun by 464–471, and 480 begins a third eight-bar group, this one also recalling the Scherzo. But this third push is cut off at its third measure. Bars 482–489 are an eight-bar group that pushes us hard ahead. But just where the evoked future might take place, the horn call summons the Scherzo back into motion. Because the last thirty bars somewhat resemble the development section of a sonata form, one might expect something like a recapitulation that would release the tensions worked up in those measures. The harmonic wrench, the frustrated voice leadings and the rhythmic hiatus at bar 490, however, make it hard to hear the Scherzo reprise as the target of the forward push in the preceding measures. Instead of fulfilling the aspirations of the Trio, the Scherzo simply sweeps them away.

We may summarize the second subsection of section two by noting that in it the listener undergoes two different processes simultaneously. On the one hand, the third wave, in spite of the jolts in bars 460, 464, 469, 472 and 482, seems more consistently to be heading toward something (whose actualization, it turns out, is cut off by the Scherzo reprise) than the second wave, and the second sustains aspiration longer than the first. On the other hand, the change from aspiration to aimlessness is increasingly less gradual as we move through the three waves. The change undergone during the course of the first wave is experienced as transformation, and categories like struggle and fulfillment are meaningful at the beginning, but gradually lose their force. By contrast, the analogous change in the third wave is experienced as conflict between a struggle toward achievement and a refusal to aspire. But because of the jolts and the renewed struggle which never seems to acknowledge the fact of the jolt, the nature of what would count as achievement becomes less and less clear as the third wave progresses. At its end it is still aspiring mightily, but in aspiring toward nothing in particular it is as disintegrated and aimless as is the end of the first wave.

In section one, befogging the focal power of downbeats dims expectation as an aspect of temporality. During each of its seven waves, this feature amounts to a kind of aimlessness — the sense that whatever is coming is irrelevant to the present. But at the end of each wave, we hear the arrival of precisely that which convention would have had us to expect. In section two, the waves of the second subsection invert this relation between convention and aimlessness. Their four- and eight-bar groups seem very much to be conventional, future-evoking gestures, but again and again the future they evoke does not happen because the conventional past is continuously forgotten; again and again a new phrase, conventionally pressing to the future, acts as if it had no past, and consequently aimlessness sets in at the end of the wave. Although the waves of the second section do not have the closed endings that endow each wave of the first section with self-sufficiency, the waves of the second section live as little from their past as do those in the first part. In both sections, each new wave seems to arise from and ride on its own impulse and not to respond to an instability in or forward thrust from the past.

(3) Section Three

The third section of the Scherzo, like the second, begins by reprising section one. In bars 490–526, as in bars 1–47, three self-sufficient waves roll by. The next two subsections are, like their section-one counterparts, introduced by the stamping motif. While subsection two closely follows its prototype, subsection three never gets from the stamping motif to the Scherzo's main theme, but as in bars

202–309 (section two), the stamping motif generates a counterpoint that recalls the Trio's theme. During the third subsection enough other motifs from the middle section of the movement are used that the force of that section — together with its aimlessness — is felt again. There are a few four-bar groupings (584–587, 602–605 and 609–612) and even an eight-bar group (614–621), but each of these is followed not by the future it has tried to evoke but by goalless wandering. The listener is reminded of the aimlessness suggested in subsection two of section two, and the similarity of the motivic treatments reinforces this association.

But during this drifting, the stamping motif is never far away and is usually explicitly present with its connotation of introducing something. Thus bars 580–632 recall both section one and section two. They combine the introductoriness of the stamping motif from section one with the aimlessness of the section-two endings; they combine looking toward a future with having no future. What is introduced commences in bar 633: a derivative of the Scherzo's main theme in the violins and the Trio theme in the bass instruments (compare 633 to 121–123 and 195–196).

As a reprise of the Trio, bars 633ff. might lead us to expect that the conventional periodic structure of the Trio would now prevail and that the tension of the impossible combinations in 580–632 would disappear. But after four four-bar groups, each of them cohering into a group a little less than the previous one, we get a new form of impetuousness: the four-bar groups are displaced by three-bar groupings (bars 648–650 and 651–653) and then by two-bar groupings (bars 654–655, 656–657, 658–659 and 660–661).

These shortened groups amount to an accelerando, which compounds the effect of using the faster tempo of the Scherzo for the Trio theme in 633ff. and which presses into a second attempt to reprise the Trio (bar 662). Once again the opening of the movement makes its presence felt along with the Trio, for the cellos and basses play the horn call from bar 1 (or, better, continue the allusion to bar 1 that begins in bar 656). Once again, the music creates four-bar groups, each of them cohering less than the previous one, and then once again a series of three-bar groups, beginning with 687–689 (but note that 711–714 is a four-bar group).

Shifting from four- to three- to four- or two-bar groups has the effect of making the higher-level downbeat irregular. Like the techniques used in the first section (increasing the anacrusis to five or six beats, suspending an eight-bar process in its middle while a counterpoint group has its say and giving a melodic fragment a new place in the group), it corrodes predictability and the sense that predictability is even a possibility.

Section three integrates sections one and two in the obvious sense that it blends together reprises of them both. The first two subsections of section three reprise the first two subsections of section one; the third subsection begins as if it were a reprise of the third subsection of section one, but then extends and develops it in the same way that the waves of section two do. Similarly, the two attempts to reprise the Trio (633–661 and 662–763) blend the Trio's motif with numerous motifs from both sections one and two.

Less obviously, but more importantly, section three integrates the first two sections in the sense of presenting the futurelessness and self-sufficiency of the waves in the first together with the aspiring and then aimless non-self-sufficiency of the waves in the second in such a way that one feels there is no difference between these two processes. The first section exemplifies the kind of process in which first the self is lost to the extent that it moves in a futureless world and then the authenticity and uniqueness of the self is lost as it falls into the conventional they-self. The second section, by contrast, exemplifies the kind of process in which a conventional they-self pushes toward a future that would actualize it and then lapses into futurelessness. The third section overrides this apparent incompability by exemplifying both of these process, mixing them together without in any way contrasting them. It thereby suggests either that there is no real difference between futurelessness and the conventional way of aspiring to a future, or that the difference is irrelevant in light of some other aspect of reality.

Like section two and unlike section one, the third section has clear, conventional groupings that seem to be evoking the future. But by imperceptible stages the groupings, by bar 726, have become so irregular — as irregular as the downbeats in section one — that we give up listening for them. In spite of the fact that groupings — whether two-, three-, four- or eight-bar groups — continually intimate an incipient regularity, fragmentation and aimlessness are in fact maximized. The irregularities of section one, the dual function of the Scherzo in section two (serving both as the reprise of section one and as the Trio's trio), and the sublimation of flow into mist throughout section two have moved us toward a world in which the expression "that which is to come" has little meaning. By integrating the first two sections, suggesting that the contrast between aimlessness and conventional future is only apparent or in the end irrelevant, the third moves us even further into a temporal process that is shorn of its future.

(4) Coda

But the very act of seeing that temporality is futureless asserts the future as its opposite category. One could not recognize futurelessness unless one had a concept of the future. Someone who lives a temporal process that is genuinely both futureless and directed toward a conventional future could not be so clearly aware of the non-differentiation between them as section three has made us. As if the very vividness of the section-three temporality thus contradicted its meaning,[24] the coda undoes it all. Or it does the same thing again in a different way — a way in which recognizing futurelessness does not affirm the future as a category after all.

The coda divides itself into two waves (764—790 and 791—819). The powerful climax in 783—790 and the new appearance of the opening horn call in 791 articulate the division. Until the climactic passage, the coda moves along in regular, forward pressing four-bar groups. The tempo is so fast that each measure as heard consists of four measures as written. But someplace we lose a beat (that is, three beats as written). By 791 it is clear that it has been lost, but Mahler so covers over the loss that one cannot say precisely when it slips out. The four-measure units are clear and regular from 764 to 779. Beginning in 783, the strings, trumpets and trombones make four-measure units, which end just before the second wave of the coda begins. See Figure 33.

FIGURE 33

Sketch of Mahler, Fifth Symphony, third movement

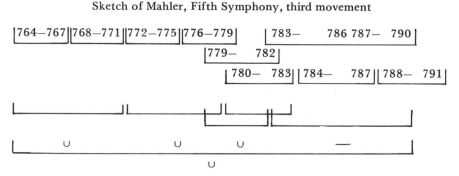

These groupings leave only three measures (780—782) between them, but the listener is not aware that a measure is missing because bar 779, the last bar of the previous four-bar unit, is also the first bar of the violin—trumpet—trombone four-bar grouping. One does not, however, decisively locate the loss of the measure with this overlapping, because the horn figure that strikes up in the upbeat to 784 makes four-bar units (784—787, 788—791) that behave as though 780—783 were a group (not 779—782, as the violins, trumpets and trombones would have it). The second of the horns' two four-bar measures is, of course, cut off by their own call in 791, and for them, the overlapping occurs here, not in 779.

This sort of overlapping means that a future arrives before the present that is evoking it has become the past. In other words, the listener is not permitted to hear a distinction between that which is and that which is to come. Mahler is not, of course, the first composer to telescope one phrase into another. But other composers do it for its witty effect: it humorously contradicts the way we usually construe the temporal process. Or they do it to intensify an urgent thrust forward. Mahler, by obscuring the fact that it is happening at all, does not seem to be appealing to any norm and so he cannot be said to be contradicting one. To be sure, the music presses ahead, but the non-distinction between the fullness of the present and the thrust toward the future is exhibited (as it has been before in the movement) as no less "normal" than what we usually take to be the usual distinction between them.

The second wave of the coda whirls along in regular four-bar groups (which, like 764—771, 772—779 and 783—790, make themselves into eight-bar groups; see Figure 34). The last four bars of 807—814 overlap the first four bars of 811—818. Not an uncommon feature, these overlapping groups are a higher-level analogue to the

FIGURE 34
Sketch of Mahler, Fifth Symphony, third movement

791—94   795—98   799—802   803—06   807—10   811—14   815—18   819—

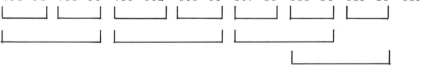

four-bar groups that overlap by a measure someplace in 779—791. And again, Mahler does not permit his listeners to hear the resulting coincidence of future and present as anomalous. He hides the fact that it is happening by sharpening the profile of the two-bar groupings within the four-bar units. Beginning at bar 807, the two-bar units are so conspicuous as to suggest that the music is now moving twice as fast, that is, in two- instead of four-bar measures, while it continues to move in four-bar measures as well. This ambiguity distracts attention from the other ambiguity, namely that of the overlapping eight-bar groups.

Moreover, bars 814—819 allude clearly to the opening of the movement (818 = 1 and 814—817 = 3—6) and its groupings so that we hear two different two-bar groupings simultaneously. We hear the two-bar units indicated in Figure 35a because they continue a pattern, established by the immediately preceding measures, of putting the focal measure on odd-numbered measures; at the same time we hear the two-bar units shown in Figure 35b because of their

FIGURE 35
Sketch of Mahler, Fifth Symphony,
third movement

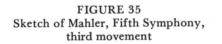

a) |813—814| |815—816| |817—818| |819—

b) |814—815| |816—817| |818—819|

identity with the motif heard at the beginning of the movement (although 815—816 is also identical to the horn in 16—17, where bar 16 begins a four-bar group). The effect of this ambiguity is to make the Scherzo end both wobbling and standing upright. The ambiguity of two different two-bar groupings, like that of moving in both two- and four-bar measures, pulls attention away from the overlapping eight-bar groupings and has the same effect on the temporal process.

The last completed four- or eight-bar group ends in 818. Bar 819 stands alone. It is the first measure of an eight-bar unit whose last seven bars consist of silence. The sound stops while the movement's process keeps on going. That is, the movement ends before it is over. It evokes a future whose only content turns out to be the memory of itself. The obverse of Mahlerian phrases that are underway without ever having begun, the music stops without having finished.

The character of this ending is critically important to the coda and indeed to the whole movement. The coda is the movement's most exciting passage; it gathers all the movement's motifs into a final, frenetic whirl, and unambiguously confirms D as its underlying tonality. And the coda is the most consistently goal-directed, forward-moving part of the movement. In its first wave, bars 783—790 (or 784—791) constitute a strong focus, to which 764—771, 772—779 and 779—782 (or 780—783) are anacruses (see Figure 33). That is, 764—782 press toward a specific future (like the waves in section two and unlike those in section one), and 783—790 actualize that evoked future (like the conventional closures in section one and unlike the unactualized aspirations of section two). Thus, while section three suggests that the contrast between sections one and two is apparent, not real, the first wave of the coda affirms the reality of the contrast by resolving it.

At the same time that the coda's first wave comes to an ending, it presses forward as a whole into the next wave, for its ending, while a genuine response to its past, is mobile. The second wave also presses toward a coming event. Bars 799—806 are a satisfactory response to bars 791—798. Bar 806 ends unstably, pressing forward. The following measures, which at first repeat 805—806 and then repeat only 806, compress and intensify this forward pressure. The groups in bars 807—814 and 811—818 are overlapping anacruses to the final climax.

But just where the final focus ought to be, we get only three notes, and they are metrically unstable (as in bar 1, we tend to hear the third note as the downbeat). The beginning of the culmination is articulated, but the event itself fails to spread itself out over time and actually take place. Or it takes place in the silence of the next seven bars. The music abandons us with the feeling that temporality is futureless after all, and that the contrast between sections one and two is apparent after all. The first wave of the coda, which affirms the reality of the contrast, has evoked a gesture which denies it. And the feeling of futurelessness takes the form of the horn call that opens the movement, spinning us back into the futureless process instead of protesting against it and denying its ultimacy. The last bar lets us feel the non-differentiation between having conventional goals and expecting nothing but, unlike section three, it does not attenuate futurelessness.

(5) The Movement as a Whole

In the first section each wave begins as if it had no past because the prior wave has had no future, and each wave has features that erode the thetic quality of some of its first beats, thereby eating away the sense of predictability and of coming events as possibilities to be synthesized with the present. In the second section, the waves of the second subsection begin as though they were pressing to some specific future. In the first wave, this pressure gradually turns into aimless drifting; in the second wave, the movement toward a concrete culmination turns into drifting less gradually, but the drifting is somewhat less aimless; in the third wave, the change from future-directed struggle to futurelessness comes as a jolting shock, and the sense of moving toward a specific future is never obliterated. The evoked future, however, never materializes. The third section reprises the first wave of the first section, then transforms a reprise of the second wave of the first section into a reprise of the second section in such a way that the temporal process it exemplifies is in effect indistinguishable from that in both the first and second sections. Then the coda undoes this integration by whirling us into a process that moves toward a future (unlike the first section) and actualizes its past (unlike the second section). The process which the movement unfolds is highly original. It successfully suggests a new kind of coherence, or rather, it is successful until the very last measure, when actualizing this coherence is cut off with a gesture whose associations with the beginning of the movement suggest that the whole cycle will go on again. Without getting anywhere. Again.

In spite of the regularity of its four-bar groups, the coda seems to be the wildest, most self-oblivious part of the movement because the tempo is increased to a frantic level and because motifs from all sections of the movement fly past in what seems to be an arbitrary succession. This frenetic, Dionysian confusion is at odds with the sense that the music is moving toward a goal — the sense that its process resembles that of a self moving toward the actualization of its decisions and thus of itself. Consequently, during and at the end of the coda we are living both with and without a future. We are living both as rationally choosing and as impulsively driven creatures that both do and do not make a distinction between themselves and the vital processes in which they participate.

The movement presents this combination again and again, and one wonders what, if anything, controls the succession of these combinations. Is it a progression or a series of impulses? Although phrase groupings, motivic unity, motivic development, rhythmic constancy and tonality enable various passages, some of them fairly long, to cohere, none of these techniques has an overarching power that would forge the movement into a single, comprehensive whole. The first and second sections are one another's obverse; they are bound together by the complementarity of opposition. To the extent that the third section integrates this opposition — or carries it to the point of non-differentiation — it would seem to be a step forward, a kind of progression. The coda presents the opposite kind of non-differentiation by first resolving the opposition and then suddenly, in a single flash — the last bar — reinstating the kind of non-differentiation exemplified by the third section's second subsection.

The movement from the first section to its obverse in the second to their non-differentiation in the third to their resolution and, at the same time, renewed non-differentiation in the coda does not disclose the operation of some principle; this procession is not•guided or propelled by some sort of necessity. Nor is it chosen; the process is not at all like a self deciding to be in a certain way and to do certain things. Nor is it completely arbitrary; though there is no single thread of continuity, there are threads of continuity, and they overlap, disappear and reappear. The movement through its sections, like the movement within its sections, both affirms and denies futurelessness.

Such is Scherzo's picture of life. It is a process that consists of opposites that turn out to be only apparent, yet also real. It is a process whose resolution consists of happening to recognize — being forced to and yet also choosing to and yet really neither being forced nor choosing to recognize — that opposites are only apparent, but because one is always in and never above the process there is no final recognition of the illusory character of the opposites; and because the recognition must happen again and again, each time as though it had never happened before, the opposition is also real and not merely apparent. In suggesting that opposition and non-differentiation are equally fundamental, the Scherzo assaults common sense and challenges the usual categories with which we think about ourselves. Yet the Scherzo does not seem to be suggesting some mystical insight, available only to a transformed consciousness. As elsewhere with Mahler, it may be that the modes of continuing embodied in the Scherzo aurally picture ordinary temporal experiencing.

3. Part Three

The future reasserts its relevance throughout Part Three — the Adagietto and the Rondo—Finale. Particularly during a passage near the end of the Finale (beginning at about bar 680), coming events impinge palpably on the present. The music here seems to be striving forward to an apex, reaching upward into grander musical spaces and growing outward into richer sonorities. Yet the climax that comes (bar 711, S:32) does not really seem to be the arrival of that which these thirty measures have been struggling to achieve. Although the brass chorale shouting the climax is splendidly glorious, it is not quite grand enough, and it seems oddly unhinged from the passage that putatively worked it up. The motivic connections are not sinuous enough, and the harmonic resolution at S:32 (going from the dominant of C to the tonic of D) is not strong enough. The listener cannot feel that the brass chorale has been generated by the preceding passage.

The brass chorale seems more to allude to the brass chorale at the end of the second movement than to project a fulfillment of that which has putatively summoned it. The orchestration, the tonality and even the melody recall the earlier chorale, whose luminosity is far more glorious and brilliant. In fact, the Finale climax is not so much a climax as the recollecton of a climax. What begins at S:32 functions as the Finale's climax not so much because it climactically actualizes that toward which the preceding passage has been striving as because it is a moment when the memory of fulfillment suddenly fills the senses and the mind.[25]

Five times previously in the movement, the music has striven toward a goal: bars 292–306, 357–372, 465–496, 550–580, and 615–622 (see Figure 36). In exemplifying forward-directed exertion, these five passages resemble one another. And the events that occur at the moment when the striving seems to usher in its goal also closely resemble one another: in each case, the putatively culminating event (like the brass chorale at the end of the movement) seems oddly unhinged from the struggling passage, and (again like the brass chorale) it recollects an earlier moment in the symphony. In short, the movement consists of one moment after another when a climax is displaced by a recollection.

It is an odd process. Other composers have given us climaxes that are also returns (as at the recapitulation in many sonata–allegro movements). The difference is that with them the return is precisely what is expected, and the return is fulfilling because it is fitted to the process generating it, while Mahler's recollections occur in the place of a gesture that would have been fitted to the generative passage. A fulfillment that is in fact a recollection seems to contradict what striving implies. If it did not occur several times before the brass chorale, listeners would probably not be able to hear and accept it there. They might well find that the movement's (and the symphony's) ending is completely unsatisfactory, and speculate that Mahler's imagination had faltered and failed to produce a satisfactory close. In order to develop terms for describing the temporal process at the brass chorale, the following sections will describe the five other striving passages and their goals, comparing and contrasting them to the modes of continuation and non-continuation in the first part of the movement. Then they will deal with the brass chorale itself, the way it pulls the movement into a whole, and the way the movement pulls the entire symphony into a coherent whole. Understanding the

FIGURE 36
Sketch of Mahler, Fifth Symphony, Finale

beginning at measure	thematic material	striving begins	climax begins	caesura at end of section
1	"Exposition" introduction			none
	section one			
24	peasant dance (a)			cadence on D, m. 55
56	fourth-motif theme (b)			bump, m. 119
	section two			
136	peasant dance (a')			bump, m. 166
167	fourth-motif theme (b')			cadence on B, m. 233
	(Scherzo and Adagietto recollections)			
245	"Striving into recollection" first wave	m. 292	m. 307 (Scherzo recollection)	bump, m. 329
330	fourth-motif theme second wave	m. 357	m. 373 (Adagietto recollection)	cadence on D, m. 415
423	fourth-motif theme third wave	m. 465	m. 497 (peasant dance and Part One recoll.)	bump, m. 526
526	fourth-motif theme fourth wave	m. 550	m. 581 (peasant dance)	none
?	fourth-motif theme fifth wave	m. 615	m. 623 (Scherzo recollection)	none
643	peasant dance sixth wave fourth-motif theme (Adagietto recollection)	m. 680	m. 711 (2nd movement brass chorale recollection)	cadence on D, m. 791

symphony's peculiar sort of coherence, one is finally in a position to characterize the temporal process that the chorale, the Finale and the symphony convey.

(1) Continuaton and Non-Continuation in the Exposition of the Finale's Two Themes

The first striving passage does not begin until after the movement has run about a third of its course. The first 233 measures constitute a kind of exposition: they end with a clearly articulated caesura (a full cadence on B), and they set forth the movement's themes and motifs and all its modes of continuation, except for the striving toward what turns out to be the non-fulfilling recollection of prior goals.

There are three kinds of continuation in the exposition: the use of four-bar and eight-bar groups to form paired subphrases, paired phrases, and paired sections, the use of a contrasting texture (namely, the fughetto that begins in bars 56 and 167) to set up a dualism which points ahead to a resolution, and the use of a violent bump (bar 119 and bar 166) to interrupt the musical flow and postpone closure.

A peasant dance strikes up in bar 24. It is cast in four-bar groups. At least it creates the sense that it is cast into four-bar groups, for as various instruments enter, they lean hard on their downbeats, insisting that they are beginning a four-bar group. But because these entrances do not come at four- or eight-bar intervals, the organization of the passage is as ambiguous and complicated as the tune itself is straightforward and naive. As the brackets below the staff in Figure 37 indicate, one hears the horn's entrance in bar 24 as the beginning of a four-bar unit. This hearing is subsequently confused by two things: the open-fifth drone in the basses is played with such a heavy accent in bars 25 and 27 that they do not readily sound like the second and fourth bars in a group. Moreover, bar 28 (horn) serves awkwardly as the first measure in the next four-bar unit because bar 28 is identical to bar 26, which is the third measure in a four-bar unit. Following these different cues, one hears first bar 24, then bar 25, then bar 26, as the onset of a four-bar group.

Hearing bar 26 as the onset of the four-bar grouping seems to be confirmed by the flute's entrance on the upbeat to bar 30, making it the onset of a second four-bar unit (see brackets above the staff in Figure 37). But this way of hearing becomes somewhat problematic in bars 32—34, which are analogous to the horn in bars 26—28,

FIGURE 37
Mahler, Fifth Symphony, Finale

because again it sounds odd when identical material functions first as the third measure (bar 32) and then as the first measure (bar 34) in a four-bar unit.

Nevertheless, the bassoon—horn—bass entrance with the peasant tune in bar 38 continues the four-bar grouping begun in bar 26, and the flute's music in bars 42ff. fits more comfortably into this grouping than into the four-bar grouping begun in bar 24. This grouping, however, breaks down in bar 52, which is so much more clearly the beginning than it is the third bar in a unit.

The four-bar units that begin in bar 24 form eight-bar units (see Figure 38). These groupings are, however, somewhat indecisive. Because of the ambiguity surrounding the four-bar groupings, listeners are less sure that an eight-bar group begins in bar 32 and that it responds to bars 24—31 as a unit than they are sure that there are eight-bar groups someplace. Eight-bar grouping breaks down when 48—51 group themselves with the preceding eight bars to make a twelve-bar unit. The answer to this twelve-bar unit and the focus of the peasant dance as a whole comes in bars 52—56. This focal sub-phrase is so brief that the passage ends very precipitously. This abruptness, together with the ambiguity about where the four-bar

FIGURE 38
Sketch of Mahler, Fifth Symphony, Finale

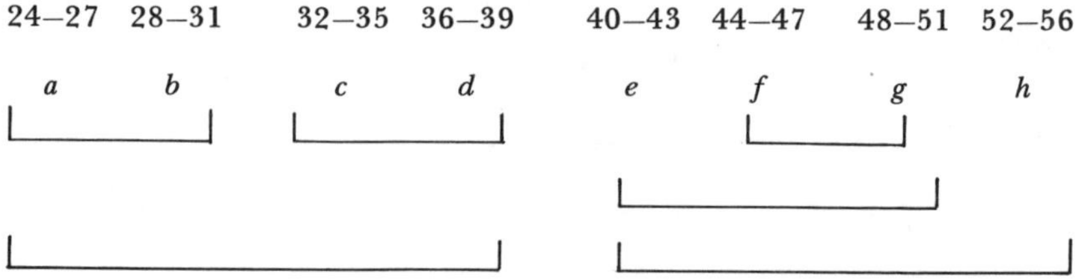

24–27 28–31   32–35 36–39   40–43 44–47   48–51 52–56

a   b   c   d   e   f   g   h

subphrases begin, generates a strong forward thrust into the next passage.

Although the fughetto texture that asserts itself in bar 56 (S:2) seems to have been evoked by the peasant dance and its residual instabilities, it does not seem really to respond to the dance. To be sure, it is responsive in the sense that it seems to burst free from the regularities involved in the dance, yet it could as easily function this way in relation to many other sets of paired groupings; there does not seem to be anything about this particular breaking loose that makes it uniquely responsive to this particular dance. Reminiscent of the stamping figures in the Scherzo and the introductoriness they imply, the fughetto does not seem so much to actualize the specific future that the dance has been summoning as to set up over against the peasant dance a new texture, a new tonal center (it quickly moves to A) and, in bar 79, a new tune (it moves in leaps of a fourth as much as the peasant tune moves in diatonic steps. The juxtaposition promises a future that will be common to 1–56 and 56ff.

Continuity within the passage from bars 56 to 99 comes from the racing contrapuntal lines and by the groups of subphrases articulated by the tune that is superimposed on the contrapuntal texture. The first two subphrases form a pair and thrust forward as a pair.[26] The fifth subphrase enters before the fourth has articulated its fourth measure, so the third and fourth cannot form a completed pair. The third, fourth and fifth (bars 88–99) are anacrustic to a coming thetic gesture. See Figure 39.

What begins at bar 100 is evoked by bars 79–99, but it is as inappropriate a response to 79–99 as the fugal texture at bar 56 is to what brought it into being. Once again, we have a gesture that refuses to actualize the future of the past that evoked it. Mahler's procedure has a significant visual analogue in Gustav Klimt's "Medicine," which

FIGURE 39
Sketch of Mahler, Fifth Symphony, Finale

mm.	79–82	83–87	88–91	92–94	99–99
subphrase	a	b	c	d	e

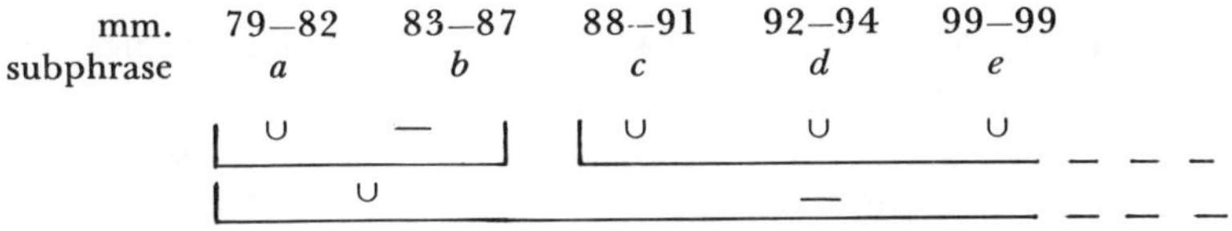

was painted for the University of Vienna ceiling in 1901. Just as each of Mahler's four-bar subphrases is fully developed within itself, so each individual figure in the Klimt is fully modeled and seems fully substantial. And just as Mahler's subphrases succeed one another without articulating a temporal process in which each event responds to the previous one and summons the next one, so also the spatial relations among Klimt's figures are as vague and formless as the figures themselves are clear and palpable.[27] Klimt's painting outraged the university faculty, and although the mood of Mahler's music is utterly different, the close analogy suggests that he too is moving us into a world that is repugnant to the rationalists' image of themselves as rational.

The passage beginning at bar 100 has the clearest pairings in the movement up to this point. Bars 100–103 and 104–107 are paired subphrases; bars 108–111 and 112–115 are paired subphrases and bars 100–107 act as a phrase paired to 108–115. The listener probably assumes that 116ff. will continue this kind of grouping and move from the subdominant of A back to the tonic of A.

Before a four-bar group can complete itself, however, this assumption is rudely contradicted by the bump in bar 119 (Figure 40). The

FIGURE 40
Mahler, Fifth Symphony, Finale

musical flow has been disrupted. A resolution of the tensions generated by the ambiguities of the peasant dance and the unresponsive continuations of bars 56ff. and 100ff. is postponed. After a second bump in bar 123, the music threads its way back to the beginning;

bars 127—130 and 131—133 repeat fragments from the introduction (reversing the order of their original appearance; see 16—19 and 10—12). The movement begins again, as it were; a second attempt to assert its ideas and let them flow to their conclusion is underway at S:5. While the reappearance of the opening material in rondos generally signifies a return to familiar and stable home territory before roaming abroad again, Mahler's music at S:5 seems to be asking listeners simply to forget the abortive first attempt to state its material, as though promising to behave in a more orderly way this time.

The second peasant dance is as foursquare as the first, and its organization is as scrambled. The closing (159—166), however, is more firm-footed and less abrupt. Because of the harmonic meanderings in bars 156—158, the *fortissimo* return of the tonic in 159 clearly begins a group, which turns out to be a pair of subphrases.

As a whole, bars 136—166, like their analogue (24—56), thrust forward, and, as before, the music that comes postpones rather than actualizes the expected continuation. The strange unresponsiveness and inappropriateness of what strikes up after the peasant dance to the material that has summoned it is even more striking this time because of the bump on the last beat of bar 166 and the abrupt shift to a new key for the new texture.

No fugal texture appears this time. Nobody follows the cello—bass lead, so instead of launching a fughetto, it becomes a running counterpoint to a graceful tune that the horns begin in bar 169. This tune is a new derivative of the leaping-fourth motif, one that fits itself into neat four-bar groups. The tidy organization and the courteous upbeats (a welcome relief to the stomping peasant dance and the downbeatishness of its sequel) at least dimly recall the Trio sections in the third movement, and motivic connections confirm the allusion (compare the descent from F to E-flat to D in bars 173—177 and the wide leaps there, and in 181—183 to bars 138—140 and 146—148 of the third movement; see Figure 41a, b).[28]

The counterpoint ceases in bar 191 when a new tonic, B, is stated. By the simple stroke of reversing the first two elements of the tune (compare 190 to 170 and 191 to 169), Mahler transforms it into an allegro version of the theme from the Adagietto (see Figure 41c and d). The passage preceding the recollection of the Adagietto consists of three pairs of four-bar groups. As Figure 42a suggests, each of these is anacrustic to some coming event. The succession of anacruses ends when the Adagietto is recollected, but, in spite of the harmonic resolution on B and the motivic connection between 169—189 and

FIGURE 41
Comparison of Mahler, Fifth Symphony, Finale, to movements three and four

190ff., the *grazioso* passage does not absorb the forward thrust of the anacruses. Partly because it begins too soon (its first two downbeats coincide with the last two of the third eight-bar group), and partly because the second violins continue the forward thrust, it seems less of an arrival and more of a continuation of bars 169—192. The continuation modifies what it extends in such a way that the eight-bar groups now create closed groups on higher levels (shown in Figure 42b) instead of functioning only as anacruses (as in 169—192).

FIGURE 42
Sketch of Mahler, Fifth Symphony, Finale

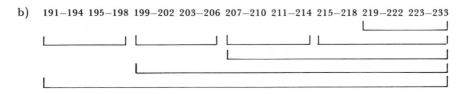

The cadence on B major in 233 conveys the strongest sense of closure of any moment in the movement up to this point. In some respects, bars 1—233 resemble the exposition in Mahler's sonata forms: we have had two contrasting ideas, each has been stated twice, and the contrast is stronger the second time through. Pursuing this resemblance, one might go on to describe 234—496 as a development section, 497—710 as a reprise and 711—791 as a coda.[29] Such a description would, however, significantly distort the movement, for as it unfolds, its shape turns out to have less to do with the dualism between two kinds of material, and more to do with the non-responsive continuations, the bumps and the recollections of earlier movements.

(2) The Striving Passages and Their Outcomes

The rest of the movement is organized, as Figure 36 indicates, into six waves by the six striving passages and the unfulfilling events that displace the goals of these exertions. Each of the first three waves separates itself from the next wave by one of the articulating devices used in the exposition: a bump (bars 329 and 526; compare to bar 119) or a full cadence (bar 415; compare to bar 233). At the end of the fourth and fifth waves, passages projecting the unfulfilling goals gradually turn into a new striving passage; no articulation separates the fourth from the fifth or the fifth from the sixth wave.

The striving passages are intensified forms of the forward thrust that characterizes the ends of the four-bar groups in the first 233 bars as well as the end of each peasant dance as a whole (bars 56 and 166). The obvious difference is that the four-bar groups and the ends of the peasant dances have a caesura of some sort that separates them from the passage toward which they are mobile, while the six striving passages flow without any articulation into the section they are generating.

The first four of the six waves form a pair of pairs. The first and third waves come to abrupt endings with bumps (bars 329 and 526) that are exactly like the bumps in the "exposition," and the heavily marked cadence on D in bar 415 separates the first pair from the second.

In all four waves, the music just after the caesura is a derivative of the fourth-motif theme of the "exposition" (see bars 79ff., 95ff. and especially 169ff.) In the fifth and sixth waves, the opening stages are also controlled by motifs from the "exposition" — the peasant-dance motif in the fifth wave and the fourth-motif in the sixth. Because throughout the movement derivatives of these two themes keep alternating with each other (and with recollections of earlier movements), one can follow Mahler's lead and call the Finale a rondo. But the label is misleading if it is allowed to distract attention from the striving passages and the climaxes that they usher in, for it is the relation of the striving to the climatic passages more than the recurrence of similar material that gives the movement its distinctive quality.

The first of the six striving passages begins about bar 292, and its climax begins in bar 307. The quality of the music at this climax seems to be more reminiscent of the symphony's third movement than it seems responsive to or shaped by the striving passage. The lack of a fit between the motif of the striving passage and the motif of its climax is underscored by the harmonic non-sequitur at 307.[30] Most of the striving occurs over a B pedal point, which, just before the climax is reached, becomes part of a dominant of A, implying a coming tonic of A. The climax is in C, flatly contradicting the harmonic implications of the striving. But because the striving is not very long or very intense and because a subsequent, more fulfilling climax may be expected, listeners are likely to be untroubled by the lack of fit between the striving and the climactic music that occurs where the goal of the striving ought to take place. The inappropriateness might be overlooked as a momentary lapse of inspiration or taste or interpreted as a deliberate interruption of a cadence did not something similar happen in the next wave.

The striving in the second wave begins about bar 357. Somewhat more intense this time, the striving stops abruptly in bar 373 with an allusion to the Adagietto (the same reworking of the fourth movement that has already appeared in bars 191ff.). The lack of fit between the striving and what happens where its goal ought to be is more conspicuous in this wave than in the first not only because the striving is more intense, but also because the *grazioso* recollection of the Adagietto is not climactic at all. In the first wave, we heard dramatic music where the goal of the striving might have been, though the climax is curiously unresponsive to the striving. In the second wave, a recollection of another mood simply displaces the climax altogether.

In the third wave, the striving is even more intense. It goes on from bar 465 to bar 496. The upward reaching half steps in bars 465ff. and 475ff. recall the striving toward the brass chorale in bars 308—315 of the second movement. This association reinforces the powerful thrust generated in bars 465—496 of the Finale by the crescendo, the persistent A pedal point, the commotion in the strings and winds and the increasingly insistent brass. What this thrust ushers in (bar 497ff.) is the peasant dance. It is reworked by the use of triplets that significantly alters the character of the music. The modification puts us in mind of those passages from the first two movements whose distinctive character is also marked by the rolling triplets and the lilting effect of triplets tied to half notes. The step-wise ascending diatonic triplets of the first movement trios and the second movement peace-questing sections are recalled by the descending triplets in the Finale at 497ff. (see Figure 43a and b), and the arpeggiated triplets of the anger music are also brought back (see Figure 43c and d). The triplets in the Finale at 497ff. are so

FIGURE 43
Comparison of Mahler, Fifth Symphony, Finale, to first two movements

pervasive that the music seems to be characterized more by its rhythm than by its melody, and the link by its rhythm to the symphony's Part One is stronger than the link by its melody to the peasant dance. In short, the earlier movements are more powerfully present than the peasant dance is. What might have been a return to the opening of the Finale, a chance to redo the peasant dance in such a way that the ambiguities of the first version are removed, and thus what might have been an opportunity to arrive at a resolution to the movement's tension, turns out to be another recollection. A memory of the past suppresses (or postpones, we may think until subsequent events disallow that interpretation) a step forward to actualizing an anticipated future.

Although the recollection leaves the striving of bars 465–496 without a response, the recollection resumes the striving, and we hear the tentative beginnings of a climactic arrival in bar 511 when the trumpet pierces the strings' and winds' triplet version of the peasant dance. The trumpet revives the motif that is used in bars 52—53 for the focal phrase of the first peasant dance. The bump in bar 526 cuts off the arrival before it fully takes shape, but the trumpets in 511—525 suggest what may be able to serve as the movement's climax, and indeed the climax that comes with the brass chorale in bars 711ff. is an expanded, complete version of what bars 511—525 adumbrate (see Figure 47). Mahler's procedure here repeats what he has done in the second movement when the climactic brass chorale at first enters fragmentarily in bar 316 and then subsequently in full dress.

The striving in the fourth wave of the Finale (bars 550—580) is about as long and as intense as that in the third wave. Like the third wave, it too leads to a restatement of the peasant dance, or rather, a new statement of the peasant dance occurs (bar 581) at the point where the goal of the striving would occur. The peasant dance cannot be heard as that goal. Three of its features make it an inadequate response to the striving. First, the long pedal point on G is not allowed to lead to a resolving C. Second, the melody of the peasant dance is harmonized in a new way that makes the melody much more tenuous (the fourth note is a dissonant here; before it was F-sharp, the third degree of the tonic chord). And, third, the texture changes radically at 581 when the striving upper strings suddenly stop playing and the upper brass take a *crescendo* into a *piano*. The upshot is that instead of arriving at a goal, the music begins wandering and wondering. A meditation on the past replaces the arrival of what has been prepared.

The wandering gives way to a new wave of striving about bar 615. This, the fifth wave, is quite brief compared to the previous two waves, and the non-arrival in bar 623 is correspondingly less conspicuous and less disappointing. The non-arrival is a somewhat altered version of what we have heard at bars 169ff. and 253ff. These earlier passages have alluded to the Scherzo's Trio (see Figure 41c, d), and the evocation of the Scherzo is even stronger in 623—642. There are motivic connections — the repeated notes in 623, 625 and 631 are reminiscent of the clarinets in the Scherzo, bars 6 and 8, and the violins in 29, 31 and 35; the swooping sevenths in 631 and 633, set up by the repeated Bs in 623—629, recall the similiar sevenths in the Scherzo's bars 434, 436, set up by the repetitions in 432—433; the lilting upbeats in 630, 632, 634 and 638 hark back to the upbeats in places like bars 15 (horn) and 47 (basses) in the Scherzo. But more than the motivic connections, it is the sense of an urbane whirl that evokes the Scherzo; in spite of the differences in meter, this part of the Finale seems closer to the Scherzo's world than to the duple-meter peasant dances of the Finale.

Bars 623—642 organize themselves into five four-bar subphrases, whose relationships are sketched in Figure 44. Because the thetic

FIGURE 44
Sketch of Mahler, Fifth Symphony, Finale

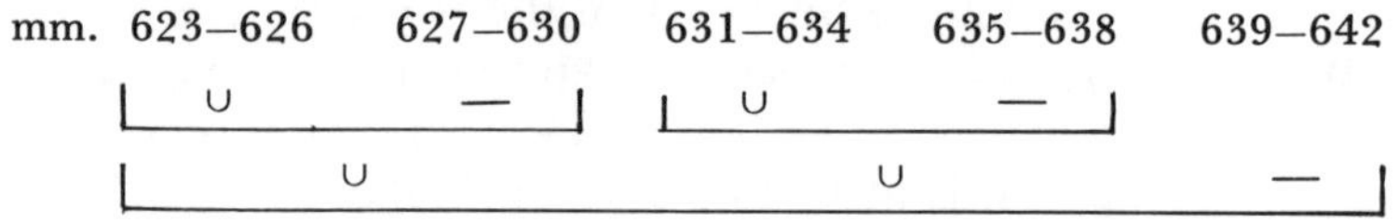

mm.   623—626   627—630   631—634   635—638   639—642

subphrase at the end is only four bars long — too brief to absorb the twofold anacrusis generating it — the section ends with considerable mobility in spite of the fact that it ends on the same tonic (G) with which it begins. The mobility links bars 623—642 to the next section, which states that derivative of the fourth-motif theme which is the Finale's version of the Adagietto theme (see bars 191ff.). The recall of the Adagietto is genuinely responsive to the mobile ending of the Scherzo recall.

The dynamic relation of the two sections weaves the Scherzo theme and the Adagietto theme into a single cloth.[31] The reminiscences are as harmonious as the prototypes are incompatible. One of the main achievements of the Finale — and it is focused in the passages from 623 to 673 — is the resolution of the tension created by the contrast between the third and fourth movements.

Resolving the contrast between a movement that runs the gamut from the exuberant to the demonic and one that runs the gamut from serenity to sensuousness is remarkable. Even more remarkable is the intimation that the apparently sharp difference between their temporal processes can be transcended. The Scherzo as a whole flirts with futurelessness in various ways, now by undermining so many aspects of regularity that one has no basis for expecting anything, now by so obstinately refusing to actualize the anticipated future that the anticipation is shattered. The Adagietto moves slowly but steadily, with few setbacks, to actualizing its goals. The subphrases and phrases form pairs with each other (see Figure 45), as each second subphrase and phrase answers straightforwardly the summons that has brought it into being. The process is surprising only in that

FIGURE 45
Sketch of Mahler, Fifth Symphony, fourth movement

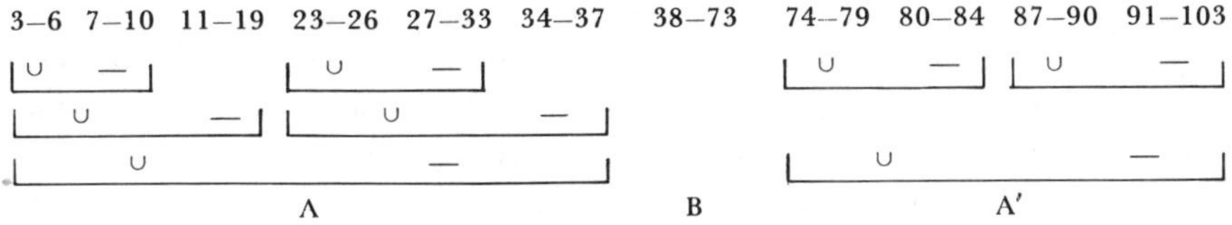

3–6 7–10 11–19 23–26 27–33 34–37   38–73   74–79 80–84 87–90 91–103

the fulfillments seem too intense for the comparatively serene phrases that have generated them; experience tells us that an intense arrival is believable only when it is the result of considerable pain and laborious effort, while the Adagietto does not linger on its dissonances nor long postpone its fulfillments.[32] And the arrivals seem too brief; the listener may well feel that such intensity ought not to be allowed to slip so quickly through one's fingers. As Bekker points out, the movement is brief enough to allow it to serve as a kind of introduction to the Finale; after all, Mahler groups the two movements together as the symphony's Part Three, and directs that the Finale begin *attacca*. By keeping the slow movement brief, Mahler prevents it from draining away the symphony's energies. Otherwise the Finale might seem unmotivated and superfluous.[33]

If the Finale in Mahler's Fifth Symphony wipes away the sharp contrast between the kind of temporal process exemplified in the Scherzo and the kind exemplified in the Adagietto by deriving recollections of them both from a single motif and by dynamically relating the two recollections in the climactic passage of the fifth wave, then one wants to know what the nature of the temporal process is that either transcends the contrast or simply displaces both members of the contrast. The recollections that have occurred where generated climaxes might have been suggest an answer to this question, and the temporal process implicit in these moments is most explicitly exemplified in the sixth wave.

Striving forward begins in this wave about bar 680. As in the third wave, a rising half-step motif contributes importantly to the push forward. The climax, a splendid brass chorale, begins at bar 711 and extends to bar 749. It is a complete gesture; two phrases, each consisting of a pair of subphrases (see Figures 46 and 47b), form a pair with each other. Actualization concretely takes place.

Or it would if it did not seem to be more the memory of a climax than a climax actually taking place. The brass chorale is a somewhat altered version of the brass chorale in the same key at the end of the second movement. The Finale chorale is far more reminiscent of the earlier chorale than it is responsive to the passage that has striven to bring an arrival into being. For it is harmonically unhinged from the preparatory passage. The striving ends on the dominant of C (705–710), summoning a climax whose tonic is C. To be sure, the dominant of D is established in bars 695–704, but in view of the fact that the preceding music has circled C by emphasizing G, its dominant, in 623–665 and then F, its subdominant, in 666–694, the dominant of D seems to be a passing detail.

Although the chorale's first subphrase alludes to the whole-step motion in the peasant dance and quotes in augmentation the

FIGURE 46
Sketch of Mahler, Fifth Symphony, Finale

711–718   719–726   731–738   739–749

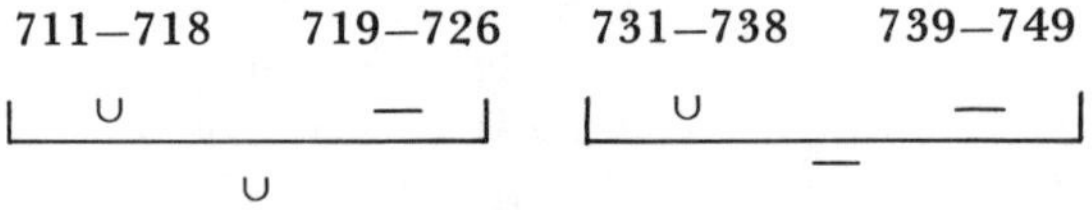

FIGURE 47
Mahler, Fifth Symphony, Finale

fourth-motif theme of bars 88–95, it binds itself even more tightly to the second-movement chorale: not only do the orchestration and luminosity keep the earlier chorale in mind, but the Finale bars 730–748 quote the second movement 500–520 almost note for note. Consequently, while the Finale chorale is the most climactic passage in the movement, the listener cannot help being aware that it is less glorious and luminous than the second-movement climax. It is shorter by eighteen measures, and its internal peaks are less well developed. It does not establish, or reestablish, the degree of fulfillment attained in the second-movement chorale. And, not resolving tensions that might have been persisting at the end of its model, it is not an extension or continuation or completion of the earlier musical event. Ungenerated by its past in either the second or the fifth movement, the Finale chorale is not a climax but a memory of a climax. Once again, a recollection stands where an evoked arrival might have occurred. But while the previous examples of this process in the movement put a non-climactic recollection where a goal might have been attained, the last wave puts the memory of an earlier climax. Here fulfillment takes place, but in the form of remembering fulfillment.[34]

The striving passages in the Finale are as clearly future-oriented as are the first subphrases and first phrases in the paired groups of the fourth movement. In both cases, the music seems to be summoning a specific actualization, and the event that seems about to take place impinges on the quality of the music moving toward that event. In the fourth movement, the summoned events take place, and the fact that they take place with an intensity that exceeds the expected level confirms rather than contradicts the relevance of the future during the summoning passages in that movement. But in the fifth movement, when recollecting displaces actualization, the process of moving from striving to its outcome turns out to exemplify a temporal process that is as futureless as that in the Scherzo, although it is futureless in a new way. When the Scherzo exemplifies future-lessness, it does so because it loses or suppresses the aspects of regularity that might form the basis of expectation. In the fifth movement, expectation is as strong and as particular as it is in the fourth movement, but the fulfillment again and again turns out to be a void that is filled by recollection. Such is evidently the nature of temporality when the temporal process of the third and fourth movements are combined and the differences are transcended.

(3) The Finale as a Whole

The temporal process conveyed by the brass chorale and its relation to the striving passage preceding it is anticipated not only in the prior waves, but also by the introduction and the "exposition." Bars 1—23 are introductory both in the sense that they adumbrate the motifs out of which the movement's themes are going to be built and in the sense that their fragmentariness generates an expectation for a succession of more securely linked subphrases. The bits and pieces of tunes in the introduction are not, however, merely fragmentary; they also relate themselves to one another in ways that anticipate the modes of continuation that will increasingly characterize the rest of the movement. The bassoon figure in 5—6 is continued in 10—12 (see Figure 48).[35] The oboe figure between the two parts of the bassoon's

FIGURE 48
Mahler, Fifth Symphony, Finale

subphrase is a non-sequitur to bar 6, a lower-level analogue to the non-sequitur of bars 56ff. vis-à-vis the opening peasant dance, and to the non-fulfilling events that stand where climaxes might respond to the striving passages later in the movement. The horn tune in 13—15 is also a recollection and continuation of the horn of bars 3—4. The clarinet in 16—20 is something of an answer to the horn of 13—15, but it is more a recollection and continuation of the oboe fragment of 7—9. In short, both 13—15 and 16—20 give us a recollection of a more distant past where we might have expected a response to a more immediate past; the temporal process that insists on itself more and more obstinately as the movement proceeds is already presented in the introduction.

Later in the movement, during the first several waves of striving, the listener may hear the non-arrivals as postponements of fulfillment; they seem to be higher-level instances of the bumps that occur in the "exposition" and elsewhere in the movement — interruptions that send us back to begin the course again with the hope that this time the music will come closer to actualizing fulfillment. The somewhat climactic quality of the non-arrival in the fourth wave and the patently climactic quality of the recollection in the sixth imply, however, that fulfillment is not only postponed, but postponed indefinitely. Because the brass chorale is climactic, but is not a climax fitted to the movement's own strivings, it becomes inescapably clear that no fulfillment to these strivings is going to be actualized. The anticipated future that has been impinging on the past during the striving passages is never going to occur.

One might expect such a process to feel disillusioning to someone undergoing it. Perhaps the most startling feature of the movement is that as Mahler presents the process, feeling disillusioned, like feeling satisfied, is displaced by feeling what was felt before. The recollection of fulfillment is presented as a kind of fulfillment, and Mahler's process must be sharply differentiated from one in which struggle produces no outcome at all or an outcome that is so different from that toward which the struggle is directed as to be worse than no outcome. To someone who believes that the purpose of struggling is to succeed, Mahler's fulfilling memories must seem to be cynical or self-deceiving attempts to paper over failure, cheap efforts to convince oneself that, in spite of the apparent waste of the energy expended during the striving, non-fulfillment does not matter. The memories may be apperceived as tokens of withdrawing from a concern for the outer-world results of inwardly determined goals. But Mahler does not present the lapses into memory at the crucial points as events that are determined either by a decision (not even a self-deceiving decision) or by causal necessity (not even psychological need). They just happen. The process the music presents resembles one in which a self unreflectively flips from consciously working toward a goal to reliving a past experience and recollecting it. The way the striving comes up again and again and always in the context of an exuberantly positive mood suggests the experience of a self that does not lose its courage or its belief in the future. There is nothing desperate or fateful about either the striving or the recollecting non-arrivals. The value of struggling is neither vitiated nor confirmed by what does or does not come about.

Mahler's process must also be clearly distinguished from one in which the past controls the future and in which what comes about is determined by what has been. Unlike the reminiscing non-arrivals, the striving sections are far more future- than past-oriented; even when they allude to prior movements, the quality of the experience felt during these sections is affected more by the anticipated future than the past. The recollecting non-arrivals consequently enter as something of a shock. Precisely because they are surprising, they do not suggest that they are implicit in the past or that the past is asserting itself relentlessly, endlessly reactualizing itself or its implications. What has been asserts itself not in the mode of being reenacted, but remembered — that is, in the mode of no-longer-being.

Nor is it the case that the past is recollected because it is more glorious than the evoked future might turn out to be. The affirmative, energetic striving certainly suggests that the anticipated future is splendid indeed. But because memory displaces awareness of the future at the moment when the future might become the present, we do not know in fact what the content of this new present might be or whether it has any content at all. It cannot be contrasted to the past or be said to be less glorious than the past because it is never actually experienced.

4.   *The Symphony as a Whole*

By alluding to passages from all four prior movements, the Finale integrates the symphony. It is, however, a kind of integration that is peculiar to the work. In the Finale to the First Symphony allusions to prior movements allow the forces that have asserted themselves before to reassert themselves and gather together in pressing toward some climax, the achievement of which functions as the goal of the entire work.[36] But the Fifth Symphony Finale does not pull the symphony into a whole by actualizing a goal that would satisfy the tendencies left unfulfilled at the ends of the prior movements. Instead, the Finale integrates the symphony by presenting a series of memories from each of the first four movements and relating them to the Finale's own process in a way that in some respects clarifies and confirms the temporal process of earlier movements and in other respects overcomes or ignores their differences.[37]

The first part of this chapter has indicated the way the second movement's chorale pulls the first two movements together and the third part has indicated how the fifth wave of the Finale overcomes the contrast between the third and fourth movements. What remains to be said is that the Finale's unfulfilling recollections convey a process that is significantly analogous to the process exemplified by the second-movement chorale. The most important aspect of the second-movement chorale is that it moves forward toward what it has already achieved, suggesting that what serves as fulfillment has already arrived before the chorale's thrust to a peak begins. The second-movement climax is therefore a moment of realizing what has already been achieved and recognizing that fulfillment has already taken place, even though striving has been continuing. This characterization of the second-movement chorale forces us into the awkward realization that the fifth-movement chorale is a recollection of a fulfillment that was itself not so much a fulfillment as a moment in which one comes to a self-conscious celebration of a fulfillment that has been previously achieved, but not yet reflected upon.

Again and again, the second movement makes it clear that decisions are always in the past, that it is what one has unreflectively decided, and not what one self-consciously thinks one is deciding, that is actualized. Like the second-movement chorale, the Finale and its relation to the second movement make the symphony as a whole suggest that fulfillments are also always in the present perfect tense. They too have always already taken place; they too have occurred before one is aware of them so that striving leads not to a fulfillment but to the memory of one, or, more startling yet, to the memory of a memory of one. Fulfillment, like decision making, is made to recede indefinitely into the past. Although fulfillment is real, it is never fully actual in a present moment. The movement toward the future is in fact a movement toward awareness of the having-happened nature of fulfillment.

The tonal structure of the symphony as a whole confirms and contributes to the image of temporality as a movement from expectation into recollection. As Harold Truscott points out, the first movement (in C-sharp minor) and the second movement (in A minor) together articulate the dominant of D; the third movement (which Mahler wrote before the other four) states the tonic of this dominant.[38] The fourth movement, in F, is an excursion into the lowered mediant of D; it prolongs D, rather than leading to or away from D. The A on which the melody of the movement ends is transformed from the mediant of F into the dominant of D as the fifth movement begins. The fifth movement does not return to the key of the opening movement. Instead, it restates the third movement's resolution to the harmonic tension generated by the first two movements together. Just as the brass chorale at the end of the Finale recalls the second-movement brass chorale, so the Finale as a whole recollects the fulfillment attained in the third movement.

To say that the fifth movement restates a resolution need not imply that the last two movements are unnecessary or redundant. It is only with the Finale that temporality as a movement from expectation into recollection establishes itself as a pattern that underlies all of experience and organizes experience into a coherent whole. The second-movement D major chorale and its place in that movement have already set forth the main lines of this pattern, but its exposition of them becomes tentative when the movement closes on A and together with the first movement projects a dominant pushing forward to D. The Scherzo resolves this dominant, but does so in a way that turns its back equally on its past and on the futures within its own course. Its futurelessness sets aside expectation that leads into recollection as much as fulfillment. The fourth movement's peaks seem to reinstate the validity of the future, but their brevity is incommensurate with their intensity. In the fifth movement, the brevity of the climax is taken a step further, in that the summoned climaxes shrink into non-existence. Unhinged from the processes generating them, the Finale peaks are as damaging to a sense that the present shapes the future as are the irregularities, unexpectedly conventional endings and disintegrated struggles of the Scherzo.

The Finale confirms a set of criteria for coherence that are startling and yet strangely familiar. They are startling because they cut across the grain of common sense that has absorbed the Newtonian assumption that the future is caused by, hence implicitly present in the past, and the (contradicting) Kantian assumption that free human decisions shape the future. They are strangely familiar in that what counts as fulfillment in our lives may after all be controlled less by the extent to which it responds to the activities, however arduous and courageous, that work to actualize fulfillment and more by our memory of previous fulfillments. That is, an event may in fact be experienced as a fulfillment more because its shape or its timing resembles the shape and timing of a recollected fulfillment than because it appropriately caps a process of actualizing a goal or instantiating a direction.

It may happen that the memory controlling fulfillment does not make a sharp distinction between events that have actually taken place and events that are imagined; both may be present forces to the extent that they are vividly present to the imagination. This sort of fulfillment contradicts Newtonian and Kantian fulfillments. But one who sets aside Newtonian and Kantian assumptions finds that memory does not need to distinguish sharply between the event as it felt while it was being experienced and the event as it is recollected when all its ramifications and effects have become known. Memory can recall the experience of an event that felt culminating as it was taking place and not synthesize it with the subsequent erosions of the culmination, or it can synthesize the recollection of an event that did not feel particularly fulfilling as it was taking place with a recollection of its subsequently manifest implications.

Memory may synthesize the recollected experience of an event with an earlier event that is believed to have been fulfilling. And then present experience may synthesize a present event with the memory of an event that is remembered as fulfilling because of the synthesis with the prior fulfillment.

It is easy to stigmatize such a movement from expectation to recollection as the mind playing tricks on itself. Karl Kraus's jab, "I have a shattering bit of news for the aesthetes: Old Vienna was new once,"[39] is directed precisely at his, and Mahler's, Viennese contemporaries who were living a temporality very similar to that of Mahler's Fifth. For them, events in 1900 were fulfilling to the extent that they were reminiscent of and celebratory of Old Vienna. That such events resembled something old was an essential ingredient of their quality, but old is precisely what that which is being remembered and synthesized with the present was not when it was taking place, unless the 1900s were synthesizing the present with the 1870s' recollection of Vienna of the 1820s.

The same temporal process is captured even more clearly in Kraus's aphorism, "I can already remember many things I am experiencing."[40] The remark gets its point from its contrast with, "I will always remember many things I am now experiencing" and "What I am now experiencing reminds me of many things I remember." Kraus's remark blurs past and present into a non-differentiation that also characterizes Mahler's movement from expectation into recollection.

Klimt's "Schubert at the Piano" (1899) presents the kind of recollection that Kraus' sarcasm is ridiculing. In his ceiling paintings for the new Burgtheater (1886–88), Klimt had reconstructed moments from earlier times in such a way that the Viennese could imagine themselves in those settings (Klimt in fact painted himself as a member of the audience in the panel of "Shakespeare's Theater"). But in his "Schubert at the Piano," the relation to the past is utterly different. As Carl Schorske puts it, "Klimt substitutes nostalgic evocation for historical reconstruction."[41] Klimt is not painting the scene as if it were contemporaneous with him, nor as if (as in Burgtheater panels) he were contemporaneous with it. That it is a scene from the past is an essential ingredient in the work; the scene is suffused with a nostalgia that presumably could not have characterized the time depicted. And the nostalgic recollection reworks the time of Schubert; as Schorske says, "The once-hated age of Metternich was recalled now as the gracious-simple age of Schubert."[42]

Klimt's "Schubert" is one of a pair of panels painted for Nikolaus Dumba's music salon. The other panel, "Music," depicts a Greek priestess, whose facial features are distinctively Viennese, and sculptures of Silenus (Dionysius's companion) and the Sphinx (the personification of feminine beauty at its most deadly). Just as "Schubert" suggests that the Viennese love for music served their recollecting sense of fulfillment, so "Music" suggests that it arises from the irrational, instinctual, impulsive energies which, as Freud saw more clearly than even Kraus, in fact controlled the behavior of people who self-deceptively saw themselves as rational and aesthetic. The juxtaposition of "Music" to "Schubert" suggests that Klimt, like Kraus, saw the nostalgia for what it was.[43]

The temporal process lived by the Viennese, whom Kraus was ridiculing and Klimt was depicting while gently criticizing by putting "Schubert" next to "Music," is one that may well accompany an awareness that the present cannot perpetuate itself and that the future is a void in the sense that its content will have to be so different from the past and the present that it literally cannot be imagined. In the case of most of Vienna's middle and upper classes, this awareness was unthematized, but those who both loved their city's culture and at the same time dimly sensed that the problems tearing apart the empire's political and social fabric fundamentally admitted no resolution perhaps lived this temporality.

Mahler's Fifth does not glorify this process; nor does it deplore it. Where Kraus stigmatizes the temporal process his contemporaries are living because they do not, he thinks, face up to the fact that their putative fulfillments are in fact the memory of a memory, Mahler presents a temporal process in which the nature of fulfillment as the memory of a memory is candidly recognized. While Kraus's jabs are directed against recollections of fulfillment which may be hiding present reality, Mahler's Fifth suggests that fulfillment may be real even though it is always in the present perfect tense; triumphant affirmation is possible even though that which is affirmed is never fully manifest or fully embodied in any present moment. Unlike the targets of Kraus' sarcasm, the Fifth begins by looking into the face of death — the counterpart on the individual level to the imminent collapse of the empire — more squarely than most of Mahler's contemporaries dared. Unlike the Second Symphony, the Fifth presents no intimation of a resurrection to contradict the first movement's confrontation with death. Unlike the Ninth, the Fifth does not transform a consciousness in which death is a controlling reality into a new kind of consciousness. In spite of the muscular cheeriness of the Finale, the force of death may still be felt at the end of the Fifth. Were it not for death, would the movement from expectation to fulfillment be replaced by a movement from expectation to recollection? Is it not precisely because finitude in all its forms — both death and the limitations and self-destructing idiocies of the imperial bureaucracy — will not allow fulfillment that recollection can, or perhaps in some sense must, step in precisely where fulfillment might have taken place?

The sense in which the symphony ends with an implicit awareness of the force of death can be specified more precisely by comparing its temporal process to the similar process in Schnitzler's "Frau Beate und ihr Sohn" (1913).[44] This novella tells the story of Beatrice Heinold, a young widow, and Hugo, her teenage son, spending what turns out to be their last summer at their villa in the Austrian lake region. At the beginning of the story, Hugo is having an affair with a middle-aged actress; in the middle of the story Frau Beate is having an affair with her son's friend, Fritz; at the end of the story, the mother and son, aware of one another's affairs, dimly aware that these liaisons were surrogates for an affair with each other, are unable to live with the knowledge that their friends and servants also know of their indiscretions, commit suicide in the guise of a boating accident. Frau Beate experiences her death by drowning as a return into the uterine fluids; the climax of her story is a recollection of the moment of birth.

In fact, the whole story is a series of recollections of the past, particularly of her life with her husband, an actor who, five years before, died of a stroke in his prime of life. The experience of remembering the past is sharply differentiated from the experience of living through the events that are being recollected. For as Beatrice is confronted with the fact that she and Hugo act on impulses that are guided by sexual passions, and not on rational, ethically motivated decisions, she also realizes that her marriage was not at all what she had imagined it to be when her husband was alive. Evidence of her husband's infidelities — evidence that hitherto she had effortlessly ignored and suppressed — now seems inescapably undeniable. She is forced to see that she was equally faithless to him; while pretending to make love to him, her sexual partner was in fact a fantasized composite of the various characters her husband enacted on the stage. Recollecting the past under the pressure of the present is actually a reworking of the past. Schnitzler makes it clear that the suicide occurs as much because the past becomes intolerable as because the future is unbearable; the past was not and the future will not be worth living. The recollection of birth is identical with death.

In moving from expectation to recollection and in making recollection a reworking of the past, the short story resembles the temporal process of Mahler's Fifth Symphony. But the relation of death to recollection is reversed, and this difference is related to the fact that where the one ends in destruction, the other ends in triumph. By placing the spectre of death at the beginning of the symphony, Mahler intimates that recollection displaces concrete fulfillment because life is finite. One's dealings with the outer world are too brief and the outer world is too recalcitrant to inwardly determined goals to permit the external world to embody the purposes of inner life. By placing death at the end of the story while making it a review of birth, as though the story were a film, run in reverse, of a person emerging from the womb, Schnitzler intimates that death comes and life is finite because recollection displaces fulfillment, or, rather, because the ultimate recollection and therefore the ultimate fulfillment is death.

Schnitzler's attitude toward this temporal process is ambivalent. He adopts the posture of the medical scientist who simply examines the human patient, observes the role of impulse in determining human affairs, and watches as the discrepancy between a person's image of himself or herself as a rational decision-maker and a person's reality as controlled by impulse leads to self-deception, hypocrisy and self-destruction. At the same time he seems also to be a moralist who deplores the fact that people do not control their impulses and who hankers after a time when it seemed to make sense to think of human beings as free and rational.[45]

There is no such hankering in Mahler. By placing death at the beginning of the symphony and shaking his fist angrily in its face, he makes it clear that the movement from expectation to recollection happens because of finitude — because of the way things are — and not because of human moral failing. The listener who hears the brass chorale in the Finale as a more or less customary fulfillment (or as an attempt at such a fulfillment) rather than as a recollection of fulfillment probably hears the work either as a naive effort to forget the death, sadness and anger of the first two movements or as a courageous effort to affirm life and meaninglessness in spite of death and the sadness and anger it evokes. Hearing the brass choir as a manifestation of either naivete or courage would turn the symphony into the kind of temporal process — a struggle for concrete actualization — after which Schnitzler the moralist longed. But it would not be convincing: Mahler's picture of death and the feelings of anger and sadness are too strong and overpowering; the naivete would seem to be foolishness, or the courage would seem to be willfulness.

Mahler is not being foolishly naive or willfully courageous. His symphony in the end is unreservedly affirmative, and yet it unflinchingly faces the reality of death. This characterization is paradoxical and the Finale chorale is heard as an inadequate fulfillment only if the listener insists on a temporal process which characterizes the ideal of people as rational decision-making, self-actualizing beings and in which fulfillment must be concrete. Listeners who allow Mahler to lead them into a non-Kantian temporality may find that the work reflects, and thereby illumines, the temporal process that characterizes human consciousness as it actually is.

The process through which the symphony leads us is similar to one of the most basic processes that Heidegger finds in human existence. Joy and peace are possible, according to Heidegger, precisely because by facing death one affirms that which is lost in death — one's ownmost self, as he calls it.[46] By this term, Heidegger means that which one most basically and authentically is. One's ownmost self is not fully actualized by any concrete fulfillment, past or future, but it is not unrelated to external events like these. Not fully manifest at any particular moment, it is stretched along between birth and death (that is, Heidegger says, it is historical).[47] Heidegger develops the concept of "repetition" to describe the ownmost self as it is stretched along:

The authentic coming-towards-itself of anticipatory resoluteness is at the same time a coming back to one's ownmost self, which has been thrown into its individualization. . . . If *Being*-as-having-been is authentic, we call it "repetition."[48]

To be one's ownmost self is to be all that one can be; the ownmost self is its own fulfillment; fulfillment must be repetition.

Heidegger sharply distinguished the ownmost self from the non-empirical ego in Kant's and Husserl's phenomenology, and so his concept is not invalidated by Sartre's (later) critique of the transcendental ego. The ownmost self that repeats itself is not the subject of a repeating consciousness; it is not the sort of thing that in principle could be like the hypothetical non-empirical self that might fully or partially manifest itself. Rather, it is the unity of the individualized human existence that stretches itself along from birth to death.

Heidegger's concept of repetition is marvelously congruent with Mahler's movement from expectation into recollection inasmuch as in the Fifth Symphony fulfillment is not a matter of the full, concrete embodiment of the free and struggling self, but rather is always a matter of having fulfilled. If Mahler's fulfillment is a matter of a memory of a memory, it is not unlike Heidegger's "repetition."[49]

Throughout this chapter, the processes projected by Mahler's Fifth have been compared to those entailed by ordinary (as opposed to transfigured) consciousness. The analogy between Heidegger's "repetition" of the ownmost self and Mahler's recollecting fulfillments invites us to see a distinction within ordinary consciousness between the ownmost self and the everyday self in which this ownmost self is not differentiated from the self that others attribute to one and that allows itself to be in the way that "one is." It is this everyday self whose concept of itself and its temporality disallows Mahler's continuity and coherence and insists on grounded events. That is, the everyday self as it reflects on itself necessarily entertains those assumptions about continuity that have to dismiss Mahler as nonsense.[50]

If the musical process of coming upon a recollecting fulfillment does indeed resemble that of the ownmost self coming upon its repetition, then Mahler's recollecting fulfillment is an affirmative ending and the glorious affirmation is appropriate to the human experience precisely because the repetition of the ownmost self is more profoundly marvelous and more authentically fulfilling than any outcome resulting from its or the everyday self's being in the world might be. While the everyday self must seek to actualize and fulfill itself in the world, the ownmost self is its own fulfillment. It is this aspect of temporality that makes possible the multiple perspective in Mahler's music that some commentators have noticed. It can be at once ironic and not ironic: the ownmost self views the everyday self's putative fulfillments from an ironic perspective and exposes their pretentiousness; at the same time, the everyday self must suppose that Mahler's recollecting fulfillment is intended to be ironic, for to the everyday self the memory of something never actually concretized can only be a pretense of fulfillment; yet the ownmost self and its fulfillment are in the end invulnerable to the acids of irony. The analogy between repetition and a recollecting fulfillment will be further developed in Chapter III where the kind of consciousness implicit in the Fifth Symphony will be contrasted to the transfigured consciousness envisioned by the Eighth.

Notes

1. Michael Kennedy, *Mahler* (1974), p. 78, typifies this defense. Robert Morgan (in "Mahler and Ives: Mutual Responses at the End of an Era," *Nineteenth-Century Music*, vol. 2 [1978], p. 76) would disagree with Kennedy: "A high degree of disjunction marks the music of both [Mahler and Ives]. The underlying continuity often appears to be cut off in mid-flight, rudely interrupted by the intrusion of heterogeneous elements. . . . Never before was this done with anything like the same frequency and exaggeration."

2. This way of describing the movement's structure does not contradict Bekker's and others' analyses of its analogy to conventional sonata—allegro form (see Bekker, *op. cit.*, pp. 181—188). The terms used in analysis of sonata—allegro form are avoided in this chapter not because they are incorrect but because they are less useful in describing the brass chorale's function than are the concepts of alternating and converging sections. Deryck Cooke, (*Gustav Mahler: An Introduction to His Music*, 1980, p. 80) says without reservation that V/ii is not a sonata—allegro movement.

3. "Mahler: A Thematic Archetype," *The Music Review*, vol. 21 (1960), pp. 297—316.

4. Following Alma Mahler's lead, Dika Newlin (*Bruckner, Mahler and Schoenberg*, 1947, pp. 178—179) associates the brass chorale here and in the fifth movement with the Protestant chorale and thence with religious mysticism. It seems odd to associate Mahler's chorale only with religious fervor and not also with outwardly visible joy and the public effects of that joy on one's relation with one's fellow human beings. After all, the chorale is as heroic as it is mystical. In this respect, Adorno's treatment of the chorale is more appropriate to its nature (*op. cit.*, pp. 159—160). Egon Gartenberg (*Mahler: the Man and His Music*, 1978, p. 304) usefully comments that Mahler "found the chorale meaningful as a symbol of majesty and triumph, proclaiming a moral universe." Deryck Cooke (*op. cit.*, pp. 15—16, 82) calls the chorale a "shout of the whole truth" — the whole truth about oneself, society, the cosmos and God, translated without remainder into objective, visible terms.

5. Cooke (*op. cit.*, p. 82) points out that this theme is melodically related to one of the *Wunderhorn* songs, "Der Tambourg'sell."

6. As Neville Cardus, *Gustav Mahler: His Mind and His Music. The First Five Symphonies* (1965), pp. 152, 159, points out, the phrase that ends in bar 316 quotes almost note for note bars 13—15 in the first of the *Kindertotenlieder.*

7. *The Rhythmic Structure of Music* (1960).

8. In *The Little Comedy*, trans. Harry Zohn (1977), pp. 147—234.

9. One might almost say of both cases that the development precedes the theme instead of the other way around. As Chapter III will point out, this procedure may also be found in connection with the Gloriosa music of the Eighth Symphony. Egon Wellesz, in "The Symphonies of Gustav Mahler," *Music Review*, vol. 1 (1940), pp. 8—9, compares Mahler's practice of stating an idea first in a vague or banal or sentimental form and then changing it in successive appearances into a final form, to Beethoven's practice of working out his themes over several years in his sketchbooks from an undeveloped shape to an admirable, memorable form. Wellesz believes Mahler's practice is an essential feature of his style.

10. The jaunty march (the term is Cooke's, *op. cit.*, p. 82) is a first cousin of the toy soldier marches elsewhere in Mahler's works. See, for example, the Second Symphony, first movement (at S:5) and fifth movement (at 11 bars after S:15) and the Third Symphony, first movement (at 7 bars after S:23).

11. In the third movement (Scherzo) of his Seventh Symphony, Mahler follows a similar procedure. Near the end of the movement (bars 417—442) he pulls the movement together by using the Trio's theme (see bars 189—208) as a consequent phrase paired to the Scherzo's second theme (see bars 54—67).

12. Figure 20, like Figure 17, shows Mahler fusing the rhythm of one motif with the melodic sequence of another. A significant trait of Mahler's style, it is analyzed in connection with the Ninth Symphony in Carl Dahlhaus, "Form und Motiv in Mahlers Neunter Symphonie," in *Neue Zeitschrift für Musik*, vol. 135 (1974), pp. 296—299.

13. One is reminded of the way Bruckner's melodies sometimes dwell on the third degree of the scale for so long that it begins to seem stable in spite of its inherent mobility. These moments — for example, toward the end of the Finale to the Third Symphony — sound like an apotheosis, a moment when something is up in the air because that is where it belongs, because it belongs to its nature not to be bound to the usual laws of cause and effect, because its distinctive quality is to transcend the ordinary.

14. Theodor Adorno, *op. cit.*, pp. 158—161, hears the chorale altogether differently. For him it is a rupture in the musical fabric, the eruption of that which is radically new and "other" to the ordinary course of the world. The course of the world is presented in the Presto sections, which know "no history, no whither, no time in which things actually happen." Lacking its own history, it drives toward the reminiscences of the first movement in the peace-questing sections. These reminiscences not only interrupt the course of the world but also "prepare the ground for the chorale vision in which the movement breaks out of the cycle of alternating sections. Only because of the motivic connections between the vision and the slow interpolations can the chorale embody the break without lapsing into chaos." Having missed the motivic connections between the anger and the peace-questing sections, Adorno also misses the

convergence of the two on each other, as well as on the chorale, and consequently does not notice the persistence of the anger motifs within the chorale. But he does notice that the authority of the brass chorale is "debased, given all the hullabaloos for which the brass choir has been used since Wagner and Bruckner," and this degradation implies that the radically new and other to the hideous course of the world only appears to take place as much as it actually takes place. Listeners are placed in the presence of the new, but at the same are reminded by the associations of the brass choir that it is only the appearance of the new that they are seeing. The new cannot actualize itself fully. Instead of hearing an "achieving" that is in fact a "having achieved," Adorno hears a rupture that acknowledges explicitly that it is only the appearance of a rupture. He is so committed to the presupposition that the temporal process consists of a non-empirical self struggling (and failing) to actualize itself that he cannot entertain the different sort of temporality that Mahler and his Viennese contemporaries are trying to project.

15. Bekker (*op. cit.*, p. 188) calls the Scherzo a "hymn to the power and indefatigable freshness of an unbounded joy in life." Cooke (*op. cit.*, p. 83) hears it as a fundamentally thrilling and exhilirating dance of life in contrast to the Scherzo of the Second Symphony, which he calls a dance of death. It may be, however, that the difference between II/iii and V/iii is not so much a difference between a dance of death and a dance of life as between a dance that is unambiguously nihilistic (Adorno, *op. cit.*, pp. 154–155, says that the incessantly self-circling *perpetuum mobile* of II/iii and similar movements is a direct image of the endless, purposeless succession of empty public occurrences that, lacking direction from a self-conscious and self-actualizing mind, are always the same in spite of the appearances of change) and a dance in which the self and the future are ambiguous, their relations to one another always sliding out of focus.

16. That Mahler is obviously using the *Reigen* as the model for this movement tantalizes one to compare the structure of his Scherzo to that of Schnitzler's play, *Die Reigen.*

17. *Op. cit.*, p. 189.

18. Wellesz (*op. cit.*, p. 15) points out that what is particularly striking about Mahler's contrapuntal style is that he sometimes lets his voices move at the same time and come to a temporary standstill at the same time and sometimes generates cross rhythms by letting a one-and-a-half beat anacrusis in one part follow close on the heels of a stressed second beat in the other part. These devices contradict traditional contrapuntal style, and that the voices survive with any clarity at all gives the lie to every counterpoint manual written before 1900. Obviously, these devices increase — or signify — the independence of the voices from each other.

19. Martin Heidegger, *Being and Time*, trans. John MacQuarrie and Edward Robinson (1962), pp. 164–168.

20. Bekker (*op. cit.*, p. 190) aptly describes bars 202–240 as "an excited burlesque game."

21. The third movement ("scherzando") of the Third Symphony follows a similar procedure. Mahler uses material derived from the opening as a brief trio (at S:16) within the Trio (the posthorn solo, from S:14 to S:17).

22. *The Fantastic Art of Vienna* (1978), p. 14.

23. At bar 462, Bekker says (*op. cit.*, p. 191), "a demonic power is unchained."

24. The dialectic is similar to Paul Tillich's analysis of despair. The more honestly and courageously one faces meaninglessness, he says, the more one affirms the meaning which is hidden and absent and for the sake of which one protests the meaninglessness. See his *The Courage to Be* (1952), pp. 46—47, 155—156.

25. Kennedy, *op. cit.*, p. 117, notices something odd about the hinge between the preparation and its climax: the preparation is repetitive and the recall of the second-movement chorale sounds contrived, he says.

26. Cardus (in *Composers Eleven*, 1959, p. 117) is jarred by the independence of the melodic parts here and elsewhere in the Rondo: "Mahler's melody is so much contending against itself that it will not blend submissively within the give-and-take limits of polyphony." Cardus ascribes this effect not to a lack of contrapuntal skill but to a deeper disharmony of spirit: "Mahler was never the man to regard music as an art to be contrived as though from the outside; if he could not feel a harmony of spirit he could not equivocate and write a dishonest musical harmony. The failure of much of his work was caused by his inability to subdue the man in him to the artist." *Contra* Cardus, it will be argued that the harsh polyphony is not a failure, for the more malleable polyphony Cardus would have preferred is subordinated to a temporal process whose viability probably eluded Cardus.

Mahler's polyphony is harsh because each voice denies the other's harmonic implications. In the Rondo, such polyphony runs above a pedal point. The pedal does not, however, compensate for the absence of a harmonic direction in the polyphony. Instead, the harsh polyphony attenuates the tonal function of the pedal. The sense of non-culmination at the various would-be climaxes throughout the movement results: the harshness of the polyphony generates tensions, but the attenuation of harmonic function weakens the listener's sense for the sort of resolution that might be fitted to it. According to Hans Tischler, "Mahler's Impact on the Crisis of Tonality," *Music Review*, vol. 12 (1951), pp. 113—121, it is this feature of Mahler's style and others like it (and not just Wagnerian chromaticism) that paved the way to atonal music; Mahler provides a link between Brahms and Schoenberg without which music history is unintelligible.

27. See Carl Schorske, *Fin-de-Siècle Vienna* (1980), p. 240.

28. Cardus (*Gustav Mahler . . .*, p. 175) describes the Trio theme as a "coy visitant" that "is raped in the movement's finale." In the symphony's Finale as well?

29. The Finale has been described as an amalgamation of rondo, sonata and fugue forms. See Cooke, *op. cit.*, p. 83.

30. Cardus (*Gustav Mahler . . .*, p. 188) acknowledges the non-sequitur by saying that the passage in 307ff. "elbows its way in unceremoniously."

31. It is not enough to say that the Finale's transformation of the Adagietto theme is "humorous" (Cardus, *Gustav Mahler . . .*, p. 186). One wants to know also the particular way it is humorous and how its humor acts on other aspects of the movement.

32. Kennedy (*op. cit.*, p. 117) hears "an unfulfilled yearning of special poignancy" in the middle section. The yearning is poignant, but it is not unfulfilled. Although the phrases extend themselves and postpone closure longer here than in the outside sections, they are not long in comparison to Mahler's other movements. Subphrases end in 42, 46, 50, 60 and 72, and, *contra* Kenedy, the resolutions are quite satisfying and touching.

33. Bekker, *op. cit.*, pp. 18—19, 26, elaborates on this point and maintains that some of Bruckner's long, intense Adagios, in contrast to Mahler's Adagietto, have a power that is dangerous, for it can deprive their Finales of a *raison d'être*.

34. At S:33—S:34 in I/iv there is a harmonic succession similar to the one at the beginning of V/v chorale: in I/iv, Mahler goes directly, without a modulation from the tonality of C to D. According to Natalie Bauer-Lechner (*Recollections of Gustav Mahler*, 1980, p. 31), Mahler said that the music demanded at that point "an enduring triumphal victory," and so the D 'chord "had to sound as though it had fallen from heaven, as though it had come from another world," hence the need for the "unconventional, daring" transition. The sense of an enduring victory is more equivocal in V/v, in spite of the similarity in the approach to the two climaxes, because the V/v climax has already been surpassed by the V/ii chorale. The First Symphony has another D major climax later in the Finale, and it is interesting to note that in the First Symphony, unlike the Fifth, the second D major climax surpasses the first. The First Symphony ordering comports with the more usual pattern for heroism and fulfillment. The First was, as Frederic Morton (*A Nervous Splendor*, 1980, p. 30) puts it, "ablast with the demonology of greatness," but it was also too "revolutionary too "modern" (see Henry-Louis de La Grange, *Mahler* [1973], p. 184), and Mahler experienced biting frustrations when he tried in 1888 to have it performed. It may be that dealing with this disappointment was related to the Fifth Symphony's reversal of the First Symphony pattern of climaxes. For in 1901— 1902, when Mahler again set out to tell the nature of greatness, his underlying presuppositions regarding the temporality in which greatness unfolds were different.

35. The bassoon figure quotes the *Wunderhorn* song, "Lob des hohen Verstandes," in which an ass judges a contest between a cuckoo and a nightingale. Cardus (*Gustav Mahler . . .*, p. 183), among others, enjoys the irony of such a beginning to the Rondo, with its "scholarly" fugues, double-fugues and "what not." For Cardus, the irony stops short of the chorale, which, he assumes, Mahler meant in earnest, even though "as usual, he protests too much" (p. 190). But the last four notes of the ass's music are a falling fourth (D to A) which, as Wellesz points out (*op. cit.*, pp. 10—11), occurs in three other fragments in the introduction (bars 11, 19 and 20—21), begins the peasant dance, anticipates the movement's fourth-motif themes and appears in the brass chorale in 714—715 and 716—717. Does the association suggest that the chorale is not the glorious outer-world victory it might appear to be? William Johnston might well see the Chorale as an instance of "Mahler's affinity with Jewish ironists who, as Kurt List puts it, 'never make a . . . grandiose statement without taking it back the next moment'" (*The Austrian Mind*, 1976, p. 138 and List, "Mahler: Father of Modern Music," *Commentary*, vol. 10 [1950], pp. 42—48).

36. See Bekker, *op. cit.*, p. 21.

37. Cooke (*op. cit.*, p. 81) hears a musical but not an emotional integration. "The symphony might almost be called schizophrenic, in that the most tragic and the most joyful worlds of feeling are separated off from one another, and only bound together by Mahler's unmistakable command of large-scale symphonic construction and unification." Paying attention to the temporal processes exempliied by the musical integration makes it possible to apprehend the emotional integration that eludes Cooke, perhaps because he is looking for a more conventional sort of integration.

38. "Some Aspects of Mahler's Tonality," *The Monthly Music Record*, vol. 87 (Nov.–Dec. 1957), p. 208. Like the Fifth, the Seventh Symphony ends in a tonality (C) that is a half-step higher than the opening tonality (B). But the resemblance is superficial. In the Seventh, the B functions as the dominant of E, the underlying and final tonality of the first movement, and not as part of a dominant of C. Truscott argues persuasively that Newlin's expression "progressive tonality" (*op. cit.*, pp. 179, 186), which she uses for Mahler's procedure of beginning a symphony in one key and ending in another, is ill chosen. See also Hans Tischler, "Key Symbolism versus 'Progressive Tonality,'" *Musicology*, vol. 2 (1949).

39. Quoted in Harry Zohn, *Karl Kraus* (1976), p. 164.

40. "An vieles, was ich erst erlebe, kann ich mich schon erinnern" in Karl Kraus, *Beim Wort Genommen* (1955) p. 433, quoted in Zohn, *op. cit.*, p. 159.

41. *Op. cit.*, p. 220.

42. *Ibid.*, p. 221.

43. Frederic Morton, whose *Nervous Splendor* is a study of Vienna in 1888–1889, points out (pp. 75–76) that many of the great creative Viennese minds at that time were the grandsons of humble artisans, small-town merchants and schoolteachers. Having broken into competitive middle-class status in Vienna, they found themselves in a "glitteringly corroded world. . . . One impulse motivated them all, namely the quest for a way out of present-day bourgeois frustration into a magic and relevatory past." Different as the past was for a Sigmund Freud, a Johann Strauss and a Georg von Schönerer, the direction of the quest was the same. Morton's generalization would have to be modified before it could be applied to 1900: by then, Kraus, Klimt, Schnitzler and Mahler were facing up to the ironies which were inherent in this quest but of which the previous decade had been less explicitly aware.

44. Translated by Agnes Jacques and published as "Mother and Son" in *Vienna 1900: Games with Love and Death* (1974).

45. Writing of Schnitzler's *Der Weg ins Freie*, Carl Schorske finds a similar ambivalence: "Schnitzler, caught between science and art, between commitment to old morals and new feelings, could kind no new and satisfying meaning in the self. . . . A despairing but committed liberal, he posed the problem clearly by shattering illusions. He could not create new faith. As an analyst of Viennese high bourgeois society, however, Schnitzler had no peer among his Viennese contemporaries" (*op. cit.*, pp. 14–15).

46. *Op. cit.*, pp. 294, 310–311.

47. *Ibid.*, p. 426.

48. *Ibid.*, p. 388.

49. It would be illuminating to compare Mahler's recollecting fulfillment to Heidegger's interpretation of Nietzsche's concept of eternal recurrence, on which Heidegger places a heavy stress: the philosopher must seek to think the connection of eternal recurrence as the supreme determination of Being and will to power as the basic character of all beings (*Nietzsche*, vol. 1, trans. David Krell [1979], p. 21).

50. See *Being and Time*, pp. 150–152, 213, 396–400, 403–408, 413–415, 429–433. See also Heidegger, *What Is Called Thinking?* trans. J. Glenn Gray (1968), pp. 8, 21, 33, 39–45.

CHAPTER II

The Third Symphony

1. Part One

Mahler sketched a programmatic description for his Third Symphony. This program, unlike Mahler's verbal summaries of his first two symphonies, antedates the composition of the symphony in 1895—1896. Mahler appears in some sense to have worked from his verbalized concept toward a musical process that would exhibit that concept.[1] Finding that listeners were misunderstanding the program, Mahler subsequently withdrew it. But, partly because the music of the Third is connotative and seems so obviously to be alluding to something outside itself, analysts continue to try to come to terms with Mahler's program.

Of these commentators, William J. McGrath is one of the most stimulating because he deals with the music, particularly the first and last movements, in greatest detail.[2] Moreover, he amplifies Mahler's own programmatic description using the terms of Schopenhauer's philosophy, which, he shows, Mahler and his friends knew and discussed. Thus, McGrath hears the opening horn call as a life-giving impulse — Schopenhauer's unconscious will — summoning inert matter to life. In subsequent sections of the first movement, he hears the lumpish material substance resisting this call and the struggle between impulse and inertia. The will triumphs over inert matter, beings come into existence, and the end of the first movement celebrates the victory. For McGrath, Part Two (the other five movements) delineates the various stages or levels of existence, beginning with the least conscious beings (the flowers) and moving by way of the more conscious animals to the fully self-conscious humans, who because they are aware of themselves can feel the pain of the will's endless striving, and thence to the angelic way of being, and finally to the culminating divine love that transcends the will's ceaseless, blind striving.

Trying to understand the symphony by amplifying Mahler's program and then connecting the music to it is an attractive approach not only because the program goes back to Mahler himself, not only because Schopenhauer's philosophy and Mahler's music seem to fit one another, and not only because the music seems patently to be referring to something, but also because it seems not to be self-referring. Most listeners have difficulty finding strictly musical relationships that would bind the movements to one another. Bekker calls them a suite of movements that have no direct relation to one another, although each is related in its own way to the Finale and through the Finale to each other.[3] Donald Mitchell, who agrees that the Third is "superficially the most loosely knit of all Mahler's symphonies," traces motivic connections between its six movements and the *Wunderhorn* song, "Das himmlische Leben," that ends the Fourth Symphony; there is ample evidence that for many months Mahler intended to use this song as the Finale to the Third, and Mitchell argues persuasively that the complex of anticipations and interrelationships between the song and the six movements of the Third would have culminated in a revelation of heavenly life had not the Adagio "assumed the dimensions of a Finale." The outcome was that the cycle of developing relationships in the Third was left "hanging in the air."[4] Deryck Cooke says that in terms of its form, the opening movement is a "total failure," and in that the Symphony's six movements fail to make a unity, it is "his one badly sprawling symphony."[5]

Two features of the first movement may support Cooke's harsh judgment. First, there are six times in the movement when the music simply comes to a halt. A dynamic flow ceases just before S:2, S:11, S:13, S:55, S:57 and S:62, and there are two more times (S:18 and S:35) when the hiatus is almost as complete. Second, while each of the various sections created by these articulations quotes motifs from other sections, no section refers to another one in the musically more significant sense of generating or being generated by it. The motifs and the sections do not even form readily discernible contrasts to one another, for it is hard to say along what axis they are at opposite ends.

Consequently, the search for the movement's unity often takes the route of identifying the ideas suggested by the music and then showing how these make an intelligible and unifying progression.

A sort of intellectual coherence compensates for the lack of strictly musical coherence, just as in opera a dramatic progression can be convincing even if one section of the music does not fulfill the previous nor generate the next section. Listening to an opera in total ignorance or indifference to its text and plot is an abstraction from the complete work of art offered to us. Similarly, for Bekker, McGrath and Mitchell, listening to Mahler's Third Symphony without paying attention to the interrelations of the images it evokes would be both abstract and unnecessarily unsatisfactory.[6]

In their descriptions of the first movement, Bekker, Cooke and McGrath concentrate on the first seventeen pages of the score (to about S:15), and one may infer that their analyses are controlled by the impression these pages make. This music is heavily laden with a sense of the mysterious. It dimly reminds us of the questions that we dimly sensed when we were children, questions that fascinated us, though we could not fathom them, and that made us suppose that growing up meant learning their secret answers: What is it that is so mysterious — what has this power? And what is it to be mysterious — what is its power like? The music vaguely recalls the vague stories from our childhood of dark forests inhabited by powers — spirits, fairies — that are partly like but mostly unlike the powers we meet in the light of day. It reminds us of things we often have wished to understand but cannot even begin to think about because we lack a vocabulary to identify and conceptualize them.

The fascination of these opening passages can lure one away from the rest of the movement. McGrath, for example, is so engrossed in them that he hardly notices the two enormous marches which together comprise about two fifths of the movement. Of the first he says nothing; perhaps he is embarrassed by its banality, on which Mahler's detractors like to dwell. Of the second march, McGrath says only that it is a celebration of the victory of Pan over lifelessness — a Bacchic procession which marches with mounting jubilation to the end of the movement.[7] Because McGrath does not talk about the musical relationship between the marches and the rest of the movement, he implies that the familiar sounding marches simply dispel the sense of the arcane. The marches seem less important because their images are less profound.

If, however, one dwells more specifically on the two marches and their details, the movement creates a different impression. For, it turns out, if one notices the motivic references in the marches to the opening passages, the internal organization of each march, the temporal process exemplified by each organization, the differences between the two temporal processes and the relationship between the marches' organizations and the way the rest of the movement proceeds, then the movement makes sense as a musical whole. The effects of the lacunae between the sections and the isolation in which each section enshrouds itself by not responding to its predecessors or generating its successors are overcome when the marches whip up phrases that are increasingly generated and generative. In short, one hears the movement as musically coherent when one feels the full force of the marches thrown against the mysterious opening sections. Images and metaphors are not needed to compensate for the putative looseness of the musical structure.

But they may be useful, even necessary, in describing the movement as a single, integrated entity, for the principle of coherence is peculiar to this movement, and conventional analytic concepts are inadequate to it. This principle has to do with the changing relevance of the future during the course of the movement. One discovers on paying attention to the variety of temporal processes projected by the various sections that the future (some coming musical event) sometimes impinges on the present, sometimes does not, and sometimes both does and does not. The future may be said to impinge on the present if what one is hearing seems to be pushing ahead or striving toward a coming event in the way a cause or a decision generates a coming event. In such cases, a sense of expectation is an essential quality of the present experience: what is anticipated is synthesized with what is currently perceived in the sense that the present is understood to be generating the coming event even if the contours of what is expected are vague and even if it turns out that what is expected does not take place. A present may be said to be futureless if no coming event impinges upon it — if it does not seem to be generating anything at all. The future both does and does not impinge upon the present when in some respects the music seems to be creating pressure toward the arrival of something (however specific or vague the something may be) while in other respects it seems to have no concern with any future whatsoever.

In so far as the opening sections of the Third seem to be generating a future, they comport with models of the temporal process like mechanistic cause or free decisions, both of which interpret the nature of reality in such a way that the relevance of the future to the present is intelligible. In so far as these passages seem to be denying the relevance of any future event, they also seem to be denying the validity of these models of temporality. This dualism is a fundamental tension, and the movement becomes coherent when later sections resolve it: at the end of the movement, the music presses toward and actualizes goals in a way that comports with that concept of temporality implicit in the notion of decision-making.

In other words, the movement's temporal process undergoes a fundamental change as it runs its course. Change, of course, is necessarily an aspect of all music, but it usually occurs within a temporal process that is consistent within a given piece. Sometimes the nature of that temporal process is not clear until the end of the piece, but the coherence of the piece is achieved when its many changes and especially its more daring ones turn out to support and be supported by, and not to contradict, the basic, unchanging nature of temporality itself. By changing the relevance of the future, Mahler's movement projects different temporal processes. If it seems incoherent on the first several hearings, the shifting temporalities may be the reason.

The following pages will focus on the transformation that occurs during the course of the movement as passages that both do and do not have a future give way to passages which unequivocally bear the stamp of the future. Instead of agreeing or disagreeing with the symbolic interpretations that Bekker, McGrath and others assign to various motifs, this analysis will concern itself primarily with the nature of this transformation; it will suggest some metaphors of the movement heard as coherent in this way; it will try to identify what the transformation metaphorically exemplifies.

(1) Overview of the Movement

Figure 49 identifies the movement's principal sections. The opening gesture is unmistakably future-directed at its beginning and is just as unmistakably futureless at its end. Then for several sections the relevance of the future to the present is ambiguous, though a sense of expectation gradually becomes stronger. It is during the first march and even more during the second one that this ambiguity is gradually but steadily displaced as a future begins unequivocally to impinge on the present.

The first three sections are totally independent of one another. They differ significantly in motif and texture, and each peters out and separates itself from the next by a gaping caesura. Each succeeding section neither responds to nor conflicts with the preceding section, for the forward thrust felt at the end of each section is so minimal that it cannot generate the next nor persist during the next as a

FIGURE 49
Sketch of Mahler, Third Symphony, first movement

Section	Rehearsal numbers in the score	Connotations
1	beginning to S:2 *	opening fanfare
2	S:2 to S:11 *	inert material resisting vital impulses
3	S:11 to S:13 *	ethereal substance resisting vital impulses
4	S:13 to S:18 **	new version of #2
5	S:18 to S:20	new version of #3
6	S:20 to S:29	exposition march
7	S:29 to S:35 **	new version of #2 (compare to #4)
8	S:35 to ?	new version of #3 (compare to #5)
9	? to S:55 *	development
10	S:55 to S:57 *	recapitulation of opening fanfare (compare to #1)
11	S:57 to S:62 *	recapitulation of #2
12	S:62 to end	recapitulation march

* complete hiatus
** nearly complete hiatus

residual force to which the new music might offer a bristling contradiction. In short, one section does not evoke the next, and even taken as a group they do not create any of the usual sorts of contrast that a later passage in the movement might be expected to resolve. It is as though the movement began three times: if it began at S:2, no one would have been the wiser (the Seventh Symphony, after all, begins with music that resembles S:2), and likewise S:11 could almost be the opening of a movement (similar passages in fact open the First and Fourth Symphonies).

At the lucunae between sections, one feels a profound mysteriousness. It is utterly unlike what we usually call expectation. That is, one may well feel a lingering impulse in all this stillness, but it would be a distortion to say that one expected the impulse to have an outcome, or that an expected outcome is the future of the impulse. What one senses here is too different from causes that have effects or decisions that have results.

Following the third section, the second and third sections are repeated in a somewhat varied form. The music does not come to a complete halt at the caesura between sections four and five, and section five flows directly into the first march. After the march, we get a second variation of the second section; this variation ends with another nearly dead stop. Then a second variation of the third section begins and flows into a lengthy development section.

The development consists of storms that completely blow themselves out. The music comes to an all but complete stop before the recapitulation begins. There are also conspicuous, mystery-laden lacunae after the first and second sections of the recapitulation (that is, sections ten and eleven), which reprise the movement's first two sections. Instead of reviewing the third section, the recapitulation goes directly to the second march, which occupies the rest of the movement.

(2) The First Section

In terms of its character and length, the first section sounds like an introduction, although it is also unlike an introduction in the way it fades away at its end into a *pianissimo* bass drum roll, making it necessary for the next section to provide its own introduction, as though the first section had not occurred at all.

The opening figure is a *fortissimo* fanfare for eight horns.[8] Although it uses the Dorian mode rather than a tonal scale, its first four bars associate themselves with conventional four-bar antecedent phrases. The music of what one takes initially to be the answering phrase, however, deviates from the standard consequent phrase by beginning without an upbeat (the typical consequent has an upbeat if its antecedent does); nevertheless, the first two bars could be the beginning of a somewhat unusual consequent. But when, in bar 7, the second half of this phrase begins by extending and heightening the first half (bars 5–6), it becomes almost impossible to imagine a satisfactory conclusion to a consequent phrase, and bar 8 decisively dissociates the gesture from the kind of structure projected by antecedent-consequent phrases. The melody of the gesture comes to an end in bar 11, returning to its opening note, although the passage does not have the kind of closure that would make it sound like a finished phrase. Then for another eleven measures, the music rocks back and forth on modal chords (that is, chords that do not have tonal functions) while the force of the non-closure experienced in the first eleven measures gradually dissipates.

The section as a whole transforms itself from a gesture (bars 1—4) that seems powerfully to be evoking a future (it seems to be heading to a goal, which, if it were reached, would be experienced as a fulfillment) into a gesture that is heavily laden with expectation (even though the anticipated future seems to have been indefinitely postponed and its contours have become quite vague) and then into a gesture that has no future (it seems to be heading nowhere at all, does not exemplify purposiveness, has no future impinging on it and cannot be followed by a gesture that would be understood as its fulfillment). During the course of the section, the process of summoning a definite future into actuality becomes the process of finding no future being evoked, as though the present were a force that so totally filled the consciousness that no future might be imagined.

In modal melodies, like the one in the first section, a note may push toward its next note, but usually not toward a note several beats in the future nor toward a final note that would be heard as closure to the whole melody. Differentiating modal melodies from tonal ones, this characteristic becomes both more apparent and more forceful as the first section unfolds and the future becomes fuzzy, then disappears. Moreover, a modal scale associates itself with that which is archaic and primordial, and this association becomes increasingly relevant as the passage increasingly suggests a temporal process that, like primordial temporality, is both pastless and futureless.

By four bars before S:2, futureless temporality is so prevalent that the music collapses into a quiet bass drum throb for four measures. But it would be a misnomer to speak of these measures as a "dead spot" as if one felt something were supposed to be happening that is not.[9]

Robert Musil's *Der Mann ohne Eigenschaften* (*The Man Without Qualities*) shows the Viennese planning a celebration for 1918, the seventieth year of Emperor Franz Joseph's reign. Those who make themselves responsible for orchestrating the fête try to think of an event whose taking place would bind together all levels of society and all the ethnic groups of the empire, without obliterating their distinctions, and in that way actualize the idea of the empire. As the novel goes on, it becomes apparent that the planners do not share a common idea of the empire. They have no way of coming to acknowledge, much less to negotiate their differences, and so the actualization of the empire is an impossibility. But as they do not and cannot know that the obstacles are insuperable, they continue to work toward their supposed goal, or go through the motions of working toward it. As the impossibility dawns upon the reader, the structure of the novel collapses; the incidents it relates have less and less direction. It is no accident that Musil did not complete it (after 1200 pages, the novel still has reached no ending). As E. Wilkins and E. Kaiser say in their introduction to the English translation, the unfinishedness may be the novel's form.[10] Musil was writing after World War I, and knew that his readers would know that 1918, far from being the emperor's seventieth anniversary, and the final coming-to-be of the empire, would see the dismemberment of the empire, Franz Josef being already two years dead. But even ending the novel by the cataclysmic war would have given it too much structure, a definite ending that would belie the temporal process that the work comes to exemplify.

Like Mahler's opening section, Musil's novel begins as though it were going to press toward a conclusion — as though its temporal process consisted of moving from idea to actuality, from projection to realization, and from a shaping self to a self manifested through what it had shaped — but trails off without reaching a culmination because, in the temporal process which the novel finally projects, culminations are impossible and to think about them and to press toward them is only to make oneself ridiculous. At the end of the novel, as at the end of Mahler's first section, we vaguely sense a lingering impulse, but we cannot imagine what its outcome might be or even that it could have an outcome because every way that we understand of moving from the present to the future has been discredited during the course of the novel. *The Man Without Qualities* is not an indictment of the empire or of the aristocrats and upper middle-class liberals who tried to preserve it; it is a hilarious parody both of the empire and of those who indict it. One must wait until later in the first movement of Mahler's Third Symphony for analogous humor: the banality of the two marches which have fun with regimental music without making fun of it.[11]

(3) The Second Section

At S:2, the second section begins. The trombones suddenly (yet quietly) flesh out the bass drum's rhythm and thereby reinvoke the whole first section and its introductory quality (see Figure 50). The trombones could either be making a foreground statement, or they

FIGURE 50
Mahler, Third Symphony, first movement

could be setting up a background for a soon-coming foreground
figure. The bassoons in the next measure could be either an answer
to the trombones' statement or the beginning of a melody against
the background adumbrated by the trombones. But the bassoons'
figure, derived as it is from the very figure (in bars 7—9) that turns
a consequent phrase into an unfinishing gesture, fails to generate a
foreground melody. The upper winds, the trumpets, the basses (in
a scale reminiscent of the scales used in the first movement of the
Second Symphony) and a trombone blast from the cavernous depths
try by turns to get something going in the foreground, but all these
prove to be fragmentary bits of sound that together create an active,
shimmering, but inchoate surface against which something can happen.

The horns' figure at 7 before S:5 we take to be one more patch of
sound in this increasingly rich background, and it is only in 4 before
S:5 that we realize that the foreground melody is finally underway.
Describing the relation of the horns to the other instruments as that
of a foreground to a background is, however, somewhat misleading.
In three respects, the distinction between a melodically less interesting
and less purposeful background to a more prominent, melodically
more interesting and goal-directed foreground does not hold here.
First, the horns' melody is rhapsodic and moves in fits and starts
without seeming to get anywhere; although it ends on D, the sense
of return to a tonic is vitiated by the use of the Phrygian mode (note
the [concert] E-flats in 4 and 8 bars after S:5). Second, the horns'
"foreground melody" has no beginning; not only does its start seem
to be one more instance of whatever the other instruments have
been doing, but also its motif is taken from the *middle* of the horn's

opening fanfare (bars 7—9), where the fanfare was changing future-directedness into presentfulness. And finally, from S:5 to 11 after S:5, the basses and cellos are just as loud as and no more rhapsodic than the horns, and so there is almost as much reason to say that the horns provide "filler" between the end of one gesture and the beginning of the next in the bass-cello part as the other way round.

Although present sounds have related themselves to coming sounds in one way at the beginning of the opening fanfare and in a radically different way at the ending, the horns' melody in section two manages to resemble both. Here (as at the beginning of the fanfare) the music pushes ahead strongly, but (as at the end of the fanfare) it is not heading toward anything in particular. The equivocal relevance of the future as well as the ambiguous distinction between foreground and background calls to mind Schopenhauer's concept of the will — a striving that has no rationality that would define its purpose. Schopenhauer calls the will "blind" and its striving "endless" because it simply wills without being able to posit goals the fulfillment of which would quell its striving. Mahler's music may be said to be an image of willing — the act of willing abstracted from willing anything in particular and from any purpose more ultimate than itself. (Mahler himself described the section using several metaphors: life breaking through, out of "soulless, petrified matter," "what the mountains tell me," "captive life struggling for release from the clutches of lifeless, rigid Nature" and the struggle between winter and summer.[12])

The section has three gestures (see Figure 51). Dominated by the

FIGURE 51
Sketch of Mahler, Third Symphony, first movement,
exposition

section two

first gesture	7 before S:5—6 after S:6	
first wave	7 before S:5—5 before S:5	
second wave	4 before S:5—1 before S:5	
third wave	S:5	—6 after S:6
second gesture	7 after S:6 —S:8	
first wave	7 after S:6 —10 after S:6	
second wave	4 before S:7—1 before S:7	
third wave	S:7	—S:8
third gesture	S:8	—6 before S:11
first wave	S:8	—2 after S:8
second wave	3 after S:8	—6 after S:8
third wave	7 after S:8	—6 before S:11

horns, the first gesture begins and ends on D minor chords. In the second gesture the trumpet comes to the fore, sliding down to a C minor chord at its beginning and ending on a B major chord. Then the horns give a varied repeat of the first gesture, the harmonies sliding down to B-flat minor, to G minor, to E-flat major and to D minor. The three gestures all have the same shape. In each one, a first wave begins with a rising figure that is repeated at a higher pitch in a second wave, and then a third wave reaches still higher and presses upward to an expected peak which is even higher, but which is not attained, for the melody sinks back down without reaching its goal.

The trumpet's gesture is more straightforward, less decorated, than the horns' gestures, perhaps compensating for the fact that the harmonies in its background are less static.[13] But neither here nor in the horn sections can the harmonies be said to make progressions. The absence of harmonic relationship from one chord to the next and the loose, constantly changing relationship between the melody and the background chords create the sense that the melody's striving and pushing has no goal. The melody asserts itself in various half-step dissonances against the background now on the strong beat, now on the weak beat, now resolving, now moving on with the expectation created by the dissonance unheeded. The trumpet melody, for example, seems at times as harmonically independent of its background as a passage from late Schoenberg, but it is not uniformly independent. It begins both its first two waves on chord tones (C of a C minor chord and E-flat of an E-flat minor chord, respectively; see Figure 52); in the first and second waves, the first two of the last three notes (9 and 13 bars after S:6, respectively) do not make harmonic sense with the background, and the last by no means resolves these dissonances. In the third and climactic wave, the trumpet rises to F–G-flat three times, and each time its relationship to the background is different. The first time (one bar after S:7), the G-flat fits in with the background chord, but this chord itself is irrational (it is a non-resolving diminished-seventh chord built on C over a D in the bass). The second time, the F cooperates with the background to make a diminished-seventh chord, but the G-flat becomes dissonant against the bass. And in the third, the F is dissonant against the background's B major, while the G-flat (= F-sharp) is a chord tone, but the rhythm of the trumpet part makes it sound as though it were not.

In short, the relation between the foreground and the background at first invites us to understand half steps against the bass as dissonances to be resolved and then vitiates that understanding. Moreover, no

FIGURE 52
Mahler, Third Symphony, first movement

single principle of succession prevails during the section as a whole. It begins and ends with D minor chords. The horns' first entrance is heard as part of the dominant to D. But the return to D at the end is not experienced as the arrival at a goal whose expectation would have guided the section as a whole. Instead, the chords along the way seem loosely and variously related to one another. It is as though the melody is simply unable to organize the background into a rationally meaningful progression. Thus, both in terms of the sounds of individual chords and in terms of the succession of chords, the background remains, in the end, unrelated to and unaffected by all the pushing and groaning in the foreground.[14] The music vacillates between evoking the expectation of a particular change and suppressing the sense of expectation altogether. Consequently, the sounds behind and beside the brass not only provide a background but also function as an independent force. Like the brass, this force, which asserts itself most conspicuously in the bass runs, presses ahead with enormous energy but with only a vague sense of direction.

At its end, the second section collapses into a bass drum throb like the one with which it began. This figure stitches the second to the third section as insecurely as the second is connected to the opening fanfare. The gaping hole between the second and third sections confirms the sense that the music of the second section is as futureless as it is forward-directed. The mysteriousness felt at the end of section one is just as palpable here.

(4) The Third Section

In terms of their temporal processes, the second and third sections are contrasting complements to one another. Through the odd relation of foreground to background, the second section continuously conveys the sense of both having and not having a future, thereby surmounting the contrast between the future-directed beginning of section one and the futurelessness of its ending. The third section (S:11) also seems to hold these opposites together, but in an entirely different way, namely, through the odd relationships of four-bar groups to one another.

The first sixteen measures of section three divide themselves into four four-bar groups (see Figure 53). The first four measures make a group that does not sound at all like an antecedent subphrase. The second group seems somewhat more like a consequent-evoking antecedent, although the nature of such a consequent is very vague. The third subphrase does not seem to actualize that which the second may have been generating; it sounds more like a new beginning and, like the movement's opening four bars, clearly evokes a consequent. This expectation, for the first time in the movement, is realized in the next four-bar group. Satisfying this expectation raises another one, namely, that this eight-bar group will generate an eight-bar consequent. But the abrupt switch from violins to clarinets and from a tonal center of D to a tonal center of D-flat treats the expectation

FIGURE 53
Mahler, Third Symphony, first movement

as though it did not even exist. Again, the music vanishes into a soft throb on the bass drum, followed this time by a long rest. Mystery supplants expectation.

The timbres of sections two and three make them contrasting complements in another sense: the sounds here are as high and light as there they are dark and heavy. To the extent that a process like Schopenhauer's willing is suggested in section three, it is as breezy here as there it is laborious. If there the will asserts itself against lumpish material substance, here it must be asserting itself (still blindly, as it happens) against mute ethereal substance.[15]

(5) The Fourth and Fifth Sections

The fourth section redoes the second section. This new version consists of a single gesture, which (like each of the three gestures in section two) has three waves. Each wave is conspicuously longer than the waves in section two, so the groaning forward pressure is sustained over a much longer span. As in the second section, the second wave (S:15 to S:16) repeats and heightens the first (S:13 to S:15), and in the third wave (S:16 to S:18) the energy reaches its peak without attaining a goal.

The forward thrust generated during section four being greater and the energy-dissipating gesture being somewhat briefer than in the previous sections, the fruitless push ahead continues to be felt at the end of the section. The momentum at the caesura distinguishes this

ending from the previous endings. Moreover, this caesura has sounds
with specific pitches (lower strings instead of bass drum), confirming
the difference and its importance.

The fifth section redoes the third section. As in the fourth section,
the forward pressure is greater here than in its prototype partly
because things happen at a faster pace (the second four-bar group
here is a conflation of the second and third groups of section three)
and partly because the basses maintain their presence, eventually
becoming a pedal point on C that strongly thrusts forward to F. This
push ahead is felt across the end of the section (S:20) and, for the
first time in the movement, no hiatus in the musical flow articulates
the division between two sections. Conventional expectation has
supplanted mysteriousness.

(6) The Exposition March

The march integrates the music of the first five sections by blending
their motifs in such a way that they seem all to be cut from the same
cloth. In this sense, the march is a response to the preceding parts of
the movement. However, the kind of temporal process it projects is
its more significant response, for at its beginning its temporal process
is just as ambiguous as that of the preceding sections, but it gradually
transforms its temporality into the kind of process in which having a
sense of direction is unequivocally possible.

The ambiguity of the temporal process at the onset of the march is
such that one cannot properly speak of its "beginning": when we
first become aware of the march, we are aware of a process that is
already underway; there is no moment in its past which we can
designate as its beginning. This ambiguity arises because the dotted
rhythms that characterize the march begin in the basses at S:20
while the violins extend the fifth section and its images of the will
asserting itself vis-à-vis immaterial substance (see Figure 54). By
about the fifth bar after S:20, one realizes that a four-bar group has
begun in the cellos and basses in the third bar after S:20. It is answered
by the next four bars in the cellos and basses, but because the last
three of these four bars recede into the background, the evoked
future seems not to happen just as much as it seems to happen. The
foreground behind which the actualization of the cello-bass future
fades is the four-bar tune begun by the clarinet (at 2 before S:21)
and finished by the violins. This four-bar group initiates a long
parade of four-bar groups, yet because its beginning overlaps the

FIGURE 54
Mahler, Third Symphony, first movement

cello-bass grouping, the march toward a fulfilling future is initially obscured. At S:21, it is not clear whether it is the future of the cello-bass or of the clarinet-violins that is relevant to the present.

The clarinet tune begins clearly in F, the tonic to which the pedal-point C, which controls the harmony at the end of section five, has been pushing. The harmonic progressions that begin at S:20, however, keep overshooting F and sinking down into D minor. The relation of dominant (C) to tonic (F), of expectation to fulfillment, is not realized until S:23. By then, a march rhythm has been dominating the texture and conventional four-bar groupings have been controlling the organization for 26 measures. The effect of avoiding the resolution of the dominant (C) is to contribute to the ambiguity characterizing the temporal process: on the one hand, the delay intensifies the thrust to F, and on the other hand, its persistence makes us wonder whether the expectation is pertinent to what is happening after all. Thus in this respect also, expectation seems both relevant and irrelevant.

As Figure 55 indicates, the march divides itself into two parts, the first with ten subphrases, the second with fifteen. As the march unfolds, the subphrases relate themselves to one another more and more strongly and become increasingly end-directed. The second part

FIGURE 55
Sketch of Mahler, Third symphony, first movement, exposition march

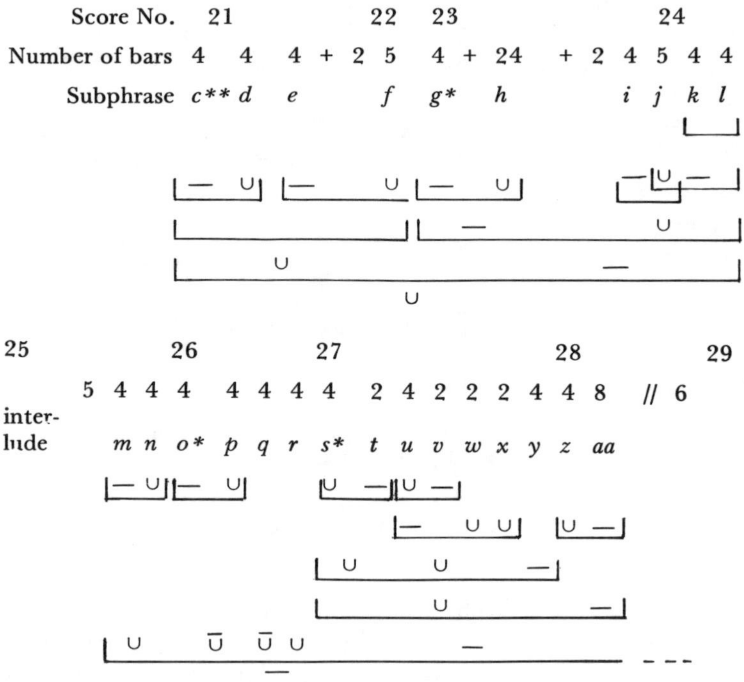

Score No.	21					22	23			24				
Number of bars	4	4	4 + 2	5		4 + 24		+ 2	4	5	4	4		
Subphrase	c**	d	e		f	g*	h		i	j	k	l		

25		26			27				28			29
	5	4 4 4	4 4 4 4	2 4 2 2 2 4 4 8	//	6
inter-lude		m n o*	p q r	s* t u v w x y z aa		

*appearances of the opening horn call and its closest derivatives
**c is the subphrase that begins two bars before S:21.

as a whole is more tightly organized and pushes more forcefully to a goal than the first part as a whole. It is these changes in the nature of the musical flow that transform the temporal process from one in which the future is ambiguously potent to one in which expectation is palpably relevant.[16]

At subphrase *s* (S:27), where D major and a fresh statement of the fanfare arrive, the march begins to attain the event toward which it has been pushing; that whose expectation has increasingly guided the struggles of subphrases *m* . . . *r* begins to take shape. As Figure 55 suggests, there are further anacrustic gestures within the actualization of this anticipated event, for it spreads itself out over a period of time, as genuine actualization must, and is not merely an infinitely short moment. These anacrustic gestures may be said to belong to actualization rather than to further preparation because the sense of uncertainty about the shape of what is expected and the timing of its arrival — an uncertainty felt during the entire march up to this point — is suddenly and drastically reduced at S:27.

The culmination, as it unfolds, is thrilling indeed, and consequently the setback experienced in the seventh measure before S:29, when culmination suddenly is swept aside, is devastating. That the arrival is cut off before it completely unfolds does not refute the assertion that during the march that which is expected plays an increasingly important role in determining the quality of what is going on in each moment. While the future is experienced as both relevant and irrelevant during the first five sections of the movement, it becomes unequivocally relevant as the march proceeds. The temporal process of the march implicitly contradicts that of sections one through five.

(7) Sections Seven, Eight and Nine

When (at S:29) the march is displaced by a reprise of sections two and three, the two kinds of temporal experience conflict openly and violently. These reprises (sections seven and eight) make it vividly clear that the temporality in which the relevance of the future is equivocal has not been permanently transformed by the exposition march into one in which the future unambiguously qualifies the present. Thus the exposition as a whole presents a dissonance between the march's temporality and that of sections two, three, four, five and seven — a dissonance that is emotionally punishing and intellectually unacceptable by our ordinary criteria of coherence.

Just as section five flows without a break into the march, so its reprise in section eight flows without a break into the development (section nine). During the development, the forward-pressing but often undirected energies of the exposition are intensified. The irrational seething and swelling at S:44 reminded Mahler of a mob milling about. The tumult and turmoil are at their most terrifying from S:51 to S:55, a section that Mahler aptly calls the "south storm."[17]

(8) The Recapitulation

The first two sections of the recapitulation (S:55 to S:57 and S:57 to S:62) reprise the first two sections of the exposition and reinstate the claims of a temporality that equivocates between having and not having a future. After the hiatus at S:62 and before section three can be reprised, the second march begins and occupies the rest of the movement. Like its counterpart in the exposition, it divides itself into two parts (see Figure 56), and the interlude between them is again marked by the woodwind turns around E that are associated with section three (compare S:25 and two bars before S:68 with S:12).

FIGURE 56
Sketch of Mahler, Third Symphony, first movement, recapitulation march

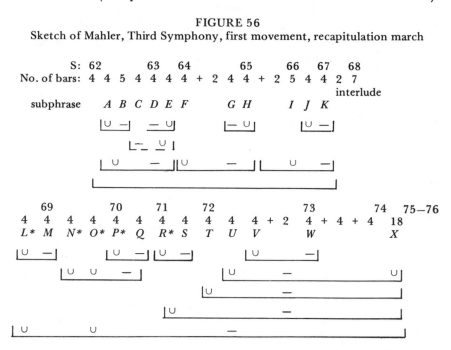

*the opening horn call and its closest derivatives

The first part of the recapitulation march, like the first part of the exposition march, suggests a temporality in which the prospect of coming events both does and does not impinge on the present. But the march reprise cannot proceed by simply repeating the exposition as though the ambiguity of forward-thrusting yet undirected energy had not been intensified in the development. The horn call from section one enters much sooner here than before (here it comes in the third subphrase, *C;* before, it comes in *g,* the seventh). In the exposition, this entrance sounds like an arrival, even though the preceeding music has only vaguely looked toward such a future (in the exposition, *c—d* are so weakly grouped with *e—f* that the listener only dimly senses that *c . . . f* might prepare some coming event, which turns out to be the martial version of the opening fanfare). In the recapitulation, the entrance of the opening call comes too soon to sound like an arrival. Subphrase *C* neither ends stably nor evokes a future, and the next eight bars are paired subphrases that continue the motif opening the march as though the fanfare group had not occurred at all. Subphrases *D—E* are not responsive to their immediately prior subphrase, but seem to have been evoked by the instability generated when subphrase *B* extends itself into a five-bar group. Thus, the contradiction between experiencing and not experiencing the contrast between what is and what is to come bristles even more palpably here than at the onset of the exposition march.

Subphrase *F* in the recapitulation restates subphrase *h* of the exposition, which there forms a group with *g,* a subphrase based on the fanfare motif (see Figure 57). Separated by *D* and *E* from the recapitulation's counterpart to *g, F* seems like a new beginning. By thus rearranging the groups that it is recapitulating, the reprise erodes the listeners' confidence that the contrast between the present (the recapitulation march) and the past (the exposition march that the present is partly recalling) is relevant to present experience; they do not know to what extent the past's future serves as a clue to the present's future.

Precisely because *F* is not grouped with *E,* it forms a group with *G* (the exposition's *h* and *i,* counterparts to the recapitulation's *F* and *G,* do not form a group with each other, although, as Figure 57 indicates, *g—h* together form a group with *i . . . l* on a higher architectonic level). *F—G* is an end-accented group, for, having heard *F* as the beginning of a group, one also hears its ending as unstable and something whose future impinges on it; *G* is heard as the arrival of that future.

This function of *G* might lead us to suppose that a transformation of the temporal process, analogous to that in the exposition, is now underway and that a temporality in which the future is ambiguously relevant is being changed into one in which the relevance of the future is unequivocal. Following *G,* however, the dotted rhythm and the tune that are used in subphrases *A* and *B* and again at *D—E* resurface and with them the clear groupings and less clear pairings that exemplify having and not having a future. In the exposition march, the subphrases dominated by this rhythm and tune seem at first to be the march proper, and then when the martial version of the opening horn call strikes up, they seem to have been introductory. But in the recapitulation, where this sort of music occurs three times (*A—B, D—E* and *H*), it does not seem to be so much an introduction to the march

FIGURE 57

Sketch of Mahler, Third Symphony, first movement. Identical and nearly identical subphrases in the exposition and recapitulation marches. Grouping of subphrases

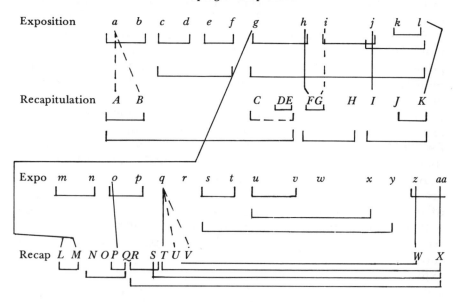

Solid connecting lines indicate identical subphrases, and dotted lines indicate similar subphrases.

proper (that is, to *C, F—G* and *I—J—K* respectively) as to be its own process to which the other subphrases are largely irrelevant. The effect of hearing alternating snatches of the two unrelated unfoldings is somewhat like that of standing on a large parade ground and hearing the infantrymen drilling (*A—B, D—E, H*) in the distance to the left, and then with a change of wind, the cavalry drilling (*C, F—G, I—J—K*) in the distance to the right.[18] Or like the moment in the last scene of Wagner's *Die Meistersinger* when the bakers barge in to the center of the reviewing area before the tailors have moved on.

During subphrases *A—B, D—E* and *H*, the future both does and does not bear on present events (although the sense that the future does not impinge on the present is weaker than it is during the faltering procession from one musically isolated section to the next during the exposition, before the march). And the force of the future is brought into play during subphrases *C, F–G* and *I–J–K*. Thus, while the exposition march begins by modulating the contrast between having and not having a future and more or less steadily moves in the direction of having a future, the recapitulation march — following as it does the stormy development — holds the power of futurelessness in play longer and sustains longer the ambiguity between having and not having a future.

But then it moves toward having a future, and it moves further than the corresponding part of the exposition. The fact that subphrases *I* and *J* evoke a future is their most important quality. Subphrase *K* actualizes that future and at the same time ends with a mobility that generates the second part of the recapitulation march (groups *L* through *X*). Subphrases *I* and *K* are restatements of the exposition march's *j* and *l,* but while the latter seem to unfold further the focus stated in *g* and seem only weakly to point ahead, the future is unambiguously relevant to the recapitulation's *I–J–K*.

A temporal process in which one struggles toward fulfillments that actually take place is unambiguously exemplified by the second part of the recapitulation march. This part of the movement is permeated with the opening horn call, now shorn of the ambiguities that characterize the beginning of the movement and transmuted into a decisively future-evoking gesture. The culmination arrives at S:74. Unlike the exposition, the reprise does not turn to D major: the recapitulation states its *T, U* and *V,* which reprise and develop the exposition's *q* and *r,* and then goes directly to *W* (at S:73), a restatement of the exposition's *x* (six bars before S:28), without going through the exposition's D major subphrases (*s, t, u, v, w*). Because the recapitulation is firmly rooted in F, the turn to its submediant (D-flat at S:74) does not attenuate the sense of culmination; in the exposition, by contrast, D is a less secure tonic than F is here, and the turn to the submediant (at seven before S:29) is a jolt that sweeps away the sense of fulfillment. The D-flat at S:74 becomes the dominant of the Neapolitan (G-flat at S:75) and part of a goal-directed progression back to F. In its haste to return to F, the progression goes directly from the dominant of the dominant (a chord built on G at the fourth bar after S:75) to the tonic, omitting the dominant (C).

(9) The Movement as a Unified Process

The second part of the recapitulation march makes the movement into a coherent whole. We have felt a strange absence of expectation at the movement's eight mystery-laden lacunae and an ambiguous blending of conventional expectation with its contrary (the result of forward thrusts that are as undirected as they are energetic) in the first five sections of the exposition, all of the development and the first parts of the two marches. This feeling is supplanted by an increasingly powerful sense of direction that arises during each of the two marches. In short, the movement as a whole goes from having no future and equivocating between having and not having a future to unequivocal goal-directedness.

The impulse for this transmutation is latent within the opening horn call. At the very beginning of the movement — that is, without the benefit of some sort of introductory gesture, as in all Mahler's other symphonies except the Eighth — the horn call summons a future, and then fades away into futurelessness. The call reappears as the focus of the exposition march (at S:27 and in a modified form at S:28). The call reappears again to announce a renewed procession toward goal-directedness after the turmoil of the development section. And it generates and permeates the recapitulation march, in which it functions both to drive toward goals and to realize the goals of other gestures. (Figures 55 and 56 identify the most explicit derivatives of the horn call in the two marches.)

But to say that the impulse for the transformation is latent within the horn call is not to say that the transformation sounds inevitable. One does not expect it, and when it happens it does not sound like the unfolding of a necessity. Just as little does it sound like the outcome of a struggle of a self-conscious agent imposing himself and his decisions on an external reality. For the arrival of a passage in which the future impinges on the present does not itself bear upon the moments in the exposition when the music comes to a complete stop, nor on the moments where the relevance of the future is confused with its irrelevance. While obviously the opening sections, whose endings have been characterized as futureless, turn out to have a future after all, expecting that future does not contribute to the experience of listening to those sections. Consequently, the movement from the mysterious impulse lingering in the lacunae between sections to its outcome is not at all like the movement from a cause to its effect or from a decision to its result.

In short, the transformation happens neither because it must nor ₐbecause it ought to. It simple happens. Instead of offering an analogue to events that obey principles or laws external to themselves or to events that are shaped by conscious choices, it exemplifies an event that establishes principles and makes decisions possible. The musical transformation more nearly resembles a world-establishing event than an event that takes place within an already constituted world. Precisely because the juxtaposition of isolated sections refuses to resemble the familiar, intelligible flow of events, it is able to suggest the unintelligible emergence of a rational world out of a chaos in which anything like conventional expectation seems impossible. Precisely to the extent that the lacunae between sections seem futureless in that they resist analogies to mechanistic causes and free decisions, they insist on the unintelligibility, indeed the impossibility of the transmutation.

The movement is often described as an aural image of the process of creation — not creation by a deity, but the process of nature making the impossible transition from a lifeless stupor to a network of articulated organisms. The description is justified not only by Mahler's own terms for various parts — "Pan awakens" and "Summer marches in" — but also by the qualities of the music itself: the opening call *does* sound like an immaterial impulse moving over undifferentiated, inert stuff, stirring it to life, section two *does* sound like the conflict between a life-giving impulse and an insentient mass; the marches *do* sound like a Bacchic celebration of the forces of summer and life over winter and lifelessness.

The most profound sense in which the movement suggests the mystery of coming to be alive, however, is the one that its shape as a whole and the coherence of its parts project: musical goal-lessness being supplanted and overcome by musical goal-directedness. As in sonata-allegro form, a dualism is set up within the exposition, although it is not a contrast of tonalities and although the exposition itself goes some distance toward resolving this tension before the end of the exposition dismisses the tentative resolution and the entire development heightens the tension. And as in sonata form, the recapitulation deals with this dualism, although its way of transcending the contrast is as peculiar to the movement as is the contrast itself. While in conventional sonata from the nature of expectation is uniform throughout the movement, here expectation comes into being, as it were, during the course of the movement. Describing the movement as an aural image of the absolutely peculiar event of a world constituting itself is one way to point to the unique musical process that the movement unfolds.

To be more specific, one may say that it offers an image of consciousness emerging. The difference between inert matter and matter that is animated by rational self-awareness is that the former experiences no contrast between what is, what was and what will be, while the latter experiences such contrasts and is constantly synthesizing past, present and expected events while maintaining their distinctiveness.

Making temporal distinctions and synthesizing temporally distinct objects of awareness are so fundamental to what we take experience to be that it seems odd to say that inert matter experiences no temporal contrasts: if it does not experience these, then it is not experiencing at all. There is, in fact, no difference between saying that inert matter does not experience and saying that it does not experience temporally. It cannot expect an object different from that of which it is now "conscious" and, if the object does change, cannot recollect that it ever was conscious of anything else. A consciousness that has no capacity for recollecting or expecting seems to be the same as no consciousness at all. Mahler's utterly goalless musical gestures — those on which no future impinges in any way at all, for example, the hiatuses dotted throughout the exposition — are an aural image of precisely this sort of non-consciousness or non-temporal consciousness, although it is a mysterious non-consciousness over which a mysterious, unidentifiable impulse hovers.[19]

The various gestures in which expectation is both evoked and suppressed and the future both does and does not impinge on the present suggest a kind of experience in which possibilities are dimly imagined and fragmentarily synthesized,[20] the less dimly and fragmentarily the more the experience is like that of human consciousness. The second and third movements give fuller characterizations of semi-conscious experiencing. In them, we experience partial goal-directedness during the course of an entire movement. Taking a cue from Mahler's preliminary titles, we learn in the second movement what the flowers tell us. For a flower is unaware of its own beauty, unable to run away from a storm, not so utterly lacking in goals as inert matter, yet not fully conscious either. And in the third movement we learn what the animals tell us. For a bird or a chipmunk or a bear is an animated flower; it can prey and be preyed upon; it can move about, as if to fulfill goals or flee from threats, but it lacks a full awareness of goals or threats or itself.

The second half of the recapitulation march, on whose clearly articulated individual moments (four bars each) both preceding and coming events impinge, exemplifies the temporal process of fully conscious experience, in which the quality of any given moment is its relation to remembered and expected (or hoped for) events. To say that this march presents fully emerged consciousness from which the second and third movements differentiate themselves in varying degrees is not, however, to disagree with McGrath's characterization of this passage as a celebration of the victory of vital impulse over the resistance of inert matter. For in the context of the movement's wobbles between not having and having expectations, between non-consciousness (or non-temporal consciousness) and various degrees of semi-consciousness (or ambiguously temporal consciousness), the appearance of fully human consciousness (or temporally articulated and synthesizing consciousness) can only be experienced as something to be celebrated. The goal of the movement — though it is not expected before it happens — is to have goals.

This way of stating the nature of the movement's coherence implies that consciousness, like the will in Schopenhauer's philosophy, involves an endless succession of short-range goals. To be conscious is to have a future. No concrete realization is so fulfilling that other goals do not present themselves; it does not belong to the nature of fulfilling goals to obliterate other goals. In this sense, consciousness, like semi-consciousness, shows the marks of a ceaseless and blind will. Although consciousness entails knowing that one has goals as well as seeing them more clearly than semi-consciousness does, the conscious person cannot see a purpose for having goals and being conscious other than that of being conscious and having goals; consciousness does not entail imagining a goal that would be so complete that meeting it would quell goal-directedness.

The fact that consciousness is endlessly goal-directed need not, however, imply the emptiness and despair that it does for Schopenhauer. Its endlessness can be seen as boundless energy and the opportunity ceaselessly to create occasions for jubilation. The first movement of the Third regards consciousness in this positive way, although the banality of the marches suggests that the jubilation may be superficial and possible only if some deeper aspect of consciousness is deliberately forgotten. The fourth movement forces this deeper aspect to the surface. It looks candidly at the negative aspects of human consciousness. It agrees with Schopenhauer, as it were, that human woe is the result of consciousness, the inevitable concomitant of endless striving both when it strives without achieving what it wants and when it achieves that toward which it strives only to discover that it still wants. But it also disagrees with Schopenhauer and reaffirms that endless goal-directedness is both the result of and an occasion for joy. Thus, in the image of consciousness projected by the fourth movement, human experience seems necessarily to fluctuate between the joy of living and the woes of biting failure and disillusioning success.

Less obviously, but more importantly, the sixth movement presents a new kind of temporal process. In it, temporal experience is transformed and consciousness is transfigured so that goal-directedness is combined with being at the goal. As goal directedness is quelled and yet continues, the tension between the positive and the negative aspects of consciousness also disappears.

2. *Part Two*

Part One ends so conclusively that it is hard to imagine a successor to it. As Bekker points out,[21] Mahler arranged for a full intermission to separate this movement from Part Two (the rest of the work) when he conducted performances of it. In many respects, the next four movements also come to a complete stop. Their endings suggest as little what will follow them, or even that anything could follow them, as the nearly total hiatuses within the first movement. In no movement does a future beyond itself impinge upon it. Although motivic interconnections link the movements, there is no dynamic thrust linking one movement to the next. Consequently, each movement must create a place for itself.[22] When the fifth movement has ended, however, the listener may recognize that each successive movement has made a place for itself by projecting a temporal process that has progressed in some sense beyond that of the previous movement. Faint though it is, the line of progress delineated by the changes of temporal process and, consequently, of levels of consciousness, going from movement two through movement five, suggests a principle of coherence that loosely ties these movements together.

Just as the marches in the first movement overcome the disruptive gaps in the musical flow and organize the movement into a whole whose principle of coherence is unprecedented, so the Finale pulls the entire symphony into a whole. Catching the listener off guard, the Finale repudiates the principle of coherence that has seemed to be emerging during movements two through five and at the same time overcomes the mutual irrelevance in which such repudiation might seem to abandon these movements. Consequently, understanding the Finale means recognizing the force whereby it pulls the work into a coherent whole. As in the first movement, the principle of coherence that emerges with the Finale has to do with temporal processes — its own and the relation of its own to those of prior movements. The interrelations of temporal processes are partly projected and partly confirmed by motivic and tonal connections among the movements. So after surveying the Finale as a whole in order to establish a vocabulary for referring to its parts, the following pages will probe these motivic and tonal relations and then try to describe the temporal processes of the Finale and of the symphony as a whole.

(1) Overview of the Last Movement

Like the second movement of the Fifth Symphony, the Finale of the Third is organized into alternating passages of contrasting music. The Finale consists of four sections (see Figure 58). Each of the first

FIGURE 58
Sketch of Mahler, Third Symphony, Finale

	first part (chorale)	second part (minor-mode theme)	climax
section one	beginning to S:4	S:4 to S:9	S:7
section two	S:9 to 14	S:14 to S:21	S:15, S:20
section three	S:21 to four bars before S:23	three bars before S:23 to S:25	S:24
section four	S:25 to end		S:29

three sections consists of two parts: a statement of or variation on a serene chorale theme in D major,[23] played exclusively by the strings in the first two sections, the winds doubling the strings in the third and the brass joining in for the fourth, and an anguished passage in the minor, in which the winds and the brass dominate.

In the first section, these two kinds of music are simply juxtaposed. The serene joy of the one contrasts violently with the searching, struggling, failing and hurting of the other. The wind and brass sonority threatens menacingly the serenity of the string sonority. The contrasts comes to a head in a climactic passage (S:7 to S:8) that connotes deep and intense pain. The second section tries to accommodate the two kinds of music to one another: the first part absorbs some elements of the second into itself, and insinuates aspects of itself into the second part. Consequently, this section is the longest of the four and has a subsidiary climax at S:15 as well as a main climax at S:20. The agony characterizing the latter climax is even more intense than the pain at the climax of the first section both because the approach to it is longer and because the twofold attempt to soften the contrast between serenity and disappointment fails. The third section makes no effort at integration: the chorale insists on itself, as though pain were to be subdued by ignoring it. The effort almost works, and the movement reaches what seems to be an altogether satisfactory close at six bars before S:23. In a sudden, impulsive surge, however, the other theme asserts itself, and without the benefit of a cautious transition, like the one that links the contrasting passages in the first as well as the second section, we suddenly feel the torment of striving and floundering; suddenly we lose altogether the perspective from which serenity may be possible. The climax at S:24 is the most devastating in the movement.

In the final section, the two kinds of music are no longer juxtaposed. Unlike the first three sections, it does not divide itself into two parts, but consists of a single sweep to the end. The chorale absorbs and accommodates the opposing motif; the strings' sound embraces the woodwinds' and brasses' sound, so that the latter enriches, and no longer threatens, the former.

(2) Allusions in the Finale to the First and Fifth Movements

As Figure 59 shows, the rhythm and the melodic contour of the chorale allude explicitly both to a moment in the exposition march of the first movement and also to a theme that pervades the Bell Chorus (the fifth movement). The connotations of that moment in the first movement have already been described; it is a gesture in which goal-directedness and the temporality of expecting a future are asserting themselves. The fifth-movement theme — as indeed the fifth movement as a whole — connotes folk-like innocence. The tempo, the brevity of the phrases, the straightforward, unproblematic phrase groupings, the little stamping accents (in, for example, the second measure after S:2), the texting (one note per syllable) and, until the end of the middle section, the exclusive use of the diatonic scale all contribute to a scene of cheery, unreflective blamelessness. The text talks about serious things — sin, weeping, mercy[24] — but the music scurries along as though it had no capacity for experiencing their seriousness. The F major of the first section gives way to the D minor

FIGURE 59
Mahler, Third Symphony

of its middle section (S:3 to S:6) with no appreciation of the possible implications of such a progression. For the coming D minor passages in no way qualify the F major phrases; the minor strains are neither expected nor unexpected. And in the concluding F major section, the memory of the minor twinges affects the mood just as little.

In this respect, the fifth movement resembles the second, whose minor passages also fail to impinge upon the cheerful serenity of the previous and coming major-mode passages. Bekker, following the lead Mahler's letters give, describes the second movement as a flower piece in which the flowers' joy in being themselves is not affected by the rain and wind they undergo.[25] They are subject to what humans would experience as pain, but do not, because they cannot, experience it that way. The angels in the fifth movement can talk about pain, but they seem to know it only from the outside, as it were, and can experience pain no more than can the flowers, who cannot talk at all.[26]

In oscillating between F and d, the fifth movement also invites comparison to the first, whose exposition begins in D minor, gives way to F major and ends in D major and whose recapitulation begins in D minor and goes to and stays in F major. In the first movement, the change from D minor to F major corresponds to a change in the nature of the temporal process. In the fifth movement, there is no such change; indeed, its temporal process is one in which the difference between what is, what has been and what is coming is recognized but not felt: the return to F major in the fifth bar after S:8 is not experienced as an arrival of that which has been expected, but as the straightforward statement of that whose coming is so certain that there is almost no difference between its not-yet-being here and its actual occurrence.

The first and fifth movements are also tied to one another by the dotted eighth-note rhythms that are used in the first movement marches and are scattered throughout the fifth movement (see Figure 60). In the first movement, this figure propels a passage which

FIGURE 60
Mahler, Third Symphony

exemplifies goal-directedness (because its cadences, dividing it into four-bar groups, are mobile) and which also exemplifies futurelessness (because each group is only loosely connected to the next). In the fifth movement, this motif again associates itself with moving toward goals. The goals are reached, but each time the course to the goal meets no impediment. There is no sense of struggle or drama. The exemplified temporality is of a piece with the process projected by the movement's tonal relations: the distinction between what is and what is coming is real, yet the passage from the one to the other meets so little resistance that there is almost no point in making the distinction. Thus, it is more unambiguously goal-directed than its first-movement prototype, and at the same time the distinction between present and future is more unambiguously set aside. It is as though the angels' intellectual knowledge of the distinction between present and future made no impact on the concrete quality of any given present.

Such is the way angels experience temporal contrasts. It is different from human temporality, different enough that humans may find it repugnant. Men and women do not want to be angels: the cherubic heaven sits so lightly to so much of reality that to humans it may seem boring and insubstantial.

Thus, several important aspects of the fifth movement — its tonal scheme, its two central motifs and its temporality — recall and at the same time recast aspects of the first movement. The Finale, through its motivic connections with the first and fifth movements, alludes not only to both of these movements but also to their relationship to each other. More specifically, the last movement appeals to the temporality of the fifth and its contrast to the temporality of the first. But the Finale also transcends both of those temporalities.

The opening passage of the Adagio consists of nine subphrases, whose organization is sketched in Figure 61. The anacrustic groups

FIGURE 61
Sketch of Mahler, Third Symphony, Finale

Score no.			1			2			3
No. of bars	4	4	4	4	4	4	4	4	5
Subphrase	*a*	*b*	*c*	*d*	*e*	*f*	*g*	*h*	*i*

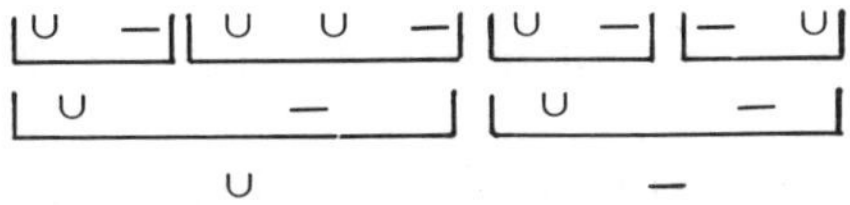

on all three architectonic levels push forward as forcefully as does the prototype of the passage, bars 1—4 of the first movement, and as do the anacrustic subphrases in the recapitulation march of the first movement. In each anacrusis the coming future is not merely relevant; it is conspicuously relevant. The contrast between what is and what is coming is a continuouly palpable aspect of what is.

At the same time, this passage shares with its prototype in the fifth movement an absence of struggle toward or longing for that which is expected. It is as though the present is so fulfilling that no coming event can enrich it, even though the coming event may satisfy an expectation that is strongly felt in the present.[27] This extraordinary combination of fulfillment and non-fulfillment is the most important aspect of the chorale. It is perhaps felt most vividly at the beginning of subphrase *d*. For at this point a four-bar thetic subphrase is expected; what we get, however, is another anacrusis, yet the non-fulfillment of the expectation is not experienced as frustration or even as a temporary inhibition that makes fulfillment, when it comes, more intensely satisfying. The non-fulfillment at *d* does not intensify the push toward what is coming precisely because it, like the other anacruses, is as intrinsically satisfying as it is forward moving.

Particularly here, but also throughout the chorale, the way the future impinges on the present in the first-movement prototype is combined with the way the future makes itself known in but has no effect on the present in the fifth-movement prototype, and the apparent contradiction between these two ways of being toward the future is transcended. If the one is an aspect of the temporal process that characterizes human consciousness and the other is an aspect of the temporality characterizing angelic consciousness, then the integration of the two must suggest a new mode of consciousness. This new kind of consciousness is barely intimated, however, before the music projecting it is juxtaposed to music of a very different sort, music in which non-arrival so intensely and painfully impinges on the present that it seems to challenge the validity of the chorale's temporal process. Evidently, the new kind of temporal process must either prove strong enough to repudiate the non-fulfillment experienced in the contrasting section, or it must somehow accommodate it too by undergoing some sort of development.

(3) Allusions in the Finale to the First and Fourth Movements

The passage that introduces an element of pain begins at S:4, the second part of section one. At first, the passage consists primarily of melodic and rhythmic fragments from the opening passage, reworked using a minor scale (compare, for example, the chorale's subphrase *d* to the first four bars after S:4, and the opening measure of the movement to the basses at S:5 and the horns at 6 after S:6). But beginning at 7 bars before S:7, a different motif gradually insinuates itself into the foreground. This motif consists of a rising scale followed by a downward droop. It has already appeared in the first movement (see Figure 62). In the fourth movement it is restated, transformed by its new context, in connection with the texts, "deeper than daytime imagined" (S:5), "Deep is its [the world's] woe" (S:8), "Woe speaks, Perish" (S:9) and "Yet all joy wills eternity — deep, deep eternity" (S:10). By using this motif, the sixth movement conjures up the first and fourth movements and their interrelationship. The sixth appeals to the way the fourth movement, like the fifth, transforms an aspect of the first movement. But the sixth also carries this transformation one step further.

In the first movement, the motif shown in Figure 62 resembles fruitless striving in that it moves forward energetically but conveys no sense of direction, and no goal is actualized; the motif participates in those passages of the first movement to which coming musical events are both relevant and irrelevant. In the fourth movement, the striving motif always comes just after a musical gesture that is

FIGURE 62
Mahler, Third Symphony

futureless in the sense that over it there lingers a mysterious impulse which is radically different from either a cause or a decision and whose outcome is to be sharply distinguished from the future of a cause or a decision. These futureless gestures provide appropriate aural images for particular words in Nietzsche's text.

They use two motifs that are also derived from the first movement. The first of these (shown in Figure 63) depicts the sleep of the

FIGURE 63
Mahler, Third Symphony

human race, cradled within the inert matter out of which it emerges. It is a restatement of the motif used at S:1 in the first movement to close the future-directed opening horn call with an utter futurelessness. The other motif (shown in Figure 64) depicts the mysterious

FIGURE 64
Mahler, Third Symphony, fourth movement

evocation of mankind out of its primordial sleep. The motif's two archaic progressions (or non-progressions) seems to suggest how utterly uncanny it is that humans, with their self-consciousness and its ability to plan ahead and synthesize what is expected with what is present, should come into being. Each of these two progressions compresses into two chords the entire harmonic progression of the first movement: the root of the second chord is a third above the root of the first, just as the first movement rises a third (from D to F) as it changes from an ambiguous blend of future-directedness and futurelessness into an explicit and undeniable future-directedness that characterizes self-awareness.

This mysterious evocation is restated at S:7, and the repetition divides the fourth movement into two parts. The first part begins with gestures that are melodically vague; as it unfolds, steps toward attaining melodic shape (using texts that tell of man awakening from the deep midnight: "What does deep midnight say?" "out of a deep dream I am awakened" and ". . . than the daytime imagined") alternate with steps backward toward melodic vagueness (on the texts, "I was sleeping" and "The world is deep, deeper . . .").[28] This part ends with the striving motif in the violins, soaring and almost reaching.

The second part makes explicit the sense in which the world is deeper than daytime imagined. It is a twofold sense: her woe is so great that it speaks, Perish, and yet her joy is so great that it wills eternity. Daytime, when things like flowers and animals are clear and definite entities, cannot imagine the capacity for either such woe or such joy as that which accompanies humans and their mysterious, future-embracing consciousness when it mysteriously emerges out of the deep midnight.

The motifs setting both the clause mentioning woe and the clause mentioning joy are derived from the first movement. The associations these motifs bring with them enrich the meaning of both woe and joy. The music setting "Deep is her woe" (Figure 65c) has appeared in the first movement at the point in section one where the opening horn call begins to transform itself from a future-directed into a futureless gesture (Figure 65a), and in sections two and four where the future is both relevant and irrelevant (Figure 65b). The music setting "Woe speaks, Perish" (Figure 65d) is the inversion of this motif. The image of woe presented here thus associates itself with both future-directedness and futurelessness and with the transformation of the one into the other. The association makes sense when we remember that, according to Schopenhauer, woe comes about because human consciousness, unlike non-consciousness and more explicitly than semi-consciousness, projects itself ahead of itself, and then experiences either the frustration of failure or the disillusionment of success; either way, consciousness expects a future than turns out to be ultimately empty, and in this new sense consciousness becomes futureless again.

The music setting "yet all joy wills eternity" (Figure 65f) is the striving motif from the first movement (Figure 65e), which also appears several times in the orchestra part of the fourth movement before it is used with this text. The use of this motif for "joy wills eternity" brings its blend of future-directedness with futurelessness to bear on this text. Thus the experience of joy, as this passage projects it, both acknowledges that ultimately the future is empty and yet still sustains expectation. Indeed, joy depends on expectation. In other words, joy is so profound — deeper than daytime or sorrow imagines — that, in spite of the ultimate emptiness of the future, expecting and striving for new occasions of happiness is as much a quality of human experience as is the futurelessness born of woe. In finding joy deeper than sorrow, Nietzsche and Mahler are repudiating Schopenhauer's basically pessimistic view of life and replacing it with a more ambiguous posture.

Although joy has the last word in the text, and although the movement's most sharply defined melodic shape is attained on this text, the orchestral closing dwells on the dreadful ambiguity of the woeful-joyful human condition. At the end, the music lapses back into the rocking which, as at the beginning of the movement, is the image of humanity cradled within the dark midnight of earth.

Such is the history of the motif that appears in the horns at 7 before S:7 in the Adagio-Finale: joy willing eternity (fourth movement) and striving in a context where it is not clear that striving makes sense (first movement). In the sixth movement, appearing in a minor-mode context and heading toward blatant, repeated

FIGURE 65
Mahler, Third Symphony

dissonances, it suggests joy willing a future with an intensity that is so excessive as to be painful. This intensity contrasts sharply to the sense of fulfillment within continuing expectation that has pervaded the opening chorale.

At the end of the section, the pain subsides even though no resolution is reached. Its contrast to the chorale, however, persists; the conflict is a continuing force that affects the rest of the movement. Among the signs of its effect are the attempts within the next passage (S:9 to S:16) to absorb the striving and pain without vitiating the serene mood created by restating the opening passage. For the violins in 3 before S:12 restate the striving motif and then, in the second through fourth measures after S:12, play it in an inverted form.

A still more significant sign of its effect is the way the second section begins. It opens with a somewhat embellished version of the first section's subphrase *c;* that is, it opens with what had been a consequent phrase, a phrase that actualizes a summoned future, as though S:9 were the future toward which the striving motif has been directing itself with such overwhelming intensity that S:7 to S:8. But of course it is not. Instead, it is itself a future-evoking phrase. One expects that future at S:10, for in section two, as in section one, the music organizes itself into paired four-bar phrases, and the first of these functions as an eight-bar antecedent (see Figure 66).

The consequent that we expect does not come at S:10. Yet the

FIGURE 66
Sketch of Mahler, Third Symphony, Finale

Score no.	9		10		11		12	
No. of bars	4	4	4	4	4	4	4	5
Subphrase	*A*	*B*	*C*	*D*	*E*	*F*	*G*	*H*

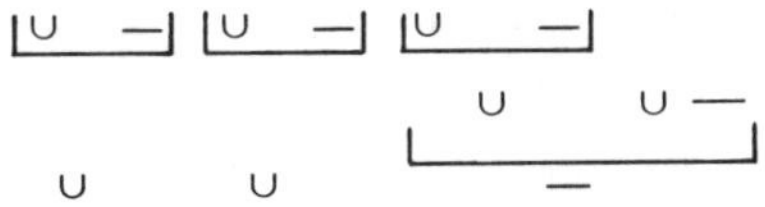

sense of fulfillment is so great that the temporary delay does not, because nothing could, intensify expectation. This phenomenon has already been experienced in the first section (at subphrase *d*). In the second section, it happens not only at subphrase *C* (S:10) but also at subphrase *G* (S:12). That it happens twice makes us feel that the resultless intensity experienced at S:8 has seeped over into this passage and manifests itself in this way as well as by beginning with a consequent phrase and by quoting the striving motif.

Just as the passage expressing a painful excess of intensity within the first section draws its motifs from the fourth movement where striving is associated with joy willing eternity (which in turn derives it from the first movement), so the second part of the second section, its climax (S:20 to S:21) in particular, is motivically related to the moment in the fourth movement where striving is associated with woe (which likewise derives it from the first movement; see Figure 65a, b). The climax of each section thus elaborates one pole of the ambiguity of the joyful-woeful human condition. Together, they project the totality of this ambiguity, which is intensified by its contrast to the chorale-like passages.

In the third section, as already noted, the striving motif asserts itself (at 5 before S:23) precipitously — without warning, without a transition. Here, as in the climax to the first section, the painful intensity and the intense pain that characterize human self-consciousness are explicitly linked with the will to bring a joyful future into actual existence: we cannot not will joy, and we cannot actualize what joy wills.

This negative aspect of the temporal process that inheres in human self-consciousness has appeared several times during the course of the symphony, each time more openly and dreadfully than the time before. It has been implied by the somewhat superficial ebullience if not banality of the tunes used in the first movement's marches, where future-directedness first unambiguously emerges. But if the triteness of these tunes implies the negative aspect of human consciousness, it does so only dimly: the implication is all but lost in the marches' glorious climaxes. The negative aspect of human consciousness is more apparent in the dark ambiguities of the fourth movement where humanity, willing a future, woe and joy are all linked to one another, each concept modifying the others. The climax of the symphony's presentation of this negative aspect is at S:24 of the Finale: here the horror of being human is at its most explicit, forceful and inescapable.

(4) Allusions to the First, Fourth and Fifth Movements in the
      Last Section of the Finale

In the last section of the Finale, we are again invited to live in a temporality in which being fulfilled and being directed toward the future are both possible. As in the beginning of the movement, once again (S:26) the motif is derived from the angels' song in the fifth movement. But while the angels brush aside pain as though they can only intellectually imagine it and not emotionally experience it, not even empathetically, and while the beginning of the movement has not yet countenanced the pain that is more intense at each of the three climaxes (S:7, S:20 and S:24), this final statement gives pain full recognition. As an equal counterpoint to the angelic motif in the trumpet, the trombone states the striving motif. Its connotation, however, is radically changed, for it takes on the rhythm of the angelic motif, with the result that its striving is relieved of the sort of longing by which fulfillment is postponed to the future and the present is endowed with only anticipatory fulfillments.

Like the three previous chorale passages, this one is organized into paired four-bar subphrases. As before, the first subphrase in each pair summons a future and, apparently paradoxically, is so rich and satisfying that it seems to need no future to fulfill it. The primary difference between this section and its predecessors is that the phenomenon of postponing fulfillment without intensifying expectation, which occurs once in the first section (at subphrase *d*) and twice in the second (at subphrases *C* and *G*) happens here with every eight-bar phrase. Another way to describe this passage is to say that each of the six eight-bar phrases begins and ends as an antecedent phrase (see Figure 67).

This process inverts the process in the first movement where subphrases begin as an antecedent and end as a consequent. Those subphrases (for example, subphrase *e* in the exposition march [7 to 10 after S:21], subphrase *j* in the exposition [S:24 to 5 after S:24] and subphrase *l* in the exposition [10 to 13 after S:24]) project a

FIGURE 67
Sketch of Mahler, Third Symphony, Finale

Score no.	26				27	28	29			30		
No. of bars	4	4	4	4	4	4	4	4	4	4	4	4	4
Subphrase	*a'*	*b'*	*c'*	*d'*	*e'*	*f'*	*g'*	*h'*	*i'*	*j'*	*k'*	*l'*	*m'*

temporality that mediates between one to which the future is relevant and one to which it is not. What is remarkable about the temporality of the phrases of the Finale's closing section is not, however, that they are unambiguously future-directed but that each postponement of the arrival of the expected future — that is, each time an antecedent is followed not by a consequent but by another antecedent — is not experienced as disappointing a hope or as intensifying a longing or as increasing forward pressure. In short, what is remarkable about this temporal process is that the richness of present wholeness is evidently too complete to permit any non-fulfillment to lessen it. It is as though the striving that characterizes the painful passages between statements of the chorale is brought forward into the closing section in all the strength it exerts elsewhere but with an entirely different effect: because fulfillment is felt continuously here, the striving is more like growth within fulfillment than growth toward fulfillment.

Serenity is combined with change, tranquility with development and forward pressure, and richness with a palpable absence. But the fusion of serenity, tranquility and richness with change, development and absence is not paradoxical, for the temporal process is one in which these are not experienced as opposites. In the temporal process that seems to be implicit in our usual concept of our consciousness, they are, of course, mutually exclusive, and must be experienced alternately, or, perhaps, they may be experienced simultaneously but on different levels. Ordinarily, serenity is the opposite of anticipating change because looking ahead to change is always experienced either as a deficiency in the present (what one expects is what one presently lacks but longs for) or as a decline (what one expects is the unwanted falling away from the consummation being experienced in the present). Where expectation involves experiencing a lack, the woe of the present is complicated by hoping for the joyful to come; where expectation involves anticipating a decline, the joy of the present is complicated by dreading its loss in the future. In our ordinary consciousness of ourselves and of the world in which we are engaged, serenity seems to be possible only when expectation is somehow suppressed. In differing from this sort of temporal process, the last section of the Finale suggests a transformation of temporality and accordingly of consciousness itself. The final section more extensively exemplifies the new mode of consciousness that the Finale's first chorale has intimated.

What is here called the ordinary concept of ordinary self-consciousness incorporates the assumptions about human nature entertained by the liberal party in Austria, which gained political ascendancy in the period just before Mahler began to compose, and by the upper-middle-class stratum of society, whose interests and self-understanding the liberal party represented.[29] Some of Mahler's Viennese contemporaries wrote political tracts and fiction that excoriated these assumptions about human nature and proposed a reconstructed consciousness. Their critique of the liberal self-consciousness and what they adumbrated to replace and surpass it may be compared and contrasted to the transfiguration that Mahler is suggesting. The following paragraphs will draw this contrast and use it to specify more precisely the kind of temporality that Mahler's Finale exemplifies.

The liberal self understands itself as rationally directed toward a future whose value will surpass that of the present. The maximally valued future will be one that fully actualizes the rational self. Until such actualization takes place, the self is somewhat disembodied, for it is somewhat alienated from its manifestations. Yet in all its various manifestations, be they more or be they less adequate, it is always identical to itself in the sense that in any given situation there is always only one truly rational thing to do and thus, to the extent that one is rational, one does and thinks what any other rational self would do. In moving toward and embodying goals, the marches in Mahler's first movement duplicate this temporality — and its naive optimism.

Mahler's fourth movement transforms several aspects of the first movement. It confirms future-directedness, but replaces naive optimism with the explicit statement that while the emergence of self-consciousness out of unconscious nature is wondrous and mysterious, it also involves an awareness of the future that is unsettling — an awareness that is incompatible with serenity. Similarly, but more pointedly and bitterly, the Pan Germans and Christian Socialists, the most powerful anti-liberal parties in Austria by the turn of the century, were disillusioned with the ideal of the rational self. They too confirmed future-directedness (they, like the liberals, sought a future that would ameliorate the woes of the present), but they regarded the notion that the impetus toward the future came from the rational planning of a ration self as naively optimistic. In agreement with Nietzsche's poem and Mahler's fourth movement, they understood that future-directedness impinged woefully as well as joyfully on the present. Rational future-directedness was therefore to be rejected.

Like Mahler's sixth movement, they envisioned a consciousness that would transcend the ambiguities of rational, liberal self-consciousness. Their presuppositions, however, contrast sharply with those of the Mahler movement, and the contrast illumines Mahler's vision. For the antiliberals, rationality was to be rejected in favor of emotion. The impetus toward the future was to be provided by the feeling of belonging to a community and losing one's will in its will.[30] Such feelings were to be aroused through what the liberal self had to regard as acrimony and demagoguery. Precisely how the community was to be defined was, of course, understood variously by the Pan Germans and the Christian Socialists, and these differences prevented them from working together effectively. But in common with one another, they seemed to think that transforming consciousness by immersing the individual, rational, future-directed self in the communal willing would blunt the distinction between the present and the future at the same time that it would provide an impetus toward a better future (though obviously not better by the criteria of rationality). In Mahler's transformed consciousness, rationality is to be transcended, not replaced. The distinction between the present and what is coming is vividly maintained, while the thrust toward the future is fused with the richness of the present.

Schnitzler's plays and stories provide another critique of the liberal self and another redoing of self-consciousness. In general, his characters come from the same social stratum as the liberal politicians and think of themselves as the liberals did: rational individuals rationally planning rational futures. But, as Schnitzler forces us to see, they are also motivated by impulses which contradict the rational ideal and whose outcomes deviate from those of rational decisions.

Because these characters cannot give up the appearance of rationality either to others or to themselves, they are driven to both hypocrisy and, what is more ruinous, self-deception. Occasionally, they come to see themselves for what they are, but never before they recognize that the process of destruction has become irreversible.

In some of his later works, and especially in *Die Komödie der Verführung* (1923), Schnitzler creates characters who come from the same social stratum yet are more nearly ready to acknowledge the place of impulse in their passage from past to future. Consequently, they seem to have given up the liberals' attempt to actualize a rational future or to direct themselves toward fulfillment. Instead of experiencing the distinction between present and future as one between a present deficiency vis-à-vis coming fulfillment, they always see fulfillments — rare as they are — as characterizing the past. The consummation of an affair cannot be duplicated, the future can only be a falling away from fulfillment, a lapse from the joyful to the woeful, and consequently the relationship is better terminated than extended into an evitable deterioration. Fulfillment must be said to characterize only the past, certainly not the future, and not even the present because one does not realize the consummation is occurring; only afterwards does one see that it has occurred.

Although both Schniztler and Mahler at first allude to and then move beyond the presuppositions of the liberal self, they differ significantly in what they move to. Schnitzler rejects these presuppositions; Mahler transcends them. In *Die Komödie der Verführung,* fulfillment can be ascribed only to the past; in the kind of temporality exemplified by the final section of Mahler's sixth movement, it is possible for fulfillment to characterize what is, what has been and what is coming, all three. This transfigured temporality is one that would be as unintelligible to Schnitzler's characters as to the liberal self.

3. *The Symphony as a Whole*

The temporal process projected by the Finale can be further amplified and specified by noting its relationships to all five prior movements. As they are occurring, these movements relate themselves to one another loosely. The Finale restructures these relationships and pulls the symphony into a tightly coherent whole. And it turns out that understanding the sense in which the six movements constitute a unity coincides with understanding the transformation of temporality and consciousness effected by the Finale.

Mahler directs that no pause interrupt the succession of the last three movements. They form a group. The fourth and fifth movements are in many respects opposite to one another: the fourth gropes continuously toward melodic shape but never attains contours that are crisp and definite, while the fifth has melodic shapes that are definite but do not grow. Because both movements associate themselves motivically with the first movement, their temporal processes represent two opposite ways of reworking and transforming the temporality projected by the first movement. The last movement transcends the contrast between the fourth and the fifth. Its chorale passages have both the forward direction of the striving motif in the fourth movement and the unconcern for arrivals that characterizes the fifth movement. The Finale's chorales have a shape that is both definite (like the fifth) and growing (like the fourth). And like both of them, its temporal process differs sharply from that of the first movement even though its most important motif comes from the opening fanfare.

The tonal centers of the successive movements are related to one another, and these relationships help to group the movements into a whole. The first movement begins in D minor and ends in F major. The second movement is in A, and the third is in C. For the most part, the fourth movement is in the Hypo-mixolydian mode, using the notes of the D major scale and A as the *finalis*. The fifth is in F major with a D minor middle section. And the Finale is in D major, without a trace of F.

The fact that the first movement ends in a key different from its opening might be construed as an instability, a harmonic tension that the last three movements resolve by reestablishing D. The interpretation does not do justice to the first movement. For in terms of its own process, its *terminus* is very much the F major section. This section, with its clearly future-directed temporality, establishes itself as the goal of the futureless and ambiguously future-directed passages, which in and of themselves point to no particular goal or resolution. When the F major closing establishes itself as a goal where none had been expected, nothing about this ending suggests that a return to D would have made a more final closure. From the perspective of the close of the first movement, one hears F as the main tonality and the D opening as an introduction to the F, rather than hearing the F as a departure from the basic tonality of D, to which one would feel the need for a return.[31] Only the superficial ebullience of the march tunes makes the end of the first movement a less than totally

convincing closure. Their military connotations seem inappropriate
to the mystery of the evocative impulse brooding over inert matter
and the grandeur of that impulse yanking matter not only into life,
but into self-aware life. The inappropriateness may be considered a
defect: if Mahler wanted a Bacchic procession, why did he use the
sound and rhythms of a regimental band? Or the inappropriateness
may intimate that self-consciousness is not only marvelous but also
somehow problematic and that its temporal process needs to be
transcended. This ambivalent attitude toward self-consciousness
becomes explicit in the fourth movement.

The second movement, in A, can confirm the tonicity of either
F or D equally well. At its end we expect a return to F at least as
much as we expect a return to D.

The third movement, a Scherzo, is more complicated. It begins
and ends in C, which confirms the tonicity of F and, by itself, would
make us expect a return to F. The fourth movement, in D, would
then be heard as a (not surprising) delay of this return, and the fifth
movement, in F, as the return and the putative Finale. What compli-
cates the situation is the Trio in the Scherzo, a posthorn solo. It is in
F, and seems to establish F as the third movement's tonic, C having
been an introductory key, for the main theme returns in F after the
posthorn solo, and stays almost entirely in F. After the return is
complete, the posthorn (which presumably can play *only* in F)
comes back. In S:26 to S:30 motifs of the Scherzo theme are blended
with elements of the posthorn Trio. This passage sounds like a coda,
and the movement seems about to end in F, when C suddenly
reinstates itself, and the movement ends in the key with which it began.

If the third movement ended in F, its tonality, like that of the
second movement, would be as possible in an overall harmonic
scheme based on D as one based on F. While a third-movement
closing on F would not absolutely predetermine that the symphony
close in either F or D, ending the third movement on F instead of C
would have made D the more predictable choice for the tonality
of the Finale. That the third movement does in fact end in C supports
an overall harmonic scheme based on F more straightforwardly than
one based on D. Thus, the fact that the third movement slips back
into C means that the Finale in D has more resistance to overcome
to establish itself; it and its transfigured temporal process are more
like a miracle.[32]

But in another respect, the tonal scheme of the third movement
offers a supporting analogy to the D Finale: that it begins in C
(minor), moves to and seems about to end in F, then suddenly yet

convincingly returns to C (major) is analogous to the way the symphony as a whole begins in D (minor), moves to and seems about to end in F (at the end of the fifth movement), then suddenly and convincingly returns to D.

While the analogy is clearly audible and palpably supports the finality of the Finale, it also raises the question of what "return" means both within the third movement and within the symphony as a whole. For if the movement to F in the first movement is not experienced as a departure from D, but rather as the establishment of that which D introduces, then the move to D at the end of the symphony cannot be experienced as a return, but rather as the establishment of that which the F of the first and fifth movements and the A of the second movement introduce. It would seem that the identity of the opening D with the closing D is more a coincidence than a return, or a return of a very unusual kind.

The same sort of return takes place when C reestablishes itself at the end of the third movement, and this event is a clue to understanding the special kind of return that takes place at the end of the symphony. In order to grasp the nature of the return within the third movement, one must first grasp the nature of the departure that happens when the posthorn Trio in F moves us away from the Scherzo in C. The Trio departs from the Scherzo most significantly in its different way of relating coming to present events and in its different allusions to ideas that are extrinsic to the music.[33]

The most obvious difference between the two sections is in their textures. The posthorn section is a straightforward melody with a background accompaniment, while the Scherzo consists of a variety of voices placed on top of one another, overlapping one another, answering one another and exchanging places with one another. The difference in texture is of a piece with the difference in phrase structure, which, in turn, is the clearest index of the difference in the way the future in each section impinges on the present.

The Scherzo opens with a background pizzicato in second violins and violas (see Figure 68). The clarinet enters in the third measure with what might be the start of a foreground melody, but turns out to be another strand of background texture. The piccolo enters in the fifth measure with what might be still another strand of the background, but turns out to be foreground melody. It spins forth for seven measures with no sense of moving toward an end or toward anything very specific. In bar 12 the piccolo is replaced, neither expectedly nor surprisingly, by three clarinets, which chirp for two bars and then yield the foreground to the flute for two bars. The

FIGURE 68
Mahler, Third Symphony, third movement

flute ends what now, and only now, proves to have been a four-bar subphrase (bars 12–15), which is separated by the change of timbre from the previous seven bars (piccolo, 5–11) and paired to them. The decisive closure in bar 15 endows bars 5–11 with a goal and organizes them, although only when they are over, into two overlapping four-bar groups: 5–8 and 8–11. By participating in both groups, bar 8 obscures both the grouping and the thrust to what turns out in bar 15 to have been the goal of both groups. The obscurity prevents any sense of what may be coming from impinging on 5–11, but still 5–11 constitute the musical past of bars 12–15. In short, during 5–11 the present seems detached from the future, but at bar 15 the present is tightly related to its past. To hear bars 1–15 is not to hear an end being summoned, yet because the passage as a whole proves to have more regularity than one realizes while it is going on, the end seems to have been summoned. Because one experiences the regularity only as a reflection on a finished process it cannot exemplify a process like that of a self in a present consciously evoking a future. Instead, the passage more nearly resembles the process that philosophers like Kant and Schelling attribute to nature: it pursues goals, but it does so unconsciously; it enacts purposes but does not know that it has them.

Or knows it only dimly, as we want to say if we compare this theme with the opening theme of the second movement (Figure 69). Here too a goal is reached (bar 19) that is neither expected nor surprising. Salient in this process is the way bars 4 and 13 seem to

FIGURE 69
Mahler, Third Symphony, second movement

close subphrases, ending them unstably so that 1—4 and 10—13 seem to evoke answering subphrases that will end more stably. Even more salient is the way bars 5—6 and 14—15 cast shadows over the future events that 1—4 and 10—13 might have been generating. Because bar 5 repeats bar 4, bars 5—9 seem as much simply to continue 1—4 as to form an answering group. And bar 14 seems to begin a group that will answer the future-evoking group in 10—13, but then bar 16 seems just as much to begin the answering group, and 14—15 are left in a never-never land between beginning a consequent subphrase and spinning forth out of 10 13. Through continuous growth, which is articulated into subphrases, a goal is reached in bar 19, but because the special quality of 5—6 and 14—15 significantly attenuates the forward thrust that 1—4 and 10—13 might have, the goal does not impinge at all clearly on the process of growth until it is over. While in the third movement's opening passage there are discrete motifs that begin and end and while its subphrases end in bars 11 and 15 with a clarity that is unexpectedly crisp, in the second movement's opening passage a single motif unfolds continuously, and one both feels that there are subphrases (hence reaching the goal is not surprising) and also feels uncertain about where they are, even in retrospect (hence the goal is not really expected either). When the second movement's main theme reappears at S:6, it is shorn of its first two bars; at S:14 it reappears with its first three bars missing. In neither recapitulation, however, do the missing measures create an imbalance or a tension. That neither reprise sounds truncated dramatizes the fact that the opening passage sounds as much like a continuous spinning forth as like a series of future-evoking subphrases.[34] The intermingling of the two ways of moving along keeps both of them from clearly projecting themselves toward a future. It is not so much that it is unclear toward what future the music is moving as that the impact of any future whatever is persistently unclear. Consequently, the second movement's opening differs even more than the third movement's from processes like human self-consciousness in which expecting a future is indispensable.

The posthorn solo in the third movement is much more like a process in which a self-conscious agent posits and moves toward a goal and awareness of the goal impinges on the moments preceding its realization. While in the Scherzo we get (or have gotten) clear subphrase cadences (clearer than in the flower movement) without having expected them, in the posthorn section we both expect and also get cadences. Its process is not, however, exactly like that of a self-aware person, for the first subphrase is tucked away inside the introductory horn call and grows out of it in such a way that we do not know a subphrase — a group with a goal — is taking shape until it is over (at 8 after S:14). Thereafter, the four-bar groupings are all responsive to their past and indicative of their future, even though the expected future does not always take place (the third four-bar group seems to evoke a paired subphrase, but in fact does not, and instead forms a group with the first two subphrases, and the three of them together evoke another pair of subphrases; see Figure 70).

FIGURE 70
Sketch of Mahler, Third Symphony, third
movement, 5 bars after S:14 to 26 bars
after S:14

No. of bars:	4	4	4	4	6
Subphrase:	*a*	*b*	*c*	*d*	*e*

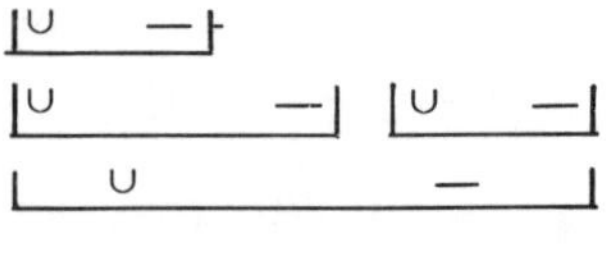

The differences among the second movement's theme, the third movement's Scherzo theme and the third movement's posthorn theme may be likened to the differences among the relevance of the future in a flower's awareness, an animal's awareness and a dreaming human's consciousness.[35] We know that Mahler himself associated the second movement with the flowers, and the third, based on a

Wunderhorn song, composed before 1892, whose text laments the death of a cuckoo and rejoices in the song of a nightingale, he associated with animals. The posthorn is associated with people who live in the woods and hills, as it signals the arrival of the mailcoach down the lane, around the bend, over the hill where the coach cannot be seen.[36] (Mahler directs that the posthorn player be offstage, and at the beginning of the solo play "as from a far distance.") The section suggests a world that cannot be seen, where things — like things in dreams — have a presence without having the definite shape and tangible form that come only with light. The future in such a world is as different from the future in the animal world, where there is joy and pain but not desire and struggle, as it is from the future in the world of fully human consciousness, where awareness of the future entails striving and disappointment as well as happiness and pain and where the future, whether hoped for or dreaded, is thus explicitly and palpably synthesized with every present. The future in the posthorn's world is in a position intermediate between the future in the animal and human worlds. In this important sense, the posthorn section provides a transition between the third and the fourth movements.

When the dream world begins, it seems to be simply juxtaposed to and contrasted with the world of cuckoos, chipmunks and bears. But then, in the section from S:17 up to S:22, the animals' world is restated in the key of the dream's world. The contrast between the two moods is considerably attenuated by the use of the same tonal center. It is as though the music, instead of contrasting the two worlds, progressed from the one to the other and stayed in the second by transforming the first into the second. One is reminded of fairy tales in which animals are endowed with quasi-human characteristics. This transformation, however, proves unstable. From S:31 to S:32 we are swept from F back to C.

The gesture at S:31 has two important connections with the first movement. It vividly recalls the gesture from six bars before S:29 to S:29 in the first movement's exposition march, which sweeps us from the goal-directed temporality characteristic of human self-consciousness back into the ambiguous relationship to the future that characterizes the first two sections of the first movement and pre-human (and even pre-botanical!) temporality. And the horn calls that begin in the fifth bar after S:31 in the third movement recall the brass motifs that are used during the first two sections of the first movement to project precisely that blend of futurelessness and future-directedness that exemplify the impossible combination of vital impulse with inert stuff. These associations are enough to make us suppose that the progression from C to F, carried out by the post-horn Trio and the Scherzo's new version in the posthorn's key, is being rejected and swept away. Yet what emerges at S:32 is not a simple return to the opening material. Although the animals insist, as it were, on their own world, and restate it in their own key (C), it is not the case that the contrast between Scherzo and Trio is reinstated (as in the typical return of a Scherzo after its Trio). Rather, the Scherzo and the posthorn theme are integrated: the open fifths and arpeggios of the posthorn theme gradually turn into the sound of the animals and maintain their presence as an integral part of the final version of the Scherzo theme. In short, the progression from the Scherzo to the posthorn is denied (at S:31), and the contrast between them is also denied (at S:32), for instead of returning to the Scherzo theme, the movement ends in the animal world transformed by the presence of dreaming humans in it. One is reminded of fairy tales in which humans are set in the animal world and endowed with quasi-animal characteristics.

This strange return is precisely analogous to the sense in which the Adagio-Finale is a return.[37] By returning to D, the Finale sweeps away the progression from D to F made by the fourth and fifth movements (a progression already made within the first movement). But the Finale does not simply return to the world of the fourth movement or the opening of the first movement, both of which are in D; it does not leave the fifth movement as a contrasting gesture sitting off to one side of the symphony's central process. Instead, the Finale derives motifs from both of the prior movements (which in turn derive them from the first movement), and its temporal process resembles both of theirs and transcends their contrast. The Finale is a return that, like the return at the end of the third movement, holds in force both that to which and that from which it is returning.

It is in this sense that the Finale pulls the symphony together. It does not hold the symphony together in the sense of being the goal toward which the earlier contrasting sections press for their resolution, for the difference between one movement and the next is not ex-perienced as a conflict requiring a resolution. Indeed, it may seem to signify progress. For as listeners are being taken from one movement to the next, they may suppose that each movement is able to make a place for itself because it signifies a step forward to a higher level of consciousness. Such a step forward would imply some sort of deficiency in that beyond which the step is being taken, and this putative inadequacy, retrospectively recognized though it be, may be taken as the propulsion from one movement to the next. The end of this line of progress would be the Bell Chorus. It is in F, and, coming after the F—A—C—D of the first four movements convincingly culminates the strong tonal progression. One may well take it to be the Finale (not unlike the Finale of the Fourth Symphony).

Consequently, for the Adagio even to begin may be something of a surprise (or an anticlimax). Unlike the second through fifth movements, which process from one to the next, the Adagio does not signify a step forward. Instead it holds together the temporal processes of the previous movements; it shows that the various preceding temporalities are all compatible and that the reality of one kind of temporality does not after all imply a denial or rejection of — or a progress beyond — the previous one. It restructures the mutual relationships among the preceding movements: by returning to the opening tonal center it undercuts the putative progress culminating in the Bell Chorus and supercedes its finality; by holding together the temporal processes of the intervening movements, it allows none of them to fall to the status of an interrupting or delaying contrast. From the perspective of the Adagio, the listener realizes that the propelling impetus from one movement to the next is not the possibility of progress to successively higher stages of consciousness, but the possibility of each of them existing and all of them existing together.

In other words, as we move through the symphony, we think we are moving along a straight line to a climax. At the end of the symphony, we recognize that we have been circling a center.[38] The impulse that moves us from one movement to the next is like the impulse that moves us from one phrase to the next in the Adagio's chorales: the impulse is not like a self struggling to actualize itself by bending a recalcitrant reality into congruence with itself, but rather like growth within fulfillment. Each movement is like an epiphany that is occasioned by a force like neither natural necessity nor moral exertion. The Finale is the recognition and celebration of this power, seen in abstraction from any particular epiphany. If the first movement exemplifies metaphorically the impossible transition from a lifeless stupor to a richly varied, living world, the Finale exemplifies metaphorically the power by which the transition is made. Mahler called this power love; he also called it God.[39]

The Adagio exemplifies this power through exemplifying a particular temporal process. It seems to draw us into this temporality; it invites us to let this temporal process — this transfiguration of the temporality involved in ordinary human consciousness — become our own.[40] In this transformed temporality, conscious striving toward goals, which is exemplified with increasing clarity by the second, third and fourth movements, does not contrast to serene fullness in the midst of change, which is exemplified by the fifth. It is a temporality in which one can be aware of the contrast between what is and what will be, but the awareness neither entails the joyful-woeful ambiguity of the fourth movement nor presupposes the emotional detachment of the fifth. It is a temporality in which what will be is evidently to be valued neither more nor less highly than the present, so that no future is to be dreaded, and the joy of expectation is no greater than the enjoyment of the present. In neither fearing the future nor expecting it to surpass the present, this temporality represents a return to the futureless and future-directed temporality of the opening, though it is a return with the difference made by the way that the intermediary temporalities have qualified and transformed both of these opposite ways of being toward the future and the way that the Finale transcends this opposition. The return is in fact a new kind of temporal process in which a new kind of futurelessness consorts with a new kind of future-directedness and neither of them attenuates the validity of the other.

Notes

1. See Bekker, *op. cit.*, pp. 105–106.

2. *Dionysian Art and Populist Politics in Austria*, (1974), pp. 133–157. In reviewing this book (*Nineteenth-Century Music*, vol. 4, no. 1 [1980], pp. 77–79, Thomas Bauman applauds McGrath's interdisciplinary approach and agrees that the Third rests on metaphysical foundations. Bauman is not convinced, however, by McGrath's argument either as a whole or in many of its details.

3. *Op. cit.*, pp. 21–22.

4. *Gustav Mahler: The Wunderhorn Years* (1975), pp. 312–318.

5. *Gustav Mahler, 1860–1911* (n.d.), pp. 15, 28. This booklet was written for the BBC's Mahler centenary broadcasts. Cooke's *Gustav Mahler: An Introduction to His Music* (1980) combines the booklet with some of Cooke's other writings on Mahler. In the 1980 edition, which is the edition elsewhere referred to in these notes, the judgment on the Third is softened: "total failure" becomes "partial failure" (p. 13). Kennedy (*op. cit.*, p. 102) takes a much more positive view of the Third, and finds that "the difficulties of the first movement have been much exaggerated."

6. Mitchell (*op. cit.*, p. 194) perhaps best sums up the matter when he writes, "Mahler was never free of doubts, torments and contradictions about his programmes — like his conducting, they were something to be resisted and denounced and yet at the same time were indispensable to him — but his own actions guaranteed that his contemporaries knew enough about his programmatic

intentions and that some sort of 'tradition' would be handed down to posterity ... One cannot discuss the early symphonies without immersing oneself in their programmes." In his article on Mahler in *The New Grove Dictionary of Music and Musicians* (1980), vol. 11, p. 516, Mitchell points out that Mahler the composer was profoundly influenced by Mahler the opera conductor. The analogy between Mahler's programs and opera plots, between the succession of his musically evoked images and dramatic progression in opera, is not merely fortuitous.

7. *Op. cit.*, p. 136.

8. Dika Newlin (*op. cit.*, p. 170) associates the fanfare with an Austrian marching song. Its similarity to the theme of the Finale in Brahms' First Symphony is probably an irrelevant coincidence. See Neville Cardus, *Gustav Mahler* ..., pp. 86, 93.

9. Probably because of the nature of this ending, La Grange calls this section "Nature's Inertia" (*op. cit.*, p. 801).

10. *The Man Without Qualities* (1953), p. xvi.

11. Mahler himself recognized the humor of these passages and thought they made the movement as a whole "humorous, even grotesque"; see Natalie Bauer-Lechner, *op. cit.*, p. 41. The regimental music, coming as it does after the weighty straining and groaning of the movement's opening sections, sounds grotesquely incongruous indeed. Freud claims that Mahler told him of a childhood incident in which Gustav's father was brutally mistreating his mother; the boy became frantic, ran out of the house, whereupon the first thing he heard was a hurdy-gurdy. According to Freud, Mahler believed that this incident accounted for the way his music sometimes goes from noble passages, inspired by deep emotions, to some commonplace melody. Freud's account is evaluated variously: Mitchell accepts it as essentially accurate, and says that Mahler was simply too hard on himself when he said that the intrusion of commonplace melodies spoiled his noblest passages (*op. cit.*, p. 74); Kennedy is skeptical about the conclusion that Freud said Mahler drew from the incident (*op. cit.*, p. 4). But however the question is eventually resolved, it is not the case that passages like the regimental marches in III/i can be exhaustively explained in terms of this incident. Whatever their origin in the composer's experience, the critic must ask about their place in the listener's experience: to what extent and in what way does the listener incorporate them into some comprehensive concept conveyed by the movement or symphony as a whole?

12. See Bauer-Lechner, *op. cit.*, p. 59, and McGrath, *op. cit.*, p. 134. Of this passage Mitchell (*op. cit.*, p. 329) writes, "Mahler obviously wanted to convey in his introduction the idea of an ice-bound Nature gradually thawing into life; and this he ingeniously does from Fig. 2 [S:2] onwards, by first exposing a texture composed of heaving, groaning motifs ... and then (around Fig. 5 [S:5] and thereafter) expanding the motifs outwards into long limbs of melody."

13. McGrath associates only the trumpet's rising stepwise motion with Schopenhauer's life-will (*op. cit.*, pp. 134–135), but in the horns' gestures as well we hear the stepwise rising figure that Philip Barford (*op. cit.*, pp. 303, 312 and *passim*) associates generally in Mahler with striving, yearning and aspiring.

14. These passages clearly instantiate what Mellers (*op. cit.*, p. 111) finds to be one of the hallmarks of Mahler's style: the way it creates a sense that melody

and harmony are at once independent of one another and yet interdependent on one another. This judgment is, of course, as impossible by the ordinary canons of coherence as the claim, made in the Introduction and in Chapter I, that sometimes Mahler writes two voices each of which is both background and foreground to the other. According to Mellers, the duality of independence and interdependence of melody and harmony is similar to the duality between Mahler's Romantic, rhapsodic, linear style and the requirements of traditional harmony and symphonic form; see pp. 112, 114.

15. Mahler's note for this section, "Pan awakens" identifies the ethereal substance as the god of fertility (as well as music), who sleeps and dreams at noonday. For a time, Mahler called the whole symphony, "A Summer Noon's Dream." See Mitchell, *op. cit.*, pp. 191, 193.

16. Here are the details of the changes in temporality that take place as the march unfolds:

Groups c through f modulate the contrast between the non-relationship of the meaninglessly juxtaposed prior sections of the movement and the very tight relationship of one phrase to the next experienced later in the movement. While the hiatuses between the movement's prior sections are so empty that they do not give even hints that anything will come, groups c through f suggest a periodic structure and a higher-level organization even though such an organization is not immediately forthcoming. For both subphrases c and e sound like antecedent phrases at their beginnings and consequent phrases at their endings, and thus preempt within themselves the function that the next groups would serve if higher-level structure were to emerge. It is extraordinary for a subphrase to be analogous to antecedent subphrases as it begins and to consequent subphrases when it ends, and this feature of subphrases c and e, more than any other feature, accounts for the way that this part of the march moves us a tiny step beyond shapelessness toward shapeliness. Both c and e begin as antecedents with a strong upbeat to their first bar (the violas' upbeat at the end of 6 after S:21 is especially important in making the beginning of e sound like the begining of an antecedent). It is probably because both of them end on the subdominant (B-flat in 2 after S:21 and 2 before S:22), instead of the more forward-pushing dominant, that they sound like consequent subphrases at their ending.

Subphrases d and f (whose tunes are similar to one another) are more like closing gestures that round out a section than like the realization of their previous subphrases' goals. Because d and f do not end more stably than c and e, respectively c–d and e–f do not make antecedent-consequent groups. At the same time, there is a hint of eight-bar grouping simply because the impulse in the violas that triggers subphrase e is so fresh that e is much more clearly separated from d than d is from c or than f is from e.

Subphrases g and h move us another small step closer to a process in which a present summons a future and responds to the past. Like c and e, g and h sound like antecedent subphrases at the beginning and consequent subphrases at the end, but in comparison to c and e, the consequent aspect is separated a little more clearly from the antecedent aspect, and the last two downbeats in each phrase almost form a consequent subphrase. Because these downbeats connote a consequent subphrase it is impossible to hear g to h or h to i as an antecedent to a consequent.

Subphrases i and j are clearly grouped with each other because of the way the tonic returns in *j* from the subdominant in *i*. But subphrase *j* is also clearly grouped with *k*: extending *j* into five measures by repeating the fourth bar gives *j*'s closing cadence a mobility that no previous subphrase has had at its ending. Thus, *j* groups itself with both the preceding and the succeeding subphrases. While prior subphrases have related themselves only loosely to either the previous or the subsequent subphrase, *j* relates itself fairly tightly to both, and, more than any of the prior subphrases in the march, exemplifies a temporal process in which the future impinges forcefully on the present.

The next few subphrases sustain without advancing the extent to which the present relates itself to previous and expected events. Subphrase *k* begins as a consequent to *j*, but it ends on the melodically mobile third degree of the scale, hence as an antecedent to *l*. Subphrase *l* begins with the same fresh impulse that separated subphrase *e* from *d* and thus cannot form a resounding consequent group. So the focus of the march up to this point is *g* — the opening fanfare redone in march time.

Because the four bars following *l* simply mark time with turns around E in the woodwinds (cf. section three at S:12) and because *m* and *n* reprise *c* and *d*, the march divides itself into two parts at this point. During the first six groups of the second part, the future steadily becomes more relevant as almost every group evokes and looks toward its future more vividly than the one before. Subphrase *o*, with its allusion to the opening fanfare, promises to be a reprise of *g* and the focus of the second half of the march, but after two bars the violins' counterpoint to the fanfare steps to the fore and ends the four-bar group with a clearly antecedent feeling. The next subphrase (*p*) extends without heightening or resolving the instability felt at the end of *o*. Subphrase *q*, like *o*, begins as though it were the arrival of that toward which the subphrases prior to it have been pushing, but it quickly transforms itself from arrival to further preparation for arrival, and *r* (unlike *n* and *p*) intensifies this push.

17. See Mitchell, *op. cit.*, p. 194, and Bauer-Lechner, *op. cit.*, p. 40.

18. The image of a parade ground is, of course, suggested by the fact that Mahler has daringly imported the sound of a military band, complete with a piercing E-flat clarinet, into his symphony. See Mitchell, *op. cit.*, pp. 326–327. The marches reminded Richard Strauss of the May Day parades in Vienna, the proletarian connotations being stronger than the military ones for him. See Cardus, *Gustav Mahler . . .*, p. 91.

19. The hiatuses between sections one, two and three may be related to the fact that for a time Mahler conceived what is now the first movement as two separate movements: an introduction ("Pan awakens") and a march ("Summer marches in"). See Knud Martner, ed., *Selected Letters of Gustav Mahler* (1979), p. 189, Mitchell, *op. cit.*, p. 191 and La Grange, *op. cit.*, p. 365. But whatever the origin of these lacunae, they must now be understood as part of the movement that Mahler actually completed, and not the movement that he thought about writing.

20. McGrath (*op. cit.*, p. 134) sees some of these gestures (namely those in section two and its reprises) as the conflict between the compulsive, blind will (the musical background) and that on which the will wishes to act. This way of describing these passages implies that the listener expects the conflict to have an outcome and that this expectation is part and parcel of experiencing these passages. This interpretation attributes to them more future-directedness than

they have in fact have. The temporal process here is more fundamentally different from both unambiguously having and unambiguously not having a future than such an interpretation recognizes.

21. *Op. cit.,* p. 120.

22. According to Bauer-Lechner (*op. cit.,* p. 59), Mahler believed that "each movement stands alone, as a self-contained and independent whole." Mahler had in mind the lack of motivic interconnections among the movements, and as Mitchell notes (*op. cit.,* p. 312), the remark was not accurate. But as a comment on the absence of a musical dynamic from one movement to the next, the remark anticipated what listeners must notice and initially find puzzling.

23. The often noted similarity of Mahler's chorale theme to the theme of the slow movement in Beethoven's String Quartet, op. 135 is too close to be accidental. Mahler's theme recaptures and perhaps even enriches the solemn joy that characterizes Beethoven's theme.

24. Mahler's treatment of weeping here is, as Mitchell notes (*op. cit.,* p. 315), one of the clearest examples of the motivic connections between the Third Symphony and the Finale of the Fourth. Compare the clarinets and horns at five bars after S:3 in III/v with the clarinets and flutes at S:5 in IV/iv. La Grange (*op. cit.,* p. 808) notes other motivic cross references between the two movements.

25. *Op. cit.,* p. 121.

26. According to La Grange (*op. cit.,* p. 366, following Bauer-Lechner, *op. cit.,* p. 60), Mahler's purpose in making the angels' music so lighthearted was to let humor represent "the ultimate that cannot be expressed in any other way."

27. Bekker, *op. cit.,* p. 133, describes the chorale as "one of those melodies by Mahler that come to periodical cadences but to no authentic close ... Each apparent ending is at once the beginning of a new progression. Together, the phrases arouse the feeling of an inexhaustible, overflowing power."

28. La Grange, *op. cit.,* p. 807, says that the movement "comes as close as any piece by Mahler to being athematic."

29. See Schorske, *op. cit.,* pp. 4—5 and *passim.*

30. See McGrath, *op. cit.,* pp. 184—187, and Schorske, *op. cit.,* ch. 3, "Politics in a New Key," pp. 116—180, and John W. Boyer, *Political Radicalism in Late Imperial Vienna* (1981).

31. It is no doubt for this reason that Mahler himself as well as the Weinberger Verlag advertisement for its first edition of the Third referred to it as a Symphony in F Major.

32. Mitchell (in his article for *The New Grove Dictionary,* vol. 11, p. 518) agrees: ". . . the ultimate D major marks the evolution of the work to an entirely new dramatic (and thus new tonal) plane."

33. Morgan, *op. cit.,* p. 76, hears the posthorn solo as a long, self-sufficient and independent section of music which is extraneous to that of the Scherzo and which sounds like an isolated moment that has "temporarily broken through from an altogether separate sphere of musical activity."

34. See Mitchell, *Gustav Mahler. The Wunderhorn Years,* pp. 320—324. The truncated reprise is one of the subtle strokes that characterize Mahler's style.

He makes brilliant use of the technique at S:18 in IV/i, at S:15 in V/ii and at S:60 in VI/iii.

35. See Bekker, *op. cit.*, p. 126.

36. The posthorn, evoking the invisible presence of both the mail from home and the passengers in the postcoach, is a typically Romantic image in the writings of Joseph von Eichendorff, Clemens Brentano and others. See, for example, Eichendorff's "Sehnsucht."

37. This important connection between the third movement and the rest of the symphony justifies the many repetitions within the Scherzo. If one does not notice this connection, the movement may sound, as it does to Cardus (*Gustav Mahler* . . ., p. 100), overdone, its length not justified by the musical material and to be explained as an "academic offering" made by a composer who is "constantly eager to prove himself an 'absolute musician.' "

38. Bekker, *op. cit.*, p. 21, describes the structure of Mahler's Second, Third, Fifth and Seventh Symphonies as a suite of movements circling and defining a center, the radius of each successive movement's orbit being shorter. This structure distinguishes these symphonies from the First, Sixth and Eighth, which are like a straight line moving to a climax, and from the Fourth and the Ninth, which mediate between the first two types of structure.

39. See Bauer-Lechner, *op. cit.*, pp. 60, 64 and Martner, *op. cit.*, p. 188.

40. Bekker, *op. cit.*, pp. 110, 135, thinks of the Finale as the revelation of love, which is the power whereby various phenomena on various levels of existence manifest themselves. McGrath, *op. cit.*, pp. 147—156, thinks of it as a revelation of a new kind of consciousness — the last in the series that begins with the flowers, and goes by way of animals, men and angels to the divine consciousness. If, however, the Adagio is heard as presenting a transfigured temporality, the difference between Bekker and McGrath may be more apparent than real.

CHAPTER III

The Eighth Symphony

1. Part One

Mahler composed his Eighth Symphony in 1906–1907, and conducted its world premiere in 1910. It was the last of his works that he heard performed. It was also the most enthusiastically received. As he dared to hope, it is perhaps his most accessible, most immediately understood symphony.[1] The form of the opening movement is firmly drawn; the beginnings of the development, recapitulation and coda are clearly marked. Bekker considers the movement to be Mahler's most frank and unreserved endorsement of sonata form.[2] With little effort on their part, listeners are taken into the exuberance and ecstasy that betoken the presence of the creative spirit.

When one looks more closely, however, into the details that generate the form and the overall effect, the initial impression of an exciting, easily understood movement disappears. And, in contrast to the immediate and overpowering effect of the sheer sound made by three choruses, seven soloists and full orchestra, the effect of the music and its structure on the meaning of the text proves to be subtle and hard to grasp. Individual images in the ninth-century Latin text are not painted by the music in a straightforward way. For a phrase of the text is often repeated with a significantly different musical motif. And a musical idea is frequently used to set significantly different ideas in the text. The effect of these techniques is not, however, so to scramble the words and the music that they become irrelevant to one another. Instead, the use of the same motif with different texts and different motifs with the same text sets up a series of dualities which, as in a standard sonata-allegro form, are articulated in the exposition, intensified in the development and removed in the recapitulation. The musical dualities organize the text in such a way that the movement becomes as much a matter of contrasting concepts as of contrasting musical gestures and tonalities.[3]

What is odd about these dualities in the exposition is that they do not seem to press forward to a resolution; the mood is so relentlessly affirmative that the dualities do not seem to be evoking a resolving future. The development section heightens these dualities and presses toward a resolution, like a conventional development, but then, oddly, resolves them before it ends, and so the development section as a whole does not press toward a resolution. If the development metaphorically exemplifies a process in which the dualities are resolved and transcended, the recapitulation metaphorically exemplifies one in which they are completely removed and even the memory of them obliterated. The metaphorical futurelessness of the exposition and development and even more the pastlessness of the recapitulation articulate a temporal process that contradicts those presuppositions with which consciousness usually reflects on itself. The movement either joins ranks with the Fifth Symphony and suggests that these presuppositions are inadequate to our actual consciousness, or, like the Third Symphony Finale, it envisions the temporal process of a transfigured consciousness. The text, of course, is pointing its readers toward a transfiguration.

(1) The Exposition

The exposition consists of three sections, the third of which reprises the first. The first and second sections each have three parts, and in both cases the third part reprises the first. See Figure 71.

In the first section, the first two parts both set the words, "Veni, creator spiritus;" the third part sets "mentes tuorum visita." (The text of the entire hymn and a translation are given in Figure 79. The two settings of "Veni, creator spiritus" approach the text in two different, gently contrasting ways. The characterizing intervals of Veni I (Figure 72) are the falling fourth (bar 2) or third (S:1) and the upward leap of a seventh. The triple meter in the third measure, which makes the accented syllable of "creator" come a beat too soon, seems to exemplify an eagerness or even impatience that the Spirit come. Nevertheless, the motif is marchlike, or at least incipiently marchlike, as though it might be the beginning of a glorious royal procession. Veni II (Figure 73) is characterized by a soaring motif.

FIGURE 71
Sketch of Mahler, Eighth Symphony, Part One, exposition

	musical structure	text	
section one	*A*		beginning of movement to S:7
first part	*a*	Veni I	beginning of movement to S:3
second part	*b*	Veni II	S:3 to S:5
third part	*a'*	Mentes tuorum visita	S:5 to S:7
section two	*B*		S:7 to S:15
first part	*c*	Imple	S:7 to S:12
second part	*d*	Qui Paraclitus	S:12 to two bars after S:13
third part	*c'*	Fons vivus	three bars after S:13 to S:15
section three	*A'*	Veni I	S:15 to S:17

Instead of simply leaping upward a seventh, it reaches upward through a series of seconds and thirds; it arrives at an octave above the lowest note in the motif (E-flat), but then surpasses this peak by reaching on to F, then continues to surpass itself by reaching on to G and then A-flat.

Because both Veni I and Veni II serve the function of establishing the tonicity of E-flat, the differences between them seem to be merely nuances. Indeed, most listeners probably take Veni II to be more a continuation of than a contrast to Veni I until, at S:5, Veni I reappears (At S:5, Veni I carries a different text, "visit the souls of

FIGURE 72
Mahler, Eighth Symphony, Part One, Veni I

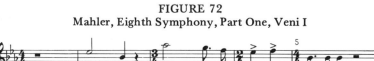

Ve - ni, ve - ni, Cre - a - tor Spi - ri - tus!

FIGURE 73
Mahler, Eighth Symphony, Part One, Veni II

Spi-ri-tus, O Cre-a- tor, ve - - - - - - - - ni Cre-a-tor, Cre-a - - - -tor

FIGURE 74
Plainchant setting of Veni, Creator

your people," which, because the music reprises that of "Veni, Creator," serves as an elaborating appositive to "Come, Creator Spirit.") In other words, it is primarily the sense of return at S:5 that makes us realize that there has been a departure and that Veni I and Veni II have in fact given their common text two rather different connotations.

Veni II seems to exemplify aspiration; reaching higher and higher, it surpasses each of the first three peaks at which it arrives, so that the listener does not expect the A-flat to be left unsurpassed; aspiration is still being felt when Veni I returns. Because Veni II soars to each of its peaks without any trace of a struggle, its continuing aspiration does not feel like a striving. Instead of aspiring toward fulfillment, it seems to aspire because it is already fulfilled; it goes on and on surpassing itself precisely because that toward which it aspires is already present. The exuberance of Veni II suggests a kind of aspiration that is more the effect of the creative Spirit within the human spirit — the transfiguration of consciousness — than a longing for it.

Compared to Veni II, Veni I has a lapidary, objective tone and seems to invoke the Spirit as something external to and different from the self invoking it. Aspiration is presented — named, as it were — by the leap of the seventh and the impatient triple-meter bar, but it is not exemplified. Veni I seems more concerned with the power and the majesty of the Spirit than with what either the aspiration for or the presence of the Spirit may feel like.[4]

Like Veni II, the first part of the middle section ("Imple superna gratia," Figure 75) moves upward and surpasses its own peaks again and again. It too may be said to concern itself with the effect of the Spirit. But the mood is different . While Veni II presents the effect of the Spirit as an uproarious exuberance, the tenderness of this passage suggests that the effect is a quiet fulfillment. This connotation is underscored by the harmonic relations. While the conventional key for the second theme in a sonata form is the dominant, a tonality that increases tension, the Imple begins in D-flat, the subdominant of the subdominant and ends in the subdominant (A-flat); these tonal relations relax the tautness of the opening section. Just as Veni I and Veni II together present the duality of invoking the Spirit and feeling his effect, so Veni II and Imple together present the Spirit's presence both as an outwardly visible effect and as an inner experience that is so profound and mysterious that no outward manifestation can express it.

The second part of the second section ("Qui Paraclitus," Figure 76) returns to the more objective, descriptive tone of Veni I. More concerned with the nature than the effect of the Spirit, it gives words to an arabesque that has appeared in the violins at S:1 as a counterpoint to Veni I. The contrast between the warm Imple passage, which is both aspiring and innerly satisfied, and the more detached "Qui Paraclitus," which appears to be growing outward but in fact does not reach beyond its opening note, is felt more keenly when the Imple motif returns at three bars after S:13 with the words, "'Fons vivus." Just as the musical relations in the first section make "Visit the souls of your people" serve as an elucidating appositve to "Come, Creator Spirit," so the musical relations in the second section make "Living fountain, fire, love and spiritual unction" serve as an elucidating appositive to "celestial grace."

The exposition ends with a restatement of Veni I (beginning at S:15)[5] followed by an orchestral pendant. In the final section, Veni II

FIGURE 75
Mahler, Eighth Symphony, Part One, Imple superna gratia

5 Bars after S:10

Im - ple su - per - na gra - ti - a, gra - ti-a, quae tu cre-a - sti

FIGURE 76
Mahler, Eighth Symphony, Part One, Qui
tu Paraclitus

Qui Pa -ra- cli-tus di - ce-ris

asserts itself only briefly (in the soaring figure for "imple" at one bar before S:16), and so the contrast between Veni I and Veni II, between invoking the Spirit and feelings its effect, does not characterize the exposition's third section.

The duality presented by Veni I and Veni II turns out to have important ramifications for the rest of the movement. Although the exposition does not present this duality violently or even crisply, and although the Veni I–Veni II duality, like the sense of aspiration within Veni II, projects no sense of agonizing struggle, still this duality keeps the movement's constantly affirmative stance from becoming overbearing or boring.[6] Consequently, it is important to feel as keenly as possible the contrast between its poles and to specify the axis along which the contrast takes place before describing the rest of the movement. One way to amplify the Veni I–Veni II duality is to compare the tension it exemplifies to a similar tension between two concepts in Christian theology. Such a comparison is particularly apt in light of the fact that Mahler's text alludes — somewhat obliquely, to be sure — to these concepts.

One of these concepts is the idea that the most basic aspect of religious experience is praise. This concept presupposes the common-sense notion that human beings and God are "other" to one another: humans are creatures of God and by nature, therefore, are not divine. A man or a woman and God are not only different beings; they are also different kinds of beings, each having its own possibilities and responsibilities. Accordingly, they encounter one another externally; each is a subject for whom the other is an object. The advent of the Creator Spirit must not be thought to imply that human beings are filled by the divine spirit in such a way that they are invaded from without and turned into something whose nature is different from human nature. Such a surrender of their spirit to the divine Spirit would seem to abdicate their freedom and thus contradict their humanity. Nor does the presence of the Spirit imply that the divine and the human spirits are so blended that together they constitute the divine Whole. Religious experience means that a being of one kind praises a being of a different kind. It does not mean that the human personal center has been supplanted by or merged with the divine personal center. As in the majestic invocation of Veni I, people invoke the presence of God as an awesome reality to whom they subordinate themselves without ceasing to be aware of themselves as distinct entities.

In contrast to this concept of religious experience as divine-human encounter is the idea that the most basic aspect of religious experience is the quickening and liberation of human depth. The most basic aspect of feeling the divine with maximal intensity is that a person's deepest self erupts into efficacy, freed from distorting ideas about itself, God and the world. The development of this concept usually suggests that to see God as an Other over against oneself is to feel a latent hostility to God. If God and his creatures encounter one another externally as different entities and distinct kinds of beings, the divine reality necessarily limits the human reality and the range of its choices and responsibility. This hostility would make human wholeness impossible, for people are alienated from themselves and from one another as long as they are alienated from the divine. People are at peace with themselves (and this peace constitutes the core of religious experience) only if they give up the idea that praise is the core of religious experience and become conscious of the divine presence in an immediate way — that is, without any concept or even awareness of anything external to the self. The separation between God and his creatures is overcome when people do not know God as an external object, but instead feel the effect of the divine presence to their deepest consciousness and find that they cannot think of themselves in any other way. Like the soaring Veni II, which is both reaching without arriving and yet satisfying, the human aspires to know the divine and to overcome the separation between the two. As it turns out, to aspire in this way is to be already aware of the divine as something intrinsic to the self; to aspire religiously is to be already fulfilled and to transcend one's sense of being divided against oneself as well as alienated from the divine.

When praise of God is thought to be the core of religious experience, human creatures are thought to be subordinate to the Creator, and the divine reality is believed to determine what shall count as the proper exercise of human freedom and hence as human fulfillment. When the otherness of Creator and creatures is set aside, the human feeling of the ultimate is thought to be both the core of religious experience and the essence of human fulfillment. The genuineness of fulfillment determines what shall count as the ultimate. In one way or another, theologicans have had to deal with the tension between these concepts: Is it the case that a person worships, praises and serves God in order to glorify God, or is it the case that the quest for a profound religious experience is identical to the search for genuine self-fulfillment? Ought religious people to understand their worship of and service to God as the performance of religious duty that is incumbent on God's grateful creatures, or ought they to understand a deep awareness of the divine as the only path to authentic happiness, a path recommended to their self-interest and charted by their best insights into themselves not so much because it avoids the divine wrath and procures the divine blessing as because it is that activity or attitude that best comports with human nature itself?

Theologicans generally answer this question by saying, "Both." Preachers, for example, typically proclaim that God is to be praised because he is divine and for no other reason, and then support this appeal by indicating how confusions and woes result from inadequate religious experience while true happiness comes with a pursuit of the divine as though the basic reason for seeking the ultimate were self-fulfillment.

Some theologians resolve the antagonism by emphasizing one pole and subordinating the other. John Calvin, for example, acknowledges the validity of the second concept in saying that the knowledge of God is that by which we grasp "what it is to our advantage to know of him" and by defining piety as "reverence joined with the love of God which the knowledge of his benefits induces."[7] Yet he subordinates this attitude to a pervasive concern with the overwhelming majesty and sovereignty of a God who is other to man or whose glorification man is purposed to serve. The more this emphasis is pressed — as it was by some seventeenth-century Calvinists — the more God becomes a monster who delights in finding his glory somehow enhanced by human submissiveness.

Friedrich Schleiermacher, for a contrary example, maintains the first concept in the sense that he never reduces the divine reality to man's consciousness of the divine, yet he consistently concerns himself more with the inner effect of the Spirit; in talking about the intuition of the divine presence, his emphasis falls on the human intuition, not on the divine that is present.[8] The more this emphasis is pressed, the more God is domesticated and the more human self-fulfillment becomes the criterion of that which is ultimate; indeed, as Ludwig Feuerbach tries to force theologians to recognize, if what the worshiping person is feeling is both the deepest self and the ultimate, then feeling the ultimate *is* the ultimate itself.[9]

Other theologians deal with the antagonism between these concepts by maintaining the tension as tautly as possible. Kierkegaard and Tillich, for example, suggest that it is inherent in the human condition to live in this unresolved tension.[10] Some contemporary theologians, notably process theologians like Charles Hartshorne and post-liberal theologians like David Tracy, seem to regard the theological task to be resolving the tension without subordinating either pole of the duality to the other. For the process theologians, the apparent tension is the result of thinking about human and divine nature in static terms instead of recognizing that both God and his creatures are continuously becoming transformed as a result of their growing knowledge of one another and their knowledge that they are known by the other.[11] Contrary to Kierkegaard and Tillich, the post-liberal theologians seem to consider the tension to be more a characteristic of thinking about human religious experience than of the experience itself.[12]

The differences between Veni I and Veni II correspond to the difference between these two emphases. The Veni I passage presents human aspiration in a single interval, and subordinates it to a blazing vision of divine majesty. The Veni II and the Imple passages exemplify aspiration in a way that makes it coincide with fulfillment; the divine is present in the sense that it is the presence of the Spirit that identifies aspiration with fulfillment (presumably, it is only when one aspires toward the ultimate that aspiration is itself already fulfilling and ultimate), and the divine as an objective reality is subordinate to the human feelings.

The point of mentioning these theological tensions is not to suggest that Mahler was aware of them or was trying to illustrate them in his music. Rather, the point is that these tensions are inherent in the process of invoking the presence of the Creator Spirit, and it is not surprising that Mahler's tension and the theological tension resemble one another. It is appropriate to his text that Mahler builds the musical duality into his exposition and uses it to generate the rest of the movement.

(2) The Development

The development is a maze of dualities. All of them are more explicit and obvious than those in the exposition, and all of them are derived from those in the exposition, though the principle of derivation keeps changing as the development unfolds.

The development divides itself into two sections, the second of which is much longer and more complex than the first. Both sections begin with a setting of "Infirma nostri corporis."[13] The first section has three parts. The first (Infirma I, S:19) and the third (an orchestral interlude, S:23) are distorted versions of Veni I. Although they differ significantly from each other, their common origin binds them together and makes them serve as a frame for the contrasting middle part, the "Firmans virtute," S:21. See Figure 77.

FIGURE 77

Sketch of Mahler, Eighth Symphony, Part One, development section

	musical structure	text	Source of motif	
section one	A			S:19 to S:30
first part	a	Infirma I	Veni I	S:19 to S:21
second part	b	Firmans virtute	Imple	S:21 to S:23
third part	a'	(orchestra)	Veni I	S:23 to S:30
section two	B			S:30 to S:64
first part	a''	Infirma II	Veni I	S:30 to S:33
second part	b'	Lumen accende I	Firmans/Imple	S:33 to S:37
third part	a'''	Lumen accende II	Veni I/Veni II	S:37 to S:64
first wave				S:37 to S:42
second wave				S:42 to S:55
first subsection		Hostem		S:42 to S:46
second subsection		Praevio	Veni I/Veni II	S:46 to S:55
third wave		Lumen accende II	Veni I/Veni II	S:55 to S:64

Infirma I portrays human weakness.[14] The music and the words
contradict one another: the text ("making firm . . .") prays for the
overcoming of the condition (physical weakness) which the music
paints. In that Infirma I is motivically related to Veni I, human corporeal frailty is set into a duality with awesome spiritual majesty. Similarly, the middle part, "making firm . . . with perpetual strength," is
motivically related to "fill our breasts with celestial grace." Just as
in the exposition, the latter (the Imple) and Veni II together form a
duality of the inner, inexpressible and outward, manifest effects of
the Spirit, so in the development "Firmans virtute" and "Infirma
nostri corporis" together form a duality of the inner effect of
strengthening (which is suggested by using the Imple motif for
"Firmans") with the outwardly visible effect (which is suggested by
musically depicting the corporeal frailty that the strengthening
overcomes).

The rest of the development (from S:30 to S:64) is a section that
consists of three parts, Infirma II (S:30, in C-sharp minor), Lumen
accende I (S:33, in D major) and Lumen accende II (S:37). The last
part has three waves: two statements of Lumen accende II, both in
E major (S:37 and S:55, the second one turning at S:58 to E-flat for
the retransition) frame the eruption of warfare ("Hostem," S:42, in
E minor) and the double fugue using both the Veni I and the Veni II
motifs ("Praevio," S:46, in E-flat).

Infirma I and Infirma II form a duality because both of them set
the same words and, even more, because both of them are derived
from Veni I. While Infirma I depicts the frailty that the divine
strengthening will, it is prayed, overcome, Infirma II suggests the act
of strengthening itself and suggests that such an infusion of power is
itself a powerful act, involving struggle, passion and even incipient
violence.

The text of Lumen accende I (S:33), like the text of Infirma I
and II, deals with a spiritual reality touching and changing a material
reality. But while the music of Infirma I focuses attention on the
corporeal weakness to be overcome and the music of Infirma II
focuses on the passionate exertion that such overcoming requires, the
music of Lumen accende I focuses attention on the effect. The music
for "Firmans virtute" (S:21) is restated by the music for Lumen
accende I; the musical restatement suggests that the later text restates
the meaning of the earlier one, that, in other words, "making firm . . .
with perpetual strength" and "may light kindle our senses" explain
and interpret one another. Like "Firmans virtute," like "Imple
superna gratia" and like Veni II, the music for Lumen accende I

soars both aspiringly and fulfillingly. But, like Imple and unlike Veni II, the aspiration and fulfillment are inward, and the outward manifestation is one of tranquility and profound peace.

Lumen accende II (S:37; see Figure 78) returns to the outwardly visible world of Infirma II; the keys (C-sharp minor and E major) are closely related, and the motifs are related to each other through a common relationship to Veni I. But while Infirma II suggests exertion, Lumen accende II suggests exuberance. The two together suggest the outside of the reality whose inside is revealed in Lumen accende I. Thus, the duality between Infirma II and Lumen accende II, on the one hand, and Lumen accende I, on the other, is an intensified version of the duality between Veni II and Imple.

FIGURE 78
Mahler, Eighth Symphony, Part One, Lumen accende II

ac - cen - de,   ac - cen -de   lu - men   sen-si-bus

The duality is complicated by the way that Lumen accende II relates itself as closely to Veni II as to Veni I. It has the falling fourths and the upward leaps of Veni I, expressing the awesome spiritual reality objectively, as something external to the person invoking the spiritual light, but it also has stepwise upward movement (9 bars after S:38) and a series of peaks (G-sharp at ten bars after S:38, then A, then B at five and six bars after S:39) that make it exemplify the same aspiration and fulfillment that Veni II exemplifies.[15] Because it alludes to both Veni I and Veni II, and weaves their motifs and connotations into a single gesture, the appearance of Lumen accende II transcends the duality of Veni I and Veni II. The first of three means that Mahler uses to remove this tension, it is one of the most significant moments in the movement. Deryck Cooke describes it as "unforgettable."[16]

Its importance is underlined by the fact that it appears at the very end of the movement, when it is played by a specially placed brass choir that cuts through the massive choral and orchestral sound. It is also one of the most prominent motifs throughout the symphony's Part Two, and in particular permeates the forest scene from its very beginning (cellos, bars 2–3, and flutes, bars 5–6) and the closing Chorus Mysticus (see, for example "ist nur ein Gleichnis," bars 7–8 after S:202, and "zieht uns hinan," bars 2–3 after S:206).

The two statements of Lumen accende II in the development are separated by two lengthy subsections, the "Hostem" and "Praevio." The contrast between "Hostem" and Lumen accende II is the most violent one in the movement. It stands at the apex of a series of contrasts that are increasingly sharp. In the exposition, the contrast between Veni I and Veni II is surpassed by the contrast between Imple and "Qui diceris Paraclitus," which in turn is surpassed by that between Veni I–II and Imple, which is surpassed by that between Infirma I and "Firmans virtute," which is surpassed by that between Infirma II and Lumen accende I. As each successive duality appears in higher relief than the preceding one, the importance of the previous contrasts as a dynamic generator of forward movement is confirmed.

The violent contrast at "Hostem" occurs just after the first attempt to overcome the movement's dualities, as though the effort had failed. Just as Infirma I suggests the weakness that the strengthening Spirit must overcome, so the disintegrating rage of the Hostem battle cries suggests how forceful must be a passage that would heal such a breach and transcend such violent antagonism if a storm like the Hostem is not to recur.[17]

The second appearance of Lumen accende II attempts to calm the storm. It is delayed by the Praevio, which functions to reinforce Lumen accende II, as it were, against the Hostem. The Praevio is, in fact, Mahler's second means for removing the tension of the Veni I– Veni II duality. While Lumen accende II transcends the Veni I–Veni II tension by presenting elements of each in a single gesture, the Praevio puts the two motifs together contrapuntally, so that the atmosphere becomes charged with the connotations of both the marching Veni I and the soaring Veni II. We see the Spirit as an awe-inspiring "captain, leading the way," and we also feel the thrill the troops feel when they see their captain, identify themselves with him, merge their will with his, and forget themselves and the terror aroused in them by the enemy. The double fugue on Praevio is thrown against the Hostem. The one is as tightly structured as the other is nearly chaotic; the one is as confident in its march forward and flight upward as the other, with its frightful shrieks on "hostem" (for example, in three bars after S:42 and one bar before S:43), is terror-stricken.

The return of Lumen accende II at S:55 sounds like the thrill of victory, the inner and outer peace and wholeness that come when the battle is done. The senses, kindled by the divine light of the Spirit, experience the release of the emotions generated by the Hostem-Praevio duality.

(3) The Recapitulation

The Lumen accende II motif persists when, at S:58, a long pedal-point on B-flat, the dominant of E-flat, leads us to the recapitulation. Here, Veni I returns with its original text. But there is no alternation between Veni I and Veni II. Instead, the two motifs are fused together, and this fusion is Mahler's third means of removing the tension of the exposition's dualities. During the reprise, the music soars and reaches upward and surpasses itself, like the music of Veni II (see, for example, S:68, S:70, S:77) while constantly referring explicitly to Veni I and its vision of the awesomely majestic Spirit. Similarly, the duality between Veni I—Veni II and "imple superna gratia" is all but completely submerged in the recapitulation. To be sure, the "Da gaudiorum . . ." (S:71) is reminiscent of the Imple motif and mood, but it begins with the Veni I motif. More significant than the allusion to Imple at S:71 is its presence as a hidden force throughout the reprise: it has been absorbed into Veni II, which has been absorbed into Veni I. In short, throughout the reprise and on into the celebratory coda ("Gloria . . .," S:83), Veni I is extended and elaborated by assimilating the mood of both Veni II and Imple.

The use of these three motifs in the development section has added to the feelings and ideas that are associated with them. While in the exposition, the invocation of the Creator Spirit (Veni I) is one pole of a duality, by the end of the development it by itself encompasses two dualities. First, because of its use in the polarly related Infirma I and Infirma II, Veni I encompasses the spectrum defined by Infirma I (experiencing the event as a miracle that is too mysterious to see or understand) and Infirma II (experiencing it as a palpably overwhelming, outwardly visible exertion). Second, because Veni I has appeared in the polarly related Infirma II and Lumen accende II, it associates itself with the whole range of events in which a spiritual force has a sensible, tangible effect, a range defined by a spiritual invigoration of the weak parts of the body on one end and by light kindling the senses on the other. Third, because of the motivic cross references, the exposition duality of Veni I–II and Imple has broadened to include the duality of Infirma I and Firmans and the duality of Infirma II—Lumen accende II and Lumen accende I, so that the Veni I-II/Imple tension now also connotes the polar relation between the event and the effect of a spiritual force touching and changing something physical. In the recapitulation, Veni I and Veni II also carry the connotations developed by the sections in which the duality between them has been, for a while at least, transcended:

when the invocation and the effect of the Spirit are blended in a single motif (Lumen accende II) or in a contrapuntal passage (the Praevio double fugue), the senses are kindled by light or the enemy is driven off.

One way to describe the enriched connotations that Veni I, Veni II and Imple carry when they appear in the reprise is to say that the coming of the Creator Spirit brings with it all the conditions for genuine human creativity. For the enemy (all the forces of injustice and oppression) is routed; physical frailty (limitations on stamina and perseverance, perhaps death as well) is overcome; our senses are kindled and inspired. All the external and internal impediments to creativity having been removed, the creature, like the Creator, becomes unendingly creative. While creativity in the world as we know it is ambiguous — it expands opportunities and at the same time has the potential for serving or inadvertently occasioning injustice — the human creativity envisioned at the end of the Veni Creator can evidently only widen and never obstruct the opportunities for others' creative activity.

In the reprise, the advent of the Spirit, carrying with it all the conditions for this sort of creativity, is inseparable from the connotations of fulfillment. It is as though to have become creative in this way were to have become all that a human being can be. Since creativity involves change, fulfilling creativity must be dynamic, though it would have none of the aspects of struggle and anguish that ordinarily characterize movement toward fulfillment. Like the kind of fulfillment exemplified by the Finale of the Third Symphony, the fulfillment suggested at the end of the Eighth's first movement must mean a growth within fulfillment. This fulfillment cannot mean acquiring a nature which one then unchangingly simply is; it involves further becoming. Such is the nature of fulfillment when it involves the inseparability of the Spirit and its effect, of divine glory and human aspiration, of the divine and human creativities.

During the reprise, Veni I and Veni II, with all these associations, are continuously and simultaneously present, while in the exposition the one alternates with the other and the absent one is present in the form of a memory or an anticipated return. Throughout the recapitulation, both the awesome sublimity of the Spirit and the soaring, fulfilling effect of the Spirit are at their strongest. Listeners are aware of both, but the sense of dualism between them disappears in an overflowing ecstasy expressed through the multiple entrances of nine choral parts (double mixed chorus and children's choir) and the seven soloists, the flowing counterpoint, and the rapid sallies into and out of *pianissimo*.[18] The entire spectrum defined by Veni I on one end and Veni II on the other is present at once. It is as though the vision of the Creator Spirit at its most majestic and the created spirit at its most fulfillingly creative did not challenge or attenuate each other anymore, as though establishing the conditions for human creativity contributed to the awesomeness of the divine as much as to the fulfillment of the human, and as though adoration of the divine contributed to human fulfillment as much as to the divine glory.

While the recapitulation is like the Praevio and Lumen accende II in that all three remove the dualism between Veni I and Veni II, there is an important difference between the reprise and the two earlier passages. The Praevio resolves the Veni I—Veni II duality in that it is a new musical entity in which the polarly related elements are presented simultaneously and the tension between them is transcended. The illumination passages resolve the duality in the same way; even though elements of the two motifs are presented successively rather than simultaneously, the musical impetus from elements of Veni I to elements of Veni II is so strong that we hear the gesture as a new entity, a single musical sweep that transcends the duality established in the exposition.

In comparison to both the Praevio and the Lumen accende II, the reprise is experienced neither as a resolution nor as a claimx. To experience an event as a resolution entails that one remember the tensions that are released by the resolution. A memory of that which is being resolved is an essential constituent of the experience. A Beethovenian climax is thrilling precisely because one experiences the contrast between the way things take place during the climax and the way they have been taking place during the passages that struggle toward such a resolution. Although Mahler's recapitulation removes the sense of duality that has characterized the exposition and the development, it is not experienced as a climax, for one does not hear it as the culmination toward which earlier passages have been struggling. Indeed, one might well take either the Praevio or the last twenty-eight bars (that is, from S:58 up to S:64) of Lumen accende II, or both of these, as the climax, for they both resolve the dualism between Veni I aand Veni II, and both are in the tonic key.[19] The sense of a climactic arrival at the beginning of the reprise is attenuated not only because its tonality and its motifs are anticipated in the preceding passages, but also because the B-flat pedal point of the retransition persists for nine bars into the reprise. The recapitulation is thrilling not so much because of its contrast to earlier sections as because of its intrinsic qualities — its way of blending awe with soaring, fulfilling aspiration. It is, in fact, surpassingly thrilling, but listeners are so absorbed by the recapitulation itself, so engulfed in its ecstatic flood, that they may well not notice that previously established dualisms are gone.

While the past of a Beethovenian climax impinges on the event that embodies the goal of the past's struggle, Mahler's reprise almost obliterates its past. The temporal process may be said to invert that of the Finale of Mahler's Fifth Symphony, in which the future is again and again supplanted by a recollection precisely at the moment where the goal of forward pressing striving might be expected to be embodied. In the first movement of the Eighth, increasingly tense dualities are not experienced as pressing forward, yet an event takes place that does resolve them. But this event is not experienced as a resolution, for the arrival of this future does not seem like an arrival. It does not contrast itself to its past; it does not depend on its past for its effect. Although the listener may be aware of the similarities and differences between the recapitulation and what it recapitulates, the non-dualistic presentation of invoking the awe-inspiring Spirit and feeling the effect of its presence is not a matter of resembling or departing from the prior duality. Caught up into the ecstatic sweep, the listener is in a temporal process whose past is as suppressed as the future is suppressed in the Fifth Symphony Finale. During the first movement of the Eighth, the future impinges very little on the present, and the past impinges so little on the character of the future when it arrives that we may say that the future, now that it is the present, obliterates the past. In the Fifth Symphony Finale, the future bears heavily on the present during the striving passages, then suddenly evaporates when a recollection of the past obliterates the future.

To the extent that our listening habits have been shaped by Beethoven, we may find the nature of Mahler's recapitulation elusive. One way to apprehend it is to compare it to Heidegger's concept of "stepping back out of metaphysics" and to the difference that Heidegger sees between the "step back" and Hegel's concept of *Aufhebung,* the "transcending elevation."[20] Hegel begins with the duality between Being and beings. To feel this duality is to feel impelled to transcend it, because to feel that Being and beings are separated is to feel that each challenges or erodes the reality of the other. Being is more real than beings if particular entities are believed to depend on and manifest the power of the former; this way of understanding the nature of reality is contradicted whenever empirical realities laugh at our understanding of Being by refusing to conform to it. Beings are more real than Being if the meaning of "to be" is collapsed into the particular entities that happen to be, if there is no power or significance that goes beyond the collection of empirical realities and if there is, accordingly, absolutely no basis for calling some entities or events "good" or "beautiful" and others "evil" or "disgusting;" this way of understanding the nature of reality is contradicted whenever human freedom seems real and one suspects that choices do not merely manifest random movements, learned responses or whimsical preferences but are in fact grounded in something ultimate and non-empirical.

According to Hegel, each age tries to hold Being and beings together in some way, but the subsequent age finds that the prior thinking has emphasized one at the expense of the other. Because of this inadequacy, the previous period's way of transcending thus becomes one of the poles of the duality to be transcended. For Hegel, the duality can be ultimately transcended only by seeing a point of non-differentiation between the two poles. Such a vision requires that one hold the duality firmly in mind, while at the same time recognizing that the content of thinking ultimately is thinking itself and that thinking itself is Being even though the thinking that is Being is also the thinking of a being.

Beethoven's reprises have been said to exemplify this sort of transcendence.[21] They marvelously and fully embody the resolution of tensions that are set up previously in the movement. These tensions imply the idea of resolution; the reprises actualize the idea. The reprises do not merely intend resolution (as though the concept of resolution were somehow behind the sounds), for resolution is concretely actual. And the sounds are not merely sounds, but are the embodiment of a concept. Neither the concept of resolution (which is the non-empirical reality that makes the sounds meaningful and which corresponds to what Hegel more abstractly calls Being) nor the sounds themselves (beings) are more real or basic than the other. To listen to a Beethoven reprise is to be in the presence of the non-differentiation between the idea of resolution and its embodiment. But although the duality is transcended, it is also sustained, for the contrast between idea (the concept of resolution which is implicit in the tensions) and reality constitutes the past to which the reprise is responding. If this contrast is forgotten, the reprise does not transcend the dualities.

Heidegger's "step back" means giving up transcending the duality, and instead simply but rigorously seeing Being in its difference from beings and beings in their difference from Being and the difference as such. Being and beings circle around each other. Instead of transcending the difference, "we follow it to its essential origin."[22] But this origin cannot be thought using concepts like "Being" and "beings."[23] One feels awestruck, and one sings and dances in celebration before that which is so radically non-conceptual that the preposition "before" is utterly inappropriate.[24] One is open without being open "to anything;" one is fulfilled without seeking fulfillment. Heidegger calls this immediate, non-conceptual, celebratory consciousness "primal thinking."

The duality of Being and beings corresponds to the duality between the Creator Spirit and his creatures. According to Hegel, the theological terms present pictorially that which he is presenting conceptually, untainted by theology's vestiges of sensuous imagery. According to Heidegger, both theology and all traditional ontological thinking, including Hegel's, are representational, for both of them represent Being as the *causa sui* that is the ground of beings. For theology, the ungrounded ground is the ultimate and the highest, and it is primal and universal because it is ultimate. Traditional ontology reverses the emphasis, sees the ungrounded ground as the universal and the primal, and says that it is ultimate because it is primal.[25] Both are representational in the sense that they both feel the need to posit a cause for beings and represent the relationship between Being and beings as analogous to the relation between two beings in which one is the cause or ground of the other. The only distinction between the Being-being relation and the causing being — caused being relationship is that in the latter the causing being itself has a cause while in the former Being is its own cause.

Heidegger's "step back" is the attempt to think Being in a radically non-representational way. As the need to posit a cause of beings disappears and the picture of the ground fades, the duality also simply vanishes. One thinks both Being and beings and their difference immediately — not mediated by any picture or concept or historical dialectical process. Hegel would have us transcend the duality by an apprehension of the non-difference between Being and beings, an apprehension that is mediated historically as Being pours itself into a concrete form, namely the totality of history, in which the idea becomes real and objective reality fully embodies the subjective idea, and subject and object, idea and reality all coincide. Heidegger would have us sustain the difference between Being and beings, but because we think each of them in an immediate, non-representational way, the sense both of a duality and of transcending the duality evaporates.

Primal thinking may be a good way to characterize the nature of the transfigured consciousness that Mahler's reprise suggests and that the temporal process of the movement as a whole implies. First, the Veni I—Veni II duality, the duality between the divine Spirit and its effect, corresponds to the Being-beings dualism. To the extent that the recapitulation continuously holds both invocation and fulfilling aspiration in the listener's mind, it sustains each as itself but submerges the dualism between them.

Second, the relation of the reprise to the exposition and development more nearly exemplifies a process like Heidegger's non-representational thinking that a process like Hegel's transcendence of duality. Mahler does not lead into his recapitulation with a struggle whose outcome the reprise could embody. He can not, for the development has already transcended the duality set forth in the exposition and intensified in the first parts of the development. The Praevio and Lumen accende II have already transcended the duality between the awesome spirit and fulfilling aspiration by embodying the idea of resolving their contrast, while still sustaining and referring to the idea of the contrast. The struggle having been won, the fullness of the present during the reprise precludes contrasting it to earlier sections. The reprise so integrates Veni I and Veni II that the ideas of both their duality and their non-differentiation disappear, and so the reprise does not present itself as a response to earlier passages. The duality simply vanishes. It is as though one were so close to Being (the Creator Spirit) and beings (those invoking him), and thinking them so non-representationally and immediately that both duality and transcending duality could no longer be thought.

If the musical duality disappears, the theological tension between glorifying God and human fulfillment also disappears. Although the full presence of the awe-inspiring Creator brings with it all the conditions for unending and fulfilling human creativity, neither is subordinated to the other. It is not the case that either one exists for the sake of the other. Each one depends on the other as much as the other depends on it. Seeing the Creator Spirit as *causa sui* and the human spirit as that which is caused distorts both of them and leads into what Heidegger would consider a distorting religious experience. The turmoil within such religious experience and the endless agony it endures result from this fundamentally objectifying, representational way of thinking the divine Spirit and the effect of his presence on human creatures.

It need not be. For while the divine quickening is the *sine qua non* and the criterion of every human attempt at creativity, still the

FIGURE 79
Text of Mahler, Eighth Symphony, Part One

Veni, Creator Spiritus,	Come, creator Spirit
Mentes tuorum visita,	Visit the souls of your people.
Imple superna gratia,	Fill with celestial grace
Quae tu creasti pectora.	Our breasts, which you have created.
Qui diceris Paraclitus,	You, who are called Comforter,
Altissimi donum Dei,	Gift of the most high God,
Fons vivus, ignis, caritas	Living fountain, fire, love
Et spiritalis unctio.	And spiritual unction.
Infirma nostri corporis	Making firm the weak parts of our body
Firmans virtute* perpeti,	With perpetual strength,
Accende lumen sensibus,	Kindle a light in our senses;
Infunde amorem cordibus.†	Pour love into our hearts.
Hostem repellas longius	May you drive the enemy far away
Pacemque dones protinus,	And give lasting peace,
Ductore sic te praevio	So, with you as captain leading the way,
Vitemus omne pessimum.**	May we escape all ill.
Tu septiformis munere	May you, the seven-fold one,
Digitus paternae dexterae.††	The finger of the Father's right hand, give us your gift.
Per te sciamus da Patrem,	Grant that through you we may know the Father.
Noscamus (atque) ⸓Filium,	(And) ⸓come to know the Son,
(Te utriusque) ⸓Spiritum	And in thee, Spirit (of them both),⸓
Credamus omni tempore.	May we at all times believe.
Da gaudiorum praemia,	Grant us the rewards of joys;
Da gratiarum munera,	May you grant us the bestowal of graces,
Dissolve litis vincula,	Loose the chains of disputes,
Adstringe pacis foedera.‖	Bind us in treaties of peace.
Gloria Patri Domino,	Glory to the Father, our Lord,
Deo sit gloria et Filio	Glory to God and to the Son,
Natoque, qui a mortuis	Who was born and from the dead
Surrexit, ac Paraclito	Rose again, and to the Comforter,
In saeculorum saecula.	For ever and ever.

---

* "Virtute firmans" in the original
† In the version of the hymn used for Pentecost Vespers, the two lines, "Accende ... cordibus" precede the two lines, "Infirma ... perpeti.
** "Noxium" in the Vespers hymn
†† These two lines ("Tu septiformis ... dexterae") are followed in the plain-chant setting by two that Mahler omits ("Tu rite promissum Patris, Sermone ditans guttura"), and these four lines follow immediately after "Et spirtalis unctio."
⸓ Omitted by Mahler
‖ These four lines are omitted in the current *Liber Usualis*

latter does not merely reflect and imitate the former; fulfilling creativity also serves as the ultimate validation of the divine quickener, as though human creativity were the criterion and guarantor of the divine glory. Consequently, the infusion of the divine Spirit is not an intrusion from without that annihilates human freedom and responsibility by displacing the human personal center, but neither is divine creativity to be reduced to human creativity, as though the two were indistinguishable and human creativity were by its very nature ultimacy itself. The inspiring and the inspired spirits are equiprimordial. The equiprimordiality cannot be thought conceptually, but it need not be if both are thought in a primal, non-representational, non-objectifying way, as Heidegger would have us to think them and as, perhaps, Mahler leads us to think them.

2.   *Part Two*

The symphony's Part Two sets the closing scene of Goethe's *Faust,* Part Two. It is somewhat ironic that Goethe should have been largely responsible for the enormous interest that the nineteenth century took in the Faust legend, yet most of the artists and composers[26] who dealt with it ignored the most obvious way in which Goethe changed the legend: Goethe's Faust is not damned; in spite of the unholy aid he accepts from the devil and in spite of the guilt he incurs during the Gretchen episode, he is redeemed. Mahler's Part Two sets the text that dramatizes Faust's transfiguration.[27] This text, together with a translation, is quoted in Figure 93.

Musical visions of redemption — what lies beyond death and the contradictions characterizing humans before they die — are always difficult to describe. None of us have any first-hand experience with that of which the music purports to be an image, and so we lack the terms that might be used in describing the new life.

Simply by juxtaposing Goethe's text to Veni Creator, Mahler directs us to some aspects of his vision. Wherever the two texts refer to similar ideas, such as corporeality or light, Mahler links them by using the same musical motif. Indeed, motifs from Part One — particularly Lumen accende II, but also Veni I and Imple — so permeate Part Two that the listener is invited to hear the entire Part Two as projecting an idea similar to that of Part One, in spite of the conspicuous differences in atmosphere and structure. If the two parts intepret each other, Faust's redemption at the end of the second cannot be unlike the ecstatic combination of Veni I and Veni II at the end of the first. To be redeemed must mean to be unsurpassably fulfilled in a way that contributes to the glorification and enhanced awesomeness of that which is primal and ultimate without subordinating human fulfilmment to the ultimate or the ultimate to human fulfillment and without merging the two into a non-differentiated unity.[28]

If it is valid to let the two parts interpret each other — if, that is, the extraordinary vision projected by the first-movement recapitulation is of a piece with Faust's redemption — then Mahler's image of redemption must be fundamentally different from those visions that see it primarily in terms of the object of consciousness. Painters and composers have typically suggested the nature of redemption in terms of an object, of which the redeemed are aware, that is so completely satisfying that the redeemed feel no longing, only peace and fulfillment. Visions like Tintoretto's "Paradise" and the angel music at the end of Gounod's *Faust* and the "In Paradiso" in Faure's Requiem subordinate the divine majesty to human fulfillment. The serenity of these paradises consequently seems self-indulgent and, curiously perhaps, somewhat boring.

For some listeners, the Mater Gloriosa music — the centerpiece of Mahler's second movement (S:106 and S:172) — evokes memories of the Gounod and the Faure. The slow, sweet melody and the timbre (harps, celeste, harmonium) make it possible to dismiss Mahler's second movement as routine heaven music of "appalling banality."[29] But if Mahler's two parts interpret one another, the rescmblance ought to be superficial, for the end of Part One would be contradicted by a vision in which the awesome divine is subordinated to human self-fulfillment. If the two parts interpret one another, redemption must mean not only or even primarily a change in the object of consciousness but a change in the way of being conscious. Mahler must be not so much painting musical pictures of the object present to the consciousness of the redeemed nor evoking the feeling that this object would evoke as he is trying to envision a radical transfiguration of human consciousness itself.

The temporal processes of Part Two support and perhaps even demand such a description of Mahler's vision. It divides itself, most analysts agree, into an Adagio, a Scherzo and a Finale, and the temporal processes of all three are so basically incompatible with the temporality of ordinary consciousness that they must be ascribed to a fundamentally new kind of consciousness.[30] In the following pages, the temporal processes of the Adagio, the Scherzo and the Finale will be taken up individually. The future seems to have quite a different force in each of the three sections, as do the past and the present, but these differences will simply be left standing until the last part of the chapter. There, Sartre's analysis of the temporality of ordinary consciousness — an analysis that characterizes the past, future and present much more completely than Husserl's does — will be summarized. By contrasting the past, future and present as Sartre sees them to the past, future and present as Mahler's Adagio, Scherzo and Finale present them, one can see that the various sections of Part Two, in spite of their obvious differences, are in fact of a piece with one another: they are complementary aspects of what may be called, following the lead of the text Mahler has chosen, redeemed consciousness.

Accordingly, the strategy of what follows will be to describe the temporal process of Mahler's Part Two, and then to contrast them to the temporality of ordinary consciousness (as analyzed by Sartre) in order to sharpen and amplify the description of Mahler's temporalities and to intimate his vision of the redeemed consciousness, characterized as it is by these processes.

(1) The Adagio

Goethe's text and Mahler's music take us into a deep forest with exposed roots and wild gorges. The scene is so remote from human civilization that civic society or farming or even hunting seems unimaginable. It opens with a shimmer that suggests the uncanny before which one can only shudder, fascinated and terrified.[31]

The Adagio consists of two parts, the first (for orchestra without voices) having five sections, and the second (for orchestra and voices) having four. The four texted sections correspond closely to the first four sections of the first part. The Adagio is usually described as a theme and eight variations. This description, while not false, obscures the way the fifth "variation" (that is, the first section in the second part), in which the shimmer comes back, sounds like a return to the beginning of the movement, and the way the next three "variations" are texted versions of the first three (see Figure 80). Moreover, the first part moves from an arrangement of its fragments that seems somewhat random to a clearer and tighter shapeliness, and the second part duplicates this process.

The sense of randomness in the first section results from the irregularly spaced entrances of an ostinato pizzicato figure in the lower strings and the imitative wind entrances that are both irregularly spaced and out of phase with the ostinato entrances. The ostinato figure is derived from Lumen accende II, although the listener may not notice the source because the ostinato figure uses the minor mode and begins on the first instead of the fifth degree of the scale (Figure 81a). The winds use a motif that consists of a neighbor-note figure (see Figure 82) that has not appeared before in the symphony plus Lumen accende II in augmented note values (Figure 81b). The neighbor-note figure is aptly called the "forest motif," but it also appears prominently in the Scherzo sections and in the "Blicket auf" (S:178) and the Chorus Mysticus (5 after S:202) at the end of the Finale.

FIGURE 80
Mahler, Eighth Symphony, Part Two, Adagio

first part		*second part*		
section:	Starts at:	section:	Starts at:	text:
1	beginning of movement	6	S:24	Waldung ...
2	S:8	7	6 bars after S:32	Pater Ecstaticus
3	three bars after S:14	8	S:39	Pater Profundus
4	S:18	9	S:53	[orchestra]
5	S:21 [Scherzo]	[10]	S:56	Scherzo, Chorus of Angels

FIGURE 81
Mahler, Eighth Symphony, Part Two, Adagio

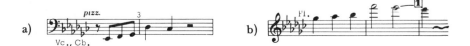

FIGURE 82
Mahler, Eighth Symphony,
Part Two: Forest motif

The texted counterpart (S:24) to the opening section increases the sense of randomness by stretching the meter. The six-beat measures make it possible for the ostinato figure to enter on weak beats as well as strong beats and for the two choruses to set their echoes of one another into different places in the measure.[32]

It would, however, be more accurate to say that the music is impulsive than to say it is unpredictable, for each fragment acts as though its impetus came from within itself. In this way, it exemplifies a mysterious spirituality — the same quality that Goethe's diction attributes to nature. By using verbs where a Newtonian scientist might use adjectives, Goethe's language suggests that nature is not a network of passive objects which people may observe in a detached way.[33] Nature consists of active forces that must seem unpredictable to the Newtonian: they do not cause effects in accordance with natural laws; they move themselves and act on other things out of their own impulses. Tree roots are in the act of clinging, crags are actively pressing down (they are not "weighty"), tree trunk thicks to tree trunk, fighting off light (they are not "close to one another"), deep holes mother protectively (not "are like protecting mothers"). Natural forces are like spiritual impulses, though they are not conscious of themselves; as impulses, they seem random to the detached observer; as spiritual impulses, they are uncanny. Nature is more an analogue to than an opposite of human, angelic or divine spirit. For Goethe, the human and the natural constitute a duality of conscious and unconscious spirit, while for someone like Kant, who explicates Newtonian presuppositions, the human and the natural constitute a duality of an inner world of freedom and an outer world of necessity.

At the beginning of the second section (S:8), a sense of purpose and forward-moving drive insinuates itself into the music. The aspiring Lumen accende II motif persists and becomes a more passionate striving. Although nature still acts impetuously and randomly in the sense that it obeys no laws external to itself, and although it does not reflect on its impulses, it now acts more purposively. The musical fragments now project phrases; the music is still impulsive, but it is now phrases, not fragments, that behave impetuously. Passion makes the impulses seem less isolated, and the scene becomes less eerie. In section seven, the corresponding section in the second part of the Adagio, the text draws an analogy between this unconscious drive and love. Two features of this solo ("Ewiger Wonnenbrand," six bars after S:32) are especially noteworthy. First, it makes an abrupt, unmodulated turn to the major mode. This shift further reduces the sense of mystery. Second, Mahler makes each phrase consist of three waves, and the first two are anacrustic to the third (these musical relations result from the melodic or harmonic mobility that characterize the half cadences in 7 and 9 after S:32, 2 and 4 after S:33, and so on; Figure 83 sketches these relations, using phrases of the text instead of bar numbers to refer to the music setting that phrase). But the third wave is no ordinary energy-absorbing focus, for it responds to its anacruses by gathering together their forward thrust. In other words, the first two waves press toward an arrival, but the arrival turns out to be also a non-arrival that summarizes and intensifies the forward drive. In the first two phrases, the text of the second wave is repeated in the third wave. As a result, both "glühendes Liebesband" and "schäumende Gotteslust" associate themselves with two different musical meanings, and their semantic meanings are made more specific by the double association: love means a longing (the second wave presses toward an arrival), and, surprisingly, love is also that which is longed for but which does not reduce the longing (the third wave is at once an arrival and a non-arrival that gathers together the forward propulsion).

FIGURE 83
Sketch of Mahler, Eighth Symphony, Part Two, Adagio, Pater Ecstaticus

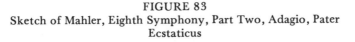

Ewiger Wonnenbrand,
glühendes Liebesband,
glühendes Liebesband,

siedender Schmerz der Brust,
schäumende Gotteslust,
schäumende Gotteslust.

Pfeile, durchdringet mich,
Lanzen, bezwinget mich
Keulen, zerschmettert mich,
Blitze, durchwettert mich,
dass ja das Nichtige
alles verflüchtige
glänze der Dauerstern,
ewiger, ewiger
Liebe Kern

The process of both absorbing and intensifying longing is exemplified not only by the first two non-arriving arrivals but also by the music for "Liebe Kern" at the end of section seven. Thus the section turns out to exemplify arrival at nothing, not only in the obvious sense that no arrival is embodied but also in the sense that by the end of the section, the listener has come to *expect* a focus that will not actualize that toward which the music has been pressing, and to feel that non-actualization is the most appropriate focus. In fact, by the end of the section the musically projected absence of arrival dominates over the forward pressure.

In the Classic antecedent-consequent phrase structure, the consequent phrase embodies that which the antecedent phrase evokes, and the process of generating and actualizing resembles the process of a self making itself concrete. In some of Beethoven's and some of the Romantics' antecedent-consequent phrases, the consequent phrase does not embody or only partially embodies that which has been evoked, resembling a process in which a self concretizes itself by failing to become fully actual and defines itself by its alienation from its inadequate embodiment. In contrast to both of these, Mahler's "ewiger Wonnenbrand . . . Liebe Kern" exemplifies a process in which non-actualization is appropriate to the force pressing toward actualization (the non-arriving foci are felt to be complete in spite of their instability), as though the self trying to become actual were not alienated from its non-embodiment and were not defined by its contrast to non-actualization. Evidently such a self identifies itself completely with pressing forward and absorbing forward pressure, which the text identifies as eternal, divine, passionate love. It identifies itself with this process so completely that there is no self independent of the process to be actualized by it, as though the subject of the process were totally merged with and submerged into the process itself. Mahler is exemplifying pure, subjectless loving.

In the next section, which gives words to section three, the text (S:39) draws an explicit analogy between the subjectless loving projected in section seven and the subjectless forces of nature. Just as the rocky cliff unconsciously presses down onto the deep abyss, just as streams unreflectively rush toward and into a violent cataract, just as the tree without any awareness of itself lifts itself up into the air, so loving reaches outward and onward though no one is loving. Though loving is almighty, it is not a predicate of an almighty being.

The phrases in sections three and eight are longer than those in sections two and seven. In sections three and eight, phrase beginnings use related motifs, as do phrase endings as well. In comparison to their predecessors, these sections have a tighter structure and more melodic definition. The size of the unit that is acting impulsively increases, but the degree of impetuousness is by no means diminished. Moreover, the increase in shapeliness from one section to the next is itself as impetuous, as little illustrative of natural or rational or moral necessity, as are the fragments in sections one and six and the phrases in sections two, three, seven and eight.

Figure 84 sketches one way of hearing the musical structure of section eight (as in Figure 83, the text is used instead of bar numbers to refer to the music). A comparison of Figures 83 and 84 indicates that the musical structures of sections seven and eight are similar. In section eight, waves once again press forward to a focus that gathers forward driving energy more than it embodies that toward which the prior waves press. The forward pressure is more violent in section eight with its jagged leaps, and the second and third phrases ("Ist um mich . . ." and "Mein Inn'res . . .") go on longer without reaching any focal wave. For both of these reasons, the nothingness of non-arrival is more palpable.

FIGURE 84
Sketch of Mahler, Eighth Symphony, Part Two, Adagio,
Pater Profundus

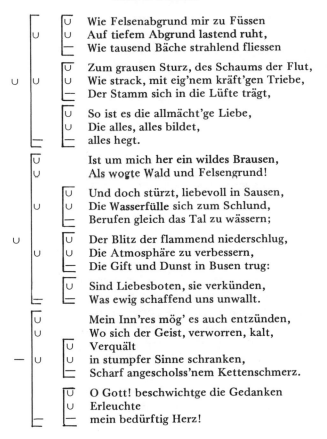

Wie Felsenabgrund mir zu Füssen
Auf tiefem Abgrund lastend ruht,
Wie tausend Bäche strahlend fliessen

Zum grausen Sturz, des Schaums der Flut,
Wie strack, mit eig'nem kräft'gen Triebe,
Der Stamm sich in die Lüfte trägt,

So ist es die allmächt'ge Liebe,
Die alles, alles bildet,
alles hegt.

Ist um mich her ein wildes Brausen,
Als wogte Wald und Felsengrund!

Und doch stürzt, liebevoll in Sausen,
Die Wasserfülle sich zum Schlund,
Berufen gleich das Tal zu wässern;

Der Blitz der flammend niederschlug,
Die Atmosphäre zu verbessern,
Die Gift und Dunst in Busen trug:

Sind Liebesboten, sie verkünden,
Was ewig schaffend uns unwallt.

Mein Inn'res mög' es auch entzünden,
Wo sich der Geist, verworren, kalt,
Verquält
in stumpfer Sinne schranken,
Scharf angescholss'nem Kettenschmerz.

O Gott! beschwichtge die Gedanken
Erleuchte
mein bedürftig Herz!

With the turn to major for the Pater Ecstaticus solo in section seven, the Lumen accende II motif begins to become more recognizable. The listener may well associate the idea of spiritual light kindling the senses and its way of overcoming the Veni I—Veni II duality with Pater Ecstaticus's words, "glühendes Liebesband," "schäumende Gotteslust" and "ewiger Liebe Kern." In section eight, the association is even stronger with Pater Profundus' "so ist es die allmächt'ge Liebe," "die alles bildet," "Sind Liebesboten," "in stumpfer Sinne schranken" and "erleuchte mein bedürftig Herz!" This last bit of the text, which Mahler treats as the focus of Pater Profundus' solo, is Goethe's closest equivalent to the literal meaning of "Lumen accende sensibus." As the use of the same musical motif makes the meanings of these texts interpret and enrich one another, the listener gradually comes to understand that the passionate loving and longing which so surprisingly resembles the unconscious forces of nature is identical to the Creator Spirit. The reappearance of Lumen accende II suggests that to love in such a way that the subject dissolves into the loving is to be illumined. The duality between loving as pressing toward a goal and loving as absorbing that pressure while setting the actualization of the goal permanently aside corresponds to the duality between the ultimate as something awesome and external to the self and the ultimate as the self's own depths.

(2) The Scherzo

Mahler lets all this sink in during a brief orchestral interlude (S:53, the Adagio's section nine). In the first part of the Adagio, section four (S:18), with its ruminations on sections two and three, is abruptly cut off by the jangle (S:21) that will become the Scherzo theme. The corresponding moment in the second part, S:56, is in fact the beginning of the Scherzo. Although the musical materials are the same (Lumen accende II and the neighbor-tone motif of the forest scene), the mood is decisively different. Suddenly, all is light and openness. Musical events become as predictable as in sections one and six of the Adagio they seem random. The world of spiritualized nature is displaced by heavenly frolics that are as lighthearted and unproblematic as those in Mahler's Third (fifth movement) and Fourth (fourth movement) Symphonies.

The Scherzo, like the Adagio, is a series of variations divided into two parts (Figure 85). Unlike the Adagio's second part, the Scherzo's merely succeed one another without any growth in shapeliness. They might become tedious did not Mahler interpolate a reprise of Infirma I and Firmans virtute (from S:76 to S:81) and Dr. Marianus's music — the beginning of the Finale — into the Scherzo, just as the Scherzo is interpolated into the Adagio (its section five).[34]

FIGURE 85

Sketch of Mahler, Eighth Symphony, Part Two, Scherzo

first part of Scherzo

1.	S:56	Gerettet ist das edle Glied . . .
2.	S:60	orchestral interlude
3.	S:63	Jene Rosen, aus den Händen . . .
4.	S:66	Böse wichen, als wir streuten . . .
5.	S:70	fühlten Liebesqual die Geister . . .

interpolation	S:76	uns bleibt ein Erdenrest . . . (reprise of Infirma I and Firmans virtute)

6.	S:81	Ich spür soeben . . .
7.	S:85	Freudig empfangen wir . . .

interpolation (first part of Finale)	S:84	(Dr. Marianus:) Hier ist die Aussicht frei (Finale)

second part of Scherzo

8.	S:121	Bei dem Bronn . . .
9.	S:123	Bei der reinen reichen Quelle . . .
10.	S:128	Bei dem hochgeweihten Orte, . . .
11.	S:136	Die du grossen Sünderinnen . . .
12.	S:142	Gönn' auch dieser guten Seele, . . .
13.	S:148	Neige, neige du Ohnegleiche, . . .
14.	S:155	Er überwächst uns schon . . .
15.	S:161	Er überwächst uns schon . . .

The angelic music jangles along without seeming to press toward any long-range goals.[35] As in nursery songs, every instance of musical openness is followed at once with precisely the expected closure. Still, longer-range goals are reached; for example, "Jauchzet auf!" at S:72 is the powerful focus of much of the preceding music (see Figure 86). But such arrivals (like those in Mahler's other angel movements) enter so effortlessly — one is so little aware of any thrust toward them — that they seem simply to occur without having been evoked. Here, as in section seven of the Adagio, there is no analogy to the process of a self embodying itself — of a self generating a future that makes the self concrete — but the reasons for the disappearance of the self are opposite. In the one, unconscious forces prcss forward, but that at which they arrive does not embody their goal; in the other, conscious forces have no goals, so the arrivals that happen cannot be understood as their achievement, and thus not as their embodiment. In the one, loving is subjectless when the goal of the process turns out not to be an actualization that would make a subject concrete but rather the intensification of loving itself; if the goal of loving is merged with loving itself, then the subject is too. In the other there is no movement to a goal of which a self might be the subject.

FIGURE 86
Sketch of Mahler, Eighth Symphony, Part Two, Scherzo, Younger angels

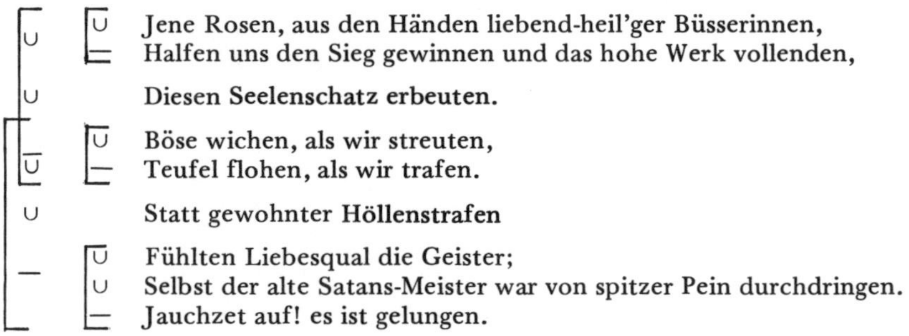

Jene Rosen, aus den Händen liebend-heil'ger Büsserinnen,
Halfen uns den Sieg gewinnen und das hohe Werk vollenden,

Diesen Seelenschatz erbeuten.

Böse wichen, als wir streuten,
Teufel flohen, als wir trafen.

Statt gewohnter Höllenstrafen

Fühlten Liebesqual die Geister;
Selbst der alte Satans-Meister war von spitzer Pein durchdringen.
Jauchzet auf! es ist gelungen.

Mahler reprises Infirma I and Firmans virtute after the fifth section of the Scherzo. Just as "Lumen accende sensibus" is associated with "erleuchte mein bedürftig Herz" so that the two texts interpret one another, so the "weak parts of our body" is made to interpret Goethe's text, "There remains a bit of earth for us to bear in pain." Mahler's treatment of the next line of Goethe's text, "Kein Engel trennte geeinte Zwienatur..." is at first a little puzzling, for the warm, gently passionate music is evidently depicting the bond between the corporeal and the spiritual and, in apparent disagreement with Goethe, depicting the bond as a positive aspect of human nature and not as a knot that needs to be cut. The puzzle disappears as Mahler goes on to make the music for "ew'ge Liebe" the focus of the passage, because then listeners see that the allusion (at S:79ff.) to Firmans virtute invites them to understand "only eternal love can separate them [the material and spiritual substances]" as meaning the same as "making firm with perpetual strength." Thus, the two allusions to Part One themes suggest that if weakness is entailed by the slightest trace of corporeality, then perpetual strength is implied by selfless, subjectless loving that purifies the spirit of its corporeal aspect — exactly the sort of loving that the Scherzo's process of arriving without exertion metaphorically exemplifies.[36]

(3) The Finale

The Finale begins before, as it will turn out, the Scherzo is completed. Dr. Marianus's music takes us into openness and light that is as much brighter than the Scherzo as the Scherzo is brighter than the Adagio. Just as the Scherzo is anticipated by the Adagio's section five, so the beginning of the Finale is inserted into the Scherzo. In fact, the first thirty-five measures of the Finale overlap the end of section six and all of section seven of the Scherzo (S:84 to S:89). A similar overlapping characterizes the beginning of the Finale's second part: the Finale resumes at S:164 with Gretchen's music, which commences just before the second part of the Scherzo is complete. In both places, Mahler's procedure resembles the frequently found device of beginning a new section on the last chord of the prior section's cadence, although, of course, Mahler is pushing that device to an extreme.

As techniques for integrating an Adagio, a Scherzo and a Finale into a single movement, the interpolations and the overlappings are masterful. Because the Scherzo appears as section five in the Adagio and because the Adagio's sections six through nine reprise its first four sections, the beginning of the Scherzo (at S:56) is heard as the counterpart to the Adagio's section five. S:56 serves both to complete the second part of the Adagio and to begin the Scherzo, just as the combination of Dr. Marianus's "Hier ist die Aussicht frei . . ." with the angels' "Sei er zum Anbeginn . . ." both completes the first part of the Scherzo and begins the Finale and the combination of Gretchen's "vom edlen Geisterchor umgeben . . ." with the children choir's "er wird uns lehren" both completes the second part of the Scherzo and begins the second part of the Finale. By alternating the parts of the Scherzo with the parts of the Finale, Mahler injects a measure of variety into the last half of Part Two, which makes it possible for him to exclude all dissonance and all heaviness without lapsing into musical tedium.

Both the Scherzo and the Finale begin as sudden elevations to brighter planes. These elevations are ungenerated. That is, there is no musical dynamic within the Adagio or the Scherzo to which the Scherzo and the Finale, respectively, are responding. Neither one is the embodiment of a future toward which the prior section might have been struggling. The opening of the new vistas simply happens, as though a new time in a new space were beginning. Yet, because of the interpolations and overlappings, the listener recognizes the new plane as also having already intersected the old. At the onset of both parts of both the Scherzo and the Finale, we have already been at the new starting place; the new world has evidently been already existing between the interstices, as it were, of the prior world.

The temporal process exemplified at the beginning of the Scherzo and Finale must be radically non-linear and non-cyclical. Ordinarily we think that ordinary time is like moving along a straight line from beginnings to endings or along a curved line in which similiar or identical patterns are cyclically repeated. Such a presupposition makes no sense when the orderly procession of points that articulate a line is displaced by a process of being suddenly elevated to a plane that is new but where we have, somehow, already been. Or, if one insists that time must be either linear or cyclical, then Mahler's music is simply confused.

The kind of temporal process prevailing at the beginning of both parts of both the Scherzo and the Finale turns out to underlie the Finale as a whole, for relationships both within and between the Finale's various sections also project a radically non-linear temporality. To accept this temporal process and to comprehend its implications for consciousness is, as the following paragraphs will try to show, to understand how Mahler envisions redemption.

(i) The First Part of the Finale

Like the two parts of the Adagio, the two parts of the Finale resemble one another, though the correspondence takes a different form (see Figure 87). While the second part of the Adagio reprises the first part, the two parts of the Finale correspond to each other in that both of them have the music for the Mater Gloriosa — Goethe's personification of loving — as their centerpiece. The first appearance of the Mater Gloriosa music (for orchestra alone, S:106–S:109) is preceded by Dr. Marianus' solo (and the chorus), "Hier ist die Aussicht frei ... Göttern ebenbürtig" and is followed by three developing restatements of the Gloriosa theme in the orchestra behind the chorus. The second appearance of the Gloriosa music (with the Mater Gloriosa singing, "Komm! ..." S:172–S:176) is preceded by Gretchen's solo (S:164, "Vom edlen Geisterchor umgeben ...") and is followed, again, by three developing restatements of the central theme.

Dr. Marianus' solo at the beginning of the Finale divides itself into three subsections: "Hier is die Aussicht frei . . ." (S:84), "Höchste Herrscherin der Welt . . ." (S:89) and "Jungfrau, rein in schönsten Sinne . . ." (S:99). The first is an objective description of the new brightness. The second describes the effect of the Mater Gloriosa — the Virgin [Mary], Queen of Heaven and Empress of the World who personifies loving — on those who see her mystery and feel her commanding and passion-subsiding presence. The third subsection is entirely ascriptive; it makes no plea, offers no promise, gives no information; it simply breathes and solemnifies the presence of loving.

FIGURE 87
Sketch of Mahler, Eighth Symphony, Part Two, Finale

first part of the Finale

1. a. S:84   Dr. Marianus ("Hier ist die Aussicht frei . . .")
                    (overlaps sections 6 and 7 of the Scherzo)
   b. S:89   Dr. Marianus ("Schönste Herrscherin der Welt . . .")
   c. S:99   Dr. Marianus and chorus ("Jungfrau . . .")

2.   S:106   Mater Gloriosa (orchestra)

3. a. S:109   Chorus ("Dir, der Unberührbaren, . . ."). First
                    restatement of Gloriosa theme
   b. S:112   Chorus ("In die Schwachheit . . ."). Second
                    restatement of Gloriosa theme
   c. 4 after S:114 Gretchen and chorus ("Du schwebst zu Höhen")
                    Third restatement of Gloriosa theme
   d. S:117   Retransition to Scherzo: Magna Peccatrix
                    ("Bei der Liebe")

Scherzo resumed
      S:121—S:164   Sections 8—15 of the Scherzo

second part of the Finale

4.   S:164   Gretchen ("Vom edlen Geisterchor . . .")
                    reprise of Imple at S:165

5.   S:172   Mater Gloriosa

6. a. S:176   Dr. Marianus and chorus ("Blicket auf, . . .")
                    First restatement of Gloriosa theme
   b. S:183   Choral restatement of "Blicket auf"
                    Second restatement of Gloriosa theme
   c. S:202   Chorus Mysticus
                    Third restatement of Gloriosa theme

All three subsections have a shape that distinguishes them from the Adagio and Scherzo sections. While in the latter, anacruses are followed by a focal phrase, in Dr. Marianus' solo, focal phrases and focal subphrases precede the music for which they are a focus (see Figure 88). What is most important about these groups is the way the focal phrase is heard, while it is going on, as an anacrusis, and the next phrase is heard as thetic when it begins; only when the second phrase is over does one realize that the focus is already past and that the second phrase has served more to round out than to articulate a focus. In other words, phrases with features like incomplete sequences, relatively unstable cadences and melodies that end on mobile notes sound as though they were moving toward a focus, although, to be sure, the forward motion is gentle, and the music is not overtly passionate. During the phrase that might state the focus, the music becomes less assertive, and the putatively thetic passage functions more as a gesture that extends and rounds out the previous phrase than as its focus. There is no arriving because the apical focus, it turns out, has been present before the second phrase begins. (In Figure 88, the symbol ‿ is intended to suggest a phrase that is initially heard as anacrustic, but turns out to be relatively stable in relation to the phrase it was supposedly evoking; ‾ indicates a passage which seems at its beginning to be thetic to the preceding or following passage but which, when it is over, turns out to have followed or preceded a thetic moment; the thetic moment itself apparently never takes place.) Just as the Adagio phrases press toward an arrival, and the arrival turns out to absorb the pressure by intensifying it and not by embodying the expected arrival, and just as the Scherzo phrases do not press forward, yet still arrive, hence arrive without exertion and without embodying the goal of any aspiration because there has been none, so the Finale phrases lead toward an arrival, but when the putative arrival appears, the music goes from preparing to sustaining fulfillment; the forward movement fades from memory, for the gentle aspiration has already projected its own quiet fulfillment.

Both the aspiring and the fulfilling aspects grow during the course of the three subsections. The growth, however, does not take the form of mounting intensity. Instead, it becomes less and less exuberant, and more and more solemnly hushed. Along the way, the melodic line becomes more and more definite — the fragments adhere to one another more and more tightly. A fully crystallized theme seems to have emerged in the orchestra at "Jungfrau, rein im schönsten Sinne," which for that reason serves as the focus of the three subsections. But its degree of crystallization is surpassed by the Mater Gloriosa section.

FIGURE 88
Sketch of Mahler, Eighth Symphony, Part Two, Finale,
Dr. Marianus and Chorus

Hier ist die Aussicht frei
Der Geist erhoben.
Dort ziehen Frauen vorbei,
Schwebend nach oben;
Die Herrliche mittenin,
In Sternenkranze.
Die Himmelskönigin.
Ich seh's am Glanze!

Höchste Herrscherin der Welt!
Lasse mich im . . . zelt
Dein Geheimnis schauen!

Bill'ge, was . . . Brust
Ernst und zart bewegt
Und mit heil'ger Liebeslust
Dir entgegen trägt.
Unbezwinglich unser Mut,
Wenn du hehr gebietest;
Plötzlich mildert sich die Glut,
Wenn du uns befriedest.

Jungfrau, rein im schönsten Sinne,
Mutter Ehren würdig,
Uns erwählte Königin,
Göttern ebenbürtig.

This section, which begins at S·106, states the theme whose fragments the Dr. Marianus music has been using less and less fragmentarily: the reach upward at the beginning of the Mater Gloriosa theme and the motif marked with an asterisk in Figure 89 have appeared prominently in the Marianus music. (See, for example, two bars after S:89, six bars after S:91, four bars after S:93 and one bar before S:100. The reach upward is isolated into prominence at 4—5 after S:99 in the solo violin).

But in spite of the fact that the Gloriosa music is the end of a progression to crystallized themelikeness, one cannot describe it as climactic, for the Marianus music cannot be said to be groping to or exerting itself toward anything. It would be more accurate to say that the Marianus passage "develops" the Gloriosa theme, although, of course the usual chronological order between statement and development is reversed. And so, the Gloriosa section is strangely like a point of departure for the Marianus music, even though it comes where a focus or climax might be. But, coming after the Marianus passage, the Gloriosa theme does not in fact depart for or take us to anyplace where it will not have already been. Compared to ordinary temporal processes, the process projected by the relation of the Marianus section as a whole to the Gloriosa theme is a convoluted one. It exemplifies on a higher structural level the same process that is exemplified within the Marianus section: the Marianus passage embodies fulfillment just as much as it aspires toward it; and the Gloriosa music sustains rather than states fulfillment.

FIGURE 89
Mahler, Eighth Symphony, Part Two,
Finale, Mater Gloriosa theme

FIGURE 90
Sketch of the Mater Gloriosa theme

And the Mater Gloriosa theme exemplifies within itself the same process. The beginning of the theme is anacrustic; its first four bars sound like a conventional antecedent phrase. But the putative anacrusis does not stop after four bars; instead it keeps growing for nine more measures. Because the theme's bars 5–6 are sequentially related to 3–4, no consequent phrase begins in bar 5. The B in bar 7 completes the echo of C-sharp–B (a motif first heard in bar 4), so bar 7 is heard as continuing the antecedent, not beginning the consequent. When bar 13 sequentially echoes bar 10, it becomes clear that 11–13 is also not a consequent, but a continuation of an antecedent that has soared and grown into thirteen measures before pausing to let a second phrase (bars 14–20) begin.

As Figure 90a indicates, the thirteen-bar phrase contains two descending lines. One starts on G-sharp; the other is an intensifying restatement — intensifying because it begins a note higher. Both descents move to the same note (B), and both end with complete repose. The second phrase sustains this repose. It is no more than a compact restatement of the first phrase, for it covers the same ground, ends no more stably (the greater stability of its ending on the tonic is offset by its shorter length), and uses the same motifs (the upward reaches in bars 14–15 and 16–17 are, as Figure 90b shows, a version in augmented note values of the motif, marked by an asterisk in Figure 89, that has been treated sequentially in bars 3–6). Consequently, the putative antecedent contains its own fulfillment. The putative consequent phrase continues and sustains the sense of fulfillment, but does not surpass the level of fulfillment achieved by its past. When we come to what would be arrival, we discover that we are experiencing the extension of fulfillment, not its beginning.

The Gloriosa theme acts as a cantus firmus holding the next three sections together. First the chorus[37] and then Gretchen sing in counterpoint to its statements in the orchestra. At S:117, the beginning of the Gloriosa theme is given words for the first time, but the tempo and the mood are those of the Scherzo. The Scherzo increasingly asserts itself until S:121, where it overtly takes over. The retransition to the Scherzo is handled so deftly that by the time it recommences, it has already been present. The process exemplified at the beginning of the first part of the Scherzo and the first part of the Finale is exemplified again.

(ii) The Second Part of the Finale

And the beginning of the second part of the Finale exemplifies it once more. Within the context of the Scherzo (its section thirteen), Gretchen puts words to the entire Gloriosa theme in its original form. After this anticipation of the Finale, the Scherzo goes on for two more sections, but when the Gloriosa theme reappears at S:172, following the powerful anacrusis of Gretchen's passionate solo (S:164), one feels that it has never really been absent.

AT S:165 Gretchen's solo puts Goethe's words ("[he] scarcely surmises the fresh life") to the music that originally set the medieval text, "Imple superna gratia." Evidently Mahler wants to suggest that for Faust to resemble the heavenly host so closely that he is not even self-consciously aware of his new life means something like our hearts being filled with supernal grace. Ordinary consciousness involves being aware that one is aware; one is aware in both a non-mediated way (so that one is literally identical to one's consciousness) and at the same time in a way that is mediated by concepts (one has a concept of this awareness and of oneself having this awareness). Goethe's text asserts that the new life — the redeemed Faust — sheds the mediated consciousness. The immediate consciousness characterizes the grace-filled heart. It also characterizes loving in the way the entire Part Two has been adumbrating; loving in a way that separates the spiritual from the corporeal is being aware in a way that separates the immediate from the mediated consciousness (the music at S:165 also closely resembles the music at S:78, "Kein Engel . . .", for Imple and Firmans are also closely related).

Goethe's text at the end of Gretchen's solo (S:170) suggests a non-mediated consciousness through the image of blinding light. Ordinarily, light enables us to see objects; here the light is so bright that all objects disappear, just as in the new consciousness all concept-mediated objects disappear. Once again, Mahler uses the musical motif to link Goethe's text to the medieval hymn. At S:171, Lumen accende II reappears: the blinding brightness of Faust's new day is identified with the Creator Spirit's light that kindles human senses. As in the first part of the Finale (at S:104), Lumen accende II is the last idea to assert itself before the Mater Gloriosa commences.[38]

Gretchen's music thrusts forward, and the Mater Gloriosa music at S:172 stands where the arrival of this thrust is expected. But once again, we hear not an arrival but a sense of extending culmination. For, although the Gloriosa music articulates the tonic (E-flat) to Gretchen's dominant (as well as the tonic of the whole symphony), its beginning does not sound like a consummation but rather like music that follows a culmination. It sustains a fulfillment that seems already to have happened. Because Gretchen's solo, with its insistent high B-flats, is the most passionate forwardly impulsive music in the Finale, the sense, projected by the Gloriosa music, of sustaining rather than attaining is the most definitive example of the temporal process that the Finale has exemplified several times before on several different levels of the music structure.

Dr. Marianus's "Blicket auf" (S:176) is a condensed version of the whole Finale (just as the last seven bars of the Gloriosa theme are a somewhat more compact version of its first thirteen). It opens with the same flash of brightness (but now in the tonic) that characterizes Dr. Marianus's opening of the Finale. It gathers together all the motifs from the symphony's Part Two: the opening figure recalls the forest motif by duplicating its rhythm (♩.♪ ♩). The motif from the Gloriosa theme marked by an asterisk in Figure 89 reappears in the fifth bar after S:176 and many times thereafter. A somewhat confined version of Lumen accende II is treated sequentially at three bars after S:178 to five after S:179. The temporal process of the Gloriosa music is replicated: the solo presses forward from its onset to S:181, when the Gloriosa theme is restated in the winds and then the strings, and as before, the Gloriosa sustains culmination rather than arriving at it. Consequently, Dr. Marianus's fervent plea, "bleibe gnädig," which is set by the Gloriosa theme, is heard as having already been answered.

The chorus straightaway repeats the same process. Beginning at S:183 it reviews and expands "Blicket auf" and works more urgently toward a culmination. The culmination that in fact sustains and extends culmination begins at S:186, where the Gloriosa music returns, this time with only the first motif, the upward reaching sixth.

The symphony is brought to its end by a choral passage, the Chorus Mysticus, that leads us through the same process one more time. "Alles Vergängliche" (S:202) and "das Unzulängliche" (S:203) take us back to the forest motif in its original form. Each of these is followed by a somewhat restrained version of Lumen accende II for "ist nur ein Gleichnis" and "hier wird's Ereignis." By using the same music for both lines of text, Mahler duplicates Goethe's appositive: "The transitory is but an image, a likeness" and "That which is fully adequate here becomes actual" interpret each other; that which is transitory is transitory precisely because it is not fully adequate in and of itself and must therefore lead into a fuller future embodiment; that which is fully adequate has no such future, hence no transitoriness. We are being given something of an explanation for the temporal process projected by the Finale sections: the passages where consummation is replaced by sustaining, rather than arriving at, a sense of fulfillment suggest that their prior passages — their putative anacruses — are not after all transitory; musical images of that which is fully adequate in itself, they could have no future that would embody something surpassing them.

"Zieht uns hinan" uses the Lumen accende II motif. Spiritual light kindling human senses is given yet another appositive. "Zieht uns hinan" is also set (at S:208) by the rising sixth of the Gloriosa theme, which appears this time in the forward pressing passage that will turn out to have contained fulfillment. The personification of loving (das Ewig-Weibliche) draws us on, but the loving-drawing theme turns out to be that toward which we are drawn. The appearance of the Gloriosa motif in this context exemplifies, therefore, the same temporal process associated with the Gloriosa music throughout the Finale.

The non-arrival that sustains fulfillment begins at S:210 when the chorus on the words "Ewig! Ewig!" sings the rising sixth motif. Mahler isolates this one word from Goethe's context ("das Ewig-Weibliche") and reduces the Gloriosa music to its first four notes. "Ewig" seems to serve as a label put on the temporal process of the whole Finale; the temporality of transfigured consciousness is exemplified most succinctly and unambiguously at this point and is identified by the word, "Ewig!"

The Chorus Mysticus begins in hushed awe, as though one were in the presence of something so majestically, terrifyingly numinous that one's feelings were suppressed and numbed. As in Veni I at the beginning of the symphony, human consciousness is subordinated to the ultimate. Although the first few phrases project a reverent stillness, they are not static. Each phrase opens up into the next one. The volume gradually increases. Imperceptibly, a sense of forward movement, resembling the striving that characterizes human consciousness, develops. At "Ewig! Ewig!" (S:210) that toward which the forward thrust has been moving has already appeared. Human consciousness has not only been fulfilled, but in having already been fulfilled, it is also transformed. Hushed awe has been changed into unbuttoned exhilaration.

The second statement of "Alles Vergängliche . . ." (S:123) exudes an exalted elation. It is not, however, the thrill of human fulfillment that is being expressed, as though human fulfillment were itself ultimate, as Veni II almost suggests that it is. Rather the thrill is that of a consciousness whose consciousness of itself has been shed and whose awareness of the ultimate is not mediated by any self-awareness. The transition between hushed awe and unbuttoned exhilaration is handled so smoothly that there is no sense of a duality between the ultimate (in the presence of which one is awestruck) and unself-conscious fulfillment (which is present as unbuttoned exhilaration). Heidegger would say that the duality could disappear only if both ultimacy and fulfillment are being thought in a radically non-representational way, for if they are thought in a conceptual way, each must be conceived as the ground of the other, and the sense of dualism and of the need to transcend the dualism would prevail. In this important sense, the Chorus Mysticus does anew what the recapitulation in the first movement has already done. Mahler confirms the connection between these passages when, at the end of the chorus, the brass choir reinvokes the presence of Veni I in a transfigured form.

Commentators like Gabriel Engel have suggested that the Creator Spirit in Part One corresponds to love in Part Two. The foregoing analysis suggests a different correlation: Part Two's redeemed consciousness, which is characterized by loving, corresponds to Part One's non-representational way of thinking ultimacy and fulfillment.

(4) Transfigured Consciousness and Its Temporality

Sartre, in *Being and Nothingness,* draws a distinction between being-for-itself, the way of being which characterizes human consciousness, and being-in-itself, the way of being of all other entities — stones, grass and human beings to the extent that they may be regarded as objects or reduced to their genetic, psychological or sociological past. Being-in-itself is unselfconscious. Unaware of itself it cannot be a subject, aware of other entities. Consequently, any relation it has with another entity is a relation as seen by an entity outside itself. The relation is external to the in-itself entity in that the relation does not qualify or inwardly affect the entity itself. What it is is no different for the fact of the relation. The entity simply is; it is identical to itself.[39]

Self-awareness — presence to itself, which the in-itself never has — is the hallmark of human consciousness. A for-itself entity (a person) sees itself; it is related to itself; it is consequently not identical to itself. It is continuously surpassing itself; it sees itself; it makes plans and sees itself making plans and identifies itself with the subject that will carry out (or fail to carry out) those plans. The act of being aware of the self transcends the self (which then becomes an instance of an in-itself) that is the object of awareness. Yet the for-itself is the very self it is transcending. Thus, the self-conscious entity is the surpassed self that, as transcended, it is not. Lacking self-presence, the in-itself entity simply is what it is; having self-presence, the for-itself entity both is what it is not and is not what it is.[40]

This bristling remark pushes language to the edge of its intelligibility. We may nevertheless accept Sartre's analysis because it rings true to the structure of our conscious experience, and being self-conscious is, after all, radically different from being an object, which ordinary language is best suited to describe.

The applicability of Sartre's analysis can be seen by considering what is involved in belief. Unlike an in-itself entity, my belief, Sartre says, is not purely and simply my belief; my belief is also the consciousness of belief. I am aware that I have such-and-such a belief; I am in a sense detached from my believing. And thus it is already no longer belief (it is not what it is); it is troubled belief; it is a belief that, being in a sense detached from it, I can doubt (it is what it is not, for it is not identical to this troubled belief either).[41]

The fissure within the for-itself, without which the for-itself would not be, is the pure negative, for it is nothing that separates subjects from themselves or belief from itself — not spatial difference, nor a lapse of time, nor psychological difference, nor the individuality of two entities that are present simultaneously. "*Nothing* can separate the consciousness of belief from belief, since belief is *nothing other* than the consciousness of belief."[42] Yet they are separate. That they are separate while nothing separates them discloses nothingness. In short, human reality establishes nothingness at the heart of being;[43] if it did not, there would be no distinction between being-in-itself and being-for-itself.

One way to indicate the nature of Faust's transfiguration, as Mahler envisions it, would be to pick up Sartre's terms and say that Faust's redeemed consciousness is partly like the unconsciousness of being-in-itself and partly like the nothingness-ridden consciousness of being-for-itself. In the redeemed consciousness, nothingness disappears without the entity becoming an example of being-in-itself. This statement contradicts Sartre's conceptuality; it joins what Sartre divides and denies the fundamental (and intuitively obvious) distinction between in-itself and for-itself entities on which his whole description of human existence rests.

The contradiction is appropriate; if Sartre's analysis were not contradicted, redemption would not involve a change in the nature of consciousness and would mean only a change in the object of consciousness. There are, of course, visions of redemption in which Sartre's presuppositions about consciousness prevail. But it seems to be the case that the more readily comprehensible are the visions of redemption, the less compelling they are. The ordinary assumptions about consciousness seem to apply, for example, to the depictions of the blessed in Renaissance paintings of the Last Judgment and to the "Wie lieblich sind deine Wohnungen" from Brahms's *Deutsches Requiem,* but many people find the painters' paradise to be boring and Brahms's bliss to be self-indulgent. Mahler seems to be envisioning a far more radical change — a change in the fundamental nature of consciousness. He seems to be envisioning a new kind of entity that is like and unlike both conscious and unconscious entities.

It is not easy to understand this statement. The best way to amplify it may be to contrast the temporal processes that would characterize this new entity to those of ordinary consciousness. It is, after all, by giving us the temporality which would characterize transfigured consciousness that Mahler projects his vision of the redeemed way of being.

Using Goethe's words, Mahler suggests that the redeemed consciousness is eternally drawn toward loving and is itself eternally loving. The Adagio suggests the character of this loving by comparing it to nature's unconscious forces which passionately pursue goals without knowing that they have goals. Natural entities, as Mahler lets them assert themselves, are not like Sartre's in-itself entities, for their goals relate them internally to other entities. Mahler's non-arriving arrivals that absorb and intensify forward thrust without embodying a fulfillment show forth the character of this loving. At these points, the nature of the past is fundamentally different from the past that the for-itself being has.

According to Sartre, there can be no past in isolation from the present of a for-itself being. It makes no sense to try to imagine a past in abstraction from a self-aware entity that might do the imagining. What the for-itself being calls its past is, without the for-itself being, simply annihilated. That is not to say, however, that the for-itself being invents the past: "It is not because I 'represent' the past that it exists. But it is because I *am* my past that it enters the world."[44] The for-itself entity does not "have" a past in the way it may "have" a coat. For while I am unequivocally not my coat, "I am me" — I am the one who has undergone this past; in being me, I am responsible for my past. "The past is the ever growing totality of the in-itself which we are."[45] But at the same time, I am not simply identical to my past; the moment when I am precisely equivalent to my past is the moment of death. A for-itself is not an in-itself entity; it must be its past in order not to be it (that is, in order to surpass it) and it must not be it in order to be it (that is, to own it and be responsible for it).[46] The heterogeneity that characterizes the for-itself way of being, already exhibited in the phenomenon of belief, appears here too.

No such heterogeneity characterizes in-itself being. Nor does it characterize the way of being that is shown forth by the loving of Mahler's Adagio. The non-arriving arrivals are, in a very significant sense, identical with their energetic, creative past. The distinction between their past and the present is obliterated not in the sense that the present (at the non-arriving foci) embodies an in-itself entity that duplicates (is precisely like) the in-itself that has been, but in the sense that the present does not actualize the goals of the past and there is therefore no question of the present for-itself surpassing the in-itself (the past) which it is. When nothing is actualized and creative energy simply persists, the nothingness that separates, for example, the for-itself subject from itself or belief from itself disappears. As energetic, creative loving does not make itself concretely actual by generating some entity that might be said to employ it, the for-itself does not turn into an in-itself; it does not become its past. Because its way of being is not heterogeneous, it persists without change or becoming. Or, perhaps better, it persists in a new way of becoming; its becoming, compared to the for-itself way of becoming, is content-less; it does not change into anything that can be specified. Because the creative loving does not generate expectations that might be un-fulfilled, the contentlessness of its becoming is positive, not self-alienating. Unlike the in-itself way of being, its past asserts its relevance onto this becoming, for the non-distinction between past and present impinges on the present during the non-arriving foci as much as the distinction between past and present qualifies the for-itself experience of owning the past.

Nothingness also characterizes the future of the for-itself entity. In Sartre's analysis, the future is not a " 'now' that is not yet."[47] The future is the unembodied but possible content that the for-itself not only lacks but lacks *in order to be itself*. The for-itself entity is always more than that to which it can be empirically reduced at any given moment, for "the for-itself *has to be* its being instead of simply being it."[48] What is called the future characterizes the for-itself for this reason. In short, "the for-itself makes itself be by perpetually apprehending itself for itself as unachieved in relation to [its being] . . . Everything which the for-itself is beyond being is the future."[49] The subject of the for-itself being — the self that is — is thus both identified with and distinguished from the in-itself which it is and owns and for which it accepts responsibility (the past), and it is also identified with that which it lacks (the future).

This sort of nothingness does not characterize the subject of loving in Mahler's Adagio. The music presses forward, but not toward an actualization of the subject, not toward the embodiment of that which it now is in the mode of lacking it. The pressing impulses do not even generate expectations whose non-fulfillments disclose the subject by their contrast to it. The music presses forward in such a way that the process it metaphorically exemplifies is one in which there is no fissure between the pressing forward and the subject's awareness that it is pressing forward because the subject is completely submerged in the forward drive. The process is temporally articulated, yet the subject and the object of the process collapse into the process itself. But though the loving that Mahler is musically characterizing differs in this way from the for-itself entity, it does not become an in-itself being. For unlike the temporality of the in-itself, Mahler's process is like one in which a future impinges on every present and qualifies a subject's every experience of itself; the loving is, after all, creative, energetic, forward-thrusting and in some sense aware that it is future-begetting.

The temporal process of Mahler's Scherzo offers a somewhat different contrast to the temporality of Sartre's for-itself entity. This contrast can be best seen by reviewing Sartre's analysis of the present. The present would seem to be definable as a plenitude of being, for "what is present *is* — in contrast to the future which is not yet and to the past which is no longer."[50] Yet the more vigorously one purges the present of what it is not (the past and the future) the more it becomes the nothing of an "infinitesimal instant." The meaning of the present, however, is not this nothing, but the presence of the for-itself to being-in-itself. Only a for-itself entity can be present to another entity, for a being that is present to something "cannot be at rest 'in-itself.' "[51] Presence entails an internal bond; the for-itself knows that to which it is present, and this knowledge contributes to the being of the for-itself. If the connection were external (as it is between two in-itself entities, which cannot be present to one another), there would be no presence. But this internal bond is a negative one in the sense that the for-itself denies that it is the entity to which it is present and denies that the bond constitutes the totality of itself. The internal bond is not a pure and simple identification.[52] In fact, the for-itself understands itself by distinguishing itself from and in a sense fleeing from that to which it is present. The "present is precisely this negation of being."[53]

The temporal process of Mahler's Scherzo does not resemble a process of a for-itself moving away from that to which it is present. The music does not establish long-range goals and characterize the present as a lack. We might say then that the blessed angels and cherubic children who are characterized by this music do not distinguish themselves from that to which they are present. In not seeking to embody something that is lacking at the present and thereby to actualize themselves, they cannot exemplify the usual process of being a self. Thus like for-itself entities, they are present to Faust and Gretchen, and unlike in-itself entities, they may be said to be "internally bonded" to them. But unlike the for-itself, they are bonded in a totally positive way, for, in not characterizing the present as a lack, they do not deny that the bond totally constitutes their being. They and their music exemplify a process in which one's presence to something else entails no flight from that to which one is present; the present loses its negation and becomes a plenitude. Such is the loving that characterizes angelic blessedness.

Both the Adagio and the Scherzo exemplify temporal processes in which the heterogeneity of the for-itself being is set aside. The in-itself is also not heterogeneous. The difference between the self-identical loving and the self-identical in-itself entity is that the former is self-related. This self-relation does not manifest itself emphatically, however, until the Finale sections. Self-relation implies both a pressing toward goals and the embodiment of those goals, an ongoing process of surpassing itself, because it sees itself and at the same time distinguishes the self it sees from the self it is in the mode of not yet being it. The Finale exemplifies both aspects of this process, but in a way that contradicts the way the for-itself is self-related: at the moment where the embodiment of that toward which the music has been pressing might take place, it always turns out that consummating fulfillment has already been present. What would be culminating moments turn out to be sustaining continuations of fulfillments, for pressing toward fulfillment has, again and again, turned out not to function as a contrast to fulfillment. In other words, Mahler may be said to be envisioning a kind of self-relation that is different from Sartre's by associating it with a different kind of temporality.

Ordinarily, self-relation means that the for-itself is aware of itself through a mediating concept — a conceptual summary — of itself, which the for-itself entity both is and is not. The for-itself experiences a gap between its concept of itself and its imagined future; more precisely, it experiences this gap as a lack and as the force of possibility. The Third Symphony Finale contradicts Sartre's assumptions about consciousness when it combines non-fulfillment with fulfillment: the forward-pressing passages in the chorale suggest a process in which a self-related self is aware of a gap between what it is and what it will be but does not experience this gap as a lack. The Eighth contradicts Sartre's assumptions even more sharply by omitting the moment of attaining fulfillment and passing directly from preparing to sustaining it: by pressing forward, the music suggests a process like one involving a self-related self (only an entity that is self-related can experience its future impinging on it); by identifying both preparing and sustaining fulfillment with fulfillment, the music is like a process that involves self-relation even though the self does not experience a gap between what it is and what it will be. The self-relation of this new kind of consciousness evidently does not involve the mediating concept that such a gap would ordinarily imply. The transfigured consciousness is aware of itself, but does not know itself (if "know" implies "conceptually aware"). Like the for-itself, it is internally bonded to that to which it is present, but lacking a concept of itself it does not distinguish itself from that to which it is present. Given the peculiar, un-Sartrian kind of self-relation that the Finale's peculiar temporal process implies, one might say that that to which the redeemed, loving consciousness is present is also a for-itself-like loving that coincides with the transfigured consciousness. Yet, for all the fullness of being which these identities imply, transfigured consciousness is evidently not static; it thrusts ahead, even though that which is thrusting and that toward which it is impelled seem, from the perspective of ordinary consciousness, to be nothing.

The Fifth Symphony leads us into and through a temporal process in which passionate striving presses toward fulfillments but in which the fulfillments turn out to be recollections of fulfillment. These fulfillments genuinely function as fulfillment, and not, like the non-arriving arrivals in the Eighth, as sustaining fulfillment. If the Fifth led us into conventional fulfillments, in which the fulfillment is like the manifestation of a self that has shaped it, Sartre's analysis would apply straightforwardly: the manifestation (which depends on its contrast to the past) both would be and would not be the self, and nothing would separate them. Because the Fifth leads us from struggling toward fulfillment to having fulfilled, Sartre's analysis must be somewhat extended: the Fifth is like a process in which the ownmost self experiences this nothing and the gap it creates in that the ownmost self self-consciously feels that the manifestation (and any putative manifestation) both is not and is identical to the self: the event that stands where fulfillment might have stood is in fact a recollection and is candidly recognized as such, yet the recollection is still a fulfillment. The recollecting fulfillment is like a process in which the ownmost self is able to repeat itself (as Heidegger would say) precisely because the nothingness involved in consciousness has come into the open and has become palpable; repetition is fulfillment because to be one's ownmost self is to be all that one can be. Where the Fifth gives us a fulfillment that turns out to be a recollection and makes palpable the gap between the self and its every embodiment, the Eighth goes directly from preparing to sustaining culmination and makes palpable the absence of a culminating moment. By doing do, it identifies preparing and sustaining with each other and with fulfillment itself. The absence of a culminating moment makes possible the fullness of consummation in which the nothingness that Heidegger's repetition presupposes plays no role.

The difference between the two symphonies is of a piece with the fact that the Fifth explicitly confronts death, while the Eighth does not presuppose finitude. In facing death, one comes upon one's ownmost self, whose repetition is fulfillment, as that which is lost upon death. Without the finitude implied by death, the Eighth suggests, consciousness loses individualization; the subject is merged with its process, and working toward fulfillment cannot be the manifestation of a self trying to embody itself. Just as the moment of attaining fulfillment disappears when the music passes directly from preparing to sustaining culmination, so the ownmost self that both would be and would not be manifest in a conventional fulfillment and that would be repeated in a recollecting fulfillment loses a concept of itself and relates itself to itself without distinguishing itself from loving and being loved.

While there are passages in the Eighth's Finale that seem at first to be thrusting forward toward redemption, it always turns out that the transformation has already taken place. The temporal processes metaphorically exemplify those of redemption itself (as Mahler envisions it) rather than the process of moving from the ordinary to the new consciousness. The distinction is an important one. The process of moving from the old to the threshold of the new would itself be characterized by the temporality of ordinary consciousness and could suggest with regard to the nature of the new only that transfiguration is the outcome of a struggle or the resolution of a longing or a radical contrast to what has been.

The difference between Mahler's Finale and the moment when the Pilgrim arrives at the gates of heaven in Vaughan Williams's *Pilgrim's Progress* aptly illustrates this difference. Vaughan Williams's arrival is a glorious, triumphant moment. But the thrill one experiences is the thrill of ending a difficult journey. The thrill of being victorious implies that one is still significantly related to that over which one has triumphed. *Pilgrim's Progress* gives us no suggestion of what being in heaven would be like if the struggle were completely forgotten. One suspects that it might be boring, that there would be nothing so glorious as the moment of arrival. Listeners who expect such a glorious moment in Mahler's Eighth are consistently disappointed. For he never offers us the moment of transformation. Instead he suggests what it is like to have been transformed.

This fundamental difference is perhaps even better illustrated by the difference between the Finale of Mahler's Eighth and the Finale of his Second Symphony. The comparison suggests itself because both use harps, organ and brass to suggest heaven and heavenlyglory, both end in E-flat, and both feature a chorus growing from a hushed opening to a mighty climax.

In the Second Symphony, Mahler's motivic treatment enables this climax to present the triumph of resurrection over death and destruction and the triumph of confident faith that there will be a resurrection over doubt and pain. The hope of resurrection is crystallized in the two motifs that are quoted in Figure 91. Both have been anticipated in the first movement. The upward rising motif (91b) is of a piece with the first movement's second subject (S:3, S:7 and ten bars after S:22); the Auferstehen motif (91a) has been adumbrated at bars 5—6 after S:16. Throughout the first movement, themes that are related to these motifs of light and serenity are generated by and are somewhat responsive to themes that are associated with death, judgment and destruction, but the themes of terror and gloom always triumph over — even swallow up — those of tranquility and hope, either abruptly and rudely (at S:4) or more gradually (at S:9 and S:24), so that the movement ends with peace dismembered and hope crushed. The themes of death and gloom

FIGURE 91

Mahler, Second Symphony, Finale

crystallize in Mahler's allusion to the opening motif of the plainchant Dies irae at bars 13—14 after S:16 in the first movement (Figure 92). The same version of the Dies irae recurs in the Finale at eight bars before S:5. In both movements, the Dies irae phrase generates a response that is associated with the Auferstehen motif (Figure 91a): in the first movement (at four bars before S:17), the motif that will bear the Auferstehen text (at S:31 in the Finale) is somewhat vaguely anticipated, while in the Finale, the responding phrase — a more or less conventional nine-bar consequent — is identical to the motif that sets "Auferstehen . . ."

FIGURE 92
Mahler, Second Symphony, first movement, bars 17—20
after S:16, Dies irae theme

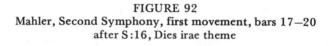

The movement from Dies irae phrases to Auferstehen phrases is one of the most significant aspects of the Second Symphony. In the first movement, the progression from Dies irae to Auferstehen, from death, judgment and destruction to peace and light, goes awry when the Dies irae reasserts itself at three bars before S:18. This process is duplicated in an expanded form in the middle of the Finale: a march derived from the Dies irae (at eleven bars after S:15) is succeeded by a long passage controlled by the Auferstehen theme (beginning at eight bars before S:16), but once again the movement toward victorious fulfillment begins to be warped when the Dies irae reasserts itself (five bars after S:17). The warp becomes particularly ghoulish at S:20, but eventually the dissonances are resolved. The music bearing the resolution is the chorus's Auferstehen, beginning at S:31. After facing a final dissonance — the difficulty of believing in the resurrection (S:39 to S:46) — the serenity motif (at S:46, compare to Figure 91b) obliterates the last enemy — fear — and the final appearance of Auferstehen (S:48) is completely victorious and untroubled. While the shape of the first movement is the alternation of death and gloom with serenity and light, ending with the destruction of hope, the Finale alternates destruction with resurrection and ends with the defeat of the negative forces. The progression at S:5 to S:6 of the Finale from the Dies irae antecedent phrase to the Auferstehen consequent phrase turns out to be a compressed version of the form of the Finale as a whole and indeed of the entire symphony.

The temporal process exemplified by the Second Symphony is

that of ordinary consciousness. While wondrous, it is no different from the process exemplified by winning a battle or overcoming hatred or subduing fear and doubt. Beyond negating negativity, the Second gives us no intimation of what the resurrected life is like. Where it suggests the progression from destruction to reconstruction and from terror to a new certainty, the Eighth Symphony suggests the nature of the new life. While the Second exemplifies the process of moving from ordinary consciousness, beset as it is with ambiguities, to redeemed consciousness, the Eighth focuses instead on the plenitude of the transfigured consciousness of loving. Although one may describe the Eighth's new life in terms of its difference from unredeemed life, this contrast plays no part in the musical process itself. One cannot speak of a victory, for a past condition over which a victory might be won has no force; it is as though the unredeemed past never happened or were completely forgotten. The consummation at the end of the Second Symphony is somewhat parasitical on its past; shorn of its dreadful memories, it would sound overdone and empty. Its past is a set of contingencies — things that happened to happen — for which it accepts responsibility and whose thrust it absorbs while distinguishing itself from these contingencies. But in the redeemed temporality of the Eighth, the past is always the past of love itself with which every present remains completely identical, just as the future implies no lack in the present, no unachieved goal, and presence means an untroubled identity with that to which it is present.[54]

Given this sort of past and future, listeners cannot be surprised that at the end of the Eighth they have not been moved through a single process, as though Part Two as a whole were the unfolding of a single structure which at the end could be contemplated as a static totality. By the canons of continuity associated with ordinary temporality, the movement is too riddled with lacunae and non-sequiturs to be considered a structure in the usual sense. The arrivals do not embody the goals of their pasts' exertions either because the past was not exerting itself toward anything (the Scherzo) or because the arrival turns out to be a sustaining continuation of its past, but the past has not in fact embodied an arrival (the Adagio and the Finale in different ways). The music continually communicates a sense of being in process; one is constantly — even at the end — kept in the midst of process and can gain no perspective outside it from which to view it. It is as though the content of the process had always slipped through one's fingers, or as though the process of loving were its own content. When we appreciate this strange sort of content and this strangely unclosed process for what they are, we are perhaps closest to seeing what Mahler saw when he envisioned the redeemed life.

FIGURE 93
Text of Mahler, Eighth Symphony, Part Two

Choir and Echo
Waldung, sie schwankt heran,
Felsen, sie lasten dran,
Wurzeln, sie klammern an,
Stamm dicht an Stamm hinan.
Woge nach Woge spitzt,
Höhle, die tiefste, schützt.
Löwen, sie schleichen stumm-
Freundlich um uns herum,
Ehren geweihten Ort,
Heiligen Liebeshort.

Pater Ecstaticus
Ewiger Wonnebrand,
Glühendes Liebesband,
Siedender Schmerz der Brust,
Schäumende Gotteslust.
Pfeile, durchdringet mich,
Lanzen, bezwinget mich,
Keulen, zerschmettert mich,
Blitze, durchwettert mich,
Dass ja das Nichtige
Alles verflüchtige,
Glänze der Dauerstern,
Ewiger Liebe Kern!

Pater Profundus
Wie Felsenabgrund mir zu Füssen
Auf tiefem Abgrund lastend ruht,

Wie tausend Bäche strahlend fliessen
Zum grausen Sturz des Schaums der
    Flut,
Wie strack, mit eig'nem kräft'gen Triebe,

Der Stamm sich in die Lüfte trägt,
So ist es die allmächt'ge Liebe,
Die alles bildet, alles hegt.

Ist um mich her ein wildes Brausen,
Als wogte Wald und Felsengrund!
Und doch stürzt, liebevoll im Sausen,

Choir and Echo
The Woodland, it sways toward us;
The rocks, they press down;
The roots, they clasp onto;
Tree trunk thickens to tree trunk;
Wave upon wave splashes;
The deepest dens shelter;
Lions, they pad silently
And friendly about us,
And honor the consecrated place,
A holy refuge to love.

Pater Ecstaticus
Eternal fire of rapture,
Glowing bond of love,
Boiling agony of the breast,
Foaming longing for God.
Arrows: pierce me;
Lances: conquer me;
Clubs: smash me;
Lightning bolts: strike me through —
That Nothingness
May evaporate everything,
And the everlasting star may shine —
The center of eternal love!

Pater Profundus
As the rocky abyss at my feet
Rests weightily on the deep abyss
    below,
As a thousand gleaming brooks flow
To the dreadful cataract of the
    foaming flood,
As straight upward, with its own
    mighty force,
The tree trunk lifts itself into the air,
So is the almighty love
That forms everything and protects
    everything.
There is around me a wild tumult,
As if forest and clift were heaving!
And yet, the profusion of waters,
    which, full of love in its rush,

Die Wasserfülle sich zum Schlund,
Berufen gleich das Tal zu wässern;

Der Blitz, der flammend niederschlug,

Die Atmosphäre zu verbessern,
Die Gift und Dunst in Busen trug:

Sind Liebesboten, sie verkünden,

Was ewig schaffend uns umwallt.

Mein Inn'res mög es auch entzünden,
Wo sich der Geist, verworren, kalt,
Verquält in stumpfer Sinne schranken,

Scharf angeschloss'nem Kettenschmerz.
O Gott! beschwichtige die Gedanken,
Erleuchte mein bedürftig Herz!

Angels
Gerettet ist das edle Glied
Der Geisterwelt vom Bösen:
Wer immer strebend sich bemüht,
Den können wir erlösen,
Und hat an ihm die Liebe gar
Von oben teilgenommen,
Begegnet ihm die sel'ge Schar
Mit herzlichem Willkommen.

Blessed boys
Hände verschlinget euch
Freudig zum Ringverein,
Regt euch und singet
Heil'ge Gefühle drein.
Göttlich belehret,
Dürft ihr vertrauen:
Den ihr verehret,
Werdet ihr schauen.

Younger Angels
Jene Rosen, aus den Händen
Liebend-heil'ger Büsserinnen,
Halfen uns den Sieg gewinnen
Und das hohe Werk vollenden,
Diesen Seelenschatz erbeuten.
Böse wichen, als wir streuten,
Teufel flohen, als wir trafen.
Statt gewohnter Höllenstrafen

Fühlten Liebesqual die Geister;

Plunges into the gorge,
Summoned to water the valley
    presently,
And the lightning that in flames struck
    down
To clear the air
Which bore poison and fume in its
    bosom —
These are the messengers of love; they
    announce
That which seethes around us,
    eternally and creatingly.
May it ignite me within,
Where my spirit, confused and cold
Agonizes within the confines of dumb
    senses,
In the pain of fast locked chains,
O God, calm my thoughts.
Enlighten my needful heart!

Angels
Rescued is the noble member
Of the world of spirit from evil:
The one who strives and struggles,
Him we can redeem.
And if love from
On high has had a part in him,
The blessed host will meet him
With a welcome from the heart.

Blessed boys
Let your hands clasp each other
Joyfully in the circle of union;
Bestir yourselves and sing
Holy feelings thereto.
Divinely taught,
You may be confident
That him whom you revere
You will see.

Younger Angels
Those roses from the hands
Of loving, holy penitents
Helped us to win the victory
And fulfill the high task
And capture this treasure — this soul.
Evil retreated as we strewed (the roses);
Devils fled when roses struck them.
Instead of the usual punishments of
    hell
These spirits felt the pangs of love;

Selbst der alte Satans-Meister
War von spitzer Pein durchdrungen.
Jauchzet auf! es ist gelungen.

More Perfect Angels
Uns bleibt ein Erdenrest
Zu tragen peinlich
Und wär' er von Asbest,

Er ist nicht reinlich.
Wenn starke Geisteskraft
Die Elemente
An sich herangerafft,
Kein Engel trennte
Geeinte Zwienatur
Der innigen beiden,
Die ewige Liebe nur
Vermag's zu scheiden.

Younger Angels
Ich spür soeben,
Nebelnd um Felsenhöh,
Ein Geisterleben,
Regend sich in der Näh'.
Seliger Knaben
Seh' ich bewegte Schar,
Los von der Erde Druck,
Im Kreis gesellt,
Die sich erlaben
Am neuen Lenz und Schmuck
Der obern Welt.

Doctor Marianus
Hier ist die Aussicht frei,
Der Geist erhoben.

Younger Angels
Sei er zum Anbeginn,
Steigendem Vollgewinn,
Diesen gesellt!

Doctor Marianus
Dort ziehen Frauen vorbei,
Schwebend nach oben;
Die Herrliche mittenin,
Im Sternenkranze,
Die Himmelskönigin . . .

Blessed Boys
Freudig empfangen wir
Diesen im Puppenstand;
Also erlangen wir
Englisches Unterpfand.

Even old Master Satan
Was pierced by sharp pain.
Rejoice! It is accomplished!

More Perfect Angels
There remains a bit of earth for us
To bear in pain,
And even if it were made of Asbestos
  (incorruptible substance),
It is not pure.
When the strong power of the soul
Has clasped matter
To itself,
No angel may divide
The two joined substances
Of the innerly bonded pair;
Only eternal love
Is able to separate them.

Younger Angels
I feel just now
Around the misty cliffs
A spiritual life
Making itself felt nearby.
Of holy children
I see a stirring host,
Free of the burden of the earth,
Companions in a circle;
And they take delight
In the new springtime and finery
of the upper world.

Doctor Marianus
Here the vista is wide and open,
And the spirit is lifted.

Younger Angels
Let him [Faust] as a first beginning,
And with increasingly complete gain,
be companioned with these!

Doctor Marianus
Women are passing there,
Soaring upward;
In their center, the Glorious One,
In a wreath of stars,
The Queen of Heaven . . .

Blessed Boys
Joyfully we receive
Him in the formative stage
For so we acquire
An angelic pledge.

Löset die Flocken los,
Die ihn umgeben.
Schon ist er schön und gross
Von heiligem Leben.

Doctor Marianus
... Ich seh's am Glanze!
Höchste Herrscherin der Welt!
Lasse mich im blauen
Ausgespannten Himmelszelt
Dein Geheimnis schauen!
Bill'ge, was des Mannes Brust
Ernst und zart bewegt

Und mit heil 'ger Liebeslust
Dir entgegen trägt.
Unbezwinglich unser Mut,
Wenn du hehr gebietest;
Plötzlich mildert sich die Glut,
Wenn du uns befriedest.

Doctor Marianus and Choir
Jungfrau, rein im schönsten Sinne,
Mutter, Ehren würdig,
Uns erwählte Königin,
Göttern ebenbürtig.

Choir
Dir, der Unberührbaren,
Ist es nicht benommen,
Dass die leicht Verführbaren
Traulich zu dir kommen.

In die Schwachheit hingerafft,
Sind sie schwer zu retten.
Wer zerreisst aus eig'ner Kraft
Der Gelüste Ketten?
Wie entgleitet schnell der Fuss
Schiefem, glattem Boden?

Penitent Woman (Gretchen) and Choir
Du schwebst zu Höhen
Der ewigen Reiche,
Vernimm das Flehen,
Du Gnadenreiche,
Du Ohnegleiche!

Magna Peccatrix
Bei der Liebe, die den Füssen
Deines gottverklärten Sohnes
Tränen liess zum Balsam fliessen,
Trotz des Pharisäer-Hohnes,
Beim Gefässe, das so reichlich

Shake off the flakes
That envelope him.
Already is he fair and tall
Through the holy life.

Doctor Marianus
... I am seeing in the light of splendor,
O most exalted mistress of the world!
Let me, in the blue
Outspread canopy of heaven,
See thy mystery.
Approve that which
Earnestly and tenderly moves the
    breast of man
And which with the holy joy of love
Bears him to you.
Our courage is indomitable
If you majestically command us;
At once our passion subsides
When you pacify us.

Doctor Marianus and Choir
Virgin, pure in the fairest feeling,
Mother, worthy of praise,
Chosen to be queen to us,
Peer to the gods.

Choir
To you, the unassailable once,
It is not denied
That those who are easily tempted
May come in confidence to you.

Carried away in weakness,
They are difficult to rescue.
Who of his own strangth
Sunders the chains of lust?
How quickly does the foot slip
Upon a sloping, slippery surface!

Penitent Woman (Gretchen) and Choir
You soar to the heights
Of the eternal kingdom;
Accept our supplication,
You who are rich in grace
And without equal.

Magna Peccatrix
By the love that on the feet
Of your divinely transfigured Son
Let fall tears as a soothing balsam,
In spite of the Pharisee's scorn;
By the jar that so richly

Tropfte Wohlgeruch hernieder,
Bei den Locken, die so weichlich
Trockneten die heil'gen Glieder —

Mulier Samaritana
Bei dem Bronn, zu dem schon weiland

Abram liess die Herde führen,
Bei dem Eimer, der dem Heiland
Kühl die Lippe durft' berühren,
Bei der reinen reichen Quelle,
Die nun dorther sich ergiesset,
Überflüssig, ewig helle,
Rings durch alle Welten fliesst —

Maria Aegyptiaca
Bei dem hochgeweihten Orte
Wo den Herrn man niederliess,
Bei dem Arm, der von der Pforte,
Warnend mich zurücke stiess,
Bei der vierzigjähr'gen Busse,
Der ich treu in Wüsten blieb,

Bei dem sel'gen Scheidegrusse,
Den in Sand ich niederschrieb —

All Three
Die du grossen Sünderinnen
Deine Nähe nicht verweigerst
Und ein büssendes Gewinnen
In die Ewigkeiten steigerst,
Gönn auch dieser guten Seele,
Die sich einmal nur vergessen,
Die nicht ahnte, dass sie fehle,
Dein Verzeihen angemessen!

Gretchen (Una Poenitentium)
Neige, neige,
Du Ohnegleiche,
Du Strahlenreiche,
Dein Antlitz gnädig meinem Glück.

Der früh Geliebte,
Nicht mehr Getrübte,
Er kommt zurück.

Blessed Boys
Er überwächst uns schon
An mächt'gen Gliedern,
Wird treuer Pflege Lohn
Reichlich erwidern.
Wir wurden früh entfernt
Von Lebechören;

Dripped sweet fragrance;
By the tresses that so softly
Dried the holy limbs . . .

Mulier Samaritana
By the well, to which already in olden
times
Abraham drove his flock;
By the pail which was permitted
To touch and cool the Savior's lips;
By the pure rich spring,
Which now pours from there
And spilling over, eternally clear,
Flows around through all the world . . .

Maria Aegyptiaca
By the consecrated place
Where the Lord was laid;
By the arm that from the gate
Warned me and thrust me back;
By the forty-year repentance,
To which I remained faithful in the
desert;
By the blessed farewell
Which I wrote in the sand . . .

All Three
You who do not deny
Your presence to these great sinners
And who elevate one repenting victory
Into the eternities:
Grant also to this good soul,
Who forgot herself only once,
Who did not suspect that she erred,
Your appropriate pardon.

Gretchen (A Penitent)
Incline —
You who are without equal,
Who are resplendently radiant —
Your countenance graciously upon
my happiness.
My beloved of early days,
No longer a troubled man,
Is coming back!

Blessed Boys
Already he grows past us
On mighty limbs,
He will amply repay
His debt for our faithful care.
We were early in life snatched
From the choir of the living;

Doch dieser hat gelernt,
Er wird uns lehren.

Gretchen
Vom edlen Geisterchor umgeben,

Wird sich der Neue kaum gewahr,
Er ahnet kaum das frische Leben,
So gleicht er schon der heil'gen Schar.

Sieh, wie er jedem Erdenbande
Der alten Hülle sich entrafft.
Und aus ätherischem Gewande

Hervortritt erste Jugendkraft!
Vergönne mir, ihn zu belehren:
Noch blendet ihn der neue Tag.

Mater Gloriosa
Komm! Hebe dich zu höhern Sphären,

Wenn er dich ahnet, folgt er nach.

Choir
Komm! Komm!

Doctor Marianus
Blicket auf zum Retterblick, alle
  reuig Zarten
Euch zu sel'gem Glück
Dankend umzuarten.
Werde jeder bess're Sinn
Dir zum Dienst erbotig;
Jungfrau, Mutter, Königin,
Göttin, bleibe gnädig!
Bleibe gnädig!

Chorus Mysticus
Alles Vergängliche
Ist nur ein Gleichnis;
Das Unzulängliche
Hier wird's Ereignis,
Das Unbeschreibliche,
Hier ist's getan;
Das Ewig-Weibliche
Zieht uns hinan.

But this one has learned,
And will teach us.

Gretchen
Surrounded by the noble choir of
  spirits
The new one scarcely sees himself,
Scarcely surmises the fresh life,
So resembles he already the heavenly
  host.
See how he lets go every earthly bond
Of the old husk,
And from ethereal raiment comes
  forth
The prime power of youth!
Grant me to teach him!
The new day still blinds him.

Mater Gloriosa
Come! Come! Rise to the higher
  sphere!
When he has a presentiment of you, he
  will follow.

Choir
Come! Come!

Doctor Marianus
Look up! All who are frail and penitent,
Look up to the saving glance
To acquire thankfully
The blessed happiness.
May every better sense
Becoming willing in service to you.
Virgin, Mother, Queen
Goddess, remain gracious.
Remain gracious,

Mystical Choir
Everything transitory
only distantly resembles what is here;
Here, that which is inadequate of itself
Becomes full-event;
That which is indescribable
Is accomplished.
The eternal feminine
Draws us to herself.

Notes

1. "It would be an odd thing if my most important work should be the most easily understood," Mahler wrote his wife after he had played a few passages of the Eighth for Mengelberg and Diepenbrock and they had responded enthusiastically. Alma Mahler, *Gustav Mahler: Memories and Letters*, ed. Donald Mitchell (1969), p. 274.

2. *Op. cit.*, p. 338.

3. In this chapter, the various motifs that set the same word will be related to one another as complements or polar opposites, and the various words that are set to the same motif will be similarly related. This method of analysis is partly derived from Claude Levi-Strauss' structural analysis. See in particular, his chapter, "Myth and Music," pp. 44-54 of *Myth and Meaning* (1979). This essay describes various dramatic situations in Wagner's *Ring* in which the so called "Renunciation" motif appears and shows that although some of these situations seem to have little in common, they are in fact complementary. In other words, Levi-Strauss identifies the axis along which they are polar opposites; the common motif discloses the existence of this axis.

4. Although Mahler does not appear to have derived either Veni I or Veni II from the plainchant version of this hymn (which was traditionally used at ordinations to the priesthood as well as at the second vespers on Pentecost), it is interesting to note two similarities. The interval of the fourth is as crucial to the distinctive quality of the plainchant as it is to Mahler's Veni I. And, like Veni II, the plainchant version exemplifies aspiration: it reaches upward (on "spiritus") after preparing the leap (by circling G on "Veni, creator"). See Figure 74. The hymn, "Veni, Creator Spiritus," is not to be confused with the more widely known, and more effusive, Pentecost sequence, "Veni sancte spiritus." Although Mahler's setting of Veni, Creator is probably the most famous one today, it is not the oldest. The text was set by Binchois, Palestrina, Praetorius, Gibbons, Bach, J.N. David and Berlioz. Since Mahler, works related to the text or its plainchant setting have been composed by Carl Orff, Richard Yardumian, Joseph Ahrens, Dietrich von Bausznern, Wayne Burcham, Heinrich Lausberg, Bernard Lewkovitch, Herman Schroeder and Heinrich Weber.

5. The exposition of Mahler's Fourth Symphony has the same structure: the first theme returns after the second theme, signaling the repeat of the exposition (or the onset of the second part of a "double exposition"), but the second theme is not restated; the return of the first theme is followed by an exposition closing and then the development. Edward W. Murphy, in his "Sonata-Rondo Form in the Symphonies of Gustav Mahler," *Music Review*, vol. 36 (1975), pp. 54-62, finds an ABA structure in seven other expositions (I/i, II/i, II/v, III/i, VII/i, VII/v and IX/i). Murphy's article usefully calls attention to significant structural aspects of II/v, VII/i and VII/v, but his analyses of II/i, III/i, and IX/i seem strained and unconvincing. In order to find the ABA structure in as many expositions as possible, he calls some gestures main themes that in fact seem more analogous to subsidiary gestures, ignores the very clear return of the second subject in the exposition of II/i, and so on. But he calls attention to the important fact that many of Mahler's themes, like both themes in VIII/i, consist of an aba structure.

6. Deryck Cooke (*op. cit.*, p. 92) is not unusual in overlooking the subtle contrast between Veni I and Veni II and failing to see that a return (S:5) implies a departure. Cooke blurs the two Veni motifs into a single characterization, "a great confident shout by humanity to the skies for the creative vision that the modern world so desperately needs." The work's greatness is lost on most of the critics who do not see the Veni I—Veni II duality as a dynamic that generates the rest of the movement. Kennedy (*op. cit.*, pp. 133-134) is typical: "The thematic simplicity and diatonic harmony are not supported by the sustained inventiveness which alone could have assured Mahler a total realization of his immense conception."

7. *Institutes of the Christian Religion* I.2.1.

8. See, for example, *On Religion*, trans. John Oman (1958), pp. 15-16, 36, 39-40, and *The Christian Faith*, trans. H.R. Mackintosh and J.S. Stewart (1928), p. 17.

9. "Once feeling has been pronounced to be the subjective essence of religion, it in fact is also the objective essence of religion . . . If feeling in itself is good, religious, i.e., holy, divine, has not feeling its God in itself?" *The Essence of Christianity*, trans. George Elliott (1957), p. 10.

10. See, for example, Soren Kierkegaard's concept of the double movement in *Fear and Trembling*, trans. Walter Lawrie (1954), and Paul Tillich, *Systematic Theology*, vol. III (1963), pp. 111-20.

11. See Charles Hartshorne, *The Divine Relativity* (1948), pp. 123-134.

12. See, for example, David Tracy, *Blessed Rage for Order* (1975), pp.43-56.

13. Gabriel Engel, "Mahler's *Eighth:* The Hymn to Eros." *Chord and Discord*, vol. 2, no. 6 (1950), p. 21, calls the first Infirma the last part of the exposition, and the second the beginning of the development proper. While not a great deal is at stake in the application of sonata-form labels to Mahler's sections, the duality between Infirma I and Infirma II is a development of the exposition's dualities and an important dynamic generating subsequent events. Recognizing, with Murphy (*op. cit.*, p. 61), that they are parts of the same section — the development — calls attention to this fact. Engel's analysis reflects the fact that a long orchestral interlude (S:23 to S:30) separates the two Infirmas, but overlooks the decisive closure to the exposition achieved at S:17 and the orchestral interlude between S:17 and Infirma I at S:19.

14. "The choir's melancholy whisper in the darkened (minor) scene tells of man's sudden consciousness of his unworthiness. The discouragement of the moment is accentuated by poignant happenings in the orchestra. Brief cries of pain issue from the piccolo; a solo violin wanders disconsolately through the gloom" (Engel, *op. cit.*, p. 20).

15. Barford, *op. cit.*, p. 312, associates Lumen accende II with other Mahler motifs in which a stepwise rising line expresses aspiration and an upward leap suddenly releases the tension generated by the scale and expresses rest. In other contexts, the rising scale expresses agonizing striving or longing, gnawing loneliness, but in the Eighth Symphony, says Barford, it suggests "upsurging inspiration" — the meaning of spiritual illumination. Barford's comparisons are helpful in specifying the process that Lumen accende II exemplifies, but because he insists that the rising component of the gesture must be stepwise, he misses the important connection between Lumen accende II and Veni II, a connection that is crucial to the dynamic process that makes the first movement of the Eighth a coherent whole.

16. *Op. cit.*, p. 94.

17. Mahler's thinking here may be compared to Haydn's in the Angus Dei of the *Paukenmesse* and to Beethoven's in the Dona nobis of the *Missa Solemnis:* they put the listener in touch with the terror of the battlefield in order to convey why and how very urgently they are pleading for peace.

18. Even the listener who refuses to be moved by this reprise cannot deny that it displays the same "instrumentation and counterpoint of infallible mastery and clearness" that Tovey (*op. cit.*, p. 77) attributes to the exposition of the Fourth Symphony's first movement.

19. For Engel (*op. cit.*, p. 22), the Praevio is the "goal of the development." The double fugue is one of the most conspicuous justifications for the vast choral and orchestral forces that Mahler calls for and that constitute the basis for Wellesz (*op. cit.*, pp. 18-19) to link this symphony with the tradition of the "colossal style" going from Benevoli's Festival Mass in fifty-three parts (1628) through the Berlioz *Requiem* and the Liszt Gran Festival Mass to the Mahler Eighth. Hans-Ferdinand Redlich (in *Bruckner and Mahler* [1963], p. 213) says that Mahler knew the Benevoli Mass well.

20. Martin Heidegger, "The Onto-Theo-Logical Constitution of Metaphysics," in *Identity and Difference*, trans. by Joan Stambaugh (1969), pp. 49-52, and *passim*.

21. See, for example, Christopher Ballantine, "Beethoven, Hegel and Marx," *The Music Review*, vol. 33 (1972), pp. 34-46.

22. Heidegger, *Identity and Difference*, pp. 65, 69.

23. *Ibid.*, p. 71.

24. *Ibid.*, p. 72.

25. *Ibid.*, pp. 60-61.

26. Berlioz, Gounod, Busoni, and, later, Thomas Mann, for example. Mann attended the premiere of the Eighth in 1910 and wrote Mahler praising the work extravagantly. See Alma Mahler, *op. cit.*, p. 342.

27. Schumann also set this passage. It is the last section of his *Szenen aus Faust* (1849). Liszt, in his Faust Symphony (1854), uses a heroic theme, which may suggest the nature of the redeemed Faust, as the climax of the first movement. The symphony closes with a setting of the Chorus Mysticus, Goethe's last eight lines. Newlin (*op. cit.*, pp. 194-196) points out some similarities, which she finds to be important, between Liszt's and Mahler's settings of the Chorus Mysticus. Redlich (*op. cit.*, pp. 214-216) hears the influence of Liszt throughout Part Two, which he describes as a dramatic oratorio "somewhat in the manner of Liszt's *St. Elisabeth*."

28. Some listeners have been bothered by Mahler's dissonant juxtaposition of a religious, Latin text to a humanistic, German text (see, for example, Redlich, *op. cit.*, p. 214). To interpret the two movements as projecting the same idea is to say that both movements challenge the distinction between the religious and the humanistic. This interpretation disagrees with that of Deryck Cooke (*op. cit.*, p. 93), who accepts the distinction as valid, though he applies it surprisingly: it is the first movement that is humanistic, in spite of its religious text, and the second movement that is actually religious, in spite of its humanistic text: "If this religious text of Part I is given a secular humanistic meaning, the humanistic text of the symphony's second part . . . is given a timeless, metaphysical meaning at the work's culmination, set as a religious chorale." In letters to his wife, Mahler himself appears to have interpreted Goethe in Platonic terms and amalgamated the Christian and Greek views of love. For him, the distinction between the religious and the humanistic evidently had no force. See Alma Mahler, *op. cit.*, pp. 332, 335, and Engel, *op. cit.*, pp. 13-16.

29. So Harold Schonberg in reviewing a performance of the Eighth (New York *Times*, February 16, 1974, p. 37). Kennedy, *op. cit.*, p. 134, is even more caustic: the Mater Gloriosa music reminds him of Mascagni's Santuzza, and the chorus's "Blicket auf" is hymned, he says, not so much to Eternal Womanhood as to the Sugar-Plum Fairy.

30. While Engel, *op. cit.*, evaluates the movement more positively than Schonberg and Kennedy, he describes it in terms of the object of consciousness and the feelings it arouses and misses the movement's radically altered temporality and the new way of being conscious implicit in this temporality.

31. Mahler opens "Der Spielmann" (*Das klagende Lied*) and his First and Second Symphonies with similar shimmers. Bruckner makes even more extensive use of this technique.

32. Goethe's text calls for an echo, presumably to suggest the cavernous depths of the scene.

33. Although Goethe came into most explicit conflict with Newtonian science in the field of optics, he was also aware that his basic approach to the study of nature was irreconcilably different. See, for example, Walter Kaufmann, *Discovering the Mind*, vol. 1, *Goethe, Kant and Hegel* (1980), pp. 35-49.

34. The view that the Scherzo is a series of variations into which the first part of the Finale is interpolated is shared by Hans Tischler, "Musical Form in Gustav Mahler's Works," *Musicology*, vol. 2 (1949) and Engel, *op. cit.*, p. 28. Redlich (*op. cit.*, p. 216n) dismisses this interpretation as *"a posteriori."*

35. At this point Mahler deviates from Goethe's text in two ways: he omits Goethe's thirty-six lines for Pater Seraphicus and the Blessed boys, and while Goethe puts "Hände verschlinget euch . . . werdet ihr schauen" before "Gerettet ist . . . mit herzlichem Willkommen," Mahler starts the Scherzo with the first two lines of the latter text and then sets the two simulatenously.

36. It is accordingly not necessary to agree with Barford (*Mahler, Symphonies and Songs*, 1971, p. 51) that Mahler did not understand the depth of Goethe's symbolism.

37. The Chorus sings a text that Goethe assigns to Dr. Marianus. Mahler does not set the seven lines of Goethe's text that come between "Göttern ebenbürtig" and "Dir, der Unberührbaren."

38. The works of visual art that most compellingly suggest the nature of redemption are not those that simply depict the blessed enjoying paradise, but those in which light is as central as it is to both movements of Mahler's Eighth. Two examples may make the point. First, the Gothic cathedral, which for medieval piety was the earthly foreshadowing of the celestial city, buttressed its roof-bearing walls from the outside so that the windows could be very large without the roof falling in. The result was that the worshiper was enveloped in walls of light-colored light, thanks to the superb craftsmanship of the artisans working with stained glass. As Otto von Simson points out, light was regarded by the medieval mind as the most direct manifestation of God (*The Gothic Cathedral* [1956], p. 53). Second, light plays a central role in some of the ceiling painting in Baroque churches which portray heaven itself breaking in above the worshipers. One of the finest examples of this convention is the ceiling fresco in Il Gesù, Rome, done in 1672-1685 by G.B. Gaulli. Clouds and figures within the fresco articulate a strong upward movement against an infinitely deep background. The painting's climax is located two-thirds of the way up its longer axis where a blinding light — the divine presence — shines forth.

39. Trans. Hazel E. Barnes (1956), p. 77.

40. *Ibid.*, p. 79.

41. *Ibid.*, pp. 74-75.

42. *Ibid.*, p. 77. Sartre's italics.

43. *Ibid.*, p. 79.

44. *Ibid.*, p. 115. Sartre's italics.

45. *Ibid.*

46. *Ibid.*, pp. 117-118.

47. *Ibid.*, p. 125.

48. *Ibid.*, p. 126. Italics are Sartre's.

49. *Ibid.*

50. *Ibid.*, p. 120. Italics are Sartre's.

51. *Ibid.*, p. 121.

52. *Ibid.*, p. 122.

53. *Ibid.*, p. 123.

54. Newlin (*op. cit.*, p. 192) misses the importance of these differences in temporal process when she says of the Eighth's closing chorus that it is a "heightened, accentuated version of the corresponding passage in the Second Symphony." See also Redlich, *op. cit.*, pp. 150-151, 216.

CHAPTER IV

The Ninth Symphony

1. The First Movement

By 1909, when Mahler was at work on his Ninth Symphony, he knew that he had a gravely serious heart condition. Some commentators have suggested that writing this piece was his effort to deal with the possibility of imminent death.[1] Whether or not the composer self-consciously understood his work in that way, the speculation accurately calls attention to the symphony's treatment of finality and to the centrality of this theme throughout its four movements. For in one way or another, a sense of being near the end or an attempt to dismiss or accept or transmute this feeling makes itself continuously present.

The first movement is a long, slow song that grows out of a single melodic kernel, usually called the "Lebewohl" or "farewell" motif. At the end of the movement, this motif has been transformed into a closely related, yet fundamentally different motif charged with fundamentally different connotations. The following analysis will try to retrace the listener's experience, identifying the connotations of these two motifs and then describing Mahler's highly original transformation of the one into the other.

(1) The "Lebewohl" Motif

"Lebewohl" is the word German-speaking people use when they expect never to see one another again. The "Lebewohl" motif consists of two descending whole steps: F-sharp to E and E to D. By Mahler's day, this motif had become a conventional way of alluding to the word "Lebewohl." Beethoven, for example, had written this word over the two descending whole steps that opened his "Les Adieux" Sonata, Op. 81a.[2] But the connection between the motif and the sense of finality is not merely conventional; the motif is also an apt metaphor for a depature. That is, its internal dynamics are such that it is a metaphorical example of a final leave-taking. To hear these dynamics, listeners must obviously be aware of the harmonic context; they must know that the first note, the F-sharp, is not the final note in a scale, but is a tone that has downward mobility to the final note, D. On hearing the F-sharp, we expect a lower note, in much the same way that we expect a noun to come when we hear the word "toward" and the context tells us we are hearing English. The downward push from F-sharp to D is not, however, nearly so strong as the downward push from F-natural to D would be. In fact, the motif begins almost balanced between the pull of the D and a resistance to movement of any kind.

A final leave-taking is the experience of feeling tied to someone, resisting movement away from this person, and at the same time feeling that the tie is about to be broken; the impending end does not weaken the strength of the bond, and the strength of the bond does not weaken the sense of imminent, final departure. In the "Lebewohl" motif, the balance between downward movement and resistance to movement makes an effective aural image of a final departure. A descent from F-natural to E to D would be a less apt metaphor for "farewell" because its downward push is stronger, and the sense of finality dominates over what is left behind. The difference between the two descents is a subtle one, somewhat like the difference between resignation and despair. When I am resigned to an ending, I accept it and continue to feel tightly bound to the other person. In despair, my strong protest against the ending distracts my attention somewhat from the positive aspects of the relationship.

As the motif unfolds, and the F-sharp is replaced by E, the downward push to D is clearer, and the sense of coming toward the end obscures the sense of involvement with others. At this point, there is no difference between resignation and despair: the ending dominates. And when the D comes, the gesture is complete. It — whatever "it" is — is over.

Measures 7 through 25 consist of the theme that Mahler spins out of this motif. In this theme, Mahler sustains the balance between the sense of a coming final end and the sense of being profoundly involved in what is about to end. He takes excursions into tunes that are reminiscent of Viennese balls.[3] The Viennese whirl of life is affirmed. It is not stigmatized as ephemeral, nor is the ending dreaded because it entails the loss of something beautiful. All these excursions are permeated with the descending whole step, F-sharp to E, sometimes beginning on other pitches (C-sharp to B, or B to A, or A to G) and sometimes decorated (as C-sharp—G—B instead of simply C-sharp to B). Each descent implies the inevitable D whose coming is delayed but never anticipated during these excursions. One way or another, the "Lebewohl" motif makes its presence continuously felt. See Figure 94.

(2) The "Ewig" Motif

The theme contained in bars 7—25 appears five more times during the movement. In its final statement, the last twenty-one measures of the movement, the motif is superficially the same, but in fact it is fundamentally transformed. We hear F-sharp to E, as in the "Lebewohl" motif, but there is no longer any pull on to the D. This motif, F-sharp to E, may be called the "ewig" motif because it is the same as the motif that sets the word "ewig" ("eternally") at the end of Mahler's *Das Lied von der Erde* (1908).[4]

FIGURE 94
Mahler, Ninth Symphony, first movement

The "ewig" motif is so brief that it is remarkable only because it sounds neither complete nor incomplete. When we hear F-sharp—E as the first two notes of "Lebewohl," we hear no closure with the E, for the E is implying a push on to closure on D; when we hear F-sharp—E as the "ewig" motif, we again hear no closure on E, but now the E is not pushing toward closure either. To say that there is not closure on the second note is to say that there is not a sense of having arrived at a point toward which the past has been moving, and to say that there is no drive to closure is to say that working toward a future in no way affects the content of the present.

These aspects of Mahler's "ewig" motif — that it is neither complete nor incomplete, that it neither has nor seeks closure, and that the sense of movement from past to future is weakened — lead us into a new kind of temporal process. Given the association of the motif with the word "ewig," one may say that Mahler's movement comes to suggest what it is like to be involved in a temporality that is eternal — what it is like to be eternally conscious. The radical difference between the temporality projected by the "ewig" motif and ordinary temporality, however, implies that this eternal consciousness means being conscious in a fundamentally new way, and not simply being unendingly conscious in the ordinary way.

In ordinary consciousness — the way of being conscious to which Mahler is suggesting an alternative — closure is essential to both the object and the subject. When I deal with an object, I expect closure in the sense that I expect what I shall see of it will fit harmoniously with what I now see and remember of it. What I think I am doing when I make a decision is to move a situation, in which various possibilities exist, to closure, and I choose that closure which in my judgment best fits the situation. In other words, I understand the present and the future by way of analogy to the past, in which closures have happened. Closure is also critical to the subject of consciousness, for the self I see myself becoming is the completion of the self I now am. The self I am now forms closure with the self I have been. Without sensing and expecting closure, the self that is aware of something and the something of which it is aware, indeed the very process of consciousness would be fundamentally different. In fact, were it not for visionaries like Mahler, we would suppose it would be impossible.

In *Das Lied,* the "ewig" motif (E—D hovering over a C major chord, neither at rest nor moving toward rest, bars 540—566) serves to resolve the fundamental tension in "Der Abschied." Arthur Wenk describes this tension as the contrast between the two major themes that permeate the six songs of the cycle: celebration of the endless renewal of life and resignation to the transitory character of life.[5] It is the contrast between the cyclic process of nature (sleeping and waking, moving into and out of darkness, dying and regeneration) and the linear process of human experience (moving toward a final departure to which there is no beyond and feeling the pathos of a final leave-taking from one's friend or from one's world). As a resolution to this contrast, the "ewig" passage does not turn human experience into a natural process (as though the end of a human life were the prelude to a renewal). But neither is the sadness experienced by a human consciousness that is absorbing the fact of its extinction allowed to diminish the ecstasy of a world that is "drunk with beauty and life." Instead, the "ewig" passage creates a new kind of temporal process that is neither incomplete (thereby contrasting to the perpetual incompleteness of cyclic nature) nor complete (thereby contrasting to the dreadful completeness of linear human experience). This new temporality is foreshadowed throughout "Der Abschied" by the way it continuously sees natural renewal as erotic and attributes erotic experience to nature (including the moon, the flowers and the brook). Not only is it erotic for a human to sense nature's fecundity, but nature itself seems to feel erotic longing and satisfaction. Although this intimation that both nature and humanity are erotic blurs the usual distinction between unconscious nature and conscious humanity, it does not bend human linearity into cyclic renewal, as though the problem of an individual's death might be solved through human reproduction or consciousness might be submerged into eroticism. Instead, it somewhat vaguely suggests a new kind of process that transcends both natural renewal and human self-awareness and anticipates the transcendence that the "ewig" passage more explicitly projects.

At the end of the Ninth's opening movement, as at the end of "Der Abschied," the "ewig" motif leaves the listener suspended indefinitely without a goal. The violins play the motif slowly several times; then the oboe plays it even more slowly (Figure 95). After the

FIGURE 95
Mahler, Ninth Symphony, first movement

oboe has held the E for four slow measures and before the E dies away, the D that is the last note of the "Lebewohl" motif is played by piccolo and strings. But the D is played two octaves higher, and because of the wide separation it does not attenuate the "ewig" motif's evocation of a perpetual absence of closure. One is simultaneously aware of "Lebewohl" and its finality and of "ewig" and its uncanny openness.

It is significant that Mahler alludes to the setting of "ewig" in

"Der Abschied" rather than to the rising sixths that carry the same word at the end of the Eighth. The associations of the Eighth's "ewig" motif with the Mater Gloriosa music make it connote the miracle of simultaneously moving toward and being already at fulfillment. Had Mahler alluded to "ewig" in this sense rather than in the sense associated with "Der Abschied," the evocation of the eternal would have contrasted more strongly to "Lebewohl" and would have dismissed its sadness more decisively. Or perhaps, he would have simply suppressed the pain of farewell. Certainly, there could have been no possibility of transforming "Lebewohl" into "ewig" — the motifs would have been too dissimilar. This transformation, which occupies the entire course of the Ninth's opening movement, allows the fullest possible weight to the pathos of leave-taking without allowing it to be the last word.

(3) The Transformation of "Lebewohl" into "Ewig"

It is only because of the context for the final F-sharp—E that this fragment sounds neither complete nor incomplete. That is, it probably would not sound this way if it were isolated from the movement as a whole. For during the course of the movement, things happen that make the E, which at the beginning of the movement pushes on down to D (articulating the "Lebewohl" motif), no longer push that way. And the transformation of "Lebewohl" into "ewig" as much as the "ewig" motif itself suggests a new kind of temporal process. Primarily responsible for this transformation are the way Mahler gradually pulls the background into the foreground, making the background into a void, and the way he gradually drains the movement of a sense of moving toward a goal, making the future into a void.

(i) Emptying Musical Space

A six-measure introduction (Figure 96) precedes the theme stated in bars 7 to 25. The bits and pieces of sound in the introduction provide a background, so that when the theme begins, we hear a melody plus its accompaniment. The texture is the musical analogue to a three-dimensional painting with a figure placed against a background. But although this introduction is halting, shadowy and tenuous, there are just enough fragments of a theme in it that, when the violins enter, we are not immediately aware that we are hearing the first notes of a theme and not just some more introductory bits of sound.[6] In other words we hear a differentiation between foreground and background, but it is less obvious than in, for instance, a Verdi aria.

At the end of the movement the differentiation between foreground and background is even less obvious; in fact, it is almost impossible to hear such stratification of sounds. It is not the case that we hear the "ewig" motif as a melody and the other sounds as an accompaniment.

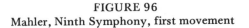

FIGURE 96
Mahler, Ninth Symphony, first movement

Rather, the "ewig" appearances in the oboe and solo violin seem to be fragments sharing or creating a foreground along with all the other fragments (except possibly the harp in 444, 446 and 449 and the cello in 444–445). It is as though the mosaic made up of these bits consisted of only a foreground set against a shimmering void.

A helpful analogy to this empty background is provided by Klimt's painting, "The Kiss" (1907–1908). In it we see a pair of three-dimensional figures placed against a two-dimensional gold background. The flat gold surface associates itself, as Klimt intended, with the gold background in Byzantine icons, where it symbolizes heaven — spiritual, non-physical space. Klimt has decorated the clothing of his figures with sexual symbolism that is so explicit and so clearly related to the painting's theme that, as Alessandra Comini says, the decoration is not decoration at all, but is in fact the content of the painting.[7]

Mahler does not go directly from a texture consisting of melody with accompaniment to a backgroundless foreground. Rather, each of the five restatements of the melody pulls another piece out of the background into itself. Indeed, it is probably because the motifs that comprise a background in the introduction are successively pulled into the foreground that they retain this function and serve as foreground motifs in the waning measures of the movement. In the second appearance of the theme (bars 47–54), a fragment played in the introduction (bar 4) by a horn is drawn into the foreground (bar 49; see Figure 97) as a counter-melody equal in significance to the melody that is being restated.[8] In subsequent appearances of this motif (for example, bars 83, 100, 187–188, 286, 414–416), it maintains its place in the foreground.

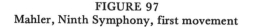

FIGURE 97
Mahler, Ninth Symphony, first movement

In the third appearance of the theme (bars 148–160), each fragment of the melody is divided between the second and first violins in such a way that they at once project the theme and also imitate the fluttering background figures played by the violas in bars 5–25 (see Figure 98). In this way, the viola figure in the background in bar 5 is pulled into the foreground.

In the fourth appearance of the theme (bars 269–278), the foreground consists of even more decorative elements that are

FIGURE 98
Mahler, Ninth Symphony, first movement

derived from the introduction and that interweave each other and swallow what they decorate. Perhaps one can say here what Comini says of Klimt, decoration becomes the content.

Before the third and fourth appearances of the theme, the introduction is restated, greatly expanded. Before the fifth appearance, the material from the introduction explodes into apocalyptic terror. When it settles down, the four-square fragment played by the harp in the introduction (bars 3–6) takes on a funereal tread; or perhaps it would be more accurate to say that the funereal tread it has had from the beginning now becomes clear. Over the notes Mahler writes as a direction to the performers, "like a ponderous cortege," and he tosses in a few trumpet fanfares like those in the dirges in his Second and Fifth Symphonies. The cortege passes by for twenty bars before the theme reappears, and it continues when the theme begins. Now it too is pulled into the foreground and becomes equal to the "Lebewohl" motif (bars 347–365). In bars 337–338 and 341–346, it is imitated in the winds with fluttering figures that recall the viola background figure in bars 5–6, thereby pulling this figure into the foreground again (it has lapsed into the background in 267–273). At the end of the movement, the last gesture in the harp part alludes at once to the harp motif and to the viola motif of the introduction, holding both of these in the foreground in the final moments of the movement.

In the final section, almost everything is foreground. The restatement of the theme begins with a wistful tenderness that remembers the past and yearns for the future that it knows it will not have. But wistfulness slips away as one instrument after another is given as the "ewig" motif — a whole step up or down.

In the stages suggested above, Mahler has made the foreground richer and more "three-dimensional," while the background has become emptier. By the final section (the sixth restatement of the theme, bars 434–454), the background has become very nearly a void; everything is foreground. It would be true to say of this section, as of Klimt's "The Kiss," that there is no background, what is "behind" the foreground is flat and has no depth; it would be just as true to say that the background is infinitely deep. Having heard a background behind the descending whole step at the beginning of the movement, one feels its absence at the end. The flatness of Mahler's musical space, like Klimt's gold, suggests a rich, vibrant emptiness.[9]

The function of a background is to define the musical space in which the foreground melody happens and thus to define the point in musical space at which the melody will sound closed. One of the most important differences between the beginning and the ending of the movement is that at the beginning the descending whole-step motif takes place in front of a backdrop that makes an expected D function as its goal, and we associate the motif with the word "Lebewohl." Partly because at the end the sense of a background is severely attenuated, we no longer hear the F-sharp–E as pushing on to D, and we associate the descending whole step that neither has nor seeks closure with the word "ewig."

(ii) Emptying the Musical Future

Mahler is not, of course, the first composer to create a texture that consists of something other than a melody plus an accompaniment. In Baroque music, for example, the voices are often woven together. They are equal to one another, and none is background. But in such music, the contrapuntally woven voices together articulate a background structure that gives the piece direction and makes a closure possible. Bach's Two-Part Invention in D Minor is typical: its two voices cooperatively articulate a D in the first section, an F in the second, an A in the third, and a D again in the fourth. We hear a background structure though we do not hear a melody against an accompaniment, and this structure makes it possible for the piece to end with a strong sense of completeness.

The first movement of Mahler's Ninth, by contrast, increasingly has less sense of direction, less sense of heading someplace. Closure becomes increasingly less expected and less possible, until at the end, the backgroundless foreground does not imply any harmonic direction, and the F-sharp–E floats aimlessly, no longer pushing on to D.

In order to become aware of this process, we must notice what happens between the appearances of the main theme. The music that separates the statements of the main theme does not connote peaceful resignation, but is despairing, anguished, angry, protesting and striving. These contrasting sections begin by turning to D minor and changing the F-sharp–E motif into F-natural–E (see bar 27 in Figure 99). Because F leans harder into E than F-sharp does, the

FIGURE 99
Mahler, Ninth Symphony, first movement

downward thrust to D is stronger in this permutation, and it lacks the resistance to movement that almost balances the pull of the D in the F-sharp–E interval. As a result, the F–E motif seems to suggest despair instead of the resignation of "Lebewohl." The new motif gives rise to an anguished figure that begins low and struggles upward (for example, bars 29–31). As if someone were saying, "No, I will *not* go gentle into that good night," the striving becomes increasingly agitated. In the first D minor section, the striving reaches a goal, and this arrival is a glorious triumph, the most thrilling and satisfying moment in the movement.

The music carrying this climax is the theme built out of the "farewell" motif. At this point in the movement, the music makes us feel that the feeling of resignation and peace is the resolution or, perhaps, the transfiguration of our earthly strivings, limited as they are by the final departure we call death.

This climax occurs in bar 47, when the movement still has 407 measures to go. Never again does the music seem so glorious. Never again does the song of peaceful resignation enter as a climax or as the goal of striving. Between the reappearances of the main theme, the anguished protest is restated; in its subsequent appearances, it simply spends itself, so that when the song of resigned peace reenters we have less and less of a sense of arrival. More and more, it simply happens.

Music can lead its listeners into two kinds of climaxes. In one kind, the music seems to be heading toward something, and then it gets there. Examples are the moments when the home key and the original theme return at the beginning of the final section in Baroque and Classical music, as well as the first reappearance of Mahler's main theme. The other kind of climax happens when the excitement or energy begins to decrease, or to increase at a slower rate, before a goal or resolution is reached. This sort of climax is common in Romantic music, and often conveys the feeling that the goal cannot be actualized; it may be real in some sense, but it permanently eludes concrete form. Mahler's Ninth gives us four climaxes where the frenzy dies away before its goal takes shape. These climaxes are even more unnerving than the typical Romantic climax. For the listener comes to feel that the anguish cannot reach a goal and that the goal is not only elusive but in every sense unreal.

The most powerful of these climaxes is the one in bars 308–313. At the moment when the energy stops increasing and begins to wane (bar 314), we get not a goal, but a restatement of the syncopated rhythm that occurs in the first measure of the movement. Obviously, the meter has not yet been defined when this rhythm (♩.♪₇♩ ; see Figure 96) is first articulated. Consequently, bar 1 can be heard as four beats in common time in which the second and third notes take place off the beat, or as a three-beat measure in which the second beat (♪₇) is only two-thirds as long as the first and third. Either way, the rhythm is unsettling, and contrasts sharply to the four-square embryonic funeral march in the harp (bars 3–6). The syncopated rhythm is played shadowily on the cellos and horns in the introduction, but when it reappears in bars 314–318

(Figure 100), it is played triple *forte* by the horns and trombones. Like a primeval blare, it has no melody, no harmony, and none of the sense of direction that melody and harmony imply. It is as lacking in energy as it is in direction; its first tone is long, then it pulsates in

FIGURE 100
Mahler, Ninth Symphony, first movement

irregular, unpredictable lengths. It so insists on its unpredictableness that the very principle of regularity on which a sense of the future depends seems to be contradicted. At the moment when a goal is most expected and most needed if goals are to make sense at all, time is frozen; the climax is the impossibility of conceiving a goal.

The funeral tread goes on, and the rest of the movement takes place within the black echo of the syncopated blare. The last of the anguished sections (bars 372—416) has very little forward-directed energy. In bars 377—390, the flute gasps a birdlike figure. It is reminiscent of the flute-phoenix that hovers over the ashes of apocalyptic devastation in the Finale of the Second Symphony (at S:29). In the Ninth, the flickering phoenix does not promise a resurrection but seals the desolation. What functions as a climax (398—399) expresses the confrontation with an empty future.

The movement is structured by the alternation between the main theme, built out of the "Lebewohl" motif, and the anguished sections struggling toward a goal. At each successive climax of these struggles, the sense of moving toward a goal is increasingly attenuated. Such a background structure not only does not give the movement a sense of direction, but in fact sucks it away. At the beginning of the movement, the main theme is heard in a world where goals are reached; then goals are expected but not reached, then they become impossible to reach, and finally impossible to imagine. At the end, the future has become empty in the sense that the present is utterly independent of the future. In the temporality of the Eighth Symphony, the present can be full and yet still have a future (though the relation of the present to the future is not the same for the transfigured as for the ordinary consciousness); here the temporal process is different: the present is either so full or so empty[10] that the future is nothing for it. Just as sucking the background into the foreground creates a musical space that is a void, so sucking the very possibility of coming events into the present creates a musical future that is a void. At the end of the movement, it is no wonder that the descending whole step from F-sharp to E sounds neither complete nor incomplete. It exemplifies metaphorically a temporal process in which one experiences no contrast between what is and what is coming.

The composer of the Ninth Symphony was a dying man. Perhaps the new way of being conscious into which the first movement leads us is his vision of what consciousness might be like after the body has died. That interpretation is possible, but, we must remember, the music does not suggest that death leads automatically to a new way of experiencing. To say that the new kind of consciousness is the goal of death would distort Mahler's process of setting goals further and further aside. At the same time, the final farewell and the anticipation of death it implies are not irrelevant to the new kind of consciousness, for experiencing them — which we do whenever we realize that we are old enough to die — allows us, though it does not force us, to move into the void in which the new consciousness happens.

As the movement runs its course, it transforms the consciousness of final separation into the kind of consciousness which knows no finality and in which one's sense of self is radically altered because one no longer closes the present self with the remembered or the possible self. The music offers no suggestion about what reality outside the self must be like in order that such a transformation be possible. The movement exemplifies the transformation only from the side of the subject. It lets us feel what the final separation is like, what the new consciousness is like, and what it is like for the one to be turned into the other.

2. *The Last Movement*

Although the "ewig" motif never reappears in the symphony, the "Lebewohl" motif permeates the last three movements as much as it does the first. In the second movement Ländler, it associates itself with a demonically whirling dance of life that is, as Deryck Cooke says, "utterly tawdry, stupid and empty." In the third movement Rondo-Burlesque, it associates itself with "a ferocious outburst of fiendish laughter at the futility of everything." But in the last movement, the Adagio-Finale, it becomes the core of a "noble, hymn-like theme.[11]

At the onset of the movement, the "Lebewohl" hymn has connotations that may be said to be an elaboration of those carried by the "Lebewohl" motif in the opening movement. By the end of the Adagio, however, a new process has superimposed itself on that of the hymn. "Lebewohl" is thereby transformed again. It is changed as fundamentally as it is in the first movement, but in so different a way that the first-movement and last-movement transformations are apparently irreconcilable.

(1) The "Lebewohl" Hymn

Straightaway, the third measure of the Finale states the "Lebewohl" motif unflinchingly, without embellishment and without hesitation, in D-flat major. From the motif Mahler spins a full phrase (bars 3–11; see Figure 101). After an interruption of five bars, a second period (bars 17–25) answers the first. The "Lebewohl" hymn appears two other times in the movement (49–87 and 126–147). As in the first movement, the passages permeated by the "Lebewohl" motif are separated by contrasting sections in the minor mode — C-sharp minor, in the case of the Finale. These C-sharp minor passages are as thin and numb as the "Lebewohl" theme is rich and passionate.

In the first "Lebewohl" hymn, D-flat is at once established as a goal, and the goal is realized in the first and second as well as the last bars of both periods. By moving to D-flat at the beginning and the end of each period and by keeping in force the goal of D-flat throughout the period, the musical line connotes a final leave-taking; the connotation supports the conventional association of the motif with that word. Along the way to the end, chromatic harmonies appear that enrich the downward descent.[12] Although they suggest that the stream of life flowing to its inevitable end is full of eddies that make it interesting and worthwhile, they never weaken the tonicity of D-flat nor hide its arrival as the passage's goal nor suggest that its arrival can be put off indefinitely. The cessation of the temporal process is its future, and this future qualifies every present along the way to the future. The excursions into chromatic harmonies exemplify a process in which the cessation of the temporal process is not allowed to preclude the pursuit of finite goals, even though awareness of their finitude is essential to their character. The voice leadings in and out of these chromatic excursions are smooth. Their fluidity suggests that the recognition of finite goals in the face of the ultimate cessation of the temporal flow cannot be thought of as a defiance of

FIGURE 101
Mahler, Ninth Symphony, fourth movement

death: while the eddies exemplifying the variegation and richness of life do not happen effortlessly, they do not take place merely to spite death. In other words, the coming futurelessness affects the present in the sense of making everything finite and making finitude an essential constituent of everything, but does not completely control the present, as it would if it prevented the pursuit of finite

FIGURE 101 continued

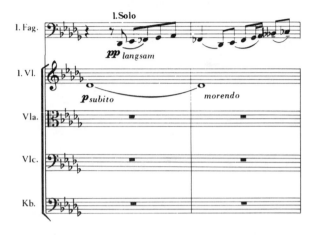

goals or if finite goals were enacted merely to shake one's fist in death's face. The temporal process projected by the "Lebewohl" hymn is one in which its subject is at peace with itself, with the certainty of its coming nonbeing and with its finite experiences. Life that ends is not worthless merely because it ends, and trying to realize valuable, though finite, goals does not need either to ignore or to defy the coming nothingness.

The second statement of the "Lebewohl" hymn (bars 49–87), like the first, establishes D-flat as the pitch to which the music moves steadily and surely, even during its still more daring chromatic excursions, suggesting again the certainty of death as well as a resoluteness to enjoy life to the fullest even in the face of this certainty. At least the first period seems to have these connotations. But in the second period (64–77), things happen that suggest that A-flat may be the goal of the musical motion as much as or instead of D-flat.

One might well ignore this hint of A-flat as a *finalis* were it not that in the third section (126–185) A-flat decisively displaces D-flat as the tone toward which the melody moves and on which it comes to rest at the end. There are, of course, other melodies in eighteenth- and nineteenth-century music that end on the fifth degree of the scale. Most of these endings differ from Mahler's in that they do not establish the fifth degree as a *finalis,* and they end without coming to rest. Their incompleteness is deliberate and unambiguous.

A-flat is reached in bar 171. At 173 the piece sounds genuinely finished: the A-flat is a genuine goal, and not a temporary substitute for one. Yet the stability of the A-flat and the musical repose on it is not that of a tonic. For while sensing the completeness and knowing there will be no note beyond the A-flat, the listener senses that the ending would sound more complete if the melodic line ended on D-flat. By establishing A-flat as a goal that is not a tonic while maintaining the force of D-flat as the melody's unrealized goal, Mahler changes not only the particular note on which completion occurs but also the nature of completion itself.

A-flat as a non-tonic *finalis* is somewhat analogous to the kind of finality experienced at the end of some antiphons of Gregorian chant. Because the finality of the A-flat and the Gregorian *finalis* is established by melodic, not harmonic, means, neither Mahler's A-flat nor the Gregorian *finalis* can be said to be tonicized. The last note of the Gregorian antiphon is sometimes identified as such by the way it is circled by preceding notes and by the way prior phrases end (either on the *finalis* or the note above it or the fifth above it). The difference between Mahler's A-flat and the *finalis* in such antiphons is that with the latter, we may know or suspect what the last note will be without feeling that any musical law or sense of appropriateness would be offended if the chant were to end on some other note, while in the case of Mahler's A-flat, any other ending would be heard either as a mistake or as a delay of the ending-yet-to-come, even though the A-flat ending projects less finality than ending on the tonic would. Perhaps a closer analogy is the ending of pieces like Schoenberg's Opus 19 *Klavierstücke,* for with each of these, one not only predicts what the final note is likely to be but also senses that any other final note would leave the piece sounding incomplete. Like the Mahler ending, Schoenberg's final notes are not a harmonically established tonic, but, unlike the Mahler, none of the Schoenberg pieces has a tonic in addition to its *finalis.*

Shifting the note on which completion is reached and, even more, changing the nature of completion alter subtly, but fundamentally, the temporal process which the movement projects. This transformed temporal process is remarkable, and the following paragraphs will dwell on it in order to let its full impact be felt. First, in order to specify more precisely what it means to say that A-flat functions as the *finalis,* attention will be called to the musical events within the last "Lebewohl" hymn that are responsible for shifting the *finalis* to A-flat. Then, in the next section, other events in the movement that anticipate, call for and lead up to a transformed temporal process will be examined. And, finally, in the third and fourth sections, the transformed process itself will be considered in terms of the events that summon and articulate it.

The process wherein A-flat is made into a *finalis* can be reduced to a single fact: during the second period of the final "Lebewohl" hymn, an ascending and a descending line in the middleground converge on this pitch. This convergence is supported by the way that the points of departure for both the ascending and the descending lines are, in turn, established by the analogous convergence, on a lower architectonic level, of an ascending and a descending line. In other words, the details of the melody, supported by the harmonic progressions, do not merely embellish the descent of a major third that comprises the "Lebewohl" motif and allow it to be repeated several times during the course of the hymn; the various melodic digressions from the basic motif also create a pattern which, in the end, becomes more prominent than the "Lebewohl" motif and which exemplifies a significantly different temporal process. This characteristic of the last "Lebewohl" hymn distinguishes it from the first one, in which the embellishments are completely under the control of the basic motif.

The second period of the second "Lebewohl" hymn is a stepping stone from the first to the third hymn: in addition to the fundamental descending motion from F to D-flat, there takes place in the second hymn a subsidiary motion descending from D-flat to A-flat, establishing the latter as a subordinate goal. As line b) in Figure 102 shows, this descent occurs in bars 64–65, and serves to prolong the D-flat of the "Lebewohl" motif.

In the second period of the last "Lebewohl" hymn, the relation between the D-flat and the A-flat is reversed: various pairs of converging ascending and descending lines establish A-flat so much more strongly than the second hymn's descent to A-flat or the third hymn's descent to D-flat that A-flat now becomes the primary goal and D-flat is subordinate to it. The details of the third hymn's converging lines are shown in Figure 103.

(2) The Tragic Fanfare

Half-step intervals are conspicuous in the lines that establish A-flat as the hymn's *finalis* (see line a) and the caption in Figure 103). These half steps are not a merely incidental detail, for they intimately relate the final "Lebewohl" to a motif that has figured prominently throughout the movement. Cooke calls this motif the "tragic fanfare"[13] (see Figure 104). Without either warrant or warning, it first appears in bars 13—14. Entering so violently, it seems to shriek a protest against the resigned peace combined with the pursuit of finite goals that is projected by the "Lebewohl" hymn; the tragic fanfare and the "Lebewohl" hymn seem to defy and invalidate one another. The tragic fanfare also sets the Finale against the second and third movements: the use of the "Lebewohl" motif in the middle movements suggests that, however much the Ländler may affirm life, ultimately human existence is unavoidably empty, futile, stupid and diabolically comical, while the tragic fanfare in the Finale urges us to believe that somehow life ought not to be so devoid of meaning.

At the end of the Adagio, the conflict between the tragic fanfare and the noble "Lebewohl" hymn disappears: in that the converging lines constituting the hymn and establishing A-flat as the *finalis* are permeated with half steps, the fanfare is absorbed into the hymn. The tragic fanfare reappears in the foreground (cello solo, bars 155—156 and second violins, bars 160—161) just before the expected A-flat is stated. But now it is played softly and tenderly, and its connotations seem to have changed radically: not only has the fanfare been assimilated into the "Lebewohl" hymn, but in being absorbed the fanfare has been transfigured. This transformation is one of the most important aspects of the movement's final section and indeed of the whole movement. The first step in delineating this transformation is to specify somewhat more precisely the connotations of the fanfare's initial form, and because it is derived from a chromatic motif that figures prominently in the symphony's first movement (Figure 105), the function of the parent motif needs to be reviewed.

The chromatic motif shown in Figure 105 pulls together into a single gesture the two contrasting motifs that animate the two main themes of the first movement: the major-third descent (F-sharp—E—D) and the minor-third descent (F—E—D). The tragic fanfare crystallizes the conflict between the F-sharp in the one and the F-natural in the other, and even repeats the interval, using a rhythm whose character reinforces the motif's tragic connotations and serves as its hallmark from its initial appearance (bars 44—45) onward.

This first appearance is part of the thrust toward the climactic return of the song of peace. Many of the subsequent statements are part of the thrusts that do not lead to arrivals. In fact, each of the successively more intense forward drives that turn out to be futile, thereby emptying the first movement of a sense of direction, has the tragic fanfare as a vital component. In two cases, the tragic fanfare

FIGURE 102
Sketch of Mahler, Ninth Symphony, fourth movement, the second
"Lebewohl" hymn (bars 64–73), second period

In this sketch and the next, a note which prolongs or embellishes another note is
linked to it by a slur; the note being embellished is the higher one on the following
hierarchy: a stemmed notehead with a quaver (♪) embellishes an unstemmed

also appears right at the climax — that is, just at the point where the forward thrust begins to ease off without having reached a goal. Figure 106 lists some of the appearances of the tragic fanfare and the climaxes with which they are associated.

In short, the tragic fanfare in the first movement has a significant role in emptying the musical future and transforming the "Lebewohl" motif into the "ewig" motif. The fanfare carries this association as well as the connotation of tragedy into the fourth movement.

Its fourth-movement form differs in two ways from the first-movement prototype. In both movements, the fanfare consists of two statements of the descending half-step motif, the immediate repetition making the fanfare more conspicuous and intensifying its connotation of thrusting forward futilely. But in the fourth movement the repetition occurs not on the same pitches (as in the first movement), but an augmented fourth higher, and the second chromatic descent is preceded by an accented lower neighbor tone. The upward leap and the auxiliary note for the repetition make the tragic fanfare a shriek of agony and anger — the diametric opposite of the peaceful resignation of the "Lebewohl" hymn. This change is anticipated in bars 234—235 (horn) of the first movement, but what are there incidental details function in the Finale as essential, characterizing features. In fact the upward leap and lower auxiliary are so central to the Finale's tragic fanfare that their absence from the fanfare's appearance in bars 155—156 is striking and seems to underscore the significance of playing it *"pianissimo, expressively."*

The second difference between the first- and fourth-movement forms of the fanfare has to do with its rhythm. In the first movement, its rhythm relates it closely to the nihilistic gesture quoted in

---

notehead (♩); an unstemmed notehead embellishes a stemmed notehead (♪); a downward stemmed notehead embellishes an upward stemmed notehead (♩); a solid stemmed notehead embellishes a hollow note (♩). Embellishing notes sometimes precede and sometimes follow the notes they embellish. A note that is embellished on one architectonic level may be an embellishing note on a higher level. A series of notes that have their stems in the same direction and that move stepwise indicates a melodic progression which establishes its last note as its goal.

D-flat controls the entire passage in this Figure. The melodic details of bars 65 (last two beats) through 68 amount to an ascent from D-flat to G-flat. The G-flat then functions as the second note in a descent from A-flat to D-flat. D-flat, the goal of the main, fundamental melodic motion in the passage, is embellished and emphasized by its lower auxiliary (the C in the last half of both bar 69 and bar 71). At the same time, the melody articulates a secondary descent from D-flat (bar 64) to C-flat (bar 66) to B-double-flat (bar 72) to A-flat (bar 73).

FIGURE 103
Sketch of Mahler, Ninth Symphony, fourth movement, the third
"Lebewohl" hymn (bars 138–162), second period

The line that ascends to A-flat begins at the F-flat below it (horn, bar 141). This F-flat is established as a point of departure by the convergence on it of an ascending line from D-flat (reached by the "Lebewohl" motif in bar 139) through the E-double-flat of bar 140 to F, and a descending line from the F that begins the second period (bar 138). As in the first two "Lebewohl" hymns, F is the point of departure for the "Lebewohl" motif in the first period, but while the background line in the first period of the first two hymns descends to D-flat, the first period of the third hymn reestablishes F by the convergence of an ascending

FIGURE 104
Mahler, Ninth Symphony,
fourth movement, "tragic fanfare"

FIGURE 105
Mahler, Ninth Symphony,
first movement

line (D[bar 128] —E[bar 129] —F[bar 133]), and a descending line (A-flat [bar 131] —G-flat[bar 132] —F[bar 133]). This reestablished F then serves as the point of departure for a descent (in the second period, bars 138— 141) to F-flat, where the descending line converges with the ascent from D-flat. The augmented octave descent from F to F-flat, incidentally, consists entirely of whole steps except for one interval (B-double-flat—A-flat); this whole-tone scale is echoed and reinforced by a descending whole-tone scale from C to F-flat in the violins' counter-melody (bars 142—143).

The F-flat of bar 141, having been established as a point of departure, moves to G-flat (bar 143, violins) and thence to A-flat (145).

On A-flat, this ascending line converges with a descending line, making A-flat the *finalis*. The descending line takes off from C (bar 147), which is established as a point of departure by the convergence on it of a descending line (the violins' whole tone scale from A-flat down to C in bars 138—139) and an ascending line (from E to F-sharp to G-sharp to A in the violins in bars 139—141 and from A [bar 145, violins] to B [= C-flat, bar 146] to C [bar 147]).

The C thus established makes its descent to A-flat entirely by half-step intervals; it goes from C to C-flat to B-flat and from B-flat to B-double-flat to A-flat. Half-step intervals also figure subtly but significantly in the process of establishing both the F-flat and the C as points of departure for the ascending and descending lines, respectively, which converge on the A-flat and make it the *finalis:* the F-flat is established by a descending scale that is in fact an embellished form of the half step, F to F-flat, and by an ascending line that articulates both the half step from D-flat to E-double-flat as well as the half step from C-flat to D-double-flat (see the sketch of the horn part, bars 139—140, in line b) above). And the ascending line that establishes C has rising half steps in the foreground (bars 145—146).

FIGURE 106
Sketch of Mahler, Ninth Symphony, first movement

appearance of the tragic fanfare	climax of the forward thrust
mm. 98—100	mm. 104—105
234, 235—236, 237—242	237—242
285, 289, 299, 306, 308	314—316
398—399	398—399

Figure 107 — nihilistic partly because of its close resemblance to the motif used in the "Trinklied vom Jammer der Erde" from *Das Lied von der Erde* for the words, "But you, man, how long will you live?" (Figure 108).[14] In the fourth movement, the fanfare's rhythm is identical to that of the "Lebewohl" motif itself. By relating the tragic fanfare to "Lebewohl," this rhythm makes the fanfare, like the hymn, an interpretation of the temporal process of living toward certain and ultimate futurelessness. But while the hymn, with the measured tread of its whole-note descent and chromatic excursions, interprets the experience of saying farewell as one that is noble and life-affirming in the face of certain and permanent separation, the fourth-movement tragic fanfare, with its closely packed half steps,

FIGURE 107
Mahler, Ninth Symphony
first movement

FIGURE 108
Mahler, *Das Lied von der Erde*, I

interprets life lived toward ultimate leave-taking as something that is so constricted and so constricting that one appropriately screams a protest against both life and death. In its transfigured form after the culminating "Lebewohl," the tragic fanfare still retains its close rhythmic association with "Lebewohl," so that the transfigured fanfare, like the transfigured "Lebewohl" hymn, continues to offer an image — but a transformed one — of the temporal process of living toward ultimate separation from everything.

In the first movement, the tragic fanfare occurs many times besides the structurally important times listed in Figure 106. It appears much less often in the fourth movement, and there all its statements are structurally significant. In fact reviewing its appearances and their function is perhaps the best way to survey the fourth movement's form. In the Finale, the tragic fanfare first appears between the two periods of the first "Lebewohl" hymn. The first period comes to a close in bar 11.[15] It consists of a pair of subphrases, the second ending as stably as the first ends unstably. The melodic downward thrust from F has utterly spent itself in the three articulations of E-flat—D-flat (bars 3,4 and 10—11). Because of these two features, the passage sounds so complete, so finished at bar 11 that one hears the rising bassoon figure in bars 11—12 as a prolongation of the final D-flat, an embellishment whose ending will surely be a fall to D-flat. The future beyond the D-flat is as uncertain as the D-flat seems certain. One cannot imagine what is coming or even that anything could be coming.

As a result, the tragic fanfare in 13—14, cutting off, as it does, the return to D-flat, sounds like an unwarranted outburst. Although it alludes to the violins' introductory gesture in bars 1—2, nothing that happens in 3—12 justifies it, and if it is to be entwined into the fabric woven by bars 3—12, subsequent musical events will have to take it into account. Absorbing it into the final "Lebewohl" hymn serves precisely this function.

Although the tragic fanfare in 13—14 comes from nowhere, it has a specific future: it leads toward the reprise of the "Lebewohl" hymn. This reprise (bars 17—25) serves as an answering period to bars 3—11. The first period ends too stably to generate an answering period; the tragic fanfare creates the future-evoking instability that pairs the periods to one another.

The second period ends just as stably as the first. The sense of completion is enhanced by the three bars (25—27) that extend the final D-flat and loosely stitch the "Lebewohl" hymn to the ensuing minor-mode section (see Figure 109). D-flat (written as C-sharp) continues to be the tonic in the new section, but otherwise the hymn and the C-sharp minor section have nothing to do with one another. There is no forward thrust from the one to the other. Although the latter's motif is anticipated by the passage (bars 11—12) between the periods of the hymn and although the turns in bars 30, 33 and 36 have appeared several times in the accompaniment to the hymn,[16]

FIGURE 109
Mahler, Ninth Symphony, fourth movement

there is no motivic connection between the melody of the hymn and the minor-mode section. Very little suggests that the two sections somehow inhabit the same world or live in their respective worlds in the same way. The texture of the one is rich and sonorous, its sounds tightly packed together; the texture of the other is thin and stringy, its three voices spread far apart. The one is hot-blooded and passionate, though the goal of its falling line is so clear and the movement to its goal is so sure that there is not a trace of striving or struggling to resist the inevitable. The other is aimless and passionless; having no future, it exemplifies precisely the temporality of the futureless void that prevails at the end of the hymn. Although one of the melodic lines in the C-sharp minor section is a rising one, it does not seem to rise to anything in particular; it hovers around G-sharp, and sounds more nearly complete on that pitch than on any other, but none of the G-sharps convey the sense of finality that characterizes the arrivals on D-flat in the "Lebewohl" section. As the hymn is an image of moving surely and certainly to a foreseen end, yet passionately affirming the process in spite of the absolute certainty of its finiteness, so the C-sharp minor passage is an image of having ended — an image of the peace of numb goallessness and blank futurelessness. If the one is in repose along the way to finality, the other is in repose without being on the way to anything. The minor section, with its incomplete completeness on G-sharp (= A-flat), anticipates the kind of completion characterizing A-flat at the end of the movement.

The minor section has three waves: bars 28—33, 34—39 and 40—48. The beginning of each wave is marked by a fresh (and unmotivated) statement of the rising figure that is first stated in bar 11. During the third wave, the line becomes a falling one, the music seems to drift even more and the texture becomes even thinner. The sense of fragmentation increases, and serves as a thrust toward the second statement of the "Lebewohl" hymn. The second hymn is heard as a return and an arrival. Thus just as the first appearance of the tragic fanfare enters without warrant and then provides the forward thrust that links the two periods of the first "Lebewohl" hymn to one another, so the first C-sharp minor passage enters unjustified by its past and then ends providing the thrust that links the second "Lebewohl" hymn to the first one.

The second "Lebewohl" hymn, like the first, consists of two periods (bars 49—56 and 64—73), each comprising a pair of subphrases. As in the first hymn, the periods are separated by a passage in which the tragic fanfare appears. As before, the tragic fanfare (bars 60—61) thrusts toward the second period. But the fanfare's entrance is different. Instead of bursting in totally without warning, it is prepared by the growth that takes place in bars 57—59, where the tension in the cellos and the violin-viola leap to F (bar 59) seem to be reaching toward some such arrival. The tragic fanfare in 60—61 is, however, only partly the outcome of its past. The climax it carries exceeds the energy that worked it up. It sounds unnaturally fierce.

In bar 88, a second C-sharp minor passage begins. It has the same connotations as the first. Like its predecessor, its beginning is only loosely stitched to the preceding hymn. Its texture is a little thicker; five voices sporadically move about, ignoring one another, each gasp being briefer than the spurts in the first minor section. As before, entrances of the rising scale three times mark the beginnings of fresh waves; this time, each wave is less sustained than the one before it. As before, one of the contrapuntally woven lines hovers about G-sharp. But — and here is the most significant difference between the two sections — the third wave does not gradually become fragmented and lead back into a statement of "Lebewohl." Instead, the tragic fanfare bursts in (bars 107—108) violently and totally without warning. It is one of the oddest, most disconcerting moments in all of Mahler's music. The very fact that the tragic fanfare is thrown as vehemently against the C-sharp minor section as against the first two "Lebewohl" hymns becomes a point of similarity between the "Lebewohl" and the minor sections; and the fact that both of them, in contrast to the tragic fanfare, are in repose and do not struggle, as it does, becomes more signficant than their differences.

Instead of subsiding, the fanfare in bars 107—108 is the basis for building to an excruciatingly intense statement — the movement's peak — of the tragic fanfare in bars 118—119.

In spite of its violent beginning and the intensity of its climax, the series of tragic fanfares in bars 107—122 is by no means a nihilistic gesture. It is not, in other words, as though Mahler were celebrating tragedy and indulging in intensity for their own sakes. For this statement of the tragic fanfare has even more intrinsic power and energy and even a stronger sense of forward direction than its predecessors have, and leads toward the final "Lebewohl" hymn in such a way that the beginning of the hymn is a powerful point of arrival.

(3) The Final Section

The "Lebewohl" hymn that begins in bar 126 adequately responds to the mighty, even violent thrusts of the tragic fanfare precisely because of the fundamental difference between this "Lebewohl" and the earlier ones that were ushered in by the tragic fanfare (namely, bars 17ff. and 64ff.). This difference has already been described: the culminating hymn absorbs the half-steps of the fanfare into its fabric and does so in such a way that points of departure for ascending and descending lines are defined, and these lines — one of them consisting of two additional, somewhat embellished statements of the fanfare — converge to articulate both a new ending and a new kind of finality. In other words, the tragic fanfare evokes the second period of all three hymns and persists as the remembered past during these periods, but during the final hymn it also exerts itself as a present force. Simply offering another peaceful but rich flow to certain finality, as in the first "Lebewohl" hymn, or flowing to the somewhat more ambiguous finality of the second one would evidently not be an adequate response to the vehemence and anger of the tragic fanfare's protest against finitude.

And as the nature of completion is transformed and the fanfare is absorbed, the fanfare is also transfigured. Just as responding to by absorbing the tragic fanfare fundamentally alters the character of the "Lebewohl" hymn, so the process of being absorbed fundamentally alters the character of the tragic fanfare. It reappears in its new form (bars 155—156 and 160—161) just before the new *finalis* is stated: at the very moment when the tragic fanfare has been completely absorbed into the texture of the "Lebewohl" hymn and when the hymn's most important feature — the completeness of its sure-footed descent from F to D-flat — has been set aside in favor of a different kind of completeness, the transfigured fanfare makes it presence explicitly felt in the foreground and delays the articulation of the A-flat *finalis* for seven measures.

The transformed fanfare enters not as an interruption (as does its prototype in bars 13—14 and 107—108) but as part of the same fabric as the transfigured "Lebewohl." And instead of thrusting ahead and functioning, as before, to make the "Lebewohl" a point of arrival, it is played softly, delicately, expressively, and its ending exemplifies the same balance of completeness and incompleteness as the A-flat ending the transfigured "Lebewohl." That is, the last note of the new fanfare does not thrust ahead to anything else; it is stable, not mobile, yet one can imagine greater stability without expecting the transfigured tragic fanfare to generate it. In short, by absorbing the tragic fanfare into the "Lebewohl," the final section takes the incompleteness and forward-thrusting aspect out of the one and the aspect of utter finality, which the life-affirming passion in the "Lebewohl" hymns contradicts and yet accepts, out of the other. The contrast between the "Lebewohl" motif and the tragic fanfare — a violent contrast earlier in the movement — has disappeared. For the transfigured forms of both motifs project the same new blend of completeness and incompleteness and the temporal process implied by this blend.

The less violent contrast between the "Lebewohl" sections and the C-sharp minor sections also disappears. For in bar 159, a rising figure introduces the second of the transfigured fanfares and recalls the C-sharp minor passages. By explicitly relating the C-sharp minor sections to the transformed "Lebewohl" and the transformed fanfare, this allusion rejects, or transcends, the minor passages' image of death as numb peace, and at the same time confirms the way hovering around G-sharp in the minor sections has anticipated the new kind of completeness that the last "Lebewohl" presents.

(4) The Movement as a Whole

The first "Lebewohl" hymn and to a lesser extent the second one as well see the final ending as the goal that destroys having a goal. All through the Finale, the tragic fanfare has protested against the finality of death and has bitterly rejected the "Lebewohl" hymn's acceptance of death and its peace in the face of final separation. The culminating "Lebewohl" is the arrival of the future summoned by the fanfare's strongest statement, and in this culmination, as in the fanfare, consciousness refuses to accept the finality of death. No other consciousness or temporality would adequately respond to the fanfare's intensity. The concluding, culminating "Lebewohl" absorbs the tragic fanfare and its protest against and rejection of the earlier "Lebewohl"'s kind of peace: D-flat — the close of the "Lebewohl" motif — no longer closes the melodic line (though it is present as the bass and root of the final harmony). A-flat is established as a *finalis* by the converging lines of the final hymn; postponing the articulation of A-flat by twice stating the transformed fanfare makes the listener even more certain that the A-flat, when it comes in bar 171, is the terminal note in the melodic line, and the viola, circling and landing on A-flat over a D-flat chord in the movement's last two bars, confirms this certainty. But this A-flat sounds both complete and incomplete. It seems complete in that to a certain extent it sounds final and one certainly does not expect a subsequent musical event that would project greater finality; it sounds incomplete in that one continues to be aware that closing the melody on D-flat would project a more final closure, even though one is also aware that a D-flat closure is not going to take place. Rejecting death as numb peace (the C-sharp minor sections), the last passage ends with an open *finalis,* an ending that carries an implied and eternally unfulfilled future along with it.

The final section, therefore, is both open to a future (while the "Lebewohl" that it transforms is not), and at the same time maintains a resemblance to the first "Lebewohl" hymn in that it acknowledges that no such future will be instantiated. To say that the terminal A-flat is an open *finalis* is to say that a future impinges on the ending (as it would not if D-flat closed the melodic line); to say that this openness is combined with finality is to say that this future is eternally unactualized. This implied, but never-to-be stated future (D-flat) is one that connotes a completely satisfying closure — a future in which all aspects of reality would have become harmoniously coherent and in which the events that have been completed are in every respect congruent with the self shaping them. In that such a future, even though it does not and cannot actually take place, affects the quality of the ending, the adumbrated and unactualized fulfillment enjoys a certain kind of reality. In such a temporality, a person is more than what death ends: a person somehow also embodies this fulfillment, even though it is foreshadowed and never enacted. The anticipation of fulfillment touches the close with joy as much as the non-actualization of fulfillment touches it with sorrow. Because one is aware that the A-flat, while open to the future, will certainly not be superceded, there is no sense of striving beyond the A-flat; both the joy and the sorrow are touched with serenity and peace.

Kurt von Fischer makes much the same point in different terms. The last forty measures of the movement consist of disjointed scraps, but the fragmentariness, he says, has a preliminary, introductory character as much as a dissipating, concluding character. Consequently, the passage points to a "not yet" at the same time that it accepts a "no longer." Fischer supports this interpretation by pointing out that the violin part in bars 164—170 quotes the vocal line of one of the *Kindertotenlieder* ("Oft denk' ich, sie sind nur ausgegangen," bars 63—69) where the text reads, ". . . in the sunshine! On those peaks the day is beautiful!" In the violas' turn around A-flat in 184—185, Mahler is remembering all the beauty and pathos that musical tradition — Bach, Beethoven, Wagner, Brahms, Bruckner, the Finale of Mahler's Third — has laid upon the slow *espressivo* turn. In alluding to the *Kindertotenlied,* the music signifies a presentiment of some ideal beauty. "Farewell, remembrance, and presentiment have, without usurping the future, become one."[17]

The temporal process exemplified by this ending and the kind of consciousness that such a temporality characterizes must be sharply differentiated from the temporality and consciousness suggested by the end of the first movement. Because the first movement begins with a temporal process in which completeness and incompleteness are palpably relevant, then goes through a process in which the tragic fanfare, along with other musical events, gradually empties from temporality any sense of moving toward a future, and comes at the end to an E (in the final "ewig") that is neither complete nor incomplete, the closing temporality is beyond the dichotomy between completeness and incompleteness. Such a temporality characterizes the consciousness of a peace which is beyond joy and tragedy and to which death cannot matter. It is a consciousness that may be described as transcendental indifference. By contrast, the A-flat of the last movement is both complete and incomplete. Instead of suggesting a temporality that does not differentiate between completeness and incompleteness, it suggests a temporality that embraces both. In that this temporal process is one in which death is a reality and it can matter, this kind of consciousness is closer to the ordinary concept of ordinary consciousness than is the kind of consciousness suggested by the end of the first movement. Nevertheless, the Finale's closing temporality also transforms ordinary temporality. For at the end of the symphony, the joy of living and the tragedy of not living out all of one's goals are maintained in the face of one another; the final temporality, in embracing both completeness and incompleteness, sustains peace with and in spite of both joy and tragedy.

3.   *The Symphony as a Whole*

The first and last movements of the Ninth present two different
transformations of the temporal process of ordinary consciousness,
including its awareness of the finitude implicit in a final leave-taking,
into a new kind of temporal process. One wonders how the two
different transformations are related. Does each challenge the viability
of the other? Is the symphony as a whole ambiguous in that in the end
it has presented two different transformations of temporality without
suggesting that they are compatible? Or does something happen that
makes one or the other more basic or more final in some sense?

The two middle movements clarify and dramatize the impetus for
both transformations. The Ländler and the Rondo-Burlesque allude
to the kinds of activities — the whirl of life symbolized by the
Strauss waltz and the Lehar operetta — that people use to occupy
themselves and hide the ultimate futility of life behind a facade of
apparently meaningful commotion. By exposing these activities to
caricature and showing how helpless they are to resist such distortion,
the middle movements suggest not only that the temporal process
is empty and meaningless but also that the emptiness, as well as the
pretense of not being futile, is ugly.

Because the first movement leads the listener to an image of transcendental indifference, it seems to be a more radical transformation
than the Finale, which maintains the relevance of the future even
though that future is unactualized and unactualizable. The more
radical transformation seems to be the more appropriate response to
the nihilism of the middle movements. The explicit allusions to the
first movement's song of peace in the most easy-going of the second
movement's three Ländler (bars 218ff. and 333ff.) support this
suggestion.

The tonal scheme of the four movements (D—C—A—D-flat) also
supports this intimation, because the first movement is more closely
related harmonically to the next two movements than the Finale is
to any of the preceding movements. Indeed, the Finale seems not
only to be unprepared by the first three movements but also to
contradict the implications of their temporal processes. For the
"Lebewohl" hymn affirms the meaningfulness of futureless activities
and the complete-incomplete ending affirms the meaningfulness of an
unactualized future, and does so in the teeth of the meaninglessness of
closure projected by the first-movement ending and the meaninglessness of what precedes closure projected in the middle movements.

The third movement has the brilliance and scope of a conventional Finale,[18] and so even to begin at all, the "Lebewohl" hymn must set itself against the sense that bitter nihilism has already had the last word. As though defying the force of the first three movements, the fourth is courageously affirmative both in moving toward and, even more, in being at closure. If the tonal center and the temporal process projected by the Finale's ending are not in any way justified or made possible by some internal process of the symphony as a whole — if, in other words, something external to the symphony must be entering it and acting on it in order to make the Finale possible — one may well regard the ending as an expression of the composer's own defiant courage.

There is, however, a way of hearing the symphony as a whole that makes the move to D-flat for the Finale seem less arbitrary and makes it unnecessary to invoke the composer's raw courage to explain the apparent inconsistency. Analysts usually say that the symphony makes itself into a whole by articulating a downward half step, D to C-sharp, the reverse of the path traversed by the Fifth Symphony, which rises a half step from C-sharp to D. For example, Bekker hears the opening and the closing as complementary movements that make essentially the same statement, each of them enriching this message by the connotations of its key, and the downward movement projected by the two together as exemplifying the same process — moving toward death — that each of them also celebrates separately:

The apotheosis of death is given in D major, the key in which Mahler had extolled first the triumph of life (the Finale of the First Symphony), then of divine love (the Finale of the Third) and then of creative power (the Finale of the Fifth). In the Ninth, we see life, love and creativity from the perspective of one who is already standing in the beyond and looks back from a higher world. To such a one, death seems to be the fulfillment of all of life's struggles and longings. Life becomes death, and death becomes life.[19]

From D major . . . the music sinks down to D-flat, the key of sublimity . . . It is not a song of mourning, but of solemn emotion, for the song discloses an ultimate vision.[20]

Jack Diether agrees with Bekker: "If a semitone rise, beginning in the minor mode and ending in the major [the Fifth], may be said to signify optimism or triumph, then a semitone fall, both beginning and ending in the major mode, may equally well signify retirement and peaceful resignation."[21]

In describing the symphony's coherence as a falling half step, both Bekker and Diether ignore the tonalities of the middle movements. They content themselves with noting motivic connections among the four movements. The middle movements could be in any keys whatsoever, and the symphony as a whole would still articulate a descending semitone. The fact that they are in C and A rather than in some other keys is irrelevant.

If one takes Mahler's choice of keys for the middle movements as relevant, however, one hears them as related to and confirming the tonality of D and thus as preparing a Finale in D. The fourth movement does not contradict this expectation: C-sharp is the seventh degree of the D major scale; C-sharp and A articulate enough of the dominant chord in D to suggest that D is still the underlying tonality. Hearing the C-sharp of the Adagio in this way implies that one is not hearing it as the Finale: one is either expecting a fifth movement that will be in D or expecting the fourth movement to make a turn to D before it ends. Listeners who let themselves be guided by their ears and not by what they see in the score or the printed program may well have this expectation. The music sustains it to the end of the movement, provided that the listener remembers the tonalities of the other movements and does not assume that they are irrelevant to the symphony's coherence. In that the symphony ends with this expectation left suspended in mid air, the work as a whole sounds incomplete. But this incompleteness is combined with completeness: as the Adagio unfolds and especially as the minor sections sustain the same tonal center, it becomes inescapably clear that the energies are too depleted for the music to yank itself up to D without sounding implausible and arbitrary. The listener comes to understand that the symphony will end on C-sharp. At the end, the musical energy is so completely spent that the work sounds altogether finished with this ending. Like the Adagio of the Third, the Adagio of the Ninth enters after a putative Finale and reorganizes the interrelations of the preceding movements. But once the Adagio has begun, the Ninth, unlike the Third, does not seem to be at its Finale. Only gradually does the Ninth make a putatively penultimate movement serve as a Finale.

The way the ending of the Ninth Symphony is both complete and incomplete is, of course, a precise analogue to the way the transfigured tragic fanfare and the A-flat *finalis* at the end of the Adagio sound both complete and incomplete. One knows that the C-sharp tonality of the fourth movement within the harmonic scheme of the symphony as a whole, like the A-flat within the melody of the closing section, is final although one can imagine an ending that would sound more final but that, one must acknowledge, will not come.

The completeness-incompleteness of the last movement and the completeness-incompleteness of the symphony as a whole confirm one another. At the end, a temporal process in which the ending is both complete and incomplete absorbs and transcends the temporal process of the first-movement ending that is neither complete nor incomplete. Precisely because the harmonic relations among the first three movements confirm the centrality of the first-movement D major and confirm that the transcendental indifference of the first-movement ending is a more appropriate response to the nihilism of the second and third movements than the Adagio is, the symphony is as incomplete at its end as it is complete. It turns out that what seems to confirm a temporality that is neither complete nor incomplete actually sets up a temporality that is both complete and incomplete.

In light of this outcome, it becomes clear that an aspect of the middle movements to which the opening movement is irrelevant is carried into the Finale. In the middle movements, one hears as a countercurrent the feeling that the activities of the everyday temporal process *ought not* be so empty and stupid as they are. Bekker aptly writes of the Rondo:

> It is a piece of caustic contempt for the world, but a scorn that has grown from a deep sense of tragedy. The one who is presenting the world in this way, who is letting it reel and race without any purpose, is one who has loved it with every fibre of his being, and still loves it even after discerning its emptiness in the mirror of death.[22]

The love for the hated world to which Bekker refers is most explicit in the Rondo's D major passage (bars 347ff.), which associates itself not so much with the song of peace built out of the "Lebewohl" motif in the first movement of the Ninth as with the candid, triumphant affirmation of the world in the blazing D major chorales in the second and fifth movements of the Fifth Symphony. The relevance of this association is somewhat confirmed by the identity of the strings' figure at the beginning of the Rondo to the anger motif opening the second movement of the Fifth.

But what is explicit in the Fifth — that death ought not to have the last word — is no more than a countercurrent in the Rondo of the Ninth. The Fifth's anger sections drive furiously forward and converge with the peace-questing sections on the shout of joy; the Rondo's refrains, quoting the anger motif, drive nowhere and alternate with episodes (109ff. and 262ff.) caricaturing a passage from Lehar's big hit of 1905, *The Merry Widow.*[23] And even in the D-major episode, the affirmation is not unequivocal. As Fischer points out, the slow turns in bar 353 and elsewhere in this episode contribute significantly to the sense it conveys of love for the hated world. For these turns carry the weight of a musical tradition that associates them with beauty, love, peace and self-fulfillment. This elevated association is, however, mocked in bar 444 when the clarinet cackles the turn and links it to Mahler's version of *The Merry Widow* music.[24] The abrupt debasement of the turn prevents the love for the hated world from becoming more than a countercurrent. Much the same may be inferred from the fact that the D-major episode is separated from and does not grow organically out of the preceding music.[25]

To the extent that the middle movements convey a sense of futility, they function as an impetus toward a new embodiment of the transcendental indifference exemplified figuratively by the first-movement ending; to the extent that they convey a countercurrent of "ought not," they are meaningless from the perspective of indifference. For from this perspective, the activities of life neither ought nor ought not to be futile. But from the perspective of the incomplete-complete ending of the Adagio, temporality again ought not be devoid of meaningful content. And, in contrast to the gimcrack of the Ländler and the pessimism of the Rondo and in keeping with their countercurrent of love for the hated world, the Finale's kind of closure confirms, "it need not be"; life ought not to be empty. In the end, Mahler backs off from the mysticism of the first movement and the nihilism of the middle movements and uses both of these postures as way stations to the Finale's affirmation of a temporality in which coming events have a force, and joy is as palpable as tragedy.

But it is not a straightforward, unqualified affirmation. Coming events have a force, but they are unactualizable, and tragedy is as palpable as joy. In facing death so squarely, the Ninth seems very different from the Third and the Eighth, and its transformation of temporality seems very different from theirs. To be sure, the fourth movement of the Third, where the curtain veiling woe is drawn aside, alludes obliquely to death, and the sixth movement sustains this allusion in order to transcend the woeful-joyful ambiguity of human self-consciousness. But the emphasis of the symphony is far more on the miraculous transition from nothingness to beings than on the dreadful transition from self-consciousness back to nothingness. Indeed, the ambiguity of self-consciousness is transcended precisely by celebrating the mysterious power, so different from causes and decisions, by which the miracle of being takes place.

The Finale presents a metaphor of this power's temporal process. It allows us to participate in at least an image of this process, and in this sense to transcend the ambiguity of ordinary consciousness and to experience reality in a transfigured way.

The Eighth takes place entirely beyond death. It celebrates the powerful love by which joy is sustained eternally; it presents the temporal process of a transfigured consciousness that has already moved beyond and in no sense sustains the woeful-joyful ambiguity.

On the basis of ordinary experience, we have no way of knowing whether the image of transfigured temporality in the Third is compatible with the vision projected by the Eighth, or indeed whether either is possible. But in comparison to both of them the temporality at the end of the Ninth seems closer to familiar processes. It is easier, and perhaps more productive, to compare the Ninth to the Fifth. In the Fifth, a recollecting fulfillment characterizes a process that is like an ownmost self repeating itself, having recognized itself as that which is to be lost in death. Repetition is wholeness; for the ownmost self to be itself is its own fulfillment. A recollecting fulfillment is still fulfillment even if — or rather, precisely because — what is remembered is not an actualization that has ever been a present reality. At the end of the Ninth, an analogous role is played by anticipating what lies beyond death — anticipating an actualization that will never be a present reality. The shift from recollecting to anticipating non-actualizable fulfillment is critical. It is exactly like the difference in temporality between the beginning and the ending of the Ninth's Adagio. For the first "Lebewohl" hymn maintains the joy of living along the way to death as much as the Fifth confirms the validity of a recollecting fulfillment. While the Fifth and the opening of the Ninth's Adagio present a temporality in which joy in the face of and in spite of death is possible, the end of the Adagio presents the possibility of a new kind of peace, a peace that combines remembrance with a sense of finality and both of them with a premonition of beauty. It is the peace of a consciousness whose temporal process makes it possible to sustain "not yet" in the face of "no longer."

In a sense, the Ninth is Mahler's culminating statement of a new temporality and a new consciousness, combining the awareness of death and the ordinary temporality of the Fifth with the transfigurations of the Third and the Eighth, exposing and transcending the differences.[26]

But only in a sense. The listener who becomes committed to Mahler's vision in the Third or the Eighth may well find that in the

Ninth Mahler has not superceded but rather has lost faith with his own vision. And Mahler wrote enough of his Tenth Symphony, and it is coherent enough and its coherence is new enough to make us hesitant about attributing any sort of finality to the Ninth.

Notes

1. See Bruno Walter, *Gustav Mahler* (1968), pp. 60–61; David Holbrook, *Gustav Mahler and the Courage to Be* (1975), *passim;* Cooke, *op. cit.*, p. 114; and Redlich, *op. cit.*, pp. 218–221.

2. Kennedy (*op. cit.*, pp. 6–7, 147) reminds us that it was Mahler's performance of "Les Adieux" when he was fifteen that convinced an estate manager in Jihlava that the boy should go to Vienna to study music.

3. Barford (in *Mahler, Symphony and Songs*, pp. 55–56), shows how closely Mahler's theme resembles Johann Strauss's "Freut euch des Lebens," Op. 340. As Morgan (*op. cit.*, pp. 75–76) points out, the straightforward diatonic character of Mahler's theme is belied by the way it forms itself out of bits and pieces into a "collage-like continuum of extraordinary subtlety and ambiguity." For Morgan, the theme illustrates an essential aspect of both Mahler and Ives: "What initially sounds familiar always ends up sounding very different from what we actually expected. The paradox implicit in this conjunction supplies the crucial point: what seems strange and extraordinary on one level does so only because, on another, it is so familiar and ordinary."

4. The "ewig" motif is often said to pervade Mahler's song, "Ich bin der Welt abhanden gekommen" — "I am detached from the world . . . and live alone in my heaven, my love and my song" (1904), but in this song the first note of the motif is always mobile toward the second. Moreover, this song is suffused with a nostalgia that holds in force the memory of the world that is being left behind. Neither it nor the peace-questing passages in V/ii nor much of V/iv, whose attitudes, motifs and dissonance treatment resemble those of the song, conveys the sort of transcendental indifference that the "ewig" motif connotes in both *Das Lied* and in IX/i. The F-sharp–E of IX/i appears in III/iv with the words, "Gib acht," but (*contra* Kennedy, *op. cit.*, p. 104), the effect is altogether different: in III/iv, the E is dissonant against the orchestra's pedal point on D and A, and is mobile, pushing on to D (or back to F-sharp). That this tension is not resolved does not mean that one does not continue to hear it as a tension; one may come to know that the tension will persist, and one may become resigned, as it were, to the non-resolution, but one can never say of it, as one can say of the E in the "ewig" motif of IX/i, that it does not push on to closure.

5. "The Composer as Poet in *Das Lied von der Erde*," *Nineteenth-Century Music*, vol. 1, no. 1 (1977), p. 41.

6. Mahler's procedure here is not novel. The second movement of his Fourth Symphony begins in the same way. In it, the introduction (bars 1–6) contains melodic fragments, played first by the horn and then the flute, that attenuate the contrast between the introduction and the theme (solo violin, bars 7ff.) that is introduced. Moreover, the introductory fragments continue in the

accompaniment to the theme, and this persistence also attenuates the sense of moving from an introducing to an introduced gesture.

7. *Gustav Klimt* (1975), pp. 14–16.

8. Carl Dahlhaus, *op. cit.*, p. 298, makes the same point more forcefully: the way the horn motive is threaded in is such that the theme is in fact a two-voice melody, not a melody with a counterpoint. For Dahlhaus, this phenomenon is possible only because the movement is a straightforward sonata form, whose exposition consists of a varied repeat, hence something like:

exposition	development	recapitulation
A^1 1–26	108–346	A^1 347–371
B^1 27–47		B^1 372–405
A^2 48–79		Coda 406–454
B^2 80–107		

The simplicity of the form makes it possible to vary the theme in extensive and subtle ways without the listener losing the connection between the varied form and the prototype. For example, a modification may be recognizable as such only because it occurs in the syntactically same place in the form as its prototype. Similarly, the procedure enables Mahler to take an accompaniment figure from the second violins in bar 24 and make it a foreground motif in the syntactically analogous position in bar 53. A different kind of example is provided by bar 221, which (using material from the secondary theme, bars 27–47) makes a single line out of what bar 211 presents as two contrapuntally entwined lines: "The impression [in bar 211] that the voices are less set off from one another as melody and accompaniment than that they together form the melody is, as it were, composed out [in 221] " (p. 299). The network of melodic connections is so extensive that they also become vague — "one can speak of a precisely composed out unclarity"; the vagueness is, however, balanced by the simplicity and strength of the formal scheme. Without the latter, the former would be mere diffuseness. With these considerations in mind, Dahlhaus concludes that Erwin Ratz ("Zum Formproblem bei Gustav Mahler. Eine Analyse des ersten Satzes der IX. Symphonie," *Die Musikforschung*, vol. 8, no. 2 [1955] pp. 169–177) and others who describe the movement as an intertwining of sonata form with double-variation form do not get to the root of the matter.

9. For a compelling argument that Mondrian's voids also exemplify rich emptiness, see Robert Rosenblum, *Modern Painting and the Northern Romantic Tradition* (1975), pp. 12–14, 32–33, 174.

10. What Barford, in *Mahler, Symphonies and Songs*, p. 59, says of the fourth movement may apply to the end of the first as well, "There is even an inverse mysticism here, an ecstasy of despair, a unity not with creative fullness and richness of life — as in the Third Symphony — but with the abyss in which all futures dissolve."

11. *Op. cit.*, pp. 117–118. Cooke reminds us (p. 116) that Haydn's Symphony Forty-five, also a Farewell symphony, likewise has a slow movement as a Finale.

12. The use of the flat submediant on the third beat of bar three, which launches

the chromatic excursions characterizing the Finale's "Lebewohl" hymn, brings to mind bar 8 of Beethoven's "Les Adieux" sonata, Op. 81a. As Cooke points out (*op. cit.*, pp. 115—116), Mahler's second movement imitates Beethoven's use of the flat submediant, and it permeates the rest of the symphony.

13. *Op. cit.*, p. 117.

14. Holbrook, *op. cit.*, pp. 155—157, points out the similarity between the tragic fanfare in the first movement of the Ninth to the passage from *Das Lied* quoted in Figure 108 as well as to a later passage in the same song in which the text tells of an ape howling on a grave site "into the sweet fragrance of life" (bars 359—361). Holbrook believes that Mahler overcame his anger at finitude (represented by the tragic fanfare) through writing the Ninth. For Holbrook, the symphony literally exemplifies self-therapy, rather than metaphorically exemplifying a transformation of consciousness.

15. Although the cadence dividing the two subphrases (bar 6, third beat) is so light that they are only weakly separated, one hears the period as consisting of a pair of subphrases because bar 7 is so clearly analogous to bar 3 in both the soprano and the bass that bar 7 sounds like the beginning of a new subphrase.

16. Kurt von Fischer ("Die Doppelschlagfigur in den zwei letzten Sätzen von Gustav Mahlers 9. Symphonie," *Archiv für Musikwissenschaft*, vol. 32, no. 2 [1975], p. 103) finds the turns in the C-sharp minor sections to be perhaps a "neutralizing metamorphosis" of the turns in the Rondo-Burlesque that are used in episodes alluding to Franz Lehar's *The Merry Widow* as well as an allusion to the "Lebewohl" theme. See pp. 292—293 and 298.

17. *Ibid.*, pp. 104—105. Fischer probably presses his point too far when he says that the figure in bars 160, 161 and 179 (which Cooke and others call the tragic fanfare) is a paralyzed, debilitated form of the turn, which at once alludes to and gives up the traditional meaning of the turn, thereby intensifying the sense of fragmentation, including the fragmentation of memory; we are dealing not so much with the tradition as with the vagueness of the tradition's traces. Such an interpretation overlooks the conspicuous role of the tragic fanfare elsewhere in the symphony, too conspicuous not to be recalled by bars 160, 161 and 179.

18. See Cooke, *op. cit.*, p. 116.

19. *Op. cit.*, pp. 339—340.

20. *Ibid.*, p. 352.

21. "The Expressive Content of Mahler's Ninth," *Chord and Discord*, vol. 2, no. 10 (1963), p. 95.

22. *Op. cit.*, p. 348. In a review of the Karajan recording of the Ninth for the Salzburg *Nachrichten*, April 19, 1981, Karl Harb criticizes Karajan for changing the Ländler completely into a *danse macabre* and the Rondo completely into a scene of elemental chaos. The Ländler, Harb believes with Bekker, should still be recognizable as such even behind the mask of the grotesque, and the burlesque must allow the charm of playfulness to persist. If either side of the ambivalence is lost, the movements seem overly long and uninspired. Barford (*Mahler, Symphonies and Songs*, p. 58) and Redlich (*op. cit.*, p. 228), for example, find the Ländler wanting, but they err in the opposite direction from that imputed

by Harb to Karajan: they fail to notice its *danse macabre* aspects.

23. See Fischer, *op. cit.*, p. 100.

24. *Ibid.*, pp. 101–102.

25. *Ibid.*, p. 100.

26. This summation comports with Bekker's interpretation of Mahler's nine symphonies (*op. cit.*, p. 354). Not realizing how much of the Tenth was complete, he believed that Mahler not only did not but could not complete a Tenth; his lifework, Bekker thought, was finished with the Ninth.

Subject and Name Index

175, 177, 178, 180, 187, 188,
192, 195, 225, 234, 244, 296.
See also Future
Explanation 6, 12, 27, 68. *See also*
Cause, Ground *and* Rationality
Extension 26, 82, 91, 92, 119, 195,
212, 237, 238
Exuberance 183, 199, 202, 210

Fanfare 39, 44, 45, 144, 156, 159,
195
Fantasy 32, 83
Farewell 268, 273, 275, 276, 291,
292. *See also* "Lebewohl" motif
Fauré, Gabriel 221
Faust 8, 31, 220, 221, 237, 238,
242, 246, 252-57, 260. *See also*
Goethe
Feuerbach, Ludwig 206, 259
Finality 46, 185, 191, 263, 267,
275, 279, 288, 290, 291, 299,
300. *See also* Closure *and*
Completeness
Finitude 127, 129, 239, 248, 277,
288, 290, 294
Fischer, Kurt von 292, 298, 302,
303
Focus 101, 225, 226, 234. *See also*
Thesis
Foreground 52, 58, 77, 78, 84, 85,
147, 148, 150, 152, 154, 172,
185, 194, 268-72, 285
Foreshadowing 56, 292
Forward thrust 58, 61, 99, 152,
153, 171, 179, 183, 187, 194,
211, 215, 224, 225, 227, 234,
240, 245, 274, 281, 287, 289,
291. *See also* Energy, Pressure,
forward, *and* Mobility
Four-bar group 79, 98, 106, 116,
152, 154, 188. *See also* Phrase
structure
Fragmentation 21, 86, 93, 97, 110,
115, 120, 135, 164, 235, 288,
300, 302
Free agent 13, 22, 32, 34, 42, 50,
130, 162, 188. *See also* Self
Free decision 7, 11-13, 21, 26, 32,
34, 42, 54, 68, 124, 142, 163
Freedom 10, 46, 205, 216, 220, 224

Freud, Sigmund 11, 38, 126, 136, 193
Frustration 171, 175
Fugue 108, 110, 134, 209, 211
Fulfillment 15, 16, 21, 34, 62, 63,
66, 70, 72, 73, 104, 113, 117,
119, 121, 123-30, 146, 155, 161,
171, 176-79, 182, 191, 202,
205-07, 210, 213, 214, 217, 218,
220, 221, 234, 236-40, 243,
246-48, 250, 268, 299
Futility 275, 283, 294, 298
Future 5, 13, 14, 51, 56, 72, 74, 76,
77, 88, 96-100, 102, 103, 108,
116, 119, 122-24, 126, 128, 142,
143, 145, 146, 154, 155, 157,
159, 161, 162, 165, 166, 168,
170, 171, 173, 175-82, 185-89,
192, 194, 195, 215, 221, 231,
244-46, 251, 265, 266, 268, 274,
276, 283, 288, 291-94, 301. *See
also* Expectation
Future-directedness 84, 95, 119,
143, 152, 173-75, 178-81, 183,
187, 189, 192, 195, 287
Futurelessness 4, 5, 14, 34, 83-85,
97, 98, 101, 103, 119, 124, 142,
146, 152, 159, 161-63, 170,
173-75, 183, 189, 192, 200, 277,
286, 288, 294

Gartenberg, Egon 131
Gaulli, G.B. 262
Generative passage 104, 161, 186,
229. *See also* Antecedent
Genius 11, 12
Gesù, Il 262
Gibbons, Orlando 258
Goal 72, 75, 93, 104, 112, 115,
116, 119, 122, 143, 147, 151,
153, 162, 164, 165, 170, 183,
186-88, 190, 192, 215, 229, 230,
234, 244-46, 251, 260, 268, 271,
273-74, 276, 279, 283, 288, 293
Goal-directedness 134, 146, 148,
156, 162-66, 168, 170, 272, 281
Goallessness 96, 133, 150, 163,
164, 172, 288
Goethe, J.W. 8, 220, 222, 224, 228,
230, 232, 237-40, 243, 260, 261.
See also Faust

Printed in Switzerland